SHATTERED KINGDOM

SHATTERED KINGDOM BOOK 1

The Realms of
Neredyn

VREAH
ISLANDS

Ackwood

SI...

GLISTENING
BLUE

Lej'Vreah

ULFRAY

HEART
ULFRA...

THE LOST
MOUNTAINS

LANDS
END

Eedwood

LEIBRATP

RUINS OF
ITHRYLAN

EAST
SEA

CALMA
DESERT

Everrun

TREE OF
THE DEAD

NISIA

Lapidos   Phornes   Khila

ILBROTT

Ilaton

White
death

The Brittle Sea

SHATTERED KINGDOM

SHATTERED KINGDOM BOOK 1

ANGELINA J. STEFFORT

SHATTERED KINGDOM

First published 2020

Ebook: ASIN B088XW7CVN
Print: ISBN978-3-903357-03-7

Typeset in EB Garamond

MK

www.ajsteffort.com

ACKNOWLEDGEMENTS

First of all to my wonderful readers, who keep asking for more, whose enthusiasm for my writing is the fuel when I am struggling to keep my eyes open late at night. Thank you for all your loving support. You are the best!

This book would never have been possible without a number of people. First of all, Marko Stankovic, who has an uncanny talent for putting my ideas into visuals and illustrations. Thank you for the map and the stunning cover.

To Dawn for patiently cleaning up my written mess and for getting what I wanted to say even when I wasn't yet able to say exactly that. I wish I could hop across the ocean for a cup of coffee and a piece of cake.

To Kathleen and Norma-Jean for real-time-reading my words. You are a tireless source of incredible feedback, and I can't say enough how much I value your words and opinions.

To Joanna who keeps encouraging me to keep with writing sprints.

To Belle Manuel for being the best critique partner I could wish for. Where have you been all my life?!

To Barbara, who has become my dearest author-friend, for her patience and kind words when I doubt myself, for the thirteen-thousand-words-days that show me what else is possible. There is always a cup of coffee waiting for you! More than one!

To my family. Thank you for putting up with me when I go through my creative tantrums. I couldn't have done it without you! I love you!

PART ONE

THE ORDER
OF VALA

After ten years in the heart of the Calma Desert, Gandrett Brayton no longer noticed the unforgiving wind drying her mouth and driving water into her eyes. She lifted her sword to strike yet again, sweat sheathing her body, top to bottom, like a second skin and making her hands slippery. Sweat—as much as her plain linen tunic and pants were part of the fashion of the roughly two-hundred members of the Order of Vala in Everrun. But the man attacking her with merciless strength wasn't one of them. His attire spoke of the outside world—a world of childhood memories and wheat fields in the north. Gandrett Brayton swirled her weapon and let it sink into the ground before her, preparing herself to propel her legs up and hit her opponent in the chest. It was a movement that always secured her victory.

But not today.

Today, Everrun's most proficient fighter found herself flat on her back before her feet could hit home.

Gandrett freed a string of curses, earning a raised eyebrow from the stranger, who, himself, seemed surprised that she was on the ground, and he kept his sword hovering before his chest as if he was waiting for something.

Already calculating her options, Gandrett looked for a weak spot. So far, her opponent hadn't made even the slightest mistake. Unlike most other fighters, he had kept his distance, delivering blow after blow without leaving his sides unprotected. He hadn't fallen for her feints, the way the acolytes at the order did, or made the mistake of losing patience. On the contrary, he had parried each of her strikes with elegant efficiency, his toned body moving as if he had never done anything else in his life.

He growled, assessing, as her gaze swept over him. Dark hair, eyes of piercing blue. Light, leather armor good for traveling. And covering his chest was a familiar pattern of burgundy and gold.

Gandrett glanced behind the man, letting her eyes widen as if she had just noticed something there—something other than the familiar sight of the lifeless desert which spread around Everrun in each direction—hoping she could fool him, and gripped her sword more tightly, pulling it down toward her in preparation for her next move. A move which would free her and put the man looming over her exactly where she was now; in the dirt.

But the man didn't loosen his focus on her. Fast as a biting snake, he set his toes on her arm, forcing her fingers to let go of her weapon, and sneered, "What a waste to keep you locked up here in Everrun."

Gandrett grimaced. "I'm not planning on staying here forever." She stilled for a moment, letting him believe she'd given up fighting, and studied the man's posture—the way he kept too much weight on one leg, a mistake. Then, with trained lightness, she rolled over and kicked into the back of his knees, making him tumble off her arm.

Before he could regain balance, Gandrett picked up her sword and was back on her feet, easing the man's weapon out of his broad hand with a swift knock of her blade. He leaped out of her reach, fumbling for the knife that was still dangling on his leather belt.

Another mistake—at last.

Gandrett's blood pumped with familiar heat as she measured how many strikes it would take to defeat him. One—she danced to the side, positioning herself with the wind at her back so the stranger would be at a disadvantage. Two—she lifted her sword above her head, easily staying out of the small knife in the man's dirt-flecked hand's reach. Three—she brought the flat of her blade down on the man's shoulder, forcing him to his knees with a blow that made the metal shudder in its wake.

Four—he was on the ground.

Gandrett loosed a breath, watching him with caution, blade at the ready.

But the man glanced up at her, a grin forming on his lips—not the kind type—and said, "I was beginning to doubt you had it in you."

For a heartbeat, Gandrett pondered whether he was mocking her, and lowered the tip of her sword toward the man's throat. But he lifted his hands from the dust, a gesture of peace despite the relentless attacks he had rained down on her.

With a flick of her foot, Gandrett shoved his knife out of reach behind her where his sword was resting between stones.

She had imagined her afternoon differently. Exercise in the training grounds behind the citadel then a run around the outer walls of Everrun. Her usual routine. Not the silent approach of an adept attacker who'd had who-knew-what in mind as she found him snooping around the city walls.

Nobody made it into Everrun without permission of the order. And nobody made it out. That was what Everrun was like. Since her very first day here. And that was what it would be like long after her last breath. Had she not spotted him trying to hoist himself up the unclimbable wall encircling Everrun, he might have given up and starved and dried out in the desert, or—which would have been the faster, more merciful death—he would have been pierced by one of the arrows of the guard.

"You could have just walked up to the front gate and requested entrance," Gandrett threw at him and earned a shrug. In response, she jerked her chin, beckoning the stranger to get to his feet, allowing him only so much space to move along with her blade as she guided him up. He eyed her with a glacial gaze.

"The Meister will be interested to know what kind of busybody was hoping to sneak into the priory." Gandrett stared the man down, ignoring the handsome face those cold eyes were set in. He couldn't be older than twenty. Twenty-five at the maximum. "Name," she demanded, her voice as sharp as the wind freeing strands of her chestnut braid.

The stranger shoved Gandrett's sword aside with a gloved hand, "Tell the Meister that Nehelon is here," and stepped past her to pick up his weapons.

Gandrett whirled around to block his path and kicked his down-reaching hands off course before he could touch the hilt of his sword.

4

She ignored his curse at the impact and flashed him her falsest smile. "I'm sure he'll be delighted." Then she crouched just enough to reach his weapons herself and collected them from the ground, never turning her eyes away from him and without lowering her sword even an inch.

He pursed his lips and fell into step as she escorted him toward the closest side gate in the wall at the tips of both his and her swords while she repeated the name. "Nehelon." She wanted to take back the word, hating that the sound of it had rung a bell. Not from the years at the Order of Vala, but from her childhood, which seemed almost like a gray haze in her memory.

Gandrett thought she heard him chuckle and pushed one of the swords against the leather on his shoulder blade just to make him move faster. The sound stopped.

She studied his powerful strides as they walked for fifteen minutes without exchanging another word, even though Gandrett was curious who he might be. A fighter, definitely a warrior. Maybe one of the most skilled she had ever encountered. But what business did he have with the order to sneak up on them? And how on earth had he crossed the desert without even carrying a waterskin or a pack of supplies? The Calma Desert spread for miles and miles in each direction, enclosing Everrun like a circle of death, a zone that isolated the Order of Vala from the rest of Neredyn. Nehelon would have been traveling the rocky, dry land without supplies for days—

Her eyes were still on his long, muscled legs as they marched, each step confident, each movement coordinated, deliberate. Then her view slid up to his back, following his spine up to his broad shoulders.

As if he felt her gaze, he glanced back and smirked. "Better than the boys at the order," he commented as if her sword wasn't just a flick of her hand away from slicing through his leathers.

Gandrett considered, for a second, the pleasure of giving her temper free rein, but smoothed over her expression, embarrassed, and denied she already hated Nehelon.

The solid, iron gate creaked open as Gandrett nodded to the guards positioned on each side above on the wall.

"What did you bring this time?" Kaleb, the younger of the two, asked with a simper, almost yelling from the tower-like reinforcements framing the entrance to the priory.

Gandrett's heart warmed at the sight of Kaleb's twinkling eyes, and she lowered Nehelon's sword to fasten it on her belt, then pushed the man forward with her hand rather than her sword.

Nehelon craned his neck to see who had spoken, his dark hair sliding back between his shoulder blades, and whistled through his teeth before he set in motion.

"Don't they feed you in here?" He gestured at Kaleb's slim, lanky frame by way of greeting as they stepped through the gate, and Kaleb and the second guard descended from their towers.

Gandrett shoved Nehelon forward, ignoring his provocations, and merely said to Kaleb, "All kind of dirt out there," as she tilted her head, making clear she meant Nehelon. "I found him snooping around the wall," she clarified. "He says he wants to see the Meister."

Kaleb gave Nehelon a look, which Gandrett knew was supposed to be dangerous, as he sized him up, but all Gandrett could see was the soft-hearted boy who she had met that first day at Everrun and trained with for ten years. Nothing about him appeared dangerous besides the black-pointed arrows peeking out from behind his shoulder.

"The Meister is busy around this time of the day," the other guard said to Nehelon, this one looking as dangerous as he sounded.

Gandrett inclined her head. "I'll bring our guest to his new quarters."

Both guards nodded, and Gandrett noticed Kaleb's mouth twitch.

The Meister wasn't busy. She knew exactly where in the lush gardens of the priory she would find him.

But Nehelon didn't need to know where she was taking him. And he didn't need to know that the 'quarters' she had mentioned were the cells in one of the two-story, stone, side buildings framing the main road to the eastern gate. That's what the order did with unannounced visitors until they could be questioned—not that many ever tried sneaking into the priory. It was common knowledge that there was no way in and no way out unless you were granted passage. That was one of the few things that made Gandrett feel safe in Everrun, despite the ghost town which lay behind the eastern gate, abandoned by its inhabitants over two-hundred years ago when the desert had still been fertile soil and the priory of the Order of Vala had been a place friendly to visitors and open to those in need.

Gandrett guided Nehelon past the citadel, its peaked tower piercing the gray sky like a needle while the thundering sound of water spilling from the roof at its base covered the echo of their footsteps bouncing off the columns that framed the front in a decorative line where the water pooled in a pond as wide as the citadel itself.

Nehelon strode forward, unimpressed by Gandrett's sword, which was still close to his left shoulder. "That guard..." He jerked his chin to the side, pointing behind him to where Kaleb had probably already climbed back into his tower. "Your sweetheart?"

Gandrett swallowed the violent words she wanted to smash at the obnoxious stranger and forced a smile onto her dry lips. Composure. If Nehelon was supposed to see anything of hers, it was composure. Kaleb was her friend, and she would in no way show the stranger that the boy meant something to her. Part of her training at the Order of Vala was to school her emotions, her hot-headedness. It was the only way to ensure she remained as good a fighter when she was under pressure or emotional strain. And even if the methods used were questionable, Gandrett was grateful that her training ensured she would give Nehelon nothing. The last time she had cried was probably the week she had been torn from her mother's arms at the age of seven. And she had sworn to herself it would be the last time the politics of Neredyn reached her, had taken something from her—

With a swish of her blade, Gandrett guided Nehelon toward one of the sand-colored side buildings. "It's open," was all she said, voice unbothered as he stopped at the narrow, black door, before she shoved him forward.

Even if the image of one of the inhabitants of Everrun escorting a captive with a sword was rare, Gandrett's fellow acolytes, the priests, and priestesses tried not to gawk as they passed by. But she could feel their eyes on her back as she crossed the threshold after Nehelon, could almost hear the whispers even if the more subdued wind inside the walls was too weak to carry the guessing, the wondering all the way to her ears.

Nehelon didn't fight when Gandrett beckoned him into one of the two narrow cells crammed at one side of the room the second her eyes adjusted to the darker light.

"Not exactly the palace at Ackwood." He launched himself onto the dusty cot in the corner farthest from the cell door, lacing his fingers together behind his head, and let his gaze sweep over the shabby interior which filled the room behind Gandrett. "But better than those inns in Nisea."

Gandrett felt her face change with interest and battled down all flaring curiosity while she shut the iron-barred cell as she asked, "You're from Sives?" Her voice sounded about as emotional as a sleeping frog. Ackwood, one of the two capitals of Sives. She hadn't heard recent news about the territory where she was born. If Nehelon was from Ackwood, he might have news about what was going on in the north.

"So now I have your attention," Nehelon commented instead of answering her question.

Gandrett bit her lower lip from the inside until it hurt and shrugged. "We don't get many visitors here."

To her surprise, Nehelon sat up on the cot, legs still crossed at his booted ankles, his eyes suggesting a challenge. "I am not exactly being treated like a visitor."

His eyes, blue as the winter sky above Sives, sparked as she stared him down, measuring, weighing, trying to read the man who had fought her as if he'd intended to slit her throat in the end and now behaved more like an annoyed, stray cat. As if he had read her thoughts, he gave her a feline grin.

"So, are you from the north?" The burgundy-and-gold coat of armor on his chest sure suggested he might be from the palace itself. Ackwood. So close to home. Gandrett stifled a sigh. All those years she'd been dreaming of one day returning to her parents' farm. The thought of it brought back the scent of grains and freshly-cut grass at high summer, of snow and roasted chestnuts in winter. And images of soft hills embedded between ever-white mountains in the west and north-east.

Nehelon didn't give any sign he was going to speak.

"Why are you here?" Gandrett didn't back down, her stare unimpressed by the glacial cold that had crept back into his eyes.

"Why don't you go stir the Meister from his daily meditation, and in return, I'll tell you the truth?"

While the desert outside the wall made the land hostile and impossible to survive, Everrun was an oasis with the water resources sufficient for five times the amount of acolytes, priests, and priestesses in the Order of Vala. Gandrett never failed to admire the lush vegetation framing the buildings of the priory, the small fields where she, among other acolytes, worked regularly to ensure the order was self-sustained and independent from the outside world.

As she rushed out the door, leaving Nehelon locked in his cell, her fellow acolytes didn't hide their curiosity, most of them halting whatever they had just been about to do, some of them nodding at her as she made her way up to the citadel.

"The Meister won't be pleased if you disturb his alone time." The bell-like voice came from the doorway of a side building. Surel moved away from the door and fell into step beside Gandrett, her onyx eyes full of excitement.

Of course Surel had heard a stranger had been brought into Everrun. Nothing slipped her notice.

"I will have to risk it," was all Gandrett replied to her friend, her mind on the tall warrior she'd left behind.

She wasn't certain what annoyed her more: that he had almost defeated her, or that he had managed to get under her skin. She shook her head at the thought, at the tightness that spread in her chest when she was reminded of her homeland, the last memory she had of her parents—weeping and pleading for *them* not to take her.

Them.

Gandrett inhaled a steadying breath, her eyes on her target as she made her way along the cobbled road, and shoved aside whatever was left of her memories from before Everrun— which were few and happy ones, mostly. So happy, the thought of them made the present even more painful. But she wasn't the only one. Every acolyte in the Order of Vala had endured a fate similar to hers.

The sun had dropped low enough that when Gandrett glanced at the pond at the foot of the citadel, she found it tinted in a pinkish-orange.

The truth. The twinkle in Nehelon's eyes when he had sent her off. A challenge. She had been training with the other acolytes in the priory for too long to not recognize a challenge. And now—

Now she found herself storming right into the Meister's time of reflection just to satisfy her own curiosity. She rolled her eyes at herself, hoping no one was watching her too closely.

The Meister wouldn't be pleased; Surel was right about that. And yet—

The girl tugged along as Gandrett entered the shade under the arches behind the columns of the citadel, her words almost drowned out by the splattering of the waterfall. "Kaleb said the guy is wearing the Brenheran coat of armor."

Gandrett shrugged, keeping her head high despite the spray of water that blew in through the arches as she neared the entrance. "One more reason to hate him," she said, her voice hard as stone.

She didn't need to look at Surel to know what the girl was thinking. Anything that wasn't the daily routine was exciting to her, a welcome distraction. Where Gandrett was a dedicated fighter, skilled with almost any type of blade one could find across Neredyn, Surel was of the gifted group of the acolytes, the few blessed ones who possessed the magic that kept Everrun inhabitable in the middle of this unforgiving land. Water magic. The ability to shape and command the element of life. The element of Vala.

Magic, not usually a human trait. And while in the beginning, even knowing that she shouldn't, Gandrett had observed the Vala-blessed with envy, she had learned to embrace her own talent—even though swordsmanship wasn't half as glorious as the sight of what some of the priests and priestesses of Vala did with water magic. She had honed it and perfected it as best she could, sparring with anyone she could get to pick up a sword and fight—until she had stopped losing. Until the Meister and some of the high priests and priestesses were the only ones who could keep her occupied for more than two minutes with a weapon.

As they turned the corner into the citadel, cool, moist air touched her face. Unlike the wind whipping over the barren land outside the walls or the calm breeze inside the walls, in the citadel, the temperature was always a couple of degrees lower than anywhere else. The Calma Desert didn't compare to the slat deserts of Phornes at the southern end of Neredyn. It didn't even belong to one of the territories of Neredyn anymore. Even if Everrun had once belonged to the Fae at some point in history, the Calma Desert had been unclaimed for a thousand years.

Surel was still at her side as Gandrett made it through the long, stone hallways, past ornately-decorated carvings that told of Neredyn's history. Gandrett didn't pay attention, not anymore, not after countless walks into the heart of the citadel.

It was only when Gandrett stopped at the gate to the courtyard garden that Surel raised a thin, black eyebrow, her golden-tan skin glowing in the sunset light that filtered in through the windows which framed the door—and crossed her arms over her chest, indicating she was going to wait here rather than face the Meister's wrath. He wouldn't punish her with violence. Not for this. She had contained a potential intruder and strictly followed protocol.

With a slow hand, fueled mostly by the annoyance at Nehelon that was still swirling inside of her, Gandrett turned the brass doorknob, the ruffled metal cool under her touch preparing her for what she was about to experience, and stepped into the windless, square space.

The Meister, perched on a small dais made of the same sandstone as the rest of the priory, didn't look up at her approach. His face was turned south-west, the direction Gandrett had entered from, and his hands rested on his knees. *Meditation*, Nehelon had said, as if he knew exactly what the Meister did in here.

Again, her mind raced back through her years at Everrun—and came up blank. Neither the name nor the face was familiar. Only the Brenheran symbol on his chest...

"It must be important," the Meister noted without opening his eyes, without any movement other than that of his lips, "if you came all the way from your run to bother me during this most sacred time of the day."

Sunset. The hour of Vala. Where the life of this day goes to rest to make way for the life of tomorrow.

As she stepped forward into the oasis of blossoms and bushes, Gandrett felt whatever force had driven her—curiosity to find out what Nehelon had to tell her—to come here at once, without even giving herself a moment to think it through, subside, leaving a mild tremble in its wake.

"Apologies, Meister." She bowed low, eyes on her dusty boots, knowing from experience that even if the Meister wasn't using his eyes, for now, he had other ways to be aware if she had followed protocol or not.

When the Meister didn't immediately react, Gandrett lifted her head just enough to glimpse at his timeless face. A face smooth yet ancient with a crown of white hair atop. A face she had gotten to know as well as her father's and mother's, better even. Only without the affection she held for the latter. And it rarely appeared as peaceful as today. Even if his eyebrows knitted together in a frown indicating she had disturbed him while he'd been pondering the fate of all of Neredyn.

Well, *this* was important, too. Even if now, facing the Meister, all urgency had ebbed away.

"Speak, Gandrett." His eyes remained closed as if he refused to dive out of wherever his mind had retreated to. Nobody knew, not even the high priests and priestesses, what the Meister truly did during those hours in the afternoon.

So Gandrett spoke. "Someone tried to breach our walls this afternoon."

The Meister's eyebrows rose, but he still didn't blink his eyes open or release Gandrett from the bow. A punishment, perhaps, for disturbing him in his ritual.

"When I confronted him, he attacked, and—" she searched for words, avoiding mentioning she had laid in the dirt before the man, "—when I was able to disarm him, I brought him into Everrun and locked him in a cell." She stopped, waiting for the Meister to react, but he didn't. Her bent back was starting to bother her even if it had been only a minute. It was the weight of the Meister's disapproval that made it so uncomfortable. Anything to not let him know his best warrior had almost failed to contain a threat's potential attack against the Order of Vala. "According to protocol," she added, shaping her words in a steady breath.

For a moment, the low sound of water trickling from stones set in all four corners of the courtyard was the only noise. Then, the Meister lifted his hands from his knees and folded them in his lap. "Did you ask him what business he has breaking into Everrun?"

Gandrett nodded to herself. Of course she had. It had been her first question, long before he had delivered the first blow with his sword. "Yes, Meister."

"And what did he say?"

Gandrett stifled a groan as the muscles in her spine began to hurt.

"He didn't tell me," she truthfully answered.

At that, the Meister's eyes burst open, icy cold burning in the blue of his irises.

"Rise," he commanded, his voice not inferior to a military commander, the only thing giving away his wrath. The wrath Surel had warned about, the wrath every one of the acolytes got to know sooner or later. The temper of the Meister who demanded nothing but impeccable performance and manners. The Meister who had replaced her loving home.

Gandrett straightened, almost releasing a sigh of relief, but at the expectant gaze boring into her eyes, she repeated what Nehelon had instructed her to. "He told me to tell you Nehelon is here."

The Meister leapt off the dais in a gazelle-like hop, his cold eyes melting at the sound of the name. "Why didn't you tell me right away?"

Despite the relief that the Meister's anger had passed, Gandrett felt a certain unease creep up on her in its wake.

He stood, the hem of his linen robes still on the rock behind him, face expectant for her to continue.

There was nothing to continue. So she stared at the Meister, unsure if his momentary change of mood was going to backlash.

"What are you waiting for?" He beckoned with one hand, dismissing her. "Bring him to me."

The cells were nothing unusual. Nothing he wouldn't be able to find a way out of, Nehelon decided as he assessed the iron-barred windows with professional fingers. Sunk into the rock front more than a couple of inches. Not solid but hollow, a tap of his index finger informed him.

Outside the windows, Everrun was as busy as he remembered it. Even the same, dull clothes on the acolytes as he remembered. The girl swaggered over the cobbled path she'd escorted him along. He couldn't help but notice that despite her young age, her body was—as far as he could judge through those linen garments—that of a fully-grown woman. He rested his shoulder against the wall, observing her movements as she disappeared from view, studying, he told himself, what it was about that girl that made her the best fighter Everrun had to offer—

And came up blank.

Average height. On the lower end of the scale, even. As he had fought her outside the wall, she had impressed him with her feline movements, her focus as she had tackled him from below, bringing him to the ground the way hardly any opponent had been able to. Not even the strongest of them. And she, *for Vala's sake*, was only a girl. Trained by the best instructors in all of Neredyn, but still a girl. Something in his male pride curled up and licked its wounds, bracing itself for her return.

As some of the acolytes assigned to farm-work strode by, carrying rakes and shovels and buckets of seedlings, he couldn't help but feel a little bit homesick. How many years had it been since—

But that wasn't why he'd come here. He'd come to get the best from the order's stable and convince her to help him. However, he needed to do it now that she already hated him. He had seen it in her eyes—as skilled as she was with disguising it, he was better in reading it.

Nehelon stood like a statue and watched, watched the sunset. Watched as the last of the acolytes hurried off the small fields and vegetable patches. Watched the cobblestones as they emptied of life with no sign of the girl returning. Watched the last rays of sun sink behind the wall, the waterfall of the citadel a hum in shades of purple, as the first doubts bit at him.

What if he had misread her? What if she wasn't curious at all regarding what he had to share? What if the Meister didn't truly care after all these years...

"You seem awfully cheerful." Her voice, heavy with sarcasm, startled him.

He growled.

Nobody startled him. No one. If anyone startled anyone, it was him. Him, who crept up on people, surprising them when they assumed they were unobserved. Him, who had the advantage of having his sword ready when others were still comprehending what was going on.

"No need to get all worked up," she flashed her teeth. "The Meister says if I don't get your ass over to him before the sun sets entirely, I'll have a problem."

Nehelon returned her gesture and bared his teeth. "It was starting to get a bit frosty in here..."

Gandrett raised her eyebrows as if daring him to have meant that she was the source of the frost. Then, she grabbed the key from her pocket to unlock the cell.

"Stay back." The girl balanced her sword in one hand as she lifted the other to open his prison.

He watched her with a frown. "You still need *this*," he asked and gestured at the blade, "even if the Meister confirmed he knows me?"

The girl didn't seem convinced. "The Meister may have been delighted to hear your name," she said, smoothing her expression over once more. "Doesn't mean *I* trust you."

Her attitude almost made him bark a laugh—almost. Then he remembered he needed her.

Nehelon's face was tight except for that tiny pull on the corner of his mouth that made Gandrett want to shut the cell door in his face the moment she had opened it.

"So I am not getting back my sword?"

Was he honestly asking that? She felt the reassuring weight of Nehelon's weapons, which she had strapped to her belt, leaving her to carry her own sword in her hand. "Not if it is up to me. You might backstab me the second I turn around." She stepped back to let him march out the entrance and cocked her head as he stopped right where she was holding the door, less than a foot from her. "You surely tried earlier," she added with a shrug, referring to their initial encounter.

"And... is it up to you?" he asked, unimpressed.

Gandrett mentally stomped a foot in response and beckoned him to get moving. "The Meister can't wait to see you." Her smile was as false as she believed herself capable.

As she escorted Nehelon back through the now-empty street of the priory, the winds of the Calma Desert had turned the sky thunder-cloud gray, laced with the first shades of night. Small windows in the residential quarters on the western side of the citadel flickered on as the acolytes and priests returned to their rooms to clean up and change for the common dinner they had every night.

Nehelon's strides, powerful and graceful, gave Gandrett the impression she was walking next to a force of nature. But however much it tugged on her nerves, she didn't turn her head to take a real look at him. She wouldn't grant him the satisfaction of seeing her curious or even intrigued—for even with all of the dust and grime from traveling distributed on his clothes, his hair, there was something fascinating about him simply because he had almost defeated her. She frowned.

"Doesn't suit you, you know?" Gandrett felt Nehelon's gaze as if someone was holding a torch close to her face. "Leaves wrinkles."

Gandrett suppressed the urge to use the sword in her hand to get him to stop talking.

As if feeling her irritation, he fell silent and didn't speak until they entered the citadel.

"This is as cold and unwelcoming as I remember it."

At his unexpected statement, Gandrett's head involuntarily turned, and she found him gazing at the torch-lit hallway with carvings of Neredyn's history, the thundering of the waterfall a constant background melody.

"You've been here before." Not a question.

Nehelon's head turned, and he faced her for a moment, his eyes muddy-gray in the mixture of fading daylight and orange flames. He gave her a brief nod before he returned his focus on the walls again. "You could say so."

"When?" Gandrett prompted.

A low chuckle was the only answer she got before they made it to the courtyard at the center of the citadel.

A breeze, unusual for the heart of Everrun, touched her face as she stepped outside, half an eye surveying Nehelon at her heels and the sword in her hand—appearing loosely and casually gripped to the untrained eye—ready to flick into the young man's thigh should he turn out to not have good intentions—

"My friend!" The Meister threw his arms open, immediately rising from the stone dais.

How very unusual it was for the Meister to show emotions like this. The smile on his face, wide and welcoming, was as alien as the rush in his footsteps as he moved to meet Nehelon—who had picked up pace and was now walking in front of Gandrett, who was still deciding whether he was a threat or just the greatest fool in the world.

She watched the two men embrace between the blossoming greenery and again felt the urge to comment when the Meister caught her eye over Nehelon's shoulder, his gaze saving her from embarrassing herself and, worse, from potential punishment had she not been able to hold her tongue. "Leave us, Gandrett," he motioned with one hand as he clapped Nehelon's back. "But stay close." He slowly pulled out of the other man's embrace, his eyes full of the dancing light of the band of fire lighting the courtyard from the edges of the gravel which enclosed the vegetation in the square space. "My friend and I have matters to talk through."

With a low bow, Gandrett retreated back inside and paced the hallway for a minute, debating whether or not it was acceptable to spy on the head of the Order of Vala and his mysterious visitor, before she settled at the windowsill next to the door and peered inside through the stained glass.

The small clear segment that was low enough for her to see through opened the view on an animated discussion. Nehelon, expression so tight earlier, was smiling broadly and openly, an expression which turned his already handsome face into outright beautiful. Gandrett bit her lip and scowled.

Who was this man to simply be allowed to upturn the rules that were valid for everyone who traveled to Everrun? How could he attack one of the Order of Vala and yet be welcomed with a hug by the very same Meister who had set those rules in stone?

As she watched them, the Meister, his face so unusually bright, pulled Nehelon down by the arm as he sat on the edge of the dais, suddenly looking old. His back, normally straight and unyielding, his shoulders, now slumped. While beside him, Nehelon's muscled body, forearms resting on his knees, dark hair falling in his face and hiding those piercing eyes behind a wavy curtain, displayed the epitome of strength and youth. And as they spoke, both faces slowly grew weary. What were they talking about?

Gandrett's head grew heavy as the sky turned darker, and she played with the plain iron pommel of her sword, which she had laid down beside her on the windowsill. She was still in her sweaty clothes, dust and dirt making the sand color appear darker in places. Her stomach growled. On a normal day, she would sit across the table from Kaleb and next to Surel, digging into whatever stew they offered for the evening, quietly smiling at Kaleb's grin's and ignoring Surel's jabs in her ribs at every one of them.

Life at the Order of Vala was easy, in a way. Every year at Vernal Equinox, the Fest of Blossoms—Vala's holiday—four children joined the order. And four left to take on their duties wherever the Meister assigned them. The children were collected from the territories of Neredyn. One child from each human territory except for Sives, the north. Gandrett's homeland. Sives usually sent two children: two symbolic, for each of the twin capitals—Ackwood in the west and Eedwood in the east. Gandrett shuddered and shoved the thought far down into the black depths of her memory.

Life at the order was obedience, training, worship. Obedience toward the Meister and his rules, training in swordsmanship or, for the gifted ones, magic. And worship of Vala. Every chore, every lap around the city, every sharpening of her blade, was in worship of Vala. That was the life she'd been sent into, and that was the life that had shaped her, sculpted her, inside and out.

Her calloused hand picked up the sword and weighed it while she watched reflections of flickering firelight dancing on the worn metal. Fancy swords were for nobles, not for members of the order who were destined to serve their entire life. Their lives a sacrifice on behalf of each ruler in Neredyn to Vala, the goddess of life and water. A glance at Nehelon's sword at her hip told her enough to know that he came from a bloodline worthy of setting jewels into the hilt and pommel of their swords. She ran a finger over the crimson crystals and frowned.

Gandrett didn't count the minutes the two of them spent conversing between the greenery, lost in her own thoughts, and pushed away from the windowsill only when the Meister called her name loudly enough to make it clear she'd been summoned.

"Get our guest to more suitable quarters for the night," the Meister ordered, his face returned to normal, as Gandrett popped her head into the courtyard, ducking under the short palm tree at the side. "And give him his weapons back."

Behind the calm posture of the Meister, Nehelon smirked at Gandrett, the look in his eyes letting her only guess that whatever their discussion had been, it had been to the young man's satisfaction. It made Gandrett want to stick out her tongue, but she bit it instead, preventing herself from falling out of grace with someone who seemed to be favored by the head of the Order of Vala.

"Thank you, Meister." He bowed low as the Meister glanced over his shoulder, a serene expression decorating his timeless face.

"We will talk tomorrow, my friend," was all the Meister said before he nodded a silent dismissal.

Gandrett didn't wait for Nehelon to join her at the threshold before she started out the door after a hurried bow. And even if her face was smooth and emotionless, she heard it in her own footsteps crunching on the stone floor, expressing how the tension was there, how she couldn't stand to have him out of sight even if, for now, he was unarmed. It went against her nature to turn her back on an opponent—even if technically he wasn't an enemy. Not if the Meister had welcomed him with open arms. She had never seen him do that in ten years.

"You could have taken the front gate," she hissed when she felt him close enough behind her to not have to speak up. "I am sure the guards would have let you pass..." she searched for words that wouldn't make her sound so bitter "...you know, if the Meister is a friend of yours, I am certain you'd have gotten immediate passage into our sanctuary."

A low snort was all the answer she got, and her mind instantly spiraled into what might have made him choose to make that sound rather than parry with words. He had certainly exceeded doing so earlier.

"You don't think so?" She prompted.

And got another sound that this time wasn't entirely identifiable—and had Gandrett peeking over her shoulder.

Nehelon's face was unreadable, tight again, all hints he was capable of the smile she had seen him flash earlier wiped away.

For a while, they walked in silence, the only sound the waterfall before the entrance arches, rolling like a harbinger of the storm that was brewing above the priory.

When they crossed the yard, leaving the pool at the foot of the citadel behind them, the first drops of rain speckled the ground, making Gandrett choose the long route along the side of the citadel that had the shortest distance to the residential building, and crossed through the tightening rain in a jog with Nehelon catching up to her side in a few elegant strides.

"You must be someone special," she sniffed, letting her own features distort at the gesture, a sign of how little she cared—tried to, "if the Meister welcomes you to Everrun with open arms... and without insisting on a cell." They ducked under the roof of the residential building.

Nehelon chuckled, a sound that mixed with the noise of the thick blotches of rain now hitting the building from a sharp angle, forced by spikes of wind that usually remained outside the wall.

Inside, after inquiring with Nahir—the housekeeper and one of the few who had been there for decades to comfort the new arrivals every spring—where to best bring the Meister's guest, Gandrett led him up the stairs to the second floor, where the ceilings were higher than at the other floors and the rooms equipped with more comforts.

"This might not be what you are used to." She opened the carved, wooden door and gestured into a room with an antechamber and an adjacent bathing room. Simple but more than double the size of her own chambers. Not that any of the acolytes had the luxury of their own bathing chamber. "But it's the best we've got."

She half-expected to get a mocking comment, but to her surprise, Nehelon stepped past her, careful not to brush against her side as he slipped into the room, and inclined his head. "It's more than I expected." His face loosened a bit as he strode through the pale blue antechamber, and he peeked into the spacious bedroom. "Better than the cell, for sure." He turned and leaned against the doorframe.

Gandrett eyed him for a moment, unsure of what to make of him, half-anticipating he might still attack her. Then, tense to the core, she reached down to her side to free his sword from her belt and held it out to him.

"I brought you to the Meister," she said, voice terse. "Now you owe me the truth."

"You can put that over there." Ignoring her request, Nehelon jerked his chin at the slim, wooden table next to the door and, much to Gandrett's relief, not showing any signs he was going to grab the blade and leap at her. His face remained unreadable, controlled, as if he had spent a lifetime hiding his emotions.

"The truth," Gandrett reminded him as she took a cautious step then lowered his weapon onto the scenes of Neredyn legends painted in pale blue and shades of brown.

Nehelon pointed at her own blade. "Yours, too." His mouth tightened as he watched her hesitate then lower the second blade beside his.

"Worried I'll attack you?" she asked with the mildest satisfaction, but didn't even get a chance to gloat as Nehelon responded, "Even with both of them, you wouldn't stand a chance."

There it was again, that mocking grin and cold eyes—not cold, cautious, calculating. Distant.

"Our short history suggests otherwise," was all Gandrett said as she dumped her blade onto the table, closed the door, and dropped into one of the wooden chairs beside it, crossing her arms.

And that was that.

"So, the truth," she repeated, keeping her face indifferent.

Nehelon's sharp eyes weighed on her, sizing her up, measuring, reminding her of her dirty, sweaty clothes and making her unfamiliarly self-conscious. She knew that when she took the effort and combed her hair and—for the holidays and ceremonies at the temple-rooms of the citadel, wore her only dress—she cleaned up well. But right now, what Nehelon must be seeing was a wildling in linen rags.

As if he'd heard her, he averted his gaze and strode over to the small window at the wall to Gandrett's right where he observed the splattering rain.

"The truth is, Gandrett Brayton, I have come to get you out of here.

The girl's eyes widened at the mention of her name. She hadn't introduced herself. She didn't need to. It had taken him a week on horseback to reach the border of Calma—not a natural border but a border where the lush forests of Ulfray and the lakes at the ruins of Ithrylan ended as if someone had cut them off with a knife, turning the other side of the cut into wasteland. From there, it had been three more days before he had made it to the ghost town at the east of Everrun, all of which he had spent absorbed in thoughts of how to best find out if Gandrett Brayton truly was what the Meister had promised—what he was looking for.

"Don't look at me like that." He could tell the difference in the way she had eyed him before and the way she did now.

The distaste, the mild mockery, they were both swept away by that simple detail—he knew who she was. And being trained by the best warrior in Neredyn—best human warrior, at least—Gandrett understood the attack, his appearance at the wall at the exact time she took her afternoon run hadn't been mere coincidence.

He turned back to the window, giving her a second of space to sort her thoughts, her expectations of this conversation.

He was aware of the stakes involved. The stakes that Tyrem Brenheran, Lord of Ackwood had placed on Nehelon's shoulders and sent him on this mission. And now that he had confirmed that at least Gandrett's fighting skills were what he had been promised, it was time to figure out if the rest was true as well.

"You have been here before," Gandrett repeated what he had avoided confirming or denying earlier.

"Of course I have," he bit at her. He needed her, he reminded himself. He had to keep his tongue under control, his temper. With a too-swift motion, less adapted to his human environment than usual, he turned and faced her, only to find intent eyes staring him down. How he hated to need her. To need anyone. "But it has been a while..." He played with a string on his leathers and cursed himself for having to do this. "It's none of your business, Gandrett."

The bold use of her first name dulled the fire in her gaze enough to hate himself even more.

He couldn't forget this girl had not seen the outside world for a decade. Her last memories of it probably—hopefully—as blurry as the rain-splattered window beside him. And if she remembered...

"So, what truth is it you've been dying to share with me?" She blinked as if shuttering away that moment of being unsettled. If she did remember, she showed no sign.

"You should choose your words more wisely when speaking to someone who is offering you a shot at freedom," he growled, his temper rising.

At that, Gandrett snorted. "Freedom?" She unfolded her arms and placed both hands on the armrests of her chair. "What is freedom?"

Her words hit him right in the chest. But for nothing in the world would he let her see, even guess what lay behind that face he chose to wear—a warrior's face, cunning, unfeeling.

"How will you get me out of here?" she eventually asked, her own face mirroring his, her words carrying a bitter note. "If you have been here before, you know that there are only two ways to get out." She held up one sun-tanned hand, counting for him. "One, you are a visitor. You come; you go. Two, you turn of age and are sent on a mission." She pursed her lips as if thinking. "But, wait... I have one more year to go until then, and even if I get sent on a mission, my life will always belong to the order." Her eyes searched the ceiling in a quite skilled display of someone who was having an epiphany. "So, no, Nehelon—if that is even your real name—now, the second way to get out of here is to be dead."

He could hardly watch her. Seventeen and so bitter, already tested by life to a degree hardly any child in Neredyn was. And she didn't even know the half of it. Of course there was no way she could trust him. Not that he deserved her trust. So for now...

"It is my real name," he simply said, leaving any emotion out of it.

"Nehelon, Lord of—?" she prompted.

"What makes you think that I am a lord?"

A nod at his sword was all the response he needed. How observant she was. The hilt, gold and set with jewels in the color of the House of Brenheran, gave away where his alliances lay even if it didn't even come close to where he hailed from.

"I have convinced the Meister to release you from your training early to assist in a matter of utmost importance instead." The words sounded like a joke rather than a real offer, especially given she had just schooled him in how little she thought she could ever attain freedom.

Gandrett fell silent in her chair, face calm despite the disbelief.

"I am to work with you?" she asked, looking about as happy as a fish swimming in glass shards.

"You are to work for me," he clarified and leaned against the windowsill, posture deliberately aloof. "That is if you agree to the terms the Meister and I agreed on."

Had he thought Gandrett was unhappy earlier, he now saw what a truly horrified look did to her otherwise pleasant—if dirty—face. Her supple lips thinned, and her eyes, big and clear—even if their color wasn't identifiable from a distance and in this light, tightened as if she was chewing them off from the inside.

"Not that you have much of a choice, really," he added with a quiet hope he would see what she was capable of if she were to kick back her check on her fighter's temper.

Gandrett was still fuming as she ascended the stairs to the top level of the building where she shared a room with Surel. Her lips were almost bloody from gnawing on them so she wouldn't rip Nehelon's throat out.

So the Meister was selling her to Nehelon like a prize pony. Even worse, lending her to the upsetting warrior. To give back after the task was fulfilled so the Meister could send her on another mission and another and another—until she no longer was able to fight. And then? What would become of her? Would she live with the priests and priestesses of Vala, serve them like so many of the former acolytes... at least the ones who hadn't died on their missions?

She stomped down the narrow corridor, footsteps enhanced by the creaking wood that made an uneven floor, and flung open the door to her room with a push of her free hand.

"By Vala," Surel started on her bed as she took in the expression on Gandrett's face. "What happened?"

But Gandrett shook her head, dropping on her own bed, and sat wordlessly for half a minute, focusing on the reassuring weight of her sword in her hand.

She hadn't struck Nehelon. She was glad she hadn't. But even if she had controlled herself enough to simply turn and leave rather than tell—or show—him exactly what she thought of the proposition, she knew there would be consequences.

"Maybe you should eat dinner before you tell me," Surel suggested, eyeing Gandrett's blade with the same respect the other apprentices did. Even if Surel's primary skill was water magic, she had been trained in the basics of sword fighting, the same way all of them had—and she had sparred with

Gandrett and lost countless times. "I am sure Nahir can whip something up for you."

Gandrett shook her head. Hunger was the last thing on her mind, but freedom...

Freedom tasted like a forbidden fruit on her tongue. And Nehelon had offered it—even if it was temporary.

If she should find herself able to live with that one painful detail of the conditions—she'd work for him. The Lord of Ackwood. Lord Tyrem Brenheran. The man who had given the order to take her from her parents and ship her to Everrun.

No matter how prestigious everyone thought it was to get chosen—everyone made themselves believe it was to get chosen—it wasn't. Not anymore, not when it was your family. When it was you being publicly sheered and dipped in cold water and consecrated in the name of the goddess. And by his order, Tyrem Brenheran had sealed her fate.

"Do you ever think of what comes after our life here?" She lifted her head and studied Surel, who seemed unsure about how to answer her question.

Of course, Surel as a water mage would have a good life, maybe even become a high priestess one day, be able to make some demands and have a comfortable life—as long as she never went against the order's orders. And as long as she never fell in love.

For Gandrett, as a fighter, a warrior, going on a mission would likely mean that her life after here would be short. Too short to even figure out what having a life would mean.

"There is plenty of time for us before we need to face it," Surel reminded with a raised eyebrow.

"For me," Gandrett admitted, "there might not be that much time after all.

The water mage sighed and padded across the room to take Gandrett's sword from her hands. Then, she enclosed the still dirty fingers in her own. "We'll deal with it when the time comes."

And so, Gandrett told Surel about the conversation she'd had with Nehelon, the offer to escape Everrun a year earlier—and step into the service of the man who was responsible for her ending up here at all.

With enough patience to make Gandrett wonder if the girl had fallen asleep beside her, Surel listened, her golden-tan face serious.

Gandrett didn't need to add that she hadn't agreed to anything, and Surel's reaction was similar to her own. Only Surel didn't hold back her thoughts.

She cursed violently, words that would have the Meister punishing her for blasphemy, and Gandrett, for the first time this day, felt a real smile creeping on her face. She leaned her head against Surel's and sighed.

"What will you do without me when you're gone?" she asked and nudged Gandrett's side.

Gandrett had to agree. Who would calm her when she was internally storming? Who would make her smile? Who would she confide in—if Surel and Kaleb were no longer available?

The first light of dawn and a rumbling stomach had Nehelon sitting upright in his bed—a bed. How many days since he had slept in a bed? The softness of it was almost wrong in its feel after a long journey on horseback and sleeping under the stars.

There were no servants in Everrun, so he rolled out of the linens and folded them before he headed for the bathing room and got dressed. The night before, he had spent an hour in the bathtub, scrubbing off the dirt of his journey, and had ended up laying down in bed without dinner. A decision he now regretted.

His morning routine was simple: the same exercise every day to keep his body toned and breakfast after so he would function for the day. Today, the routine had to wait. He tied his leathers on the side, flung the Brenheran coat of arms into the basin to wash later, then picked up his sword from beside the pillow where he had stowed it the night before. On his way out, he glanced at the sky—the storm and rain had made way for a bright, orange sunrise—then snuck down the one flight of stairs and made his way to the back door, Unlike when exiting at the residential building's front, this way no one would notice him slipping away.

The priory was just waking up when he made his way past the back of the citadel and through the lines of side buildings where Gandrett had locked him in a cell. The eastern gate lay just behind those, but he didn't risk sneaking around them, instead hoisting himself up at a window to climb up the second floor with nothing but his fingers holding onto the small gaps between the stones. Years. It had been years since he had done that here in Everrun, but his hands seemed to remember as if it were yesterday.

It didn't cost him much effort to reach the roof and the tiles, shabby as they were, held fast as he set one cautious foot after the other, ducking over the rooftops and toward the wall. The biting wind hit his face at almost the exact moment he reached his goal. Far enough from the eastern gate, Nehelon leaped over the gap between the last house and the wall and flung himself over so he hung from the top of the wall, just out of sight of the guard towers overseeing the ghost city at his feet. The drop to the ground let his blood heat. It was—as always—a combination of skill and luck that he didn't break any bones and that he wasn't discovered before he could make it to the safety of the withered buildings beyond the wall. A town once—a city with the priory adjacent in the west. He could almost hear the merchants in the ruins of the market he sought cover in, could almost smell the fruit and vegetables that had once been sold here. But even if it broke his heart to see this town—his town—in ruins, he didn't let it slow him down.

On and on he moved, through the blacksmith quarter, toward the north-eastern end, the rising sun mercifully casting shadows over him as he made progress, keeping him hidden from the guards on the wall.

There, just before the last scattered ruins, he had left his two horses and his pack. He had made it to this shelter three nights ago and decided to stay in the ghost city of Everrun before he would seek out the Meister and find Gandrett. He wanted to take his time, learn about what had changed around the priory, how many people entered or left the wall these days—not many, he'd notice—before he came to claim what the Meister had promised: his best fighter to assist in the mission that lay ahead of him. A reliable fighter, bound to a code of silence just like him, and with no connection to the outside world. Someone uncorrupted.

The thought hurt as he became fully aware that bringing Gandrett back to Sives, bringing her into Lord Tyrem's court would corrupt her in no time, and if he didn't manage to secure her trust and her loyalty by then, she might as well become a liability. He shuddered.

Stomping hooves greeted him as he entered the centuries abandoned stables, and his black mare gave a grumpy huff as he came to her empty-handed.

"If it makes you feel any better, I haven't eaten since I headed out yesterday, either."

The horse gave him a disdainful look then gnawed on the mane of the slightly smaller bay gelding, who seemed marginally happier to see Nehelon and whinnied softly as if voicing a question.

"Yes," he nodded at the horses, "I found her."

The mare paused the social fur-gnawing to give him a warning look.

"And, yes, we can stay in proper accommodations for a couple of days."

The mare blinked her depthless eyes before she shook her head, then her neck, followed by her whole body like a wet dog, making the gelding buck.

With quick fingers, Nehelon gathered his pack. Then, he rubbed the horses down with a fist-full of leftover hay before he threw on bridle and saddle and led them out the half- caved-in building. Thank Vala, what was left of the roof had provided enough shelter that neither horses nor belongings had gotten wet during the storm.

The sun had climbed the horizon in the east where far beyond the desert, the ocean seamed the continent when Nehelon hoisted himself into the saddle.

"Not far," he announced and kicked the mare's flank who, with the gelding in tow, fell into a steady trot.

⁂

Gandrett couldn't remember when she had fallen asleep.

After what had felt like hours of tossing, Surel had tiptoed across the room and laid down beside her, putting one arm around Gandrett's shoulders. It had always been like that. Since they had both been brought to the priory, they had watched out for each other. They had comforted each other. Even if emotions had no place in their daily training or during their chores, if it hadn't been for Surel, Gandrett didn't know if she would still be sane. She was the bubbly well where Gandrett was the fierce storm. And Kaleb—

Kaleb was the brother she had left behind in Alencourt when Lord Tyrem Brenheran's men had come to tear her from her home. When she looked at Kaleb, she saw her brother's gray eyes, his blond, curly hair, his freckles. Andrew probably didn't even remember he had a sister. He had been too young, only four short years.

Beside her, Surel stirred then yawned and rolled to her side.

"You look like the dead." She raised an eyebrow, her black eyes blinking against the morning sun.

Gandrett climbed out of bed with a frown. "I feel like the dead." She didn't stop at the small mirror in the corner next to the plain, wooden desk but scooped up two fresh sets of clothes from the chair by the door where Nahir dropped them every night.

Surel had made it to an upright position, her eyebrow still arched toward her hairline as she observed. "Do you want to talk about it today?"

She hadn't last night. She hadn't wanted to spill every thought, her anger, everything. And even though she had shared about the *offer* Nehelon had presented, her mind was still in too much turmoil to verbalize her thoughts. "Thanks for the offer." She tossed Surel a set of clothes and forced a smile. "But the only thing that will help is Nahir's special recipe."

Surel bobbed her head. When they had arrived that spring ten years ago, Nahir had heard them weep through the night, and in the morning, she had been waiting at their door with a tray of cookies. Plain raisin and oatmeal cookies. And they had tasted as if Vala herself had made them.

Gandrett headed for the bathing rooms and freshened up, changing into the practical linen pants and tunic before she combed through her waist-length hair and braided it back.

When she returned to the bedroom, Surel was dressed and ready, her raven hair flowing freely down to her shoulders. Unlike the fighters' brown belt, she was wearing a pale blue one of the Vala-blessed, symbolizing water.

Gandrett strapped her sword to her hip and stepped into her boots.

As they headed downstairs, she found the house was already buzzing with life, most of the acolytes swarming to the dining hall on the ground floor.

Kaleb waved them over to their usual table in the corner where the three of them were unbothered by the world, his eyes expectant, and straightened a little. But while Surel joined them at the table, Gandrett screened the room for the messy black-gray hair of the housekeeper and, when she didn't find her, trudged to the kitchens across the hall where Nahir hid her secret stash of cookies.

"It is either that time of the month, or the talk with that visitor didn't go well."

Gandrett stopped her hand midair, reaching for the cookies, and turned around to find Nahir leaning at the stove, apron white with flour in places, a cup of tea in her hand, and gave her a knowing look. "Which one is it?"

The housekeeper pushed away from the stove and set down the cup before she brushed off her hands in the rag on her shoulder, immediately hurrying to the cupboard at the other end of the sun-lit room.

"I moved them," she whispered, glancing over her shoulder as she pulled a small, wooden footstool toward her with her toes then stepped onto it, too short to reach the top shelf without the extra inches. "Kids are starting to sneak in here during the night and emptying the box." She produced a round, wooden container from the cupboard and shook it, which resulted in a soft rattle as if to prove a point.

She spoke in her heavy accent. The accent of the Nasha nomads, a people that had been living and striving in these lands long before Calma had turned into a desert. These days, the few Nasha left had retreated to the south to live at the feet of the mountains.

"With the new kids coming in in a couple of days, I'll need to triple my production, or I won't be able to do a thing for them when they're homesick." Nahir's chubby cheeks raised as she smiled broadly, the gesture filling Gandrett's stomach with mixed feelings.

The new ones... The novices. Each year, on Vala's Day—the Fest of Blossoms as they called it in the north—when day and night were equally long, the four new ones were brought in. And every year, the crying and whimpering filled the residential building for days, if not weeks. There was nothing much anyone could do... other than to help Nahir hand out cookies and soothing words.

Gandrett did it every year since that first anniversary of her consecration. It didn't change the fact that another four kids were torn from their homes and committed to a lifetime of service, but it helped her deal with the melancholy that hit every year as if someone set a timer for it.

Nahir reached into the box and handed her a cookie. "Don't tell the others where I'm hiding them," she whispered and pulled out two more cookies and put them on a small plate, which she placed on the counter, "For later," before she stowed the box back on the shelf.

The comforting taste of sweetness and familiarity filled Gandrett's mouth, wiping away the heavier thoughts—for now.

"The visitor," she finally said, earning a knowing look from Nahir.

"I knew the second you marched him past the guards that he was trouble."

Gandrett cocked her head, wondering if there was something she hadn't noticed. But again, the elderly woman nodded and gave her that look.

"If you'd been wandering the lands for as long as I have—if you'd seen what the world is like outside those walls," she nodded toward the window beside the shelf that gave a clear view of the western gate and the cobbled roads that led past the citadel to where she had locked Nehelon up, "you'd know that there is more to him than just that pretty face."

Gandrett felt her brows rise.

"And I am not necessarily speaking about the good kind of *more*." Nahir pushed the plate of cookies toward Gandrett, who hadn't noticed she had finished the palm-sized one she'd held in her hand a moment earlier. "That man has secrets." She gave Gandrett a conspiring glance.

The next cookie was gone in two bites.

Gandrett was aware that it was one thing to tell Surel about the Meister's intentions to lend her to Nehelon, but to tell Nahir... Even if she loved the woman like a mother—because of the lack of the latter. Nahir was the only person living and working in Everrun not because she'd been sacrificed, but because she chose to. She had spent her childhood with the nomads at the border to Phornes, and at some point—she had never shared the full story, but Gandrett suspected a man had something to do with it—she had shown up at the order's doorstep, and the Meister had taken her in, given her this job, this new life. For all that is worth, the Meister had a humane side buried deep down somewhere. She had seen it with Nahir, and she had seen it with Nehelon the night before.

"The Meister seems to trust him," was all that Gandrett said.

And the shrug she earned from Nahir was enough to tell her she didn't.

The blond-curled boy wasn't at the gate this time, but the second one was and had, together with a broad-built acolyte, taken up their positions in the narrow towers.

The sight, familiar as it was, made him sick. Children. Even if they were almost of age by human standards, by his own standards, they were little more than fledglings. Even if they had trained for ten years within these walls, none of them had seen a battlefield. None of them had killed or seen their loved ones being slaughtered. Nehelon's face hardened as if it could change the memories in his head.

"Nehelon, guest of the Meister." He inclined his head an inch, unpacking his manners for a moment.

While the new guard returned his nod and waved him forward, the other one scowled. He remembered that yesterday he had behaved like scum—only to challenge Gandrett, to see how she handled things. But the guard didn't know that.

"So I've heard," the boy said, voice more controlled than his face, and pulled the mechanism to open the gate.

A gust of wind followed Nehelon and the horses into the priory where everyone had taken up their chores once more. While some acolytes were sawing grains, water mages were manipulating the rainwater in the soil to pool around the seedlings. It brought back memories of his years in Everrun, in this very priory. A time when the Meister had just started his own journey in the Order of Vala.

Nehelon didn't bother climbing off the horse as he steered the mare toward the stables on the right, followed by the second horse, nose close by his thigh. No one asked why he was here, or why he had brought two horses, as he halted and slid off his mare then led both animals inside. Instead, two acolytes were ready to take the reins, leading each mount into a shack with stacks of hay and buckets of water. The Meister had probably instructed them. Nehelon smiled.

He hadn't had to sneak out this morning. The guards would have let him pass to get his things and his horses, but it was so much more fun to sneak out like the old days. He caught one of the acolytes returning his smile and barked something at him, sending the boy running off with his mare's bridle.

Gandrett played with the pommel of her sword as she walked up to Nehelon's door. The tenth hour, sharp, the message had said, and knowing how fast word got around here at the priory, she made sure she arrived a good time earlier just so the Meister wouldn't have a reason to punish her.

She had long been done with her oatmeal cookies when one of the younger acolytes came running with a piece of paper with the Meister's zig-zaggy handwriting speaking of urgency. So Gandrett had dropped her book—prayers to Vala— and anxious to be on her way, she had almost run over Kaleb, who had come to check on her after she had ditched him at breakfast. A few awkward words had been the result, and his cheeks had burned as she promised to sit with him at dinner that night. Empty words, she knew, for if Nehelon had it his way, she might no longer be here for dinner. A shudder ran over her back as she approached the carved door on the first floor, footsteps muffled by the thick rug that was unique to this level of the building.

She hadn't even lifted a hand to knock when Nehelon's voice sounded through the wood, beckoning her to enter, the cold tone of it making her hair stand.

What was the worst thing that could happen? She straightened her back and smoothed her tunic. Nothing—nothing could happen. At least nothing worse than what had already happened. The Meister had lent her to the man with that taunting gaze.

She took a steadying breath and brushed back a loose strand of hair then opened the door with more force than necessary, only to stop dead on the threshold—

There stood the man who had almost defeated her, the man who had glanced at her with glacial eyes, who had wielded his sword as if it was the only thing he'd ever done in his life, and—

And he spoke to a bird. Crouching on the floor, one hand resting on the windowsill, and perched on one finger sat a fat, gray bird, tweeting cheerily.

Gandrett was about to turn on her heels and leave when Nehelon, his face hidden by a curtain of dark hair, whispered something at the bird then flicked his hand and watched the creature take flight.

"Where else did you think I get the news from in this godsforsaken place?" His words were as icy as the day before, but his brow lifted as he tore his attention away from the window and turned to look at her.

Gandrett's eyes involuntarily shuttered. Nehelon had changed out of his leathers and was now wearing black pants and a tunic of equal color but with subtle embroidery at the collar and around the buttons and on the sleeves. His hair was washed, wavy, giving him a more civilized look than the dirt and leather the day before. But what struck her wasn't his outfit but his face: clean and with the slightest bit of emotion—even if she had no name for what was playing in his eyes, it did something to her stomach that reminded her of nausea, but a surprisingly comfortable kind of nausea.

"Not gods-forsaken," she gathered her thoughts and corrected him, remembering at that instant just how much disdain she held for the man across the room, who slowly and gracefully rose to his feet.

He cocked his head as if he couldn't believe she had just replied in such a way, then leaned against the windowsill. "I haven't seen any sign the gods—the male gods," he clarified, "have any interest in this place."

For a moment, he paused as if waiting to see whether Gandrett would be able to hold her tongue this time.

She was.

"But the goddess—Vala—she is here. I can tell by the storms that keep circling Everrun like a stroke of her hand, and the magic in the citadel, the magic in some of the acolytes."

The words weren't what had Gandrett gaping at him, for once forgetting she was doing exactly that. He ran a hand through his hair, and though she'd promised herself to face this man at her strongest, not giving him a flicker of herself, what he exposed when his fingers slid absently through his hair, pulling it back behind his ears... pointed ears.

5

While Gandrett was still gawking, Nehelon's face turned ashen with realization. Even if the dark strands had fallen back into place, covering what he had exposed, Gandrett knew by the look on his face that he was aware she'd seen them.

Fae. He was Fae. And he had made a fool of her all this time...

Gandrett swallowed and browsed through what little she had learned about Fae. Magic. They had magic. And not just the simple kind the Vala-blessed possessed.

While among humans, only those blessed by the goddess at their consecration had magic, there was one territory in Neredyn where magic—in all of its varieties—was as common as bad stew in the human territories: The kingdom of the Fae. A kingdom feared for over a thousand years, its nobles dormant in the evergreen forests of Ulfray, sworn to remain behind the lines where the magical green ended. Sworn by an oath that was as old as the desert around Everrun. And bound by a magic more ancient than the forgotten islands in the west.

That magic—the magic of the Fae, was feared. And if someone, anyone but the ones blessed by Vala, showed any signs they had it, they were exiled to Ulfray, leaving what happened to them up to whatever Fae were still alert enough to deal with them. And the legends she'd heard in her childhood, the legends even told by Nahir, didn't suggest they were a merciful people, but a cruel one, killing for sport and feasting on their prey's fear.

Gandrett's heart slushed in her throat, racing as if it could escape without her feet, but Nehelon's gaze—

From the look on his face, he was calculating the best way to put her down before she could work up a scream. The fastest way. Maybe a blow to the head with his steel Fae hands. Or rip out her throat with his perfectly white, now-bared teeth. She couldn't muster the courage to turn her back to him and run. For the first time in her life—for the first time since that day she'd been torn from her mother's arms—she couldn't think, couldn't breathe.

So as she kept staring, gawking bluntly, Nehelon stared her down, a warrior no longer, but a predator assessing the kill he was about to make.

Cold sweat covered Gandrett's neck, and she forced her mind to function, to remain calm—or to return to that detached mode she went into while fighting.

As if the memory of herself wielding a sword broke the chain on her mind, her body started following her orders again, but there was something else holding her back. An external force—

And then, the door behind her shut so fast she could hardly see it move.

But Nehelon was still standing where he had been a heartbeat ago, his lips parting over his teeth in a feral smile that didn't allow for much hope.

"You're Fae," Gandrett finally gouged out the words, and she wasn't surprised her voice was shaky... or that it sounded like an accusation.

Because it was.

It was an accusation. If he was Fae, he was bound to dwell in Ulfray where the trees were growing over the dormant people. The dormant danger, the threat her ancestors, and their ancestors before them, had fought to contain, to banish from the human realm.

"How observant you are," was all that Nehelon replied. But she could tell how powerful he was from the way everything about his demeanor, his posture, his movements, had changed. No longer slow and graceful—human. But quick, fluid, lethal.

Gandrett fought against the invisible hand—not a hand, a wall, a layer, solid as rock, yet transparent as air—magic—enclosing her and, again, found herself unable to move.

Nehelon's grin widened as if he found something indescribably amusing and pushed away from the windowsill, eyes never blinking. Not even once.

Gandrett's hand strained to reach for her sword, but the invisible grasp didn't allow so much as a quarter of an inch. Sweat was plastering her hair to her neck and was trickling down her back and chest, leaving stains on the pale fabric.

"You're afraid," he mused as if that was something to ponder rather than the effect of his involuntary revelation.

He took a stride toward her, then another, and another, pushing Gandrett's heart to its limits as it raced in fear, until he stopped one short step away, towering over her by over one head and glancing down at her as if he had just discovered a very pleasant dish.

Had her chest not started to ache, her eardrums not throbbed from the thundering of her weak, human heart, she might have noticed to a full extent how different Nehelon looked compared to what she had seen that first time she had laid eyes on him. His face was smooth planes and sharp angles, sun-kissed. And heart-wrenchingly beautiful. With eyes, cold and calculating, that had nothing to do with the smile on his full lips. He was Fae, and it was obvious on every inch of his gods-damned, chiseled features. As if someone had pulled off a layer of disguise, a veil to conceal the damning reality.

"Good," he said as if to himself, making Gandrett's eyes shutter as she realized she wasn't only staring from fear, but with a kind of morbid fascination.

"Here is what will happen, Gandrett Brayton." His voice was a symphony of shimmering velvet. And lethal like a butchering knife. Gandrett shrank back against the wall of magic enclosing her, finding herself in the exact same position. "You didn't see what I am. You were never in here. You missed me in my chambers and went right to the citadel to see the Meister and meet me there." He flashed his teeth as he leaned closer, staring her down. "You will go upstairs, pack your things, then meet me at the citadel. When we step in front of the Meister, I will do the talking. And you will agree to everything I say. Every demand, every condition of my bargain with the Meister, you will nod your consent." His face was an inch from hers, breath hot on her cheeks, gaze hard and deep like blue diamond. "Understood?"

Gandrett nodded, finding her head to be the only part of her body capable of moving. There was nothing not to understand in his words.

"If you linger, if you speak to anyone, if you try to make a run for it," he added, voice low and clear. "If you try, I will know. I will come find you. And you will regret you ever met me."

Again, Gandrett's head bobbed as if compelled by his words. Not that she needed another reason to regret having met him. It was already ingrained in her system to hate him, to fear him, to put as much distance between him and whatever was dear to her. But that didn't matter now, did it?

As if he suddenly lost interest, Nehelon turned around and strode to the armchair by the bedroom door, leaving her standing like a petrified doll. "Now is the time to swing your pretty legs and run upstairs," he said, flinging himself into the chair, and watched her with mild amusement as he crossed one ankle over a knee. And when Gandrett didn't react, he barked, "Now."

Like a bolt of lightning, his voice tore through her core, almost making her fall forward as he lifted the spell on her. Nehelon bestowed on her a mocking grin before he gestured at the door and cocked his head, not needing to say anything else prior to Gandrett's survival instinct kicking in again, and she reached for the doorknob behind her, never taking her eyes off the Fae male lounging in a chair across the room as if he didn't have a care in the world.

andrett ran, ran, ran, not looking left or right as she climbed up the stairs to her room. She prayed to Vala that Surel wasn't there for fear she would ask questions. Questions which cost time to evade when she wasn't allowed to give answers.

She might have grown up away from the world, but she was no fool, understanding that the Fae could hear through walls, that they could smite humans at a whim without lifting as much as a finger. If she talked, Nehelon would know. She was certain of it. He was probably down there, straining his Fae ears to pick up every step of hers.

Gandrett quickened her pace as she made it to the dim corridor, out of breath, not from the physical strain but fear, from the feeling that she was being watched. Only a couple more steps, and she'd be able to fulfill Nehelon's first order. Pack her things.

She ditched a girl who had a room at the other end of the corridor, noting her curious glance from the corner of her eyes—no one ever saw Gandrett out of breath. She had become so much a master of her own strength and stamina that no one at the order was able to engage her into fighting long enough to push her to her limits. Not even the Meister. Not anymore.

But Gandrett didn't give any sign she had seen the girl, instead rushing on to her room and slipping inside, closing the door and leaning against it, taking a deep breath.

Thank Vala, the room was empty.

Another breath. This couldn't be happening. The Fae were banned. They were bound to their own lands, to the shades of their trees, to their forests. How had Nehelon gotten out?

Then it hit her that that wasn't really the question she should be asking herself. The one that begged an answer: What did he want with her?

Unable to gather a clear thought, other than she needed to hurry, Gandrett pulled out her spare set of clothes, what few toiletries she possessed, bundled them up in her worn nightgown, and stowed them in her satchel. She grabbed her narrow, leather vambraces from the shelf—the only piece of armor they were allowed in the priory, and slipped them over her hands then pulled her sleeves over them so no one would notice them.

When she had hidden them, she halted and sat on the bed. What was she doing? She couldn't just sneak out of the priory with the Fae male. What if he was just on the lookout for his next snack? And what if she ran? How fast would he catch up with her? Would she even make it through the night?

The scars spread on her back and arms spoke volumes about how much she could handle—whether they were from sparring accidents or from the frequent occasions the Meister got dissatisfied. But could her body endure the brute strength of a Fae?

She shuddered and rested her head in her palms for a short while—just a couple of breaths, she told herself. But the shrill tweeting of the fat, gray bird on her windowsill made her jerk upright.

"Shoo, shoo." She fanned her arms at the creature. The same bird Nehelon had been talking to. Nehelon's messenger.

The feathered beast cocked its head at her and clicked its beak as if telling her to follow through with her promise.

Promise. Gandrett snorted and threw the strap of the satchel over her shoulder. It hadn't been a promise, but she had been threatened. Vala help her. That Fae had intimidated her into submission and now had sure sent his fat, feathered spy to know if she was talking to anyone.

Gandrett's gaze fell on the desk where her prayer book was sitting, still opened to the page she'd been reading when the messenger had summoned her. Not the book but the pen behind it. If only she could leave a note for Surel to tell her what had happened. But she had to get away from the bird first—

With a glimpse over her shoulder, she made sure the creature hadn't moved, and finding it still round and curious on the windowsill, she stepped closer to the desk, hiding both book and pen from its view, then snuck the pen into the book and closed it before she turned back to the room and stowed the book—its inconspicuous spine turned toward the bird—into her satchel.

The bird chirped and seemed to jerk its head toward the door, beckoning for her to hurry.

Gandrett's fear was sparked once more by the thought of the Meister's disapproval.

There was only one more thing she wanted to bring. The only thing worth bringing if she really thought about it: the thin necklace her mother had slipped into her hands as the men had come to take her. She had hidden it in her fist all the way through the consecration and then to the priory. And unlike the rest of her belongings, nobody had found it and taken it away before she had been able to hide it in a small hole in the wall behind the edge of the desk. Every night, for the first two years, she had held it in her hands so she could fall asleep. And every morning, she had put it back into its hiding place. Today, for the first time, she slid it over her head and hid it under her tunic. She wouldn't leave behind the only possession of her mother's. Not if she could help it.

The bird chirped again. But Gandrett was already out the door and stomping down the stairs.

There was nothing she could do. Just go and put her fate into Vala's hands. Except—

She stopped at the kitchen doors and found the room empty. There was a small space under the counter where Nahir normally stowed her footstool that was out of view from the window and in the blind spot of the door. Gandrett darted through the kitchen, eyes on the window, half expecting to find the fat bird spying, and sought cover under the ledge. She pulled out the prayer book, the pen almost slipping from her fingers as she tried to scribble a note, then ripped out the page and folded it into a tiny square before she let it disappear in her fist—just like the necklace—and crawled out into the open.

The bird landed on the windowsill as she half-straightened, and she dropped the pen, hands still close enough to the floor so the bird wouldn't see them, then shrugged at it. "At least let me get some provisions." With all the confidence she could muster, she reached for the top shelf and pulled out the cookie box, holding it out for the bird as if mocking it by offering a cookie through the glass.

The bird screeched in response.

But Gandrett's hands had already pulled the box back and were now replacing the cookies inside with the note she'd written for Nahir, the only one who'd find her message.

On the windowsill, with the sun on its dark feathers, the bird was chirping angrily as she wrapped the cookies in a dishcloth and shoved them into her satchel.

Gandrett didn't care. All she cared about was that someone knew that she was in trouble.

The gravel crunched under his boots, loudly and violently, as Nehelon crossed the back of the yard. He filtered out the noise of the waterfall and focused on the few acolytes whose chores took them to this part of the priory. They were young—way too young to be working so hard. At least they weren't carrying heavy buckets of water. The Vala-blessed were taking care of that by simply having threads of liquid floating alongside them as they marched up and down the fields.

Different from Fae magic, Vala's magic was designed to aid her people with planting and maintaining crops. Water, the element of life. He stopped pacing for a heartbeat and let his senses test for the girl's footsteps—or her heartbeat; he would hear her heartbeat long before her footsteps if it kept hammering violently the way it had in his chambers. The shock in her eyes would have been enough to alarm anyone. An expression like that on a fighter like her... it was even worse than the occasional shriek of fear when someone spotted his obvious Fae-traits. Rarely. It happened so rarely. Usually, his glamours held up, but with Gandrett... he couldn't tell what it had been that had him letting his control slip...

No one heeded him a look, probably afraid of the ire in his face and rolling off him in idle waves as he paced the side of the building.

Where was she? The tenth hour, the Meister had said in his note. She had little time to make it.

Nehelon wasn't certain how he would feel if he held up his end of the promise—the threat. He had threatened her like a brutalizing bastard. Had tapped deeply into his Fae instincts and let them take over, caught by surprise as she'd broken through his glamour.

How he had hoped he could use the time at the priory to get to know her a little, to understand what kind of human she was so he could slowly build her trust until she was ready.

Yet, now—

Now there was no going back. Not until they were safely away from all civilization, until he could even attempt to release her from the leash he'd put on her by his threat. He had made her see him as a monster—and for good reason. Now there was no way she'd ever trust him. Especially not if she knew all the legends about his people.

He kicked a stone in frustration.

The bird-messenger zoomed into view, aiming toward him, before he spotted *her* emerging from the residential building, carrying nothing more than a leather satchel. He gulped down the urge to wrap her in his magic and force her motions to be faster. He knew just how unaccommodating the Meister could become when he felt behavior wasn't up to his standards. But he stopped and straightened his spine, shoulders back and chin up, giving her a lazy smile as she approached, sweat beading her forehead.

"Here I am," she panted, still out of breath, affected by the magic he'd used on her.

Humans didn't react well to his abilities. He'd seen it before. No wonder they were still shunning everyone who wielded magic other than the sacred one Vala had gifted them.

"If you're looking for applause, you're looking in the wrong place," he simply said and turned on his heels, beckoning her to follow him.

He didn't turn to demonstrate power, how little afraid he was of her, but because he couldn't bear seeing how she cringed at his words. And he hadn't used those because he meant them. He had spoken like that because, now that she had seen what he was, fear was the safest measure to control her.

He brushed imaginary dust from his shoulder and glanced at the stables as they approached the entrance of the citadel. His horses—their horses—were ready. Disgruntled at the short pause under a safe roof but ready to take on the journey ahead. His things were packed. He had even changed back into his leathers to be prepared for all eventualities—

That initial sword fight with the girl, how easily she had parried his attacks, how she had felled him like an old, sick tree... It had been quite unsettling. Even if he had eventually let her win intentionally, all part of the plan, the extent of her skill and strength still had been a surprise.

He didn't check over his shoulder—didn't need to—as they entered the citadel and progressed through the cool stone corridors. His Fae hearing was all he needed to locate the girl's exact position, which foot she was setting down. His own footsteps were a sigh against the floor as he kept the pace fast enough to make the girl jog to keep up with him. He did it as much to take away any chance for her to confront him as he did to not have to see the fear in her gaze, the sheer terror that spoke through every twitch of her muscles, every blink of her widened eyes. It was, as after hundreds of years, suddenly as though looking into a mirror again.

At the corner of the Meister's study, Nehelon halted, turned around, and let Gandrett catch up with him. He locked her to the spot with a cold gaze the second she stopped, in a movement like a shying cat, and said, "You don't speak. You don't even open your mouth. All you do is nod and bow until we leave this gods-damned place."

R ow after row after row of books. The Meister's study
had always fascinated her. All the knowledge tucked
away onto feeble, aged pages. Today, her interest in
them piqued. She noted every tear in the spines, every blemish
in the leather, every cord that dangled down over the shelves,
emerging from the books where they marked pages. Blue and
purple and brown. The thundering of her heart hadn't changed.
And after she had almost bumped into the Fae male, she could
hardly control the shaking in her body.

Where was Gandrett, the cunning fighter? What impossible corner of her mind had she withdrawn to?

The sound of the Meister clearing his throat called for her
attention, and she set one weary step forward from the threshold where she had yielded. She bowed.

Nehelon, on the other hand, was already lounging in the cushioned chair across from the Meister, who sat at his carved desk, a pen between his slim fingers.

"Sit, Brayton," the Meister ordered and, to Gandrett's surprise, beckoned her to the vacant chair next to Nehelon's. She swallowed for two reasons. First, never in her time at the priory had she been invited to sit in the Meister's presence. Second, the chair was less than a foot from Nehelon's. She couldn't find it in her to sit so close to the predator.

It's all right, she wanted to say, *I can stand*—or, *I'd rather stand*. But Nehelon shot her a look that promised violence if she didn't obey. And for a moment, she considered whether it was worth it. If defying him and losing her life then and there wouldn't be the better option. But her survival instinct was still in full blossom, and so she took a quick step toward where she'd been ordered and stiffly sat down.

"It has come to my attention," the Meister opened, "that your particular skills would be of value to my friend Nehelon." He smirked at the Fae warrior next to her, giving no hint he was aware that he understood in whose presence they sat. "We have agreed—" he gave Nehelon a nod, to which the Fae replied with a brief drop of his chin, "—that you will venture on a journey with Nehelon to assist him with a particular issue that has demanded utmost secrecy." Another look was shared between the two men. Not men. One man and a male. Gandrett swallowed the words that were rising in her own throat, the scream for help that had been building in her lungs since that first moment she had spotted the ears. Her eyes darted to the right, examining Nehelon's hair where the anatomical detail which had given away his secret lay. And once more, she entertained the thought of selling him out. Telling the Meister. Screaming it from the top of the citadel. Nehelon surely couldn't take on the entire order at once: the priests and priestesses, the warriors, the water mages, and... she noted Nehelon's raised eyebrow as if he was following her train of thought... and children. Most of the people here were children, and she couldn't risk their lives. Not to save her own.

Nehelon's eyebrow lowered. "I have informed Miss Brayton of our deal." He took the opportunity to keep his reply short to get out as quickly as possible, Gandrett was sure, to not waste any time or give her any spare moment to escape blind panic and make up her mind.

"And what does *Miss Brayton*—" he spoke her name with bemusement, as if putting the little word *Miss* in front of it made it a well-told joke, "—have to say to the offer?"

She hadn't been aware it was an offer, Gandrett wanted to say, but the muscles in Nehelon's thighs tightened, and the hand resting on the cords of steel curled into a fist, demonstrating how easily he could crush her.

"Miss Brayton accepts," he said with a voice as bright as the sunshine that filtered in through the stained glass windows. "To all the terms of the deal," he added.

All the terms. Gandrett wished she knew what that meant other than her being a slave for however long Nehelon needed her for whatever task. But she didn't dare ask. Not now when his deadly Fae hands were less than a foot from crushing her if he felt like it.

It made Gandrett's hair stand, but as he shot her a warning look, her chin jerked down in a shaky nod.

"Then it's settled," the Meister clapped his hands once. "You will fare with Nehelon to the East of Sives where you will become part of Lord Tyrem's—" he paused for a moment as if searching for the right words, "—special guard," he finished with a smile. A smile that, especially when returned by Nehelon with an equally feral one, couldn't mean anything good.

Gandrett felt herself inching toward the door in her chair but, at Nehelon's attention, dropped her head again in a bow.

"And it will be an honor for Miss Brayton," Nehelon added, his gaze now boring into hers as if saying, *you know what will happen if you don't play along.*

"An honor, indeed," she repeated and inclined her head at Nehelon, everything in her body burning with helpless rage and fear, and was eternally grateful for the years and years of practice that had gained her control over her features. At least control enough to be able to look like she meant what she was saying. And what she meant *was* that it would be an honor. An honor to give her own life in order to protect the innocent in this priory.

Nehelon didn't speak as he led the way to the stables at a speed that made her stumble on the cobbles, and she wasn't a clumsy maid but a trained fighter—even if she felt like one less and less as they put distance between them and the place where the Meister had taken a heavy-looking, coin-clinking, velvet bag from Nehelon's hands as payment for the *lost vessel* to Vala.

One more year. It would have been only one more year, and she would have had a chance to get out. Even if still a lifelong member of the Order of Vala, but still, away from the desert, away from the limited space to move, the limited faces to greet and the questions of what else lay behind those barren lands.

One of the younger acolytes was waiting at the stables, a smile on his face, and informed Nehelon that the horses were ready, which triggered Nehelon to flash a smile and lead Gandrett right past the stables to the wooden bars behind, where horses were usually readied for messengers or the rare visitors of Everrun. It was something Gandrett had learned very soon—that no one came to Everrun without an agenda. There were no tourists here.

As Nehelon pointed at a well-fed bay horse, beckoning her to get on while he mounted his black mare, the bells of the citadel announced it was time for the daily prayers. When Gandrett glanced back over her shoulder, the boy at the stable doors was already running toward the sound as they all were. Everyone in the priory took part in the morning prayers. Even Nahir. And as Gandrett watched them all bustle into the citadel where they would fill up the temple rooms, her heart emptied. Her hope, slight and brittle as it might have been, crumbled. This—the timing of when to hold that meeting—ensured no one would be outside to witness how she and Nehelon vanished from the priory, and when the prayers were over, they would be long gone and too far to catch up. Especially with no one knowing where they were headed.

With a sigh that tore into her frightened heart, Gandrett climbed into the saddle.

The sun had long climbed to its pinnacle and Nehelon hadn't said a word. He hadn't given her a glance but held the reins of her gelding safely in his hands as he led the horse alongside his black mare. They had made it through the gate by Nehelon handing each guard positioned at the watchtowers a small note, which the Meister had personally signed in his study. Gandrett had no idea what the notes said, but judging by the way the guards had waved them through after they had read them, wishing them, "May Vala guide you," Gandrett was certain they wouldn't spend another thought once they were out of sight.

Then they rode through the ghost town beyond the walls of the priory. Everrun—the real one. The ancient city of which its abandoned ruins spoke of war and decay.

Gandrett knew the first couple of rows of houses from her afternoon runs, but never in her ten years had she meandered further from the priory than that. *Not safe*, was what the priests and priestesses said. *Shaelak himself took the city and may still be wandering the streets.*

Shaelak, the god of darkness.

Gandrett hadn't dared stray further, for fear of what she may find or what may find her in those dead and empty streets and alleys. With Nehelon at her side, no matter how afraid she was of him, there was an advantage to his deadly power and strength. If stories were to be believed, even the gods feared the Fae—

Nehelon sat straight like a needle, his chin high, one hand on his sword, the other one leading both horses. He hadn't looked at her once since they had left the safety of the priory, and he hadn't told her his plans for the travels—not that Gandrett would be able to make anything from the plans. She hadn't traveled since she had left Sives. Her stomach growled audibly—probably sounding like an avalanche to Nehelon's Fae ears—but Gandrett didn't speak. She didn't complain about her empty stomach or her thirst or that her legs were sore from her linen pants, which weren't made for riding, or the fact that her head was beginning to ache in the baking sun. She didn't add the wind to the list, for the wind was what she had grown accustomed to over the years, training in the priory of Everrun.

And as the sun climbed further along the sky, shifting to the west, tinting the mountains in the north-west in orange and gold, exhaustion took over fear, and Gandrett no longer pondered the stories she had heard about the Fae's bloodlust, about their cruel nature, about why they were still called the *fair folk*—

Her eyes cautiously peered at Nehelon's profile to study his features in the warm light of the sunset. It was like that moment when she had noticed his pointed ears: his face was different, not human as much as it had seemed in the Meister's office or when they had gotten onto the horses and headed out of the walls. He was radiant even with the dust of riding on his cheeks, lips full and sensual, and his hair, black and smooth, falling to his shoulders, hiding those treacherous ears. And eyes—

Gandrett froze as she found Nehelon glaring sideways.

Fear flooded her system yet again, silencing all of her needs until darkness fell.

They only reawakened as Nehelon finally halted both horses without indication of where to find shelter for the night or if that was even his intention. And as he watched Gandrett scan their surroundings—still the mostly flat land that they had been following all day long, without a tree or even a boulder to find shelter from the biting wind—he shrugged and slid off his horse in a graceful swing. "This is as good as anywhere," he announced and dropped his mare's reins to the ground before gesturing for Gandrett to get off her horse, wearing a look impatient as a vulture circling a carcass. Gandrett shuddered at his stare.

If it only were as easy as he'd made it look. Her body was well trained for sword fights, for running, for climbing... but for riding? Her legs almost didn't obey her will when she lifted them—heavy as the boulders she'd desired as shelter—and slithered down the side of her horse, fingers holding on to its neck for fear her knees would buckle under her weight.

Nehelon laughed coldly, probably enjoying seeing her in pain—it wouldn't surprise her; he was Fae after all—and

Gandrett faced him with bared teeth, prepared to throw a nasty comment at him, when the Fae male reached behind him for the waterskin dangling from the saddle of his horse and handed it to her.

"I keep forgetting how high-maintenance humans are," he mocked, eyes glimmering in the silver light of the rising moon.

Gandrett wanted to spit at him, but her mouth was dry as the cracked soil beneath her unstable feet, and so she silently took the waterskin from his hand and led it to her mouth, about to drink greedily. But she halted—

Nehelon hadn't drunk from it. What if it was poisoned? What if his intention was to drug her?

"You think I would use poison if I wanted to get rid of you?" he asked, face stone-cold as he watched her hold the waterskin hovering above her mouth.

His tone was enough to make it clear that if he wanted her dead, he would find other, more creative ways of making that happen. Gandrett swallowed once then put the waterskin to her lips and drank.

"Not so bad, is it?" Nehelon didn't take his eyes off of her the entire time she was drinking, as if he was studying something curious, a creature he had never seen before and found fascinating.

Gandrett didn't reply but handed him the half-drained waterskin, her eyes squinting in a gesture she was hoping said, *it's the least I expect that you'll water and feed me when you drag me through the desert.* The look in his eyes, the tiniest bit of amusement glimmering in the silver light, told her he'd understood.

Without a word, he dropped the waterskin to the ground between them then pulled his pack off the horse, dumping it on top.

Gandrett watched him in disbelief. "You are really planning to stay here for the night," she said, coming to a realization. As he didn't deny it, Gandrett's eyes anxiously darted around, hoping she had missed something earlier, a small boulder to hover behind while she relieved her bladder. He couldn't be serious. Then there was the wind... it was still whipping through the air, unbroken by trees or bushes. With the sun gone, the temperature would drop to a point too low to sleep unprotected—

Nehelon eyed her, face tight, as if he was realizing just how *high maintenance* humans were.

"You are aware that if you don't poison me, I might freeze to death overnight," Gandrett pointed out. There wasn't any wood for a fire, either. Even if there was, it would be like a beacon for the predators of the desert—not that she wasn't already in the presence of the worst predator of all.

The Fae male simply shrugged and unsaddled the horses, letting Gandrett sway on her aching legs. Then, he took a step back and lifted both hands.

At first, there was a slight shudder beneath Gandrett's feet, and the horses whinnied as they trampled closer together. Then the ground began shaking.

Gandrett hadn't heard of earthquakes in this region, but as a child in Sives, she had experienced a mild one, and this... It was more than triple what she remembered. She waited for Nehelon to notice it, too, for the horses to panic—

Yet, while the animals stood close to each other, eyes darting to the sides as if they were waiting for something, Nehelon closed his eyes, and as he turned over his palms so they faced upward, the dust-dry soil rose in a circle around them as if a giant insect was digging underground. It rose one foot, two...

until eventually, the wall reached Gandrett's waist, enclosing them like a miniature of the wall they'd left behind at the priory.

Gandrett was still taking turns staring at the wall and at Nehelon, who had reopened his eyes and looked slightly smug as he prowled past her to stroke the horses' necks.

That—she gaped at the power of his magic, at what he had just produced from flat, barren ground—was the reason why it was wise to fear him. That power. If he could easily create a crater the size of the pond at the priory...

She didn't even want to consider what else he was capable of. And she had the slight impression she might find out for herself if she so much as brought it up. But as she crawled back to her feet, having dropped to her hands and knees on the rattling ground from fear it would crack open right beneath her and swallow her, she found Nehelon watching her with moon-lit eyes, half-annoyed, judging by the thin-pressed curve of his lips.

"You should have seen yourself," he said and raked his fingers through the mane of his horse, "like a beetle on the ground." With efficient steps, he crossed under the neck of the mare to get to the side of the gelding where he started unbuckling bridle and saddle. "Almost as if you believed something in the wide, flat land could fall on your pretty head." He smirked at her over the horse's back, teeth catching the moonlight.

Gandrett felt her fear subsiding as anger at the impossible Fae male threw itself above it in layers woven of shame and annoyance. "You think I'm pretty," she bit at him before she could stop herself, an attempt to hide any emotion.

But Nehelon's face went blank at her words, and he shook his head as if he was trying to shake off a spider in his hair. "That's beside the point," he threw at her, crossed the space between them, and dropped the horse's gear on top of the mare's which was right beside Gandrett's foot. "I think you're pathetic."

Gandrett had expected many things including torture and death at his hands, but what she hadn't been prepared for was this: cold insults. And even less, that they would hit her right in the heart. He knew nothing about her, and just because he may have bought her from the order for a bag of coins, he didn't have the right—

She turned slightly and assessed the protective walls he had created without even touching the soil and debated scowling, but she was too exhausted, her legs still sore and her bones aching from riding in the wind and cold all day long. Without another word, she stalked to the point farthest away from him and laid down on the ground, ready to ignore him.

Nehelon chuckled at the other side where he was laying out the horses' gear to dry off from the mounts' sweat. Then he lifted a pack from the ground and chucked it toward her.

It landed half a foot from Gandrett's head, making her cringe back toward the reassuringly-solid wall, her hand reaching for the empty spot on her belt where her sword had been hanging this morning—the one which was now dangling from Nehelon's hip like a toy copy of his jeweled blade. "Why don't you just knock me over the head with it?" she barked, "At least then I'll sleep."

Nehelon roared with laughter—not the happy kind—and prowled to her side to pick up the pack and open it. "Here." He extracted a blanket and dropped it on the ground before her, followed by digging deeper to pull out a small bundle wrapped in cloth. "You think I'd spend a fortune to get you out of there just to let you freeze and starve the first chance I get?"

His gaze made clear he didn't expect an answer as he tossed her the bundle, one eyebrow rising in obvious surprise as she caught it with one shaky hand.

Close, he was too close. And the power, that brute strength, it enveloped him like a brewing storm. Gandrett sat back on her heel, praying that her fear wasn't written plain on her face... Even if it wasn't, the relentless thrumming of her heart was enough for his Fae ears to pick up on her rising panic as her eyes searched the earthen wall for a way out.

Not that running made any sense with someone like him. He'd have her in his grasp before she even reached an exit. Now Gandrett scowled. Not at him but at herself. She had been trained better than to flinch at the sight of a seemingly insurmountable obstacle. She wasn't the best warrior in the priory for nothing.

Gandrett felt his gaze on her as she opened the bundle and pulled out a piece of dried meat, but she didn't look up to give him the satisfaction of seeing her wonder if this was even edible for humans—or if it might even be human meat. Instead, she made her hand lead one chunky slice to her mouth and took a bite.

Nehelon chuckled again and leaned closer, lowering his head enough to look into her eyes. "I told you, poisoning you now would be a waste of money."

For some reason, his words were not reassuring.

She looked pale in the morning sun, nestled into the rough blanket he'd offered her the night before, strands of chestnut hair that had slipped from her braid tangled around her head. Pale. The hard lines of fear and frustration had left her features the second exhaustion had swept her into a restless sleep. He had watched her all night, his Fae senses— even over the constant wind—allowing him to tell when her heartbeat had slowed enough to consider sleep himself, and he had turned his eyes on her the second she drifted off.

Gandrett. How little she was like he'd imagined her. Nothing like it. He had expected a raw diamond, and what he'd found was a bitter lump of coal. Intriguing in its own, dark way, but nothing like the bright crystal he had imagined. He had seen it in her face—pretty as it may be—as she had tried to hide her scowl from him. With all her skill and all her training, there was one thing she lacked: heart.

And now, for hours he had been studying her, spying on her while she'd been resting, not taking a minute to rest himself as he guarded the horses and his most treasured belonging—not his. That of Tyrem Brenheran. Something in his chest stirred, unfamiliar and unwelcome. He smothered it and decided it might be for the best. If fear, obedience, and discipline were the only things she knew—had known for a decade—trust might not be what he'd need to get her to work with him.

And yet, something was there on her features in her sleep that told him not to trust what she was letting on. She had been trained by the best, by the Meister himself—a training very few received. Even with his Fae senses, he couldn't look inside her mind or inside her heart. While her thoughts he might be able to draw from her through torture, what was inside her heart she'd have to give willingly.

He got to his feet, pulled off his blanket, and flapped it over her shivering body instead. Then, with a last look at her, he strolled over to the horses, where he stretched out on the cool ground and closed his eyes, sensing the sounds of the desert night retreating before the climbing sun.

Nehelon was sitting on the ground, cross-legged, chewing absently, when Gandrett opened her eyes to find herself not half as freezing as when she had fallen asleep and was curled up under more weight than she remembered. Behind him, the horses were saddled, their noses in a heap of hay of a size that made it difficult to believe it had been transported in one of the packs.

With a groan, Gandrett sat up, her legs still sore and her back aching from lying on the hard ground. She couldn't remember when she had fallen asleep, only that her dreams had been full of collapsing houses and men carrying leather pouches stuffed with coins. With a slow hand, she reached for her pounding head. Water, she needed water—

"Looking for this?" Nehelon held up a waterskin and let it dangle in his broad hand by way of saying good morning.

Gandrett observed him through squinting eyes as she tried to make out his features against the morning sun. He was fully dressed in his leathers, letting the sun warm his back, at least, that was what it looked like. He could have been praying to Shaelak himself, considering what he was.

Then, it came back to her, the fear, the unease, the legends and myths, and she cringed back against the wall until—

The weight on her, the blanket—two blankets. She'd only had one blanket when she fell asleep, and now...

"*Thank you* is the word you're looking for." He rose, graceful as a tree growing from the ground, and as solid, then prowled over to hand her the waterskin. "I thought I'd better deliver the goods unharmed," he added in a whisper as he stopped and bent down close enough his breath touched her ear. With one hand, he grabbed the blankets and pulled them off her, leaving her sitting in her linen clothes.

Gandrett shivered. Which made Nehelon chuckle as he returned to the horses where he folded and packed the packs, leaving only a small bundle out. "You can have breakfast on horseback," he explained, looking at the bay horse while gesturing at her.

To her surprise, the horse crossed the earthen circle in a trot and stopped by Gandrett's feet.

"Up, up, up." Nehelon clicked his tongue, and the horse stomped its foot beside her, making her bolt upright and fumble on her clothes.

It was embarrassing having to ask, but, "I don't assume you will allow me enough time to..."

Nehelon just lifted a hand, and the wall crumbled in front of him and his mare, leaving a gap wide enough for them to stroll out.

"Let me know when you're done," was all Nehelon said when he was out. Then he snapped his fingers, and the wall reassembled, leaving Gandrett behind with the gelding.

Great. Gandrett looked at the horse, which was eyeing her expectantly.

"I can't pee while you're watching," she whispered at the animal and walked a couple of steps away to an angle where she hoped neither the horse if it turned its neck, nor Nehelon, whose broad shoulders and black, wind-torn hair were visible, would see her.

She slipped down her pants and crouched to relieve herself—not an easy task considering the sensitivity of the Fae male's senses. Gandrett swallowed her pride and thought of running water.

It was only when she was done that the horse stomped its hind leg impatiently enough to make her hurry back to her feet and climb into the saddle, not without releasing a low curse at her sore muscles.

"Done," she called unnecessarily, for the moment she was in the saddle, Nehelon turned his head and asked over his shoulder, "Better?"

Then he held a hand out to the side, and the circle enclosing Gandrett and her horse crumbled to the ground, leaving nothing but a ruffled imprint of the arrangement.

"We have a lot of ground to cover today," he informed her and held out the bundle in his hand—a loaf of bread. "You better start eating so we can talk."

Gandrett gobbled down the bread until almost half the loaf was gone. Neither her protesting muscles nor Nehelon's incredulous gaze allowed her to stop until her belly was full enough that she believed she could make it until nightfall without eating anything else.

She handed him the rest of the bread, bundled back into the cloth, and mentally prepared for a long, hot day, biting wind, and more insults that would strain her physically and mentally.

As they made their way north, Gandrett knew which way they were headed because the mountain range separating the continent in the middle appeared to their left, leading to Fae territory in the west and human territory in the east.

"Ithrylan?" She asked, almost yelling the name with relief. "You are taking us through Ithrylan."

There were only two ways to get to Sives. The path west of the mountains led through Ulfray, Fae land, dangerous due to the possibility of running into one of them—Gandrett shuddered at the mere thought of meandering through the Fae forests then remembered that she no longer needed the Fae forests to run into one of them—while the east path led through Ithrylan, which was merely cursed land. Once the bright beacon between the human realms in the north and the south, it lay now rotting and whispering the stories of countless deaths—and yet, it was the safer options. At least the dead didn't kill.

Nehelon measured her face, his own features like stone as he nodded and slowed his own horse just enough to ride beside her. Today he hadn't taken the reins of her mount, but the bay had trotted after the mare without any effort on Gandrett's side. If she had tried to get him to break away from its traveling companions, she didn't believe the horse would obey.

"What do you remember of Sives?" His question came as unexpectedly as the sudden stillness of the air.

Gandrett inhaled the dry, clean air, buying herself time to consider if she should give him part of the truth. But as she turned to him, to her surprise, she found a thin line of concern pulling his perfectly-arched eyebrows together. He cocked his head and smoothed over his expression as if he was just realizing there was something readable on his face.

"So?" he prompted.

The small, wooden farmhouse in the heart of Sives popped into her head, the smell of grains in the summer, the scent of the air after it rained on the meadows, the blossoms of the fruit trees in spring, the buzzing of insects—

She closed her eyes—a brief blink, elongated by a fraction of a second, but enough to be immersed into childhood memories. Her father, as he bent over the plow, strapping the horses to the machine, his smile when he noticed she was watching, her mother's call to return to the house for lunch, her brother—

"Nothing much." Gandrett shrugged and swallowed the tune of the lullaby her mother had used to sing to them when they were little, the warmth of her embrace that seemed to envelop her now that the wind had for once subsided. As if the gods knew her thoughts and were mocking her, the wind started its endless howl and carried away the moment of comfort even if it had only been in Gandrett's mind, replacing it with images of the men who had torn her out of her mother's arms. "I was seven when they took me." Her voice was stable. A trained habit, to speak without emotion, and despite the terror of being in the presence of a deadly creature, terror can hold someone captive only so long before it becomes the new norm and the mind adapts.

Nehelon didn't comment, but something in his face changed. Not that it became warmer or gentler, maybe even understanding—no. There was a grim sort of relief written in his eyes that was about as appropriate as having to pee in his presence.

Gandrett directed her eyes at the sun-kissed mountain tops. Witnesses of the ages and almost untouched by men, they formed a barrier between the lands. She had seen them once before from up close: the journey to Everrun, the one and only journey in her life so far. She could almost feel the rattling of the carriage that had brought her into the green heart of the barren land they were now crossing, and again she was seven, heart pounding from fear, fingers reaching for her shaved-off hair—

"Ten years," Nehelon commented, eyeing her hair-entwined hands. "It has grown out beautifully."

Gandrett's mouth opened and closed, trying to find something smart to reply, and came up blank. His face, once more, had changed, a crack in the mask of stone he'd been wearing since the moment he'd revealed his secret.

That alone was enough to ask, "You said I was going to be in the service of Lord Tyrem Brenheran," she swallowed the disgust at the taste of the name on her tongue, "but that I am to work for *you.*"

Nehelon held her gaze, that crack in his mask gradually sealing.

"What will I be doing, exactly?" she asked, for lack of better wording. So far, he had given her nothing besides that the task would be of utmost importance, but neither he nor the Meister had mentioned what it actually was she would be doing. Why she had been bought out...

"I will share in time."

Gandrett huffed and wondered if she had truly expected to get an answer—a real answer.

Nehelon didn't speak again until nightfall when he raised another earthen circle as a shelter, handed her food, and let her sleep without taunting this time. No snide comments or mocking.

On the third day of riding, the landscape changed, and Gandrett knew it was only a matter of time until they would ride through grass-covered lands and see streams and forests lining the roads. But first, they needed to cross the ruins of Ithrylan, its two towers silently hovering on each side of the valley that led them out of the desert.

"We cross right in the middle," Nehelon glanced up at the ruins—each tower like a giant shadow in the distance, miles and miles apart. Twin towers. One sitting in a lake right where the Fae lands met the mountain range, the other crumbling away where the chain of mountains ended dropping into the East Sea.

Gandrett's gaze followed his. He could tell by the slight shift in her posture as she took in the gargantuan, stone structures, which seemed to be forming a gate of otherworldly size. Not for travelers but for armies the count of thousands and thousands and thousands of men.

In the evening sun, the girl's face looked flushed, alive, the grim expression replaced by awe for once. Nehelon allowed himself to take in the hues of pink and orange painting her skin, and the palette of reds bouncing off her hair, before he nudged his horse forward, Gandrett's gelding following suit.

He could feel them, the horrors of the battlefield as they rode on, the countless lives that had been lost on that very soil, as if the dead were calling out for him. And the same way he had ignored it on the way to the priory, he shut out the sensation now. They were too close to Ithrylan to stop for the night, and if they continued at a steady pace, they would make it to Elste before nightfall. The closest village to the ruins where some merchants and traders held residence as well as some shady creatures of the realms. He had passed through on his way south, glanced at the bright window and the small tavern from outside, and decided that with a human in tow, it would be a good place to stay for a night to clean up and get a proper meal in her belly.

The absolute silence was the first thing he noticed. Then Gandrett's gasp sounded at the shadow darting at them from the side. Nehelon's sword was in his hand at the same moment he held out Gandrett's plain blade to her. She grabbed it without taking her eyes off the giant desert lion zooming at them at neck-breaking speed.

"Stay close," he growled, eyes on the lethal cat darting at them.

Gandrett had never seen any of them. Heard, yes, but never actually seen. They were the reason they didn't stray from the priory or explore the ghost city of Everrun. But what she beheld when she watched the animal's elastic movements had her already picturing it dodging Nehelon's sword and going right for his throat. For a fraction of a second, the thought gave her a weird satisfaction. If the desert lion was busy with Nehelon long enough for Gandrett to land one blow—just one well-positioned blow, she could be rid of the beast and the Fae who had purchased her for the man who had ordered her admission to the Order of Vala. The man who, by his order, had taken her childhood away. And her entire life. Maybe it was justice that now that she was skilled to a degree no one but the fighters of the order achieved, he had to pay handsomely for her.

But freedom—

She took a defensive position atop her horse, prepared to fight as she had been trained to do. One blow.

The cat was racing for them like an arrow. Had either of them had a bow on them, one well-placed shot, and the cat would be down, but with their blades as the only weapons, the cat came dangerously close, its eyes not on the Fae but, as Gandrett realized to her horror, on her.

Her hands were steady as she assessed the movements, the weak spots in the cat's anatomy, its throat, its neck, the soft part on the back part of its abdomen...

She was still sizing up the death on paws as the cat leaped, and as it catapulted itself toward her, it slammed into an invisible wall and dropped to the ground where it remained motionless. She gaped, her mind lagging behind what her eyes beheld. "How—?"

With a flick of his hand, Nehelon indicated it had been him.

"Magic," was all Gandrett was able to say. He had done it with his magic. An invisible shield.

And then, shame came over her. While she had been calculating the odds that the desert lion may rid her of her new master, he had actually saved her life. She should be thanking him, but her mouth remained immobile and didn't comment when Nehelon slipped off his horse and strolled to the unconscious cat with the comment, "As I spent my savings on you," wearing a twisted grin and a shrug, "their furs pay well," and drove his sword into the animal's chest then skinned it.

Nehelon could taste the horror and disgust in the air between them. Good. If only for a second, he'd seen it there in her face, the hope the lion would go for him and end him. And she would have let him bleed out and made a run for it. He checked her expression as he rolled up the desert lion skin and tied it to his saddle, her features slowly returning to the schooled indifference she wore most of the time.

He could still hear it. The thrumming of her heart as it raced in her chest. She had trained with swords and fought people, but had she truly ever been exposed to the threat of a wild cat-like the ones living in those ruins? Had she ever killed? From the look on her face, she didn't have that type of blood on her hands. Her fighting so far had been all in training, sparring; not the real thing. Though, even when she had found him climbing the wall, he hadn't doubted for a second that she was capable of driving that blade through his chest or slitting his throat. The Meister had been right. And if she were to assist him in his mission, he would need both sides of her—the virtuous vessel to Vala as much as the ruthless fighter who was ready to let a powerful opponent bleed out.

Without another look at the carcass lying in a puddle of blood, he mounted his horse, and once more, they set in motion.

The sun was slowly disappearing, and no other threats were within hearing distance as they were almost out of the desert. Almost. Before them, right where they passed between the two towers of Ithrylan, a seam of spring grass spread to the north as if someone had drawn an arbitrary line in the dirt, forbidding the grass to grow beyond it.

Beside him, Gandrett gasped at the sight, forgetting her self-chosen muteness, and commented, "The Meister told us about it, but I never believed..."

"Never believed it was true?" Nehelon finished for her and found her head bobbing from side to side in a definite no.

"Never believed it was possible," she corrected.

Her incredulous look almost let him forget the blood on his hands and leathers, but as he glanced down at the cushion of greenery, he caught a glimpse of his crimson fingers and decided that as soon as they got out of Ithrylan, he would find a place to wash up and let the horses have some well-deserved grass.

"I heard the legends as a child that the Calma Desert was not a natural desert but one caused by a war... some magic gone wrong..." She chose her words carefully. "And then, the Meister kept speaking about Vala's circle of safety for the children. A ring of barren land to keep out any danger for her sacred vessels. I didn't see it on the way to Everrun all those years ago..."

He could tell by the way her nose crinkled that she hated it, the thought of having been sacrificed, of being a vessel, of belonging to anyone. It was there in her eyes, the secret yearning for freedom, the years and years of discipline and order. And that despite the clear title she held, an acolyte of the Order of Vala, a fighter, she was so much more—and she didn't even know it.

G andrett couldn't remember what a village looked like, so she set one shaky step after the other, guided by Nehelon, whose broad shoulders hid what lay ahead of her. But what lay around her, what she could see...

What she could smell...

And taste in the air...

And the sounds, so new and yet an echo of a long-lost life...

"Let me do the talking," Nehelon ordered over his shoulder, and for once, she was grateful for his demand. For Gandrett was in no shape for talking, wouldn't even know what to say, what anyone would expect of her—

The wooden buildings of Elste reminded Gandrett of the outskirts of Eedwood. She had been there once—the day of her consecration—before they had handed her off to the Order of Vala. And the people, even if darker in skin tone than in Alencourt where she had grown up, spoke the same language, a dialect she had difficulties deciphering at first, but it was her language. The tongue of the north.

She absorbed every word she could overhear as they approached the center of the town, their horses already taken care of in the stables close by, and took in the colorful attire of the townsfolk. Despite the late hour, most people seemed to be out on the streets where music was streaming from the open windows along with the smell of roasted vegetables and freshly-baked bread fanning in the light breeze. Even with night fallen upon the town, the air remained a lovely temperature compared to the rough cold of the desert nights. Gandrett smiled, her nervousness only second to her anticipation of warm food, a bath, and a soft bed to sleep in.

The dark wooden tavern door groaned as Nehelon pushed it open. He almost entirely filled the doorframe with his height, his muscled arms and broad back, his hands casually dangling near his sword and knife, always prepared, even if a flick of his fingers would probably be enough to make the building collapse. Gandrett followed suit as the Fae male stepped inside and walked up to a blackened bar where a middle-aged woman with a low-cut blouse was cleaning glasses.

"Sit there," Nehelon hissed at Gandrett and nodded at a small, crooked table near the kitchen entrance, "and wait for me."

Gandrett did as she was told, her eyes assessing the rest of the room. People were eating and drinking, all of them dressed in something better than usual travel clothes.

As she relaxed her back in her chair, her hand resting on her hip just above the hilt of her sword, which Nehelon to her surprise hadn't demanded back, she felt eyes on her and scanned the room.

She was familiar with the feeling of being stared at; for the simple reason that she was the best fighter in the Order of Vala—the Meister had told her that even with all the fighters on missions, she remained the best. Not that it had earned her any privileges; just envy. People can be cruel when they envy someone. So, when she noted the men's gazes on her, sizing her up from the table next to hers, studying her from head to toe, Gandrett turned her focus right at them, a challenging flicker in her eyes, and said, "Never seen one of us around here, have you?" She noticed how they eyed her linen uniform, giving away where she had come from as much as a coat of armor would.

"Never seen one as pretty as you, for sure," the shortest of them said, his eyes watery from too much ale and his words drawn out to a lull.

Gandrett knew then that it might have been better to remain quiet, for the men all grinned at her widely, some with less yellow teeth than the others, but there was something in their gaze that told her she wouldn't make it out of there in one piece—not if it was up to them. And raising attention might not be what Nehelon intended. So Gandrett stared down the men—no fear on her face—and waited.

That was when Nehelon stepped between the two tables, closer to her side and towering over the men, and said with a grin. "You should be honored to have a Child of Vala in your midst at the Fest of Blossoms.

The men shrank at his mere size.

With a casual gesture, Nehelon pulled out the chair at the head of the table and settled down between Gandrett and the men, blocking her from view. His eyes remained on the men, for once freezing someone else with their diamond-cold.

Gandrett hid her smugness. For one, because she knew that she could have taken on the men, especially when they were drunk, but observing the world shrink at Nehelon's obvious power? How could she not have noted the instant she'd found him climbing that wall? Maybe he had purposely hidden it, like the glamour that made his features look less... she couldn't even tell less *what*. Since the moment she had discovered he was Fae, it was like that glamour was coming on and off like a costume he slipped into when needed. Right now, he seemed to need to impress those men and appear more like the powerful male he truly was. Gandrett couldn't help but feel a pang of affection for him. Even if she didn't need it. If she could defend herself. He was doing it for her.

As if he felt her stare, he turned to face her, one eyebrow raised as if questioning why the sudden interest.

Gandrett lowered her gaze to study the patterns in the wood of the table. "I know, it would be a waste of investment if you let them drag me behind the tavern."

Nehelon's hands lay in front of him on the surface, considerably clean after he had washed up at the stables.

He kept his gaze on her even as the barmaid set down two bowls of steaming stew and two mugs of some honey-colored liquid. The woman wiped her hands in her dirty apron and bent down to inform Nehelon that she had found a room for them.

He nodded and handed her a small bag of coins, eyes still on Gandrett as the woman disappeared back to the counter.

Much to her surprise, Nehelon didn't return to brooding silence but kept his face polite as he picked up his mug and drank deeply. "Bothenia ale," he explained as he noted Gandrett's questioning look.

Bothenia, or what they called it in Sives: the potato of the poor. Her parents had drunk bothenia ale on the holidays, unable to afford better. With a shaky hand, Gandrett picked up her own mug and led it to her lips.

The taste was bitter, making the inside of her mouth feel like leather. She grimaced.

"Not the milk and honey you're used to from the priory, is it?" Nehelon commented, his voice authentically amused.

The sound alone was enough to make Gandrett look up.

It was probably the first real emotion she had seen on his features. His lips, tugging upwards on the sides, gave away that there was something deep down in the Fae male that wasn't designed to destroy, but to live. It was enough to give her the courage to ask, anyway, "How do you know so much about the order?"

She had considered asking before, during the hours of riding in silence. But whenever she had glanced at him, ready to speak, his cold glare had made her reconsider. Not that she backed down easily, but with a ticking Fae male time bomb as a conversation partner, she found it better to not take any risks.

The amusement remained—superficially. Behind the hard blue diamond of his eyes, a hint of nostalgia broke through. "Everything in time, Miss Brayton," he said formally, the mention of her last name like a private joke to him curling his lips a little more. He lifted his mug again to drain it. And that was that.

Gandrett ate in silence, the vegetable stew a welcome heat in her empty stomach. What she would have given for Nahir's rice-and-spice dishes, for Kaleb's smiling face across the table, Surel's elbow in her ribs for every grin she drew from the boy.

When dinner was done, Nehelon drained his ale, pushed away from the table, and got to his feet. He flashed a feral smile at the men who were still eyeballing Gandrett as she rose with him and followed him to the counter where the barmaid held out an iron key and instructed them to take the stairs and follow the hall to the very end.

The darkness didn't hide anything from him, but he felt Gandrett stumbling and cursing lowly behind in the lightless stairwell. He found their room and shoved the key into the lock, clicking it open with one swift turn before he stepped into the candlelit room.

Gandrett stopped on the threshold, taking in the same thing he did—

One bed. Wide enough for both of them to lay without noticing much of the other. But still, one bed.

"Come in, and close the door," he said, keeping his voice low. All kinds of people came to a trader settlement like this, and not only the noble ones. He had seen enough scum on the streets, scanning the new arrivals—especially Gandrett's curves—and potentially already plotting to ambush her if he let her out of his sight for even a minute. Thus, he'd insisted on one bedroom to host both of them, even if he'd much rather prefer a night of solitude. He had even paid the barmaid handsomely to give them a room with an integrated bathing chamber—overpaid, he now realized when he looked around the small space adjacent to the sleeping area. He hoped that she would do better at the second task he had paid her for.

Gandrett was beside him a breath after the door closed, her eyes weary at the sight of the bed.

"Take a bath," he ordered and sniffed. Days of riding through the heat and dust, nights sleeping on the ground had left their odor on her, and now that the constant wind was no longer scattering the smell, or the scent that bread and ale and stew wasn't covering, it pooled in his nose.

Not unsurprisingly, Gandrett walked right to the bathing room and locked the door behind her.

Bastard. Gandrett couldn't think anything else for a long minute until she took a whiff herself and had to admit he was right. She reeked of sweat. And if his senses were truly more sensitive than human ones, she even pitied him. Still, he had no right...

Fueled by anger, she half ripped her satchel and clothes off, her sword clanking on the stone floor as she dropped everything in a heap, then turned on the water and stared into the bubbly flow until the small bathtub was filled enough to soak and scrape down her whole body.

With one hand, she tested the temperature while the other reached for the soap on the rim of the tub. *Milk and Honey*, she read the label and chuckled as she slid into the water, hair and all, and released a groan of comfort at the heat enclosing her sore body.

She could hate Nehelon all she wanted, but he had given her something no one else had in a decade—a private bathing room. She tuned out every thought that threatened to push to the front of her mind and closed her eyes.

11

How long could a human girl bathe? It wasn't a rhetorical question. He had seen the women at court disappear into their bathing chambers and remain for hours and hours, servants scrubbing down their bodies with soft sponges and massaging their scalps with fine soaps and oils.

But this was a shabby tavern with a couple of rooms for shady travelers. Money paid—no questions asked. How long could a human girl remain in a sub-standard tub?

And why, by the gods, did it bother him that she still hadn't come out?

A knock on the door interrupted his pacing, making him leap across the bed to quickly reach the entrance.

It was the barmaid herself, a bundle of cloth in her hands and a knowing smile on her lips as she scanned the room behind him, her eyes not finding the girl. Her glance returned to his face, and her eyelids shuttered before she flashed him a tentative grin.

"In case she returns." She handed him the bundle, rough skin brushing his hand. "And if she doesn't..." She let him finish the thought as she turned around looking at him from under her lashes.

Nehelon nodded his thanks—for the clothes, not the offer of a warm bed—and shut the door behind the woman. It wasn't that he hadn't noticed her supple body, her assets plainly displayed with her low-cut blouse. And it wasn't because of the mild lines on her face. He'd had them all—young, old, pretty, mousy, the shy, the bold, the rich, the poor... All of them had their advantages and disadvantages. On his journey south, he might have even considered taking her offer, but then something had happened—

Gandrett had happened.

And she had broken open something in him that had been sealed for a long, long time.

She had seen him. *Seen* him. And it had shaken him. Deeply. All that cunning, careless, audacious self he had been displaying these past years—decades. And no one had gotten a glimpse of what he was. He had traveled the lands, never stopping until Ackwood. Until he had met a broken man and sworn an oath to help him.

He unfolded the bundle, extracting a simple gown and fresh underthings from it—the size seemed about right—then laid out the clothes on the bed before he pulled out his own set of fresh garments from the pack he had brought and put them on the chair by the window.

Outside, the town—town was too much of a word for it, the village—of Elste was still full of life, people starting the Fest of Blossoms early—Vernal Equinox. The holiday of Vala. Tomorrow there would be celebrations all over Neredyn, and for the first time in ten years, he would feel the guilt ease off his shoulders.

The click of the bathing room door saved him from a journey down the pain of memory lane.

The girl padded into the room on bare feet, her body wrapped in a thick, generous towel, wet hair hanging over her shoulders and her back, down to her waist. He stifled a cough at the sight and turned around to pick up the clothes he'd procured for her, tossing them at her before she could say anything. Then, he crossed the room, avoiding the desire to let his eyes wander to the seam of her breasts visible above the towel, grabbed his bundle from the chair, and slid through the half-open bathroom door behind her.

She had washed her clothes and hung both sets of them on the edge of the bathtub. With the steam in the room, they wouldn't dry overnight, so he used his magic to summon a breeze. Just enough to ensure she'd have something comfortable to wear when they got back in the saddle.

He grabbed a washcloth and cleaned up until any proof of their ride through the desert and their encounter with the desert lion had disappeared.

When he returned to the bedroom, Gandrett was sitting in the chair, blanket slipping off her shoulders, exposing that she was wearing only her underthings. She was fast asleep, face relaxed for once, not full of fear or dismay or of that hidden melancholy he had been observing those past

days. He gently slid one arm across her back and one under her knees, and he carefully carried her over to the bed
where he tucked her under the heavy blankets and spread
her hair around her head so it could dry. Then Nehelon
grabbed the blanket that the girl had been wrapped in and
laid down with it on the floor at the foot of the bed.

12

andrett woke to the dulled sound of music and the
happy chattering of people in the streets below the
window. With heavy limbs, she sat up in the middle
of the soft bed—how had she gotten there?—before she leaned
forward to scan the room for Nehelon. The bathing room was
open with no sign he was inside.

Keeping the blankets wrapped around her, Gandrett
climbed a little further toward the end of her bed, to find the
view of the freshly-dressed Fae male sprawled on the floor, fast
asleep, one hand on the sword beside his head. She froze so as
to not wake him. It was like the glamour had slipped again in
his sleep, more thoroughly this time, revealing to a full extent
his stunning features.

He must have carried her into bed and picked the floor for himself. This creature who never held a kind word for her...

Spellbound, Gandrett studied him. The high cheekbones, the strength of his jaw, the curve of his lips, sensual, soft, his eyes framed with a fringe of thick, black lashes casting shadows on his cheeks in the morning sun. But what was more beautiful than any of his visible features was that peace. An expression she hadn't even believed was possible on the usually so cold and stone-like face. So fragile, she almost reached out to brush his cheek with her fingertips. Almost.

Then, she noticed his hair had slid back to expose his pointed ears. Fae ears. And the urge subsided.

Slowly, carefully, Gandrett slid out of bed, grabbed the plain brown gown from the backrest of the chair where Nehelon must have hung it, and tiptoed into the bathing room to get dressed, to find her acolyte uniform almost dry on the rim of the bathtub where she had left it last night.

She considered putting it on but slipped into the simple, brown gown, preferring dryness over comfort at this point. The morning air would be chilly, and she didn't want to risk getting sick.

Besides, it was the Fest of Blossoms today. She had heard what people expected of Children of Vala on that day. Some even pilgrimaged to the priory to receive blessings from the high priests and priestesses. Gandrett doubted Nehelon would agree if they were held up because of her. Besides, she wasn't a priestess. A blessing from her was worth about as much as buying one of the lucky charms the traveling merchants had sold in Alencourt the day she had been taken.

To her surprise, the dress fit. More tightly than anything else she'd ever worn, but it was clean and warm enough. She was half-done when there was a knock on the door—not the bathing room one—followed by rustling and Nehelon's voice barking for whoever it was to leave whatever it was at the door. An array of clattering dishes followed suit.

Gandrett chuckled at his tone. Not the cold, calculated one he used with her, but an authentically disgruntled one similar to what Surel sounded like when woken early.

When she entered the bedroom, fully dressed, hair yet to be braided, Nehelon was handling a tray of steaming tea and fresh breads. He looked up over a plate, eyes wide as he took her in.

Gandrett merely smoothed out her skirts and sat down on the edge of the bed. "Good morning."

Nehelon's eyes were still grazing over her, not the way the men's had at the tavern last night but with a look somewhere between disbelief and surprise.

"This is what I look like when I'm clean," Gandrett explained and took the tray from his hands, watching his throat bob as she did.

He sat on the chair by the window and watched her set down the tray beside her on the bed.

"Compliments of the house," he said, voice raw. "For the Child of Vala."

Gandrett mustered a smile and nodded her thanks, then picked up a cup, filled it with a wonderful-smelling herbal infusion, and handed it to him.

Nehelon's eyebrows rose. "A peace offer?" he asked with a grin similar to the mocking ones before she had found out his secret.

Gandrett, however, brushed her hair back over her shoulder and shook her head. "Nice of you to let me have the bed last night," she merely said, and she saw it in his eyes, the facets of blue diamond sparkling, even as his face tightened a bit, that he realized it had been *his* peace offer. "Plus, it's Fest of Blossoms today. We are supposed to share meals and enjoy ourselves."

His grin turned into a tentative half-smile. "Even with the savage who bought you from the priory?"

There it was. The cold truth told from his sensual lips. Gandrett's heart thundered in her chest, and by the way his face changed, she knew that he regretted having reminded her.

Gandrett wasn't done. "How come no one has noticed what you are?" She asked, curious to find out how he had been navigating his life in human realms without getting caught.

He just shrugged. "The glamour works on most humans," he explained and pointed at his face, which slowly dulled, taking away the radiance—not that anyone could ever miss how handsome he still was, but the full extent of his beauty had been hidden behind whatever spell he was using.

With swift fingers, he reached up and pulled back his hair, showing ears now round as any human's.

Gandrett sucked in a breath.

"When it slipped that morning with you—" He studied her face, eyes curious, not cold, but as he leaned a tad closer, Gandrett moved away.

"I understand if you are afraid of me," he said lowly, some emotion filling his eyes as he still measured her face. "This is not how I thought things would turn out."

"How did you think they would turn out?" she asked into the silence that was spreading between them. "You could have just walked in through the front gate of the priory instead of provoking a sword fight. That would have been an idea."

She swallowed, watching him take a sip of tea, darkness in his eyes brewing like a storm. "How would I have ever known if you were worth the money?" he plainly said, a grin decorating his lips. And even though he smiled and spoke and drank tea like a normal person, he had paid the Meister dearly for her temporary service. The bag had been heavy and probably filled with gold.

"And, am I?"

"That remains to be discovered," he responded, his smile turning feral. "Let's see how you do in your assignment."

She tried not to be offended.

It hadn't changed: Gandrett was afraid of him and for good reason. But she was even more afraid of not knowing what lay ahead of her. "When we arrive in Ackwood," she cautiously asked, "what will I be expected to do?"

Nehelon eyed her, conflict rushing over his features, and Gandrett expected him to return to his stone-like mask, but he surprised her with a low sigh and flash of desperation in his eyes before he made up his mind and spoke, "You will help me free Lord Tyrem's lost son."

Nehelon heard her heart stutter as he said it. Fear. It was there in the pace of her heart, in the moss-green of her eyes, which widened at his words. Otherwise, she was a fortress of calm. Almost dangerously calm.

He should have waited, given her time to adjust to the new situation, let her gain trust...

Trust. He shook his head at himself. One night of handing the comfort of the soft bed over to her and picking the floor instead, gentlemanly as that may be, didn't turn her into a sudden ally. Maybe if she had never found out his secret, then she might have trusted him by now. He might have had the time to win her over to his cause, and not drag her out of Everrun like a slave.

"Lost son?" Her low voice shattered through his thoughts.

He nodded, for lack of words to spell out what they were to do, of the horror he had done before.

"That's a job for mercenaries, not for a Child of Vala," she pointed out.

But he shook his head. "I don't know what you remember from when you were little..."

Her face tightened, making him shudder.

"Sives has been at war for a long, long time. Not Sives," he corrected, "but the houses."

Gandrett gave him a nod. "Brenheran in the east and Denderlain in the west," she noted.

"While they have been splitting the rule over the lands for generations, they have been working against each other for decades, making the people of Sives suffer, starve. To finance their feud, they have been raising taxes on the people. They have been selling the grains needed for their own people to the regions in the south, to Phornes and Lapidos."

He watched the girl's eyes grow wider and wider as he spoke.

"They taught you history and politics in the priory, didn't they?" he reassured himself with the question and got

106

the nod from her he had hoped for. She knew. About the Brenherans and Denderlains, who had been marauding the land of Sives, each of them on their own strive for power. "The conflict has gotten worse over the past years since the House of Denderlain abducted Lord Tyrem's oldest son, forcing him to bow."

Hamyn Denderlain, the name alone was enough to make a shudder run down his spine, was a tyrant and one with the support of a magic unfamiliar even to him. A dark magic. But for now, he kept that suspicion to himself.

"Who is this lost son?" Her words were low, as if she didn't even realize she was speaking.

"Joshua Brenheran." He could tell from the look on her face that she had never heard that name before. "Lord Tyrem has done anything to keep it a secret. But he had taken ill a while ago, and even if there is Brax, his other son, and Mckenzie, his daughter, it is Joshua he wants to see on his throne before he meets his end."

She put down her own teacup, and the question was visible in her eyes before the words fell off her tongue, "Why bring me, then? Why not just march into the fortress of House Denderlain and free him yourself?"

Nehelon leaned back and glanced out the window, as if expecting someone to listen from beneath. Then, he got to his feet and sat beside her on the bed, the wooden tray between them. "Because—" he paused, fingers folding in his lap, "—this is a mission too big for one man—even a Fae," he clarified before she could argue. "We have tried and failed for four years. And now—"

Gandrett waited for his words to come.

"Now it is time to choose a different path—a path that they would never consider—and to find Joshua and bring him back." His words were flat. Clipped. Impossible for her to read a plan in them.

But Gandrett didn't ask any more details. For now, it seemed like a huge achievement that Nehelon had shared a shred of information at all.

Much to her surprise, he wasn't done yet as he said, "It was never my plan to get off on the wrong foot with you, Miss Brayton." His eyes were sincere. "When I joined Lord Tyrem's court a little over ten years ago, I didn't know I would..." He stopped and picked up a piece of bread, shoving it in his mouth.

Gandrett did the same. From the look in his eyes, she knew he wasn't ready. And if she had learned one thing during her painful years in Everrun, it was that pushing someone who wasn't ready wasn't the way to get what you needed.

They chewed next to each other, neither of them looking at the other until breakfast was done, and Nehelon got to his feet, announcing that he wanted to be on his way in order to not lose too much time on their trip north. Gandrett didn't object. The Fest of Blossoms for her remained a reminder of what had happened to her and that she was now in the service of the man who had ordered it to be her.

Wordless, she put on her linen pants under the dress so she wouldn't expose her legs while riding, packed her satchel, and followed Nehelon out the door.

Her stomach twisted at the sight of the flowers, all of them meaning it was that day of the year. That day when four kids would be sent into the desert to become something they shouldn't even know about. Fighters, killers maybe even. To endure the scolding and the wrath of the Meister. To endure the punches and the blows if they were unlucky. Like she had. That day, when families all over Neredyn grieved for the future that had been taken away from them. Gandrett swallowed her bitterness and put on a brave face. The face she had been wearing for ten years.

It took them a solid hour to retrieve their horses and get out of the town through the people dancing and celebrating in the streets, their hair crowned with flowers. Gandrett accepted the tiara of blossoms someone handed them and allowed Nehelon to place it on her head. She didn't even flinch when his fingers brushed the hair from her forehead. He hadn't hurt her so far despite his threats, and he said he needed her—for whatever reason, but it was enough, for now, to trust she would make it back to Sives safely.

And then... maybe she would run.

Rays of sun danced off the surface of the Penesor, making it a silver band of light curving through the green land. She strained her eyes, looking into the distance where the river split into two arms: one to the east and one going west, right to Ackwood, the city built on a river island. She had seen drawings and carvings of Ackwood at the priory, and maps, showing just how close the western capital was to the Fae lands. Gandrett wondered if Nehelon ever felt homesick. They had been riding for days, following the mountains to the east until they had hit the river, which they were now following toward the heart of Sives, where mountains and rivers met. Close to Alencourt where she had grown up. For she felt the soothing spring green of Sives singing to her like the lullaby her mother had sung when she was a child.

"Less than a day to Alencourt," Nehelon said, his gaze following hers.

Gandrett felt it burning in her chest, the question over whether she would be allowed to stop by her old home. She hadn't made a run so far for the simple reason that Nehelon was the one providing them with shelter and food every night. They had slept at the edge of a forest for one night, his magic enclosing them in a wall of stone and wood. The next evening, they had stayed at an inn by the river, their meal consisting of fried fish and warm slices of spiced bread. He had even trusted her enough to leave for a bit—long enough to sell that desert lion skin—and she had stayed in the room as he had asked her to. Asked her—not told her like he had so many times before.

"I know you wish to see them," Nehelon read her yearning as they continued along the river, "but now is not the time."

Gandrett's heart sank. She had hoped...

"But I have made my own conditions for this bargain on Lord Tyrem's end of my deal with the Meister," he informed her with a conspiring look. "I am aware you, as an acolyte, and even as a full member of the Order of Vala, cannot take payment," he reminded her of the rules that dictated her life—would be dictating it for all eternity, "but I thought seeing your family would be possible on the way back to Everrun." He flashed her a smile, a real one. "When your task is done, that is."

The task. Freeing Joshua Brenheran. A task that, for some reason she yet had to learn, was something she qualified for. Nehelon was still cryptic about that. But seeing her family. Maybe running wasn't worth it after all. Not that she would make it far with a Fae hunting her down.

"Don't tell the Lord I have told you, though," Nehelon added. "He likes to make that sort of announcement himself."

"To appear like the great philanthropist he is," Gandrett bit at Nehelon and watched his face cloud over.

"He is not a bad man." Nehelon shook his head as if to enhance the meaning.

"He gave the order," she countered. The order to sacrifice a child from Alencourt rather than from his own city as it should have been.

Nehelon didn't ask what order she meant. It was clear on his face he knew what she was talking about. "He had his reasons."

Gandrett didn't look north as they passed the bridge where the Penesor split into Ackpenesor and Eedpenesor. No, she kept her eyes west, on the water, and when the next day the skyline of Ackwood, with its pointed spires, appeared on the horizon, she kept her eyes on those. She didn't ask any questions until they reached the massive gate where the statue of a hooded warrior, point of his sword set down before his feet, had Gandrett craning her neck. The city was a fortress, set on an island right where the Ackpenesor met the sea in the west. On the wall above the statue, a row of guards, armed with bows and crossbows, eyed their approach.

Gandrett turned on her horse, facing Nehelon as she whispered. "Do they know?" Her eyes darted for his silky, dark hair, which was covering his ears and neck, his glamour in place.

He shook his head, and the look on his face made clear that if she dared so much as indicate what she knew to anyone, Gandrett Brayton would be a figure of the past.

The gate opened upon a lift of Nehelon's hand, the guards, clothed in burgundy embroidered with threads of gold, saluting him as if he were the lord himself.

But Gandrett's eyes went straight to the gate, which slowly flapped outward to form a bridge over the water, and the view that spread behind it. Timbered houses settled along a canal with its own little gate on the side, granting access to merchants and traders coming in by boat. The streets were busy among workshops open to the thoroughfares, the clinking of metal from the blacksmiths filling the air as much as the hammers of the carpenters. Children were running along the cobbled roads, driving wheels before them, which they steered with sticks. Children, laughing and playing, unlike the unfortunate ones whose childhood had ended two nights ago when the noble Lord Tyrem Brenheran had sentenced another one of them to a lifetime of service. A lifetime of fighting and praying.

"Stay close," Nehelon warned as he noted her attention drifting. "We don't want you to get lost in this city."

She lifted her eyes to his, trying to read the warning.

But all he did was nod at the side streets, which were darker than the main road they were following and where women in light dresses were offering their bodies for money.

"Just because something is pretty on the surface doesn't mean it's as pretty deep down." For some reason, Gandrett didn't have the feeling he was speaking about Ackwood.

The spires of the castle towered high over the rest of the royal residence. Royal because House Brenheran had once held the title of kings. As had the House of Denderlain in the east. But the kingdom of Sives had been shattered long ago, during the same war that had eradicated the fertile lands around Everrun and starved its people. The same war that had turned the gate of Ithrylan into ruins. Now, they were merely two noble houses fighting for their standing while they ruled in the east and the west, tearing the people of Sives apart and the country into ruin.

Gandrett got off her horse, shaky from all the eyes she found on her. She was still wearing that plain, brown dress Nehelon had gotten her, but she could have been in rags, and it wouldn't have made much difference. Nothing was fine enough for the palace that stood before her, a row of guards, all in burgundy uniforms, shiny armor protecting their chests and their shoulders. A carriage rolled by, decorated with ornate gold patterns, and behind the lace curtain, Gandrett spotted a woman in a colorful dress, a small hat atop her curly hair, and a fan hiding everything but her eyes.

As Nehelon beckoned her forward, Gandrett's knees went wobbly. She had been at the order for too long, and before that, she had lived on a farm, playing on the fields, not learning how to use silver tableware and pretty lace-up dresses. She hadn't even learned how to curtsey properly.

He seemed to sense her distress and offered a hand, face expectant as if he were saying, *Take it. Or I'll drag you by the collar.*

So Gandrett took it, her fingers hesitant as they touched his.

But Nehelon's hand gripped her tightly and led her forward, forcing both their hands forward between them.

"Smile," he ordered, his own face smooth and a bit amused.

So Gandrett smiled. It felt unnatural, and her eyes stung as she dragged one foot after the other forward until the palace had swallowed her, but she smiled.

The halls were cool and unwelcoming. Even if they had been bright and filled with flowers, it wouldn't have made a difference for Gandrett. It was *his* home. Lord Tyrem Brenheran's. Every banner on the wall, every portrait, every carving on the doors they passed spoke of the man who was responsible for her loss.

A pair of guards had joined them on their way in, both reporting to the Fae male in hushed voices and slipping Gandrett curious glances every now and then. They didn't ask questions but escorted them up a flight of stairs, then another, until they halted at open double doors where more guards were stationed, armed with swords and spears.

They inclined their heads to Nehelon as he led Gandrett right into the great hall made of dark, polished stone.

And there he was lounging at the end of a long, dark, wooden table. The face Gandrett knew from paintings and sketches at the order, paler and gray from bad health. A man in his late fifties, popping some type of exotic fruit into his mouth, failed to heed them a look as they entered. The rest of his court did. Men and women dressed in fine clothes and frilly gowns, gold details on layers of fabrics, eyes on not Nehelon but Gandrett, who shrank under their stares despite what she had promised herself: that she would get through this, help this man she hated so dearly, and live to see her family again.

"About time," he said by way of greeting, not interrupting his decadent snack. "My lovely wife and I were just beginning to wonder if you would ever return." The lord gestured at the small-framed lady next to him, who glanced up with an unreadable gaze, meeting Gandrett's then Nehelon's.

The latter inclined his head at the lady then bowed at Lord Tyrem Brenheran. "May I present, Miss Gandrett Brayton."

Gandrett considered curtseying, but then with the entirety of the room watching her, she reconsidered. She didn't need to embarrass herself at the first opportunity.

"Pleasure," she said drily, her face as smooth as she had learned to keep it in battle. Yes, her emotions were there. Plentiful. But her pride didn't allow for any bowing and curtseying.

That man had damned her by taking her away from her family, and now he had paid to get her here. He needed her. The life of his son depended on her. And she would not bow.

Nehelon gave her a glance that suggested if she didn't, he would knock her knees out from under her, but before he got a chance, to his credit, Lord Tyrem laughed with delight.

"Unique," he said with a voice that reminded Gandrett of the Meister when he was about to let that wrath break her.

But Lord Tyrem didn't get to his feet and pick up a rod. He didn't gesture for any of his guards to lift a finger. No. He sat and watched her with amused eyes as he beckoned her to come closer.

When she didn't react right away, Nehelon gave her a tiny push with his hand, shoving her a step toward the lord. With small yet steady strides, Gandrett walked up to him, keeping her face blank.

The lord and his court only watched her, the men with curious eyes, the guards sizing her up, trying to figure out what threat she would pose if she unleashed herself on the great hall—they had no idea that within the minute she had spent in the room, she had identified the twelve guards, apparent and disguised, and the assortment of swords, knives, and bows they were carrying. They didn't realize that it would take her less than another minute to launch herself on the table, pick up the various silverware, and throw it at the archers at the back of the room, then roll to the other side and, maybe using Lady Brenheran as a shield, wield her sword at three guards that stood right beside the lord... She didn't finish that game in her mind, for she knew there was one person she wouldn't find a way around—Nehelon. His Fae speed and strength, his magic, if he dared to use any of it, would have her on the ground before she'd reach that table. And even if she knew, if she had trained for it, to kill, to protect, to fight, she had never taken a life. And she wasn't inclined to start with it the moment she walked into her probably only shot of seeing her family again.

So she stopped close enough to reach the lord's throat with her sword if she changed her mind, flashed the men a grin, and inclined her head at the ladies who measured her for other reasons, returning her attention to Lord Tyrem, whose gaze she held, waiting for him to speak.

Lord Tyrem's eyes grazed over her in a way that made her hair stand.

"So you are Everrun's best fighter," he finally said after a long assessing silence. His eyes wandered back to her hip where her plain sword was dangling in the folds of her skirt.

"That's what they say." Gandrett focused on keeping that face smooth, calm. No emotions. They would only betray her. This man, she reminded herself, had paid to get her here. And horrible as that made her feel, to be someone's slave, her unique skills—whatever they were remained a question for another day—gave her a certain standing.

The lord hadn't protested when she hadn't shown him the respect his position demanded. He hadn't reprimanded her. All he did was observe as if he was waiting for something to happen.

"Is she really as good as they say?" he asked Nehelon without taking his eyes off of her.

Gandrett didn't dare break the stare. He wanted something. And she had it. She was in a position of power even if her dirty clothes, her uncombed hair, the soreness of her legs suggested otherwise.

Nehelon's chuckle carried through the high-ceilinged space, past the pillars, and echoed in the far corners by the stained glass windows. "Why don't you ask for a demonstration?"

So the lord lifted a hand, causing a guard to rush close to his side at the gesture, and he whispered something to the heavily armed man.

"Why don't you demonstrate, Miss Brayton?" The lord gestured for the guard to step forward, and as the broad-shouldered man did, the courtiers cleared away from one side of the table as if they were expecting to get in harm's way.

Gandrett swallowed. The guard that was approaching her in solid steps was almost as tall as Nehelon and wore a breastplate. His neck was a muscle-corded column, his features saying nothing but, *Show me, little girl, how you defeat a mountain like me.* He drew his sword, a fine blade singing in the half-light of the great hall, and gave her a taunting look.

She had fought his kind before. The older boys in the order were all eager to prove themselves, challenging her in training.

And none of them had won. Also, none of them had been a man of forty with probably two decades of experience on a battlefield. A real battlefield.

As she drew her sword, she thought of the other ones she had fought. The ones who returned from their missions every now and then, to spend a couple of days in solitude at Everrun and to report back to the Meister to get their new assignments. They came from every corner of Neredyn—except the Fae territories—and she had defeated them all. The Meister had insisted she fight them all because she had defeated anyone else there, and he wanted to know where her boundaries were. How strong she really was, how skilled. She remembered the expressions on their faces when she had them on the floor, her sword at their throats, and sometimes, her hand had shaken, eager to drive that blade home. Not because she wanted to kill, but because she wanted it to end. She never gave in to that urge.

Gandrett didn't need to adjust her stance to parry his first blow. She had been training to be balanced even if she were sleepwalking. His blade hit hers with a deafening crash. She used the force of the impact to swirl to the side and kick the man right in his ribs under his sword hand.

The man staggered back to the surprised *ohs* of the courtiers while Gandrett stood, calm like a blade of grass, waiting for him to recover.

She could have used the time to strike again and get him to the floor in one or two blows, but that wasn't what she wanted to demonstrate. Not that she could be used as a killing machine, the way so many of the Children of Vala were, but that her strength was extraordinary restraint in battle.

It had always been the one thing that her opponents lacked. The patience to find the weak spot, the skill to parry strikes until the weak spots became accessible—

The guard barked something at her. More a cry of rage than words. He was the sort of man who wasn't used to being toyed with.

When he pulled a knife from his belt, both arms extended with deadly blades, Gandrett stood and waited, assessing the way he shifted his weight. He was bulky, strong, yet slower than most of the boys at the order. If he managed one blow—just one, single blow—she would be out cold.

So Gandrett crouched and swirled the same moment the man threw himself at her, both hands grabbed the hilt of her sword as it touched the floor, a counterbalance for her legs as she launched them up in the air, her feet darting right between his blades, hitting him in the chest.

She landed like a cat, sheathing her sword at the same moment the metal of the breastplate hit the floor, both his blades clattering to the stone beside the massiveness of the guard. With light fingers, Gandrett picked them up and had them at his throat before he could recover from the impact.

"You're lucky you're wearing this," she clicked the tip of his sword to the breastplate, "or I would have broken your sternum." He stared at her, wide-eyed. "Or ribs," she continued, "or both."

Then there was absolute silence, save for the man's panting.

Gandrett lowered the blades, took both hilts in one hand, then held out her free one for the mountain of a man. He grunted but took it and, to his credit, let her lift him without any scowling.

Her back protested as he let her haul his full weight, but she didn't let it show. She tugged until the man was back on his feet then handed him back his weapons and turned to Lord Tyrem.

The lord was studying her with vivid eyes, as was the rest of the room.

Gandrett felt Nehelon's stare on her but didn't turn until the slow clap of hands from the back of the room caught her attention.

From the shadows by the door, a handsome young man dressed in black and gold strolled up to the table, his boots clicking on the stone floor, and gave her a long, deep look with a pair of curious, emerald eyes.

"There is nothing more beautiful than an artfully accomplished victory," he said as he stopped right in front of her.

Gandrett held his stare, hand casually slipping closer to her sword.

"Oh, I am not going to fight you," he whispered and leaned forward, close enough for his breath to touch her cheek. Then he turned on his heels and joined Lord Tyrem at the table, taking the seat across from Lady Brenheran.

Gandrett watched him settle down, his tall figure folding into the carved wooden chair, his wavy, black hair, short enough to end at the gold-embroidered collar of his jacket, dancing as he leaned back and glanced at her over his shoulder.

In the silence that followed, Nehelon prowled to Gandrett's side and said to the lord, ignoring the young man's stare, "Did I promise too much?"

Lord Tyrem only leaned back in his own chair and stared. It was his wife who gave Nehelon a nod of approval.

"Show Miss Brayton to her chambers," she ordered, and Nehelon inclined his head, beckoning Gandrett to follow him. But she didn't move.

"I understand, Lord," she gritted her teeth at the word, "that you have paid the Meister handsomely to get me out of training early in order to help you with a mission that has failed before."

Lord Tyrem's gaze chilled, his features hard, making him look like an old man. To her surprise, the pointed glare wasn't meant for her but for Nehelon, whose features hardened equally as the gaze hit him, his back straightening as if he was tensing to attack—with words rather than his swords or magic.

"It seems you're more talkative abroad than you are in your own court," the young man in black noted with a grin.

Nehelon and the Lord Brenheran ignored him.

Gandrett bit her tongue. What Nehelon had told her about the mission... she realized it hadn't been for him to tell. And he had told her anyway. He had told her what the mission was and that it had been unsuccessful for several years. As for the how—it was only that detail he had left her in the dark about. That, and about everything else.

"The nature of your mission, Miss Brayton," the lord said between gritted teeth, "is a matter to be discussed in private."

Gandrett felt them. The eyes on her. Nehelon's weighing heaviest of all.

Lord Tyrem clapped his hands, "Out, everyone out."

In an instant, the courtiers were on their feet, marching for the door with variations of disgruntled expressions on their faces. Some of them awarded her a cold look on their way out.

When only Lord and Lady Brenheran were left alongside with the black-dressed, black-haired young man, Lord Tyrem Brenheran eyed her for a long moment, again measuring her as if he wasn't done with his verdict.

"Sit," he ordered, and Nehelon grabbed Gandrett by the arm and pulled her into a chair far enough from the three nobles that even the length of her sword couldn't reach them. Gandrett let him.

To her surprise, the Fae male remained standing behind her, probably there to keep her in check in case she got any ideas—

"Eat," Lord Tyrem offered and gestured at the fruit platter to her left.

With a slow hand—slow enough not to startle anyone, or trigger Nehelon's alarm bells—Gandrett picked up a piece of the same fruit she had seen the lord had eaten before and shoved it into her mouth.

Delicious. Juicy. It was simply delightful. She had never eaten anything like it. An explosion of sour and sweet...

It was only when the young man three chairs left from her raised his brows that she realized there was liquid dripping down her chin. She halted, eyes darting for a napkin and finding none within her reach.

The young man picked up a piece of cloth embroidered with the crest of House Brenheran and handed it to her with a pitying smile. "They train you well in combat," he said, his eyes wandering to her chin then her hair, her dirty clothes, and at last, to her hands greedily clutching a second piece of the nameless fruit. "But that's about everything they train you in."

A low chuckle rose from behind her, and she felt the urge to turn and stomp onto Nehelon's Fae feet.

But she cooled her temper and said with the friendliest face she could muster, "Better savage and alive than sophisticated and dead."

Gandrett could swear Lady Brenheran was suppressing a smile, but her features smoothed the moment Lord Tyrem spoke again, "Miss Brayton." He straightened in his chair, resting his forearms wrapped in sleeves of burgundy velvet with buttons of gold on the table. "You were summoned here for the sole purpose of retrieving my son—" His eyes darted to the side at the young man who had called him father. "—my eldest son, Joshua, from my enemies."

Gandrett fashioned a surprised face as she pulled the napkin from the young man's hand and wiped off the juice, hoping that it was convincing enough that Nehelon wouldn't get into trouble. For some reason she couldn't quite understand, she cared.

"That," Lord Tyrem continued, "is the mission that has failed before as Nehelon has described it so well." A cold glance at the Fae male behind her. "That is the mission *he* has failed at before would be the correct way to put it."

She could feel Nehelon tense behind her.

"That's why I made sure we have the best weapon we can in order to get back Joshua. There is a reason why the Meister picked her." His tone was different from how he had spoken to her—neither the cold, clipped words, nor the heavy ones that had slipped him at Elste. Here, inside these polished stone halls, his voice was an intricate texture of sound and meaning. Gandrett wanted to turn in her chair and see his face, discover if it had equally changed or remained the same as what she had studied during the long journey from the priory. "I fought her at Everrun, and I can attest that she is the best. You have seen her demonstration. She can defend herself. She can fight the strongest of your guards. She—" he paused, all eyes but Gandrett's on him, "—she even defeated me."

Gandrett felt a tug on the corners of her mouth and suppressed a smile. She had.

"Now it's only about getting her to be..." He searched for words. "To be acceptable for Denderlain court."

Lord Brenheran nodded as he looked Gandrett over like a prize pony. "I see."

Beside him, Lady Brenheran sought Gandrett's gaze as if she was trying to tell her something. An apology maybe... But the lady averted her eyes too fast to be reading too much into it.

"There is a lot of work to be done, Brax." He glanced at the young man, who gave a nod as well, his eyes lighting up despite his otherwise cool expression.

Gandrett tried to make sense of their words, her heart picking up speed. "Denderlain court?" She finally peered over her shoulder to find Nehelon frowning. "I thought I was to free Joshua Brenheran. A mercenary mission."

The lord laughed before Nehelon could explain. "If it were a mission doable by mercenaries, believe me, our own guards and mercenaries would have managed." He shot a look of dismay at Nehelon. "*He* would have managed," he added, his chin jerking at the male.

It was clear in the lord's voice and the way Nehelon almost invisibly cringed that this was personal for him. Her success was personal for him.

She took a steadying breath and straightened, placing the sticky napkin on the table before her. "What am I to do to bring Joshua home?"

14

"Seduce Denderlain?" Gandrett coughed at Lord Tyrem Brenheran. His wife flinched beside him but said nothing. "You are aware, *Lord*," she raged, her calm facade crumbling in the wake of the lord's words, "that I am a Child of Vala. Trained in swordsmanship. Trained for combat." She paused, inhaling deeply through her nose, and exhaled through her mouth once. Twice. *You, yourself, saw to it that I was sent to the priory as Sives's stupid sacrifice,* she wanted to say. But she held those words in, throwing little daggers through her gaze instead.

The lord acted as if sending a girl of barely eighteen to seduce the enemy for information was something he did every day.

"A disguise," Nehelon said behind her, his deep voice clarified. "Not a job."

Brax Brenheran grinned widely as if he was enjoying the spectacle. Nehelon shot him a pointed glare.

"For some reason, House Denderlain knows every face of my guards, male or female. There is no one I can send who they won't identify right away; and send back with a missing limb in the best case, execute on the spot in a worse case." He looked her straight in the eye, face fierce with a hint of fatherly concern. "Worst case, they torture my guards, my mercenaries." His gaze shot to Nehelon and back. "I don't want to know what they are doing to my son." Lady Brenheran reached for his hand at that, her face tight. "Hamyn Denderlain is not a man to hold back his blade." There was a deep sadness in his eyes, and rage—the rage of a father who was helpless, who could do nothing but watch as his son was taken from him, hurt, potentially tortured—

Gandrett's head sunk at that last memory of her own family. The pleas to choose someone else, to leave their daughter with them. This man before her, sitting in his castle with his wife and son, feeding on imported fruit, fighting on the expense of his people—the people of the west of Sives. She focused on the silverware before her, swallowing any emotion. She had to keep a clear head.

"We need to infiltrate the Denderlain court and find out Joshua's whereabouts. Last time my men tried to get him, Hamyn moved him just a day before they arrived and had a party of soldiers waiting for them instead."

Nehelon shifted behind her, but Gandrett didn't turn, didn't want to see what was there on his face, if it spoke of pain, of torture, of a history that had driven him to agree to make her nothing more than a courtesan...

"And where exactly do you expect I find Joshua?" she asked pointedly. "In Hamyn's bed?"

"I like her, Father," said Brax to the lord and chuckled darkly. Then, he turned to her, shaking his head. "It's a disguise, Miss Brayton," he repeated what Nehelon had said before. "Nobody expects you to actually get that far." His gaze swept over her once more. "And it's not Hamyn we expect you to seduce but his son and right hand, Armand. You need to win his trust so you can sneak around and find Joshua. And with Armand's trust, his affections—" He didn't need to continue.

Gandrett swallowed and looked down at her brown gown, shabby compared to anything she had seen in this palace so far, and became very self-conscious. She knew enough about boys to understand Brax's assessing glance. He was studying her curves, and the dress, even if plain and unrevealing compared to what some of the courtiers had worn, what Lady Brenheran was wearing, showed off the generous curve of her breasts, her slender waist. Heat rose in her cheeks as she noticed they were all looking now. Even Nehelon, who had stepped forward and stood by her side, face unreadable.

With another deep breath, Gandrett shook the feeling of being an exotic animal to be sold at an auction. "I am a Child of Vala," she repeated, implying precisely what it meant and reminding the four people in the room of exactly that. "I was forced at the age of seven to swear an oath to be faithful to the goddess and the goddess only. I am sworn to the Order of Vala, and that will be my sole company for the rest of my days." Nobody had to point out just how bitter she sounded, how little she had wanted that oath. How little she wanted that life.

Even Brax Brenheran lost his grin at her words.

But Tyrem Brenheran, no matter how understanding his eyes were, simply said to Nehelon, "I didn't pay a fortune for a girl who shies away at the sight of men."

Nehelon squared his shoulders ever so slightly, as if reminding himself of something, but didn't speak.

He saw their looks, Lord Tyrem's and Brax's. And he could tell they agreed with what he, himself, could no longer deny. Below the plainness of her dress, the girl's body was as if made to draw men's stares. She was perfect for the job—especially her skills in sword fighting, her uncanny way of knowing just how to put her opponents on their back. Once she'd made her first kill, she would be unstoppable.

How exciting it was to come across someone skilled and strong enough to maybe even take on him.

But seducing Armand Denderlain to win his trust, even if it was just a decoy...

He remembered that first time Lord Tyrem had hatched the plan. Find Joshua by infiltrating the palace. Armand Denderlain, Hamyn's right hand and commander of the guard, was suspicious of every new addition to his fighters, every new courtier, so there was only one way to get her close enough to him without having to introduce her as a servant.

Maybe they would plant her at one of Denderlain's parties, Armand was known for always looking for a new face. He was sure Armand would not miss her undeniable beauty.

"I don't shy away from anyone," Gandrett clarified, her cheeks stained in a shade of red that reminded him of the wild raspberries in the forests of Ulfray.

Brax's eyes sparked as he noted the fire in Gandrett's gaze. Not a Child of Vala—a warrior of Vala.

"You may have *bought* me from the Meister like a common slave," she said, her voice deadly calm, "but I am nobody's whore." She paused, letting her words sink in, and to Nehelon's satisfaction, Lady Crystal gave a short nod of agreement. "I will do what I can to save your son. I will risk my life because that is what I was trained for. I will even slip into make-up and flimsy dresses to get it done."

Nehelon waited for what was coming, they all did. For the smug look on her face promised there was a condition.

She could taste the tension in the air. The anticipation. All of them were still looking at her—at her face now. Into her eyes. Lady Brenheran had even nodded her agreement. Now it was time to play the cards right. The Meister—painful as his lessons might have been—had taught her one or the other thing about how to navigate herself in situations that demanded wandering off the path of Vala. She could negotiate—would negotiate.

"A year," she said coolly.

And Lord Tyrem's eyebrows rose, as did Brax Brenheran's and Lady Crystal's. Nehelon's face, however, remained unreadable.

"What ever do you mean, Miss Brayton?" Lord Tyrem asked when Gandrett left them guessing for a moment longer than his patience held.

Gandrett kept her face blank. "When I bring home your son Joshua," she said, sounding as reassured as if she were telling Nahir that she wanted more oat cookies, "I want one year with my family."

Beside her, Nehelon's arm twitched the slightest bit. He knew that she was taking what he had already negotiated with the lord and stretching it, testing how far she could go, to gain as much from the bargain as she could. Something more valuable than any gold they could pay the Meister—time with her family. Seeing her mother's smile, hearing her brother's laugh, looking out the window and finding her father on the field with the fat ponies that pulled his plow—

If Lord Tyrem was offended by her question, he didn't show any sign. All he did was turn to Nehelon and say, "So far, she exceeds my expectations in every regard but manners." Then to Gandrett. "If..." He gave her a stern look. "If you manage to pass as a lady in Denderlain court," his eyes bore into hers, fierce. A warrior, a father, betting on the only horse available to save his son and pushing it, daring it, threatening it to win. "If you bring home my son in one piece," he leaned back, "I will grant you a year."

Somehow, he didn't look like he believed she would manage.

"Show the *Child of Vala* to her chambers." He nodded at Nehelon, who promptly reached for her arm and pulled her up.

"Come, Miss Brayton," he said with a professional tone, "I am certain you can use a bath after the strain of our journey."

Gandrett ignored as he sniffed at her before he walked her from the room.

The double doors of her chambers were guarded, one heavily armed man on each side. Gandrett had flashed them each a smile as Nehelon walked her in—not at the tip of his sword the way she had done with him at the priory but with mere words of caution.

"Don't even think about running," he had said with a feral grin.

Gandrett interpreted his words as, *If you want to live long enough to see your family again.*

He had left her to take a bath and get some rest with the reminder that the guards outside wouldn't be the only ones monitoring her chambers. And while both of them knew it would take more than two or three guards to stop her once she made up her mind, they also knew that he, with his Fae senses, would be the first to come after her the second she went missing.

Quiet footsteps interrupted her thoughts, and she looked up to find a woman in a simple dress—still more fashionable and of a better fabric than her dirty, brown one—enter the bedchamber where Gandrett was standing and studying the burgundy and gold tapestry. The woman stopped and curtseyed then hurried to the dresser, head down, and opened it to pull out a variety of fabrics.

Gandrett watched, her mouth open. She had heard about servants, about noble ladies having someone tending to them. But never had she believed anyone would see to her needs.

The woman turned toward her, curtseying again. "We didn't know what size you'd be," she said with a low voice, half-blushing as she studied Gandrett's body, "so we brought some underthings and something to sleep in...just until we get some clothes made for you tomorrow."

Gandrett's eyes followed the servant's hands as she reached into her apron, and her instincts went on red alert... For a second, until the woman extracted a tape measure and stepped closer.

"If I may," she lifted the item in her hand and waited.

And waited.

For a moment, Gandrett just stared. Then she realized what the woman meant and fumbled with her dress.

"My apologies, Miss Brayton." The servant took another step. "I can help you with the dress if that makes it easier."

Gandrett stopped. "What's your name?" she asked the woman and tried to smile, something Nahir had said once coming to her mind. *Treat your servants like the people they are—people, who through their hard work, make your own life easier. Respect them.*

The woman looked up with hazel eyes. "Eugina."

"Thank you, Eugina." Gandrett pulled off her dress in one sweep, folded it over a chair, and held out her arms to the side for Eugina to take measure. "I haven't worn a proper dress in—" Over a decade. "A long time." She wasn't sure how much the woman knew about where she had come from, what her purpose at the palace was, how dangerous she could be. So she smiled again.

Eugina, obviously relieved that Gandrett wasn't a fire-breathing monster like some ladies—according to Nahir—were, wrapped the tape measure around Gandrett's chest, waist, hips, then measured the length of her arms, shoulder to floor, and every other detail that Gandrett never knew was necessary in order to fabricate a dress.

Then, with another curtsey and the promise that she'd have something to wear by tomorrow, the woman left.

Gandrett loosed a breath. Her own chambers. Not just one room shared with another acolyte but one bedroom, a private bathing chamber, an antechamber. Her eyes darted from surface to surface, marveling at ornate carvings, burgundy and gold patterns, and the thick rug covering most of the dark stone floor. She marveled until her chest hurt from the ambivalence of it. Beautiful, yes, but it all belonged to the man who had taken her childhood away.

And if she was honest—the only thing keeping her here was knowing that if she tried to run, Nehelon would end her with a flick of his hand. She couldn't care less about Joshua Brenheran. No one had cared when she had been taken from her parents. People in the streets had cheered when the dark-clothed, hooded men had picked her from her home. She couldn't remember faces, just the fear when it had settled in that she would never return.

If she ran now, she would make it to Alencourt in two or three days on foot.

A glance out the open balcony doors told her it would be easy. With her acolyte-uniform on and some strips of fabric from the dress to wrap her hands with, she'd climb down the rough stone to the garden below and disappear in the blossoming bushes, following them until they lost themselves near the palace walls.

A low laugh from above caught her attention. Reaching to her side for the sword she had dropped on the chair alongside her dress, Gandrett swirled around, her hands gripping thin air, and earned a clap from Brax Brenheran who was leaning on the balcony rail one level above.

"Denderlain court will be in turmoil if this is to become your usual attire," he said, a mischievous grin lingering on his sensuous lips. He leaned forward, hair dancing around his face like onyx silk. "Not that it doesn't suit you." A wink.

Gandrett suppressed the urge to throw the flowerpot in front of her at him and hastily retreated into the room.

"I mean it," he called after her, his chuckle outlasting her quick exit, and Gandrett silently thanked Vala he didn't see her turn crimson.

With quick fingers, she sealed the doors and padded to the bathing chamber where the mirror told her that her face was about as pink as the flowers she had debated throwing at the Brenheran-boy.

The next morning, Nehelon found her fast asleep, only her head, one shoulder, and one arm peeking out from under layers of blankets she had wrapped herself in. The chestnut of her hair spilled over the pillows, a stark contrast to the cream silk her cheek was resting on.

For a long second, he held his breath and studied her face, so much softer without the boiling fury she kept locked in all the time. Her lips were parted, life-giving breath flowing in and out in a slow rhythm—almost too slow for a girl her age. But then, she was fit and her stamina built; he noticed her pulse was as low as his own when he rested.

Quietly, Nehelon took a step toward her bed, reassuring himself that all he'd do was take a better look, assess his newest weapon from up close, study the muscles in her bare shoulder and arm before she woke and sneered at him again.

She had been so brave the night before, tackling and defeating Mike in one agile strike. And she had shown nothing of what it cost her, the effort of keeping her emotions in.

She had done a great job. No one had seen it but him, his Fae senses letting him smell just how much she hated Tyrem Brenheran. How she despised all of them for what they were asking of her—not asking. Demanding.

The scent of cherry blossoms and orange oil filled his nose as he stopped beside her bed. It was a scent that was familiar from the ladies at court, and yet—there was something different about the combination when it mixed with the scent of her skin and her hair. Something intoxicating.

As if steered by an invisible hand, Nehelon bent down, eyes closed, and inhaled deeply.

"What are you doing?" Gandrett's voice, too close by his ear, made him jump.

What *was* he doing? Nehelon's eyes widened as he found Gandrett's face mere inches from his, those moss-green eyes revealing flecks of gold in the morning sun. Her gaze was everything but the calm, breakable girl he had spied dreaming. Fury, cold and hot at once met him as he braced himself to pull away from that scent—

"Get out of bed," he barked the first thing that came to his mind. "You won't find out Denderlain's secrets by sleeping late." With a spin on his heels, he propelled himself upright and faced the balcony, his eyes on blossoms opening to the warm light outside. A view that would catch his attention on other days if it weren't for the soft thud of blankets, the sigh of silk against skin, the quick pace of Gandrett's heart as she padded across the room with so little noise he found himself turning to check where she was going.

And found himself staring at a stripe of bare skin between a cascade of chestnut waves above her waist and honey-colored fabric covering everything downward from the curve of her hips.

"Find somewhere else to look," she demanded with what sounded like mild amusement.

How she knew he'd been staring, he didn't know.

Nehelon was sitting at the table when Gandrett emerged from the bathing chamber back in her acolyte uniform. After an hour-long bath the night before, soaking in the luxurious tub, breathing the fruity scent of the soaps and oils on the tray by the door, she had fallen into a comatose sleep.

And woke to a close-up of the Fae male who didn't seem to be able to make his mind up whether he was there to help her or to torment her. She shuddered at the thought of his diamond-blue eyes... and the dark waves that had caught the morning light... were still shining in a rainbow of copper and onyx...

His eyes scanned her, mouth tight.

"Not up to your standards anymore?" Gandrett commented at his frown.

Now that she knew what her task was, however little she liked it, and she had negotiated her own condition—a year with her family, a whole year before she'd return to the Meister's will—she found it easier to face the Fae male. Even forgot for a moment there what he was as his mouth twitched as if he was holding back a grin.

How she would like to know what it took to coax a real laugh from him.

"They haven't delivered you new clothes?" he merely asked.

Gandrett picked up her sword and belt from the chair where she'd left them the night before and added them to her hips, aware of Nehelon's eyes on her.

"What are you thinking?" She asked, unable to read him.

"You shouldn't be wearing this."

"Why?" Gandrett grabbed her mass of hair and twisted it until it was one long chord then bound it to her neck with a string of leather. "Thanks to your wonderful gift," she gestured to the dirty brown dress on the chair, "I still had a spare set of these." One hand pulled on the pale linen tunic on her chest. His eyes followed there, too. "What do you suggest, I go in my underthings?"

Her memory rewound to Brax's melodious chuckle and the spark in his emerald eyes while Nehelon's lips finally curled upward for a fraction of a second before he knitted his brows together again. "I'm certain Brax wouldn't object."

Gandrett said nothing.

"Even if you are to pass as a lady, we want to take slow steps, getting you to walk, talk, and act like one."

There it was, a punch in the gut. A reminder of what she was about to do. The boundaries she might need to cross... even if she'd never share a bed with Denderlain. His trust. She needed to gain his trust so she could sneak around and find Joshua. Nothing more, nothing less. The young lord's protection rather than his undivided attention.

Nahir had told her the first time she had bled, when her breasts had just started to form and her hips had widened enough to distinguish her from the boys her age, that she would grow into a beautiful woman. And Nahir had seen enough of the outside world—travelers and more—enough Children of Vala who had grown into adulthood under her care. She had warned Gandrett that, first, the older boys at the priory would fight for her attention, then when she went on missions, it would be the men out there... And she would one day need to learn to either wield that femininity like a secret weapon or find ways to conceal it. So far, she had chosen the latter. While Surel had chosen the other path. Surel...

Her heart sank at the thought of her friends who were probably worried about what had happened to her. Even if the Meister had informed them she'd been dispatched early on a mission, the note in the cookie box must have been found by now. With a glance at Nehelon, still frowning but otherwise tame enough, she was wondering if she had overreacted, if maybe he wasn't as dangerous as she thought.

"So teach me, Lonnie," she said in a whiff of boldness.

Not unsurprisingly, Nehelon didn't as much as blink at her challenge. But something else became apparent. A silent defiance that was so uncommon for the otherwise calculated male.

Lonnie? Nehelon wanted to grab the inkpot before him and throw it out the window.

One breath, another one, and another one. He counted. When he reached ten, with a sideways glance into the garden, reassuring himself there was no one within sight, he got to his feet and crossed the room at Fae speed, and pinned her against the wall before she could even notice he had moved.

Lonnie. I will Lonnie you.

Gandrett looked up at him with the same calm face she had worn the night before when she had bargained with Lord Tyrem—a whole *year*. By the gods—if she was scared, her eyes didn't tell. But her heart? It raced in her chest, galloping. He tightened his grip.

Her scent climbed back into his nose, filled his mouth as he leaned closer, baring his teeth, and debated unleashing his magic on her to give her a taste of what happened when people called him *Lonnie.*

16

The air swept from her lungs as Nehelon crushed into her, locking her against the wall with a firm grasp at her wrists, his chest flattening her into the stone behind her. His eyes—there was nothing left of the cold, calculating gaze she was used to.

"You might have gotten a good bargain with Lord Tyrem, but don't get cocky." He squeezed a little harder, as if to remind her she wouldn't escape his grasp. Not if he didn't allow it. His breath was hot on her face, and his scent—

She had never noticed, never even considered how different he would smell from anything she knew. Maybe that was part of the Fae allure—that, and the striking beauty that broke through the glamour as he growled, "Here are some ground rules: you meet me in the training pits at dawn. You don't wander around the palace by yourself—a guard will escort you everywhere," his eyes sparked with ferocity, "even when you take a break to piss."

Gandrett didn't feel the wall behind her or the hardness of his fingers as they encircled her arms.

"You will spend the mornings exercising and sparring and your afternoons learning how to charm Denderlain. Am I clear?"

Gandrett pondered while she marveled at the Fae face before her. "Are you going to teach me how to charm people?" she asked, unable to control the grin that flashed on her lips. "I'm sure you'd be a great teacher, considering how well you handled me." She winked, something inside of her pushing her to keep going, to provoke him. Just to see that glorious wrath of the Fae male for a minute longer. Anything, she noticed, was better than the contained, cold travel companion she'd spent too many silent hours with.

It seemed to take Nehelon all the strength he had to not make it her throat as he bit the air between them, more predator than anything. And she shuddered against the stone behind her, suddenly very much aware of how dangerous a game she was playing.

"That *pleasure*—thank the gods—goes to someone else." With those words, he let go and stalked to the doors where he paused and glanced over his shoulder. "Don't come out until you are wearing either fighting leathers or one of those gowns that are equally dangerous as your blade." With those words, he smoothed over his face, Fae features disappearing in the glamour that settled over him once more, and left.

It took Gandrett a minute or two to recover. What was she thinking to provoke a *Fae* male?

She rubbed her wrists, noticing the hurt his grasp had left behind. A reminder of what he was, how little she could do about it. And even now that she had gotten her assignment from Lord Tyrem directly, she was stuck with Nehelon even if it was only for training.

With a sigh, she grabbed a whetstone from her satchel, flung herself back onto the bed, and sharpened her sword.

Eugina came at noon with a tray of delicacies Gandrett had never seen in her life, announcing that it was an assortment of fish from the East Sea and that Nehelon wished her to become accustomed to the taste. The servant left her alone with the food, and by the time Eugina returned with heaps of frilly fabrics, Gandrett had tried almost every one of the slimy fish dishes and deemed none of them edible.

"You'll get used to it over time," Eugina commented as she dropped her carrion on the wide, burgundy sofa.

Gandrett set down her fork and picked up the glass of juice before her and drained it, just to get some sugar into her system, then nibbled at a piece of bread as she watched Eugina smoothen out the bundles of burgundy, purple, and midnight-blue.

"They don't serve fish in the desert," Gandrett explained and, at the knowing look on the servant's face, wondered if she'd said too much.

"Don't worry, Miss Brayton," Eugina said. "I will keep your secret." She gave a warm smile as she picked up the dirty, brown dress from the chair and placed it in a basket by the door.

Gandrett measured the woman for a while, wondering what secret she meant, that she was from the order or that she didn't like fish. But Eugina returned to the table and offered, "I will have one of the girls bring you some stew from the servants' kitchen. It's hearty and warm and will give you the energy you need to deal with the lord's chancellor."

"Chancellor?" Gandrett prompted and shoved aside the tray at the prospect of something that would fill her stomach.

"Nehelon Sterngrove," Eugina said and curtseyed. "I thought you knew..."

Gandrett endured the cold touch of disappointment. Disappointment about what? He had come to retrieve her from Everrun for Tyrem Brenheran, and even if it had felt at points like he wasn't entirely happy with the task she'd been assigned, what had she expected he'd do about it? The lord's chancellor.

As Gandrett didn't respond, Eugina returned to the dresses, unnecessarily shaking them out. "The chancellor asked me to put proper clothes on you the second they were ready," she continued, and Gandrett turned to watch her finally pick the burgundy one and hold it up for Gandrett to examine. "Is it to your liking, Miss?" she asked and moved a step closer, displaying the soft velvet that was cut high enough to show nothing more than the collarbones of its bearer.

Gandrett shrugged and stood. "It doesn't matter what I think," she murmured, "as long as the *chancellor* is happy."

Chancellor. How had a Fae ended up being a human lord's chancellor? She hadn't given his position in the Brenherans' court a real thought until now, too busy fearing what he would do to her if she exposed him or weighing her chances of running. She had been so absorbed in hating Lord Brenheran that it hadn't occurred to her, Nehelon could be more than a mere mercenary. The thought of the contained fraud as the lord's closest advisor was something she wasn't sure she could stomach.

Mechanically, she got to her feet and took off her acolyte uniform to make way for the cascades of burgundy in Eugina's waiting hands.

The bodice hugged her like a second skin, skirts falling to the floor in soft waves. Eugina adjusted the sleeves until she was satisfied, then wrapped a wide, golden belt, set with rubies and emeralds, around her waist. Gandrett flinched at the tightness of the garment but didn't complain.

She let Eugina braid her hair and put on the burgundy silk slippers without comment. Everything was for the sole purpose of seeing her family again.

"Where can I find the chancellor at this hour of the day?" she asked when they were done, but Eugina didn't need to point her anywhere, for the door opened, and Nehelon Sterngrove stood in the doorway, arms crossed over his chest and eyes cautious.

Nehelon didn't know why he had returned to Gandrett Brayton's chambers, and now that he found her clothed in a garment that left that delicate neck exposed from shoulder to shoulder, something tugged on his stomach. He couldn't tell if it was in a good way.

Eugina noticed him as the girl froze where she stood. So she knew who he was in this court. One less thing for him to reveal to her. He could have told her from the start, could have played with open cards, but then—then he would have had to reveal that his intentions of choosing her had nothing to do with saving Joshua Brenheran. Even if Joshua Brenheran was vital for the future of Sives. A kingdom without a king. A land split and plagued by war for centuries with no prospect of peace. Tyrem Brenheran was the first lord since the kingdom had fallen apart after the Great War of Neredyn, who offered a chance at peace. That was why he had chosen the grumpy lord over his meandering through the lands and was still in his service. That's why he had done his duty every year for over a decade and retrieved the children from their homes on Vernal Equinox. That's why he had taken *her*.

His chest tightened at the glare Gandrett shot at him. She had no idea how right she was about it. To despise him. It was one of the reasons he had chosen not to reveal his identity to her right away, the shame that still lingered after ten years, the fear in her eyes when he had torn her from her mother's arms, the pleas in the woman's eyes when he had taken her child—

Gandrett stood still, unyielding under his gaze. He had asked her on their journey here what she remembered about her life before the order, and she had given no sign she remembered that he had been there that day her childhood had gone to Hel's realms. How often he wished the god of death would take his revenge on him, but he was still there, roaming the realms of Neredyn as he had been for hundreds of years. So he blinked away his guilt and stepped forward, all arrogance and coldness, a shield against what tried to break free within him, from what he had to do.

"What a lovely surprise, *Chancellor*," Gandrett said sweetly. So sweetly it tasted bitter in her mouth.

Nehelon didn't give a sign he had heard the twist on the sound of his title as she had spoken it. He just took a step into the room, arms dropping to his sides, exposing his muscled chest clothed in a clean, white shirt, a burgundy jacket hanging open as if he hadn't cared to finish dressing. He looked human, the glamour properly in place, no sign of his pointed ears, even now that his hair was bound at his neck, leaving them exposed.

"Miss Brayton." He inclined his head just enough to give his demeanor a gentlemanly touch. Gandrett knew his manners were as much a glamour as the roundness of his ears. As he took another step closer, he dismissed Eugina with a word of thanks then waited in silence until the servant had left.

"Is something the matter?" Gandrett asked as all he did was stare at her, seemingly lost for words.

Nehelon shook his head. "I just thought—" he paused, cleared his throat, "—that I'd check in." He smoothed his jacket as if he was only noticing he hadn't buttoned it. "You know, make sure you got something to eat..." His voice trailed away as his eyes fell on the belt. "I see you got clothes."

"No leathers or armor," she pointed out. "So you'll need to wait your turn until tomorrow at dawn." She saw it there in his eyes that her cocky words didn't flare the same fury as they had this morning but, instead, some sort of discomfort that was impossible to understand. "You are still up for training, right?"

Nehelon nodded and turned his head, listening to something only he could hear with his Fae ears.

A moment later, the door burst open, and a young woman with hair the color of sunshine and familiar, emerald eyes swept in, the train of her black gown flaring behind her. "Where is she?"

The girl stormed into the room, sizing up Gandrett with keen eyes as she maneuvered to the table, gracefully dropped into a chair, and pulled Gandrett's abandoned tray toward her. "No wonder they want me to teach you manners if you are too barbaric to recognize the fine tastes of Sives's seas."

Gandrett shot Nehelon a look that was meant to ask whether he or she were going to draw their swords, but Nehelon was already prowling over to take the vacant chair across from the girl. "And good day to you, Mckenzie," he growled, somewhat annoyed.

It was a relief to know there was something between furious and emotionless with the male. But the way the girl he had called Mckenzie leaned back and shuttered her black lashes-framed eyelids gave Gandrett the feeling that there was some history there that she'd rather not know about.

"I know that it makes your miserable life a bit more bearable if you spend your time where the radiance of beautiful women can touch your heart of stone," she looked up and winked at Gandrett, "but—what are you doing here?"

Nehelon snorted and folded his arms, studying the tray on the table rather than meeting the young woman's gaze. "Gandrett Brayton, meet Mckenzie Brenheran, daughter of Lord Tyrem and Lady Crystal Brenheran..."

"Yes, yes," Mckenzie interrupted him, impatient, and stood. "And you are the famous Gandrett Brayton." She prowled toward where Gandrett stood too far from her sword to casually grab it.

"Famous?" Gandrett mouthed at Nehelon, who shrugged.

"Well, it's not easy to get this man on his back," Mckenzie chirped and reached behind her to pat Nehelon's shoulder. "Trust me," she grinned the smile of women who had secrets to share, "I would know."

Gandrett stifled a cough and silently wondered why Nehelon hadn't already pinned the woman against the wall and bitten her for behaving the way she did.

To her surprised, she found Nehelon shrinking slightly in his chair.

"Let me know if you ever need help with that," Gandrett offered with a generous smile and got a bright one from Mckenzie in return.

If that woman made Nehelon uncomfortable enough to shrink, Gandrett decided she liked her.

"It's not so much what I need help with but what *you* need help with." Mckenzie approached her with appraising eyes, gaze lingering on her chest. "Not that there isn't already enough that is gods-given..."

Nehelon coughed lowly.

"You are dismissed." She waved her hand at Nehelon without heeding him a look, and Gandrett watched the male obediently rise and prowl from the room, not without a slight bow before he withdrew through the double doors.

Mckenzie reached out an arm, wrapped it around Gandrett, and squeezed her once, leaving her to wonder if she should be concerned or glad a stranger was this welcoming.

"I am so happy you're here," she whispered, all smiles dropping from her features as if she had taken off a mask. "I was wondering how much longer Father would let this go on—let men march into Eedwood and unnecessarily lose lives." Her expression grew somber.

Gandrett didn't speak. One thing she had learned at the order was that information was as crucial to defeating and enemy as a sharp blade—sometimes even more.

"As a member of the Order of Vala, you are sworn to secrecy, Gandrett, aren't you?" Mckenzie asked and sat on the sofa by the gowns, examining the fabric.

Gandrett was aware that there was little common knowledge about the specifics of the order. Only the numbers of vessels and that they were sacrificed on behalf of the kingdoms to gain Vala's favor. Later, the sword fighters went on missions for the order, and the Vala-blessed were installed as priests and priestesses throughout the territories—all but Ulfray.

"We all swear the oath to Vala when we enter the order." *My life I give to serve and love no other than the goddess. Each drop I drink, each drop I sweat shall be in her honor. My loyalty lies with my brothers and sisters of the order from now until my last breath. No secret will leave my lips, or I will gladly lose my voice, I will give my heart to no one but the goddess. Let this water cleanse my soul so*

I may be worthy of serving the goddess of life. To Vala, I belong, from now until eternity.

She remembered every word, for she renewed it every day at morning prayers with bitterness and the silent hope that, one day, her life would be her own.

Had renewed it... until that day Nehelon had practically dragged her from the priory. What did that make him, a slave-master or a savior? She fell silent, studying the gold embroidery on her sleeves until Mckenzie spoke again.

"You are our last hope," Mckenzie admitted with a voice that didn't compare to the bubbly woman who had entered her chambers only minutes ago. "If you can't get Josh back..."

Gandrett didn't know why she did it, but she reached out her hand, taking Mckenzie's in her own. The woman's emerald eyes told of the nights of crying over her lost brother, the days of hoping for his return, and the moments of disappointment, followed by those nights of crying again.

"I don't know if it means anything to you when I promise I will do my best to get your brother back."

Mckenzie's lips tightened into a smile of gratitude as they looked at each other for a moment before she retrieved her hand and clapped. "Let's get you in shape, then."

After three days, the training with Nehelon every morning was getting boring. He hadn't managed to show her anything new, provoke her in a way that let her lose control of her fighting calm. All he did was bark commands and study her every move as if he, himself, couldn't believe the level of dexterity and stamina she had achieved at the age of seventeen. After a week, she had fought and defeated the most skilled warriors in Lord Tyrem's guard, but Nehelon didn't give her a day of rest. He was there every morning when she entered the training grounds, and he stayed there when she left after hours of sweat and strain. She never showed him when she got tired, and he never asked. Neither of them brought up the incident in her chambers even though his eyes followed her around the pit as if he was trying to solve some riddle.

Gandrett tried not to think about the meaning of it. She was there for one purpose only—her family. She would see them again if she did well enough to be unleashed on House Denderlain soon.

As for the lessons with Mckenzie, they were making the muscles in Gandrett's jaw, and her head, ache as much as her limbs did from the training with Nehelon. First, she wasn't used to smiling. Second, none of the reasons Mckenzie named for those pleasant—and fake—smiles seemed worthy of half a thought. Whether it was a list of topics men liked to ramble about that she was supposed to be impressed with, or the jokes they made at other men's cost, Gandrett, for the first time in her life, saw the value of her oath to Vala, of remaining faithful to the goddess alone.

"And that is only the beginning," Mckenzie informed her with authentic amusement. "You will spend some time with my brother to feel more at ease with what you learn with me."

"Brax," Gandrett remembered. The same emerald eyes, but while Mckenzie had taken after her mother—supple body and round, rosy cheeks—Brax's features were sharper; pleasant, handsome, yet more angled and somehow more mature.

"My twin-brother likes to think of himself as the subject of the dreams of all ladies here at court..." she paused, giving Gandrett a knowing look, "and outside the palace."

Gandrett heard his melodious chuckle in her mind and damned herself for having stepped out on the balcony in her underthings. Nobody could know.

"And... is he?" she cautiously asked.

"A gentleman never tells," Brax's chuckle, the real one, sounded from the door.

Gandrett felt her face turn pink and didn't dare turn to face him.

"We really need to do something about the guards out there, Gandrett," Mckenzie sharply said. "Wouldn't you agree? They seem to let anyone in."

"Otherwise, *you* wouldn't be sitting here," Brax countered, flashing a grin at his twin while he prowled to the table where he sat and examined the bowl with the remainders of the stew Eugina had snuck into her room earlier—the way she had every day since Gandrett's arrival. His nose crinkled.

"Aren't you supposed to be somewhere, impressing someone?" Mckenzie sighed and folded her hands in her lap. Gandrett mimicked her, memorizing the movements for the next time someone stormed into her room to disturb whatever conversation she was having. She had already copied most of Mckenzie's standing and sitting positions even if walking like a dancer wasn't working just yet.

Brax shrugged, the collar of his black jacket rising to his hairline. "Whoever wanted to be impressed will need to wait for another day." He spoke as if whoever that was wouldn't have any more regrets than he did. "There are more important matters to tend to." He leaned forward, resting his forearms on his thighs as he took a good look at Gandrett and grinned. "As I can see, you have upgraded your attire," he noted, dimples forming beside his curling lips. "Not that I minded the alternative." He gave her a look that made color stain her cheeks anew.

Was there a lever she could pull to shut him up?

"How is our new *lady* faring?" he asked his twin with interest, his eyes not leaving Gandrett's face.

Arrogant bastard. Gandrett wanted to yell, but clasped her hands together instead.

"I haven't seen her fight, but—" Mckenzie started.

"I have," Brax cut her off and winked. "Quite some skill."

Gandrett wasn't sure she imagined the hint of admiration in his emerald eyes.

"Good, but as for the foundation for her... other skills..." Mckenzie cocked her head at Brax. "Well then, if she continues at this pace, Josh will rot in Eedwood for the rest of his life." The tone of her words was joking, but Gandrett noticed that that somberness had entered the emerald of her eyes.

Brax studied her for a moment, probably reading the same thing, and heaved himself up. "Good thing I came by then." He prowled toward where Gandrett and Mckenzie were sitting on the couch and looked down at Gandrett. "How would you feel about a walk in the gardens, Miss Brayton?"

Mckenzie gave him a warning look that made Gandrett reconsider her initial longing for a change of scenery.

"What? I'm sure I can teach her one or two other things you can't, sister." He said it with a sensuous smile that made Gandrett's core tighten.

She lowered her gaze.

Cunning. That's what he was. Insidious.

"See," he commented, gesturing at Gandrett's averted eyes, "she needs my help. Now. If we want Josh back any time soon."

Something in his tone told Gandrett he wasn't offering his help for his brother's sake.

Mckenzie got to her feet with a sigh—"Fine."—and left the room with her promise to be surveying the gardens from her balcony.

So, with a squeamish stomach, Gandrett returned her gaze to Brax and drew from her new arsenal, "Help me up, will you?"

Nehelon set down his pen and stared out the narrow window. All bedrooms in the palace faced south-east, and so did his. The window of his adjacent study overlooked the ocean of blossoms that the gardens were at this time of the year. Cherry blossoms amongst others. The memory of the scent—her scent—filled him for a weak second before he returned his thoughts to the letter he was writing.

It had been months since he had sent an update. Too long.

As he picked up his pen and dipped it into the crystal jar of cobalt ink before him, footsteps carried toward him from the garden.

Again, he found himself glancing out the window.

There, by the pear trees, Brax Brenheran's familiar figure strode beside a lady in midnight-blue. He wouldn't have heeded the woman a second look hadn't he recognized the gown. With a hand so fast no human spectator could have seen, he pushed the window open a bit further and examined the scene.

He could only see their backs, but it was obvious, even from this angle, that Brax had sought her company for her alluring curves and her graceful movements. Familiar movements.

He held his breath and listened harder to their murmured conversation, finding his heart picking up pace as Gandrett's voice filtered to him through the blossoms. "Do tell, Brax." A quiet laugh escaped her lips—a sound he had never heard from her. With him, all she did was growl and scowl and avoid any conversation unless necessary. "I'd love to hear that story."

Brax's hand rested lightly on her back, just above the golden belt she had worn that first day he had found himself in her chambers. A belt-like shackles to a girl like Gandrett Brayton. Her wild nature, even if superficially tame, couldn't be locked, couldn't be shackled. He had learned that over those past days of sparring with her, of studying her. She was feline when she fought, graceful and deadly— even if the tip of her sword had never sliced into its aim. Nehelon already dreaded for anyone who put themselves in her path.

His eyes, still on her slim waist, strained to memorize her shape. So far, the most revealing thing he had seen her in was that burgundy gown from the first day. And that had been modest compared to the midnight-blue fabric that highlighted her curves with its silken shimmer.

When she was with him, she was wearing fighting leathers and weapons, and they suited her well. But this—

A growl rose in his throat as Brax's fingers brushed over her back while he plunged deep into a meaningless story of court councils and debates.

Gandrett's quiet laugh pierced him like a knife. What was it about Brax's words that amused her so much?

Nehelon closed the window with so much force the glass vibrated in the frame. Then, he picked up his sword and fled to the training grounds.

A branch of white blossoms held Gandrett's attention. At least that was what she told herself.

"You didn't even notice I stopped talking a minute ago," Brax commented, eyeing her with amusement.

Gandrett considered denying it. She had done so well playing along, implementing everything Mckenzie had taught her. She had nodded and smiled the way Mckenzie had instructed her. Listen, encourage the men to continue speaking. Let them lay their heart at your feet while you keep your back straight, your posture impeccable, your face interested.

She had stomached it for a long time, all the while wondering how society at any court worked if women were supposed to hold their tongue. At the order—even with all the horrible traditions—men and women were treated equally. They were expected to do the same chores whether it came to cleaning out the stables or fighting with a sword. Their words had the same weight, and they were punished the same way. They both had the same chances to climb in hierarchies.

"Am I really that boring?" he asked, a sly smile on his lips, emerald eyes sparkling.

Gandrett gave him a challenging look. "I am sure there are women who enjoy your company despite your talking."

She started walking again, Brax at her side in an instant.

"You know, if you act like that with Armand Denderlain, you might lose your tongue," he cautioned her, his tone still teasing despite the heavier note of his last words.

"What are the women that you normally spend time with like?" she asked, hoping for anything that would distract her from his face.

He shrugged and mentioned a list of traits that Gandrett deemed weak. Then he glanced at her from the side. "Jealous?"

"Like mad." Her natural tone was the opposite of the pleasant chime Mckenzie was teaching her, and Brax noticed that she had switched to that real-self, too.

"They are boring, Gandrett. Something to make days pass faster, nights dreamless. Something to forget how lonely the heir to my father's title truly is." As Gandrett looked up at him, he put a grin back in place. "And they certainly don't talk to me the way you do." He winked and quickened his pace. "You do realize that you need to get used to the flirting," he commented at her blush.

Gandrett touched her cheeks in embarrassment. "Mckenzie already told me that."

"Of course she did," he turned and walked backward, watching her as she set one foot after the other in a perfect copy of Mckenzie. "She is the better teacher."

"Why am I spending my afternoon with you, then?" Gandrett inquired and wasn't sure that was a good question to ask.

Brax chuckled. The same melodious sound that had been following her in her dreams. She smothered the nervousness that rose in her stomach.

"Because I want it that way."

Entitled bastard. Gandrett collected herself. "Is that how you treat your women?" she asked, her tone as cunning as his. To Hel's realm with everything Mckenzie had taught her. Brax struck a nerve, and she couldn't help herself when she smirked at his hesitant response.

But he wasn't hesitating from lack of something to say. "I have never respected a woman enough to treat her like that." He turned around, leaving her with the view of his broad shoulders and straight back. The walk of a noble, no matter how much of a mischief maker he was.

"You respect me?" Gandrett clarified and earned a stomach-squirming chuckle. She knew what that laugh looked like on his lips and didn't want to plunge into the sensation it instilled.

"You are a Child of Vala," he explained with a glance over his shoulder and turned into the corridor of cherry trees. "No man should ever touch you."

His words were like little daggers, especially when she knew they were true. And yet—

"What if all this training actually works? What if I do win Armand's trust... and more?"

"You mean, if he falls for you?" he rephrased. He didn't need to mention that what he was really saying was, *What if he touches you?*

"You are the best fighter Nehelon has ever seen. You'll find a way to defend yourself."

Gandrett didn't know what to make of his words, but she followed him into the cherry trees through the falling night and let him lead her up the stairs to her chambers.

"You have no idea how much hope your presence at court instills in my family." Brax indicated a bow, not giving Gandrett a moment to respond before he fashioned a grin and reached for her fingers, sending an explosion of conflicting sensations through her body—"Goodnight, Miss Brayton."—then bent down and blew a kiss on the back of her hand.

The guard escorting her to her daily training at dawn was as quiet as she was at that ungodly time of the day, which gave her a couple of minutes to erase the blush on her cheeks that surged up every time her mind wandered back to Brax's lips brushing her skin. Thank the gods, when they arrived, Nehelon, for a change, wasn't there before her, and the young guard turned to her and said, "Thank you for doing this."

Gandrett pretended not to know what he was talking about. She wasn't sure who exactly knew about her mission, how secret it truly was. On that first day, Lord Tyrem had only dismissed his court when they were to discuss the details of his plan. But he had let them watch how she defeated the giant of a guard by his table. So she remained quiet, waiting for the guard to reveal more.

"Joshua used to train with us every morning, Miss Brayton," he said, his eyes scanning the sand-covered space where she would soon be going up against the Fae male. "It was a shock when he was taken. And we have lost too many men trying to retrieve him."

Gandrett placed her hand on the hilt of her sword. "Is Denderlain really that dangerous?"

She couldn't tell what it was that instilled enough trust to ask if she was truly going on an impossible mission.

The guard nodded. "Hamyn Denderlain is not only dangerous; he is ruthless. And his son..." He gave her a look that said enough. "It's good you have Brax and Mckenzie to prepare you. It would be a shame if we lost you, too."

Gandrett held his gaze. "What's your name?" The tan, brown-eyed man blinked.

"Kyle."

"Thank you, Kyle," was all she could say to him before Nehelon appeared in the gate and came toward them in powerful strides, his sword already drawn as if today he wasn't going to waste any time talking.

Kyle inclined his head and disappeared the way he did every morning, leaving Gandrett with a couple of seconds before Nehelon was upon her.

She didn't draw her sword. It was something Brax had pointed out during their walk in the gardens, that the tighter and flimsier the dresses got, the less of a chance she would have to store a weapon... and it would get harder to retrieve as a sword. So she let Nehelon come toward her, and her hands curled like the claws of a desert lion while she hoped that he would yield his blade instead of cutting her down. From the look on his face, the latter was exactly what he intended to do.

The first strike hit her on the arm. Too slow to avoid the Fae male's blow, the flat of his blade made her scream out in pain. Nehelon pulled back, giving her enough time to regroup, then attacked again with a snarl.

"I thought we were here to train, not for you to kill me," Gandrett hissed at him as the flat of his blade bit her ribs this time. She panted through the pain. It wasn't anything new to her. At the priory, pain was the cost of improvement as much as it was of disobedience. A lesson engraved into the skin on her arms, on her back, on her legs in a pattern of thin scars that no one would ever see since no one would ever get close enough to get a good look.

Nehelon wielded his sword over his head. "Not my problem if you don't defend yourself." His eyes were hard diamond, his face cold the way she had memorized it on their journey. There was no pity in his eyes, no curiosity the way she had seen over the past weeks at their training. Only rage—channeled through his muscled arms and the steel of his sword.

Gandrett swirled to the side and found her balance just before Nehelon struck again. Keep moving, that was what she had to do. Always stay in motion. A moving target was more difficult to hit. So she started dancing through the sand, her feet as light as the wind—the way she had at the priory for the Fest of Blossoms.

Nehelon halted, sword mid-air, and watched her as if she had gone crazy. "What is that?" he asked, his emotions about as visible on his features as on the flat stone walls behind them.

Gandrett didn't stop. "I am not going into the palace of Eedwood as a fighter but as a lady," she pointed out. "Maybe it's time I started acting like one." She put on a smile that made her cheeks hurt. "Dance with me, Sir," she held out a hand, dancing in her spot for a while, letting Nehelon assess her from head to toe.

"No." He shook his head, dark hair swinging with the movement, and brought his sword down on her once more.

But Gandrett was already spinning away,

What was she doing? Nehelon had fought many opponents, too many, in his hundreds of years, but he had never encountered—well, *this*.

Gandrett was *dancing*. On the training grounds. With little shame over how she swung her hips. And with her ease of movement, she grinned at him. *Grinned.*

His sword missed. Once, twice, thrice. And still, Gandrett grinned. And danced as if she were in a trance, strands of hair coming loose from her braid, flying around her head as she spun.

What had Brax done to her?

When he had returned from exercising down here the night before, he had spied Brax and Gandrett, still in the garden, talking. He had observed them from afar, letting himself believe he was just watching out for Lord Tyrem's heir just in case they never got back Joshua.

Brax had returned her to her chambers like a gentleman. He had kissed her hand the way Nehelon had seen him do with every other woman in court. The fury had lingered through the night, had woken him early this morning. What was it about Brax Brenheran that she found pleasure in spending time with him—worse, talking to him? She didn't talk to Nehelon. Didn't smile at him. Didn't laugh in his presence. Only now, that frantic grin that reminded him of the ceremonies of the Order of Vala. Of those brief years at the priory in Everrun. That grin wasn't for him—

He swung his sword anew, fighting his anger rather than the dancing girl before him. And once more, he let himself miss. Couldn't bring himself to strike the untamed beauty before him.

And it hit him. That he had let his blade touch her, that he hadn't held back his Fae strength when he had brought down the flat of his blade on her arms, on her thigh.

She hadn't yielded. Hadn't reached for her own sword. Had screamed, yes. And he had mercilessly struck again. What had *he* done?

As he lowered the tip of his sword into the sand, Gandrett swirled right in front of him and flashed her teeth before her fist connected with his throat, sending him staggering back. Her boot followed only moments later, bringing him down. And when she straddled him, his arms tucked tightly to his sides between her knees, that grin was real.

Mckenzie couldn't stop laughing when Gandrett shared the news of what had happened. Of course, Gandrett had left out the details of her own bruises. Nehelon hadn't just struck her with the blade. He had battered it down with all his strength—his real strength, not the subdued, human-like version of his strikes.

"No wonder he is going up against you every day," Mckenzie roared with laughter. "He is a sore loser."

So far, Gandrett had done a good job avoiding the topic of Nehelon during her lessons with Mckenzie. She had seen the explosiveness when both of them were in the same room and wasn't certain if she knew the reason it would help any of them.

"You should have seen his face." Gandrett herself chuckled. A sound that she was getting used to. Even if most of the times it was the fake laugh of a delighted woman intending to earn the attention of a man. She had practiced that on Brax in the gardens. Had hardly listened to anything he'd said, her mind too occupied with the scent of blossoms, the buzz of insects, the lush grass under her feet. And then, there was the nervousness that rose whenever Brax smiled at her with that sensuous mouth. That used up part of her resources, too.

She cringed as she sat down at the table and rested her hands at its carved edge. Eugina had brought lunch earlier: fish and a small bowl of stew. Gandrett had gotten used to fish enough to not gag at every bite, and Eugina seemed to feel safe with reducing the amount of stew, day by day. It helped that Mckenzie kept her company during her meals—even when it was mostly to correct her way of eating, of drinking, of sitting, of using her napkin, of basically everything Gandrett did.

There was a small, shiny box sitting beside the tray full of empty dishes today. Gandrett had noticed it earlier but... after this morning's events, had been too upset to find herself interested enough to take a look.

Now that her stomach was filled, her anger at the male subsided, and she was curious enough to pick it up.

The lid came off easily, exposing an assortment of chocolates. Gandrett's stomach tightened with excitement and sadness all at once as she lifted the box to her face and inhaled the smell. The last time she had tasted chocolate was the last Midsummer Solstice before she'd been brought to the priory. Her parents had afforded a piece for each of them for the celebrations in honor of Nyssa, the goddess of love.

"Who is it from?" Mckenzie wanted to know, her emerald eyes peering past the chocolates at the folded piece of parchment that was tucked in-between the box and a rose-petal-sprinkled chocolate.

Gandrett at first didn't understand, but when she found Mckenzie's eyes, the mischievousness was enough to understand she thought it was from a man.

"Who would send me chocolate?" she asked casually, suppressing any emotion that would send her down that path of happy memories—bittersweet memories.

"The question is: who wouldn't?" Mckenzie positively glowed with curiosity. Gandrett's palms turned sweaty. "Haven't you noticed how they all look at you?" Gandrett didn't fail to hear a certain jealousy ring in the young woman's voice.

She had noticed their gazes when she crossed the hallways in her fighting leathers every morning and returned sweaty and dirty before noon. She had never given it much thought. As for the rare occasions that she left her chambers in something that informed the world she was a woman, the glances were more obvious but nothing that she wasn't used to. People had stared at her in Everrun for the sole reason that she was their top fighter. The admiration in their eyes was for the level of skill Vala had allowed her to achieve and nothing else.

Here, in this palace, it seemed Vala was not as omnipresent as at the priory. Not every step taken was to serve her, not every breath taken in her honor.

"If you don't look, I will," Mckenzie threatened with a giggle.

"No," Gandrett held up a hand, keeping her from reaching over, then took the note from the box and opened it.

The handwriting was elegant and reminded Gandrett of the spires of the palace. *I would have stolen a kiss last night, but I didn't want to upset Vala.*

All air left her lungs as she read the message again. And again.

"Who is it?" Mckenzie pushed and plucked the note from Gandrett's hands with swift fingers.

And gaped at what she found.

"What did you do to my brother?" Mckenzie asked, beaming.

Gandrett's cheeks went hot. *Brax.* "Nothing."

The look on Mckenzie's face made clear she didn't believe it.

"You wicked creature charmed Brax," she claimed and leaned back in her chair, fair hair bouncing along on her shoulders.

Gandrett wanted to sink into her own chair. Better to have the ground open beneath her feet and swallow her. "All I did was follow your advice, smile, nod, laugh at the bad jokes." And secretly ogle at his handsome face.

Mckenzie laughed. "Brax never sends chocolate," she informed Gandrett. "With all his various women, he avoids sending anything at all."

Gandrett ignored that feeling of horror and excitement that rose with Mckenzie's depiction of Brax Brenheran. Instead, she thought of that moment Brax had bid her goodnight, one hand behind his back, the other reaching for hers. The warmth of his breath on her skin when he'd indicated a kiss on the back of her hand.

She retrieved the note from Mckenzie and placed it on top of the chocolates before she closed the box and stored it in the small bedside table. She didn't know how long it would take until she returned to her family, but she knew she would bring them chocolate when she did.

It took several days to be able to look Brax in the eye without blushing. The young man, however, never mentioned their conversation from the walk in the park—nor the chocolates or note, for that matter. In the meantime, most of Gandrett's days consisted of training with Nehelon and lady-lessons with Mckenzie, who was becoming somewhat of a friend, if she could call anyone in this court such. After all, Lord Tyrem had bought her like a slave for that mission.

"You are not paying attention." Mckenzie nudged her elbow. "One step forward and one back. Spin and sideward to the left." She spoke in the rhythm of the music performed by two musicians in the corner of the room. "How can you fight like a goddess but trip over your own feet when you dance?"

Gandrett struggled to follow Mckenzie's instructions, the woman's fair hair flying as she spun, too preoccupied with the music filling the room. It touched her heart on a level she had believed she'd left behind at her parents' farm. The sound of Sives's folk-music. "Probably because I never learned to dance." She set one unstable step to the side, then another. "I wasn't aware they played this type of music at court."

Mckenzie eyed her through the arch of her raised arms. "It's the one thing both courts have in common. The music of Sives. The music that dates back before the kingdom was torn apart."

Gandrett turned slowly, avoiding the yearning to fall into the frenzy of Vala's dance of life. The dance she had performed in Nehelon's training grounds. She suppressed a chuckle. He had avoided speaking to her since that day. Just the necessary orders at training, some instructions concerning when and where to meet the next day, his eyes cautious for once as if he didn't want her to act like that again. Besides the bruises that were almost healed, it had earned her some space from the unpredictable Fae male.

"The houses of Sives don't forget their history," Mckenzie explained, oblivious to Gandrett's train of thoughts. "They don't forget that these lands once had one strong king who ruled over all of Sives, from Ackwood to Ithrylan, in peace. The music speaks of those times." She hopped from one foot to the other.

"And each of the houses still believes that one day they will rule over all of Sives," Brax finished her sentence from the threshold where he had joined them unnoticed.

Gandrett stopped her attempts and watched him saunter to his twin sister, whose hand he took, leading her in a small circle until she faced him. "Let's show Miss Brayton how it's done." He flashed Gandrett a smile over his shoulder, shook a stray strand of hair from his forehead, and led Mckenzie in curved lines and hops through the room.

Gandrett observed, shamed by her lack of skill, and focused on Mckenzie's feet rather than Brax's eyes, which he kept on her as he danced as gracefully as he walked. She had spent three weeks at the palace in Ackwood, and as she watched them, she didn't feel any closer to passing for a lady than the day she'd arrived. Maybe it was that no one told her when she would make her journey to Eedwood or how she would get to meet Armand Denderlain, but she felt afloat in the strangeness of this court-life where people chit-chatted over fish-delicacies and danced just for pleasure. It was a life that she had never known, would never fully understand when all she had learned was that pleasure is something for lords and kings, and she was a servant of the goddess.

So her feet remained still while the others danced.

Nehelon heard the music first then the multiple voices coming from the small dining hall. He had been on his way from his daily meeting with Lord Tyrem where he had reassured the man and Lady Crystal that Gandrett was making good progress. He had even brought up that he'd observed her in her interaction with Brax and that from afar, she had appeared as ladylike as any other lady here at court.

Lord Tyrem and Lady Crystal had agreed that it was time to act soon; every day lost was a day too many. Nehelon didn't mention that he had taken his time testing Gandrett's fighting skills, reassuring himself that whatever happened, she would walk away from Denderlain and live. That he had hoped by now she would have shown signs of magic—and not the silly games of the water mages of Everrun, but magic. Real magic like his. Every day he procrastinated, the mission was a day lost for Joshua Brenheran while it was one day won for Nehelon to find out if he had been right about her.

So he followed the music, knowing whom he would find at the source, and prepared himself to tell Gandrett that by the end of the week, she would be dancing with Armand Denderlain.

When Lady Crystal Brenheran summoned her, Gandrett wasn't sure what to make of it. She hadn't seen the lord or the lady who had bought her to retrieve their abducted son since that first day at Ackwood. Now that she was standing before Lady Brenheran, it was hard not to see the similarities with Mckenzie.

Fair hair the same shade as Mckenzie's; emerald eyes, even if the lady's weren't sparkling like the young woman's, but troubled. Her burgundy dress made a stark contrast with the fair skin above the neckline. Bulky necklaces of gold wound around her throat, making Gandrett wonder if the weight of them wasn't throttling her.

"You asked for my presence," Gandrett curtseyed—something she had mastered through countless hours in front of the mirror, staring at her new self—the mask she was wearing from head to toe. The mask of a lady.

Lady Brenheran gestured for her to step closer but remained seated on the sofa by the window, a book in her hand.

"Nehelon has reported progress on your..." She searched for words. "Well, the new you." Her slender, gloved hand gestured at Gandrett in general.

Gandrett once more felt like a prize pony. "And has he spoken true?" she asked, keeping her voice the melody she had adopted from Mckenzie—light, charming, without any sign of the constant inner debate whether all of it would buy her a chance of getting Armand to talk if her sword or a pointed dagger wouldn't be the wiser option. As for now, she held her tongue, smiled like a lady, and took a step closer, turning slightly to the sides to give Lady Crystal a clear view of how confidently she was wearing the moss-green gown Mckenzie had picked out for her.

Lady Crystal got to her feet, eyes on Gandrett, seemingly making up her own mind about what she saw.

"My son Brax informed me you have mastered the basics of the dances popular in Sives's courts."

Is that so? Gandrett cocked her head.

"Most certainly he praises your gracefulness." The lady spoke as if that surprised her.

Gandrett suppressed a chuckle. Over the past days, she had made progress under Mckenzie's and Brax's guidance, but it was nothing near what she needed to pass as someone from a good household, worthy of the attention of a lord's heir.

"You may never join the royal ballet of Khila," Lady Crystal walked around Gandrett in a circle, her eyes assessing, measuring, probing, "but you can always fake a sore ankle if someone asks you to dance."

As with so many things, Gandrett had never heard about the royal ballet of Khila even when Khila, the capital of the southernmost territory, Phornes, was famous for its music and dancing. "My dance is with the blades." Her hand reached for her absent sword in reflex. And Lady Crystal smiled.

"It most certainly is." She stopped in front of Gandrett. "I have been watching your training with the chancellor. He is the best fighter I know—used to be." Her gaze wandered to where Gandrett's hand was still clutching thin air. "Until he brought you back. It gave me hope, seeing someone as delicate as you bring down mountains of men." Something bitter lingered in the air between them. "And you have the help of the goddess herself, the justice of Vala at your side."

Gandrett didn't dare to object, to voice that it felt like quite the opposite. That ever since she had been torn from her mother's arms, she felt like Vala had forsaken her.

"The chancellor informed you that you are to make your journey to Eedwood by the end of the week?" Lady Crystal returned to the sofa, the skirts of her dress sighing as she settled down.

Gandrett shook her head. "Was he supposed to?"

Her response put a smile on Lady Crystal's lips. "He might have been otherwise occupied."

Even if Gandrett couldn't pin down what it was, something was off about the way the lady was speaking. "I am certain the chancellor is too busy to inform me about everything in person." She couldn't explain either why it hurt that he hadn't told her. Or why it bothered her that when he had shown up that evening Mckenzie and Brax had taken turns instructing her how to dance, he had turned on the doorstep and stalked into the dark hallways of the palace.

"The House of Denderlain will have their Spring Hunt in honor of Demea this weekend." She glanced at Gandrett over the book she was now fanning before her. "You know how to handle a bow, don't you?"

Gandrett nodded.

"Then it's a good thing, Miss Brayton, that you are planning to go on a hunt in the forests of Eedwood. And too bad your bow will break just as you are planning to bring down the wolf the Denderlains are hunting." Lady Crystal's eyes flashed at her. "Just make sure Armand is there to see it." A devious smile graced her cunning face. "You can *hurt* your ankle right there in the forests too, just so you won't need to dance that night."

So that was the plan, to plant her in Denderlain court. Make her a damsel in distress and let the tyrant's son rescue her. Gandrett frowned.

"Lose that expression," Lady Crystal ordered. "It doesn't suit a lady."

Gandrett trudged from the room with little regard for how it made her look. Three days, Lady Crystal had said. Three days before she would go into enemy territory as a spy on a rescue mission. She preferred to see it that way rather than to submit to the suggestion Lord Tyrem had made. Seduce the enemy.

The guard who had escorted her to the lady's chambers was gone, but Gandrett didn't stop to wait and see if someone might take her back to her own rooms. After almost a month, she knew her way around well enough.

Her footsteps echoed in the stone hallways, the sound a mockery of the light steps she was supposed to make with her stupid silk slippers. It didn't take long until hers weren't the only footsteps that bounced off the walls. She didn't care to lift her head and glance over her shoulder to know it was Nehelon who was behind her. The soft clicking of his sword on his belt had given him away.

"I will help you prepare," he spoke so softly it made Gandrett look up.

His eyes, diamond-blue and flickering with something other than fury or mockery, were on her face. She turned away before she could figure out what it was that was shaping a crooked line between his eyebrows.

"You *have* helped me prepare for the past month." And if it weren't for him, she wouldn't be in a situation where she even had to prepare.

"You need to study the castle layout, the floor plans, the exits." Nehelon didn't raise his voice but spoke with quiet urgency as he followed her down the stairs past a row of stained glass windows in crimson and blue. "I am not going to send you in there without knowing you'll find your way out."

Gandrett turned the last corner and walked up to her chamber doors, nodding at Kyle, who smiled back, before she stepped inside, not bothering to close the doors behind her. People came and went in her room as they pleased, it seemed, and there was no door strong enough to keep the Fae male out.

Eugina had left dinner on the table. A meal that wasn't fish, judging by the delicious smell of it.

When she turned around, Nehelon had shut the doors and was sauntering toward her with lazy strides.

"I haven't *bought* you out of Everrun to let you recklessly throw away your life at Eedwood." He planted himself before her at arm's length, staring her down.

"*You* were just a messenger, delivering the goods." Gandrett waited. Waited for the fury to take over his face, for the anger to flare in his eyes, for his temper to take him over.

All he did was look at her, eyes probing. Until he finally said, "We don't have much time left. I don't want to waste it slandering each other."

His words—

Gandrett loosed a breath, the tight bodice of her dress letting it rush from her lungs the second she freed it. If she hadn't known better, she would have said the Fae male was concerned.

"Wasting time is nothing I enjoy," she eventually said after a pause that let her wonder if this was the same male before her who had mercilessly battered his sword down on her a couple of days ago. "What do you suggest we do?"

His features suddenly softened, and his glamour slowly faded as they eyed each other, both cautious, both careful, as if that sudden truce between them might burst into thin air if they as much as blinked.

Nehelon's face changed, and it wasn't only the hardness of his features that slipped but the glamour, too, allowing Gandrett to see it, all of it. The flawlessness of his skin, a sun-kissed, golden tan, glowed from up close as he took a step forward. His eyes, all facets of blue shone in the depth of diamonds. His eyebrows arched in two dark lines, leading her gaze to the side, to the waves of his hair, to what was hidden beneath it.

Gandrett held her breath as she lifted a shaky hand and reached for what she had seen and still had difficulties believing. But when he stood before her, un-glamoured, a Fae, a *real* Fae, and for once not growling at her—

He didn't move as her fingers brushed aside his hair, exposing a pointed ear, and let the tip of her index finger graze along the miraculous arch that was evidence he truly was a different species. And she could swear his heart was pounding in the silence that filled the space between them.

Nehelon didn't back away as she explored the tip of his ear. He didn't speak—

But the look in his eyes gave away that it took him everything he had not to attack her, not to scold her—or run away.

"How—?" Gandrett breathed as she studied Nehelon's face, her fingers moving down the angle of his cheekbone. His skin was like silk, like flower petals, yet rough from the wind and dirt he was exposed to every day in those training rings. From the many years he had been walking this earth. She didn't even know how old he was. In his human glamour, he looked in the prime of his years. But in his Fae form—

Gandrett had no words that could describe what she saw, what she tried to understand. His eyes held the wisdom of centuries and yet—yet his face was as youthful as if the goddess herself had blessed him with eternal spring.

As her fingers reached the end of his cheekbone and traced down toward his strong jaw, Nehelon's hand caught hers as if he had suddenly awoken from a trance. It hurt as he pulled her hand away with a rough grasp. "This," he noted, eyes solidifying as he spoke, "is exactly what I call a waste of time."

Then, he dropped her hand as if it burned him and headed for the door, hair swooshing back over his ear as he spun away from her.

Gandrett couldn't even take a steadying breath before he reached the threshold and said over his shoulder, "I should know better, Gandrett Brayton, than to try to change the course of history."

And then he was out the door.

Touch him. He had let her *touch* him. What had gotten into him? If it weren't for his promise to Lord Tyrem, to save his son, Gandrett's door wouldn't be the only one he'd shut behind him. What was he thinking, allowing to let her glimpse even a hint of him? To let her break that glamour over and over again? He should have killed her that first day she had seen his ears, when she had realized what he was. The horror in her eyes—

And yet... he needed her. He needed her to safely retrieve Joshua. To get to Eedwood and back in one piece. To return so he could prove she was who he thought she was.

His hands shook as he ripped all maps of Eedwood he owned from the shelves of his study and dumped them in a heap at the center of the room. He didn't bother to light a candle, Fae eyes allowing him to see just as well as in bright daylight, his fingers already sorting through everything that would help Gandrett prepare her escape routes. He knew she would know what to do with the maps and plans. She had been trained by the best—

Nehelon didn't show up for training the next day, leaving Gandrett's nerves to lay bare as she kept staring at the door he emerged from like a clockwork every morning at first light.

Instead, Mckenzie met her with her arms full of scrolls of parchment.

"He says it's best you take some time to look at those on your own," she said by way of greeting, a half-hearted smile tugging on her lips.

Gandrett didn't feel like taking a look at anything. Or smiling, for that matter.

Sleep had eluded her all night, and the meager breakfast Eugina had brought didn't change much about her energy levels, nor did the fact that it would be hours before she would force down some fish dish she'd rather never have known existed.

"He is going to great lengths to make sure you are prepared," Mckenzie noted, beckoning with her chin for Gandrett to follow her to the small bench near the training ring where Nehelon sometimes sat when he had her try movements.

Gandrett shrugged, the leathers on her shoulder shifting up to her ears. "He went to great lengths to get me from Everrun," she pointed out. "Why would he not make sure his prize pony lives up to his promises?"

Mckenzie gave her a sideways glance as she flattened one of the scrolls between them on the bench. "You are not his prize pony," she said and picked up another scroll, opening it just enough to peek inside. "He really wants you to succeed." She dropped the scroll she was holding and looked at Gandrett instead. "He cares."

Gandrett avoided showing any of the conflicted emotions that welled up inside her chest. All night long she had tried to understand what had happened. Why she had followed that impulse to touch him. Why she had felt as if a wall had broken down between them.

And then he had pulled it up again—iron and stone and ice—and had left her with a cryptic statement which made even less sense than anything else about him.

"How well do you know Nehelon?" Gandrett asked instead of responding to Mckenzie's words.

The young woman adjusted her sleeves with sudden interest. "Well enough to know that he cares." There was a hint of discomfort in her voice. If Gandrett didn't see the smile on Mckenzie's face widen into a real fake smile, she would have passed it off as embarrassment. But there was more to it.

So she asked, "Did he say anything?" It was a stupid thing to ask. Why would he be talking to Mckenzie about her? And why did it suddenly matter to Gandrett if he did?

She remembered that first encounter in her chambers, how Nehelon had shrunk from Mckenzie's taunting. "You and he—"

She didn't need to finish her thought with Mckenzie's sudden tomato-like skin tone speaking for itself.

"It's all right. You don't have to tell me." Gandrett didn't need to know. It didn't change anything. He didn't mean anything.

Mckenzie's hand landed on hers with her usual lightness. "I want to tell you. Friends tell friends about such things."

"Friends?" Gandrett looked up. Surel was her friend along with Kaleb. Mckenzie was the daughter of the man who had damned her to a lifetime of servitude to a goddess who forbade Gandrett from sharing her life with anyone but her. Of the man who had bought her to retrieve his abducted son, using means that would damn her in the eyes of Vala. And yet, when Gandrett looked at Mckenzie, she saw more than that. She saw a brave and witty woman who had spent her life navigating through an existence damned to a different type of servitude. A life of not having a voice, of being the pretty, dressed-up accessory for the men who surrounded her. A life that Gandrett didn't envy her for. A prison so like the one Gandrett had been pushed into.

"Friend," Mckenzie smiled and nodded at her. "I didn't believe it when Nehelon told me a girl was going to save my brother. But if anyone can do it, it's you."

"Let's see about that when I return from my mission." Light words. But their meaning too heavy to bear. So soon, a life would depend on her. And Gandrett didn't know if she was ready. To wield a sword, to fight, yes. But to ensnare Armand Denderlain's heart so she could sneak around Eedwood castle and find Joshua Brenheran—

"I used to believe Nehelon and I could be a thing," Mckenzie interrupted Gandrett's thoughts. "We had some moments, I thought, but then he left to get you from the priory and—"

Gandrett didn't dare ask what could have changed.

"It was *I* who had some moments," Mckenzie admitted. "And he might have needed a distraction." She gave Gandrett a knowing look. "It's a lonely life being a man of power. And he isn't even a lord. Just a chancellor." She pretended to be serious.

Gandrett said nothing. Couldn't.

"Joshua is different..." Mckenzie's eyes grew distant as if she was looking at her brother in her mind. "He used to prefer my company over everyone else's. He taught me how to fight when I was little—not that I am any good." She giggled. "He is my friend as much as he is my brother."

Gandrett sighed through her nose, her fingers playing with the edges of the parchment between them. Her brother... She wished she'd been around to show him how to fight.

"You will bring him back, Gandrett." Mckenzie sounded convinced.

Gandrett didn't agree or decline. She didn't speak her doubts, that when even a Fae male had failed to retrieve Joshua—

"This is Eedwood castle." Mckenzie ran her finger over the inked lines on the open scroll. The layout of the castle grounds. "I might have been brought up to smile and nod like a lady—" She looked at the lines down her nose. "—but I know how to read plans and plot as well of any of the men here in court."

They spent the rest of the morning going over the floor plans of Eedwood castle's square layout, and Gandrett spent the major part of her energy on memorizing every entrance and every exit. On the arrangement of the chambers of the

Denderlain family on the second floor, on the barracks where the guards slept, where weapons were kept, the location of the stables, the gates—

"Isn't it a bit late to join?" Mckenzie said, making Gandrett break her focus. She had been so busy memorizing every stairwell, every door, that she hadn't noticed they had company. "We were just finishing up."

Nehelon's shadow hit the bench and crossed Gandrett's lap as she bothered to look up, her face bored as she glanced at him through the intensity of the spring sun. Gandrett harrumphed by way of greeting and returned her attention to the maps she'd been studying. Good.

"Why didn't you take a hostage in return?" she asked out of the blue but didn't give him any time to answer. "You could have taken anyone close enough to Lord Hamyn and exchanged them for Joshua."

Nehelon lifted a brow, trying to ignore Mckenzie's sideways glance. Gandrett hadn't told her what had happened between them. Not that anything had happened, really—

Anything. He had expected rage, hurt, or even that Gandrett would mock him for running out on her, but this—

It was as if last night hadn't occurred. "We considered the option and deemed it unsuitable for a situation of such importance." Hadn't she felt it? The tingling at her touch. How her fingertips had made his buried Fae soul sing? "He is Lord Tyrem's heir and the only worthy one—" He gave Mckenzie a look, hoping he wouldn't come across as condescending. "—the only worthy male heir," he added for her benefit. The laws at the courts of Sives dated back to ancient times when women were not recognized as successors. Mckenzie, with her fierce heart and her sharp mind, would make for an outstanding Lady of Ackwood.

"Hold your breath, chancellor." She gave him a brief, poison-sweet smile. "I have made my peace with remaining a pearl-laden accessory for the rulers." She didn't seem even half at ease.

The young woman shook out her fair waves in the sunlight as she closed her eyes for a long second, a gesture he had observed made the courtiers' eyes spark. And from an objective point of view, Mckenzie Brenheran was the epitome of beauty, with supple curves and depthless, emerald eyes and a smile that could bring kingdoms down. That's why he had entertained the thought of seeking distraction in her arms. Why he had lingered in the hallway that night when she had asked him to. Why he hadn't pulled away when she had laid her hands on his arms and stood on her toes to kiss him. Once. Just once. And with many regrets, not half-worth the trouble of having a noblewoman set her eyes on him.

Gandrett studied him as if he were a book she'd dropped when it couldn't spark her interest. He didn't turn away from Gandrett, who seemed intent on pretending she hadn't felt how his heart had beat in his chest, simply because she hadn't shied away from him—from what lay beneath the glamour. He hadn't had that sensation since—

"Just make sure Gandrett gets to Denderlain court safely," Mckenzie added when none of them spoke. He could feel the noblewoman roll her eyes. "And when all this is over, why don't you disappear already?" Her words sounded annoyed, but he saw it in the small details of the way her eyes tightened and her throat bobbed as if she wanted to take back the words she had just spoken, that his rejection had hurt her.

He didn't respond but said to Gandrett, "My apologies for ditching you this morning. I had important matters to attend to." *My apologies for running away last night. And, it's better you don't know the matters until the time comes.* He took a steadying breath when her face showed as little emotion as a polished iron. So he turned to the woman who was as beautiful as a masterpiece painted by the masters of Ackwood and couldn't find anything on her lovely face that would hold his interest. "Thank you, Mckenzie, for keeping Miss Brayton company."

Mckenzie recognized her dismissal with a sour look, got to her feet, and threw her arms around Gandrett before doing so. "Let him help you, Gandrett," she whispered, but not low enough to keep her words from his Fae hearing. "He might be a grumpy pain in the ass, but he knows what he's doing."

With those words, Mckenzie left them in the rising heat of the ascending sun, and Nehelon's mouth went dry as Gandrett, a ghost of a smile on her lips, turned back to the maps.

He swallowed. Once. Twice. Then took a seat where Mckenzie had been a couple of moments ago.

"I spent the morning arranging for a carriage and escort to Eedwood Forest." His words sounded dull in his human voice. "You'll leave at first light in two days."

Nehelon didn't need to look up to know Gandrett had feared—anticipated and feared—this moment when the plan would be laid out for her.

It had been Lord Tyrem's decision to keep her in the dark about details until the very last moment. Now it was on him to tell her.

He had put it off that night when he had found her dancing with Mckenzie and Brax, both twins, even though by far more skilled at it, not even a shadow of the grace with which Gandrett moved.

"The Denderlains always hunt in the same part of the forest. You won't be able to miss them."

Gandrett remained silent, her hands in her lap, fiddling with the edge of a scroll.

"Mckenzie agreed to oversee your wardrobe. Brax offered to take you to the forest himself..."

"He can't." Gandrett cut him off, eyes fierce, but quickly smoothed over her expression. "I mean... It's too dangerous for him to go. If anything goes wrong with Joshua..."

"The Brenheran's need Brax as their heir, I know," he finished her sentence. But didn't fail to notice the flicker of light in her eyes. She was anxious for Brax.

Nehelon ignored the surge of anger that accompanied the realization.

"Because his life is too precious, it will be I who escorts you to the edge of the forest. You will take a horse from there."

Her eyes didn't flicker with fear for him, and the lack of it smothered the anger with a pang of disappointment.

What had he been hoping for? That she would even hold a shred of warmth for him? Her touch the night before—curiosity. She had been examining a foreign species. That was all.

"I'll need weapons," she demanded, and he wanted to tell her that he would lay all the armament he had at her feet when the time came. *If* the time ever came.

But now was not the time.

21

Brax visited her first thing that morning, hair combed, a fresh jacket protecting him from the cold breeze. Frost had eaten away the blossoms overnight, leaving wrinkled fallen petals all over the palace grounds. He hadn't found her at her chambers but spied her from the window at the end of the hallway, sending him down the stairs taking two steps at once.

He crossed the courtyard, hands in his pockets, the fingers of one hand playing with the silver chain he'd pulled from the dresser last night, his course set toward the waiting by the stables.

Gandrett was a vision in fir-green, a color that brought out the golden flecks in her eyes. Of course, he could hardly see them in the gray light of dawn. She smiled at him when she noticed him approach in a hurry, probably seeing his casual jog for what it was—an attempt at keeping himself from flying toward her.

"You thought I'd let you leave without saying goodbye?" he said by way of greeting.

Gandrett's smile widened.

It had been weeks since that first stroll in the park he had taken her on. Back then, she had marveled at the trees, at the lushness of the grass, the colors of the flowers. He had seen it in her eyes, the wonder at all the beauty she'd missed out on during her time in Everrun. And he had noticed how her cheeks had stained when he had caught her staring—not at nature, but at him.

A Child of Vala. He shook his head at himself. With all the women throwing themselves at him—heir or not—it had to be a Child of Vala.

Nehelon had warned him, the night he had brought her back from Everrun, that he was to leave his hands in his pockets with her if he didn't want to jeopardize his brother's rescue mission. So he had. Even if the first thing he'd noticed was that the girl was unlike anyone he'd been with. It was like looking into a calm lake, a surface as clear and beautiful as crystal glass, no indication of what lay in the depths beyond.

He normally didn't care, didn't want to know what lay in anyone's depths. But Gandrett Brayton was an enigma he was determined to figure out.

Even if it would have to wait until Josh returned so Nehelon couldn't make any claims.

"Is there anything you want me to tell Joshua when I find him?" she asked, not saying good morning either. Her lips were like cherry blossoms, pale-pink, and the collar of her dress, lined with soft leather, leaned like tulip petals against the slender column of her neck.

He let his gaze linger for a second before he looked her in the eye. "Tell Josh that if he doesn't get his ass over here, I'll personally dig a tunnel into Eedwood castle to go kick it." He laughed, not at all feeling like it, but he did it because it made her smile. Anything for that smile.

And if it didn't make her smile, at least it made her cheeks turn pink and her eyes shutter.

Even if she was a Child of Vala, not versatile in flirting and court chit-chat, despite Mckenzie's countless hours of getting her used to it, there was a different strength in her. A quiet beauty that had crept into his mind and lingered. And her skill with the sword...

Nehelon was a fool if he doubted anything could keep Gandrett from bringing back his brother.

Brax's fingers curled around the chain in his pocket as he studied her face in the rising daylight. "I won't tell you to be careful, Gandrett," he said and reached for her hand, watching her eyes widen slightly with that weird satisfaction of knowing his touch had some small effect on her. "But I'll ask you not to forget me while you're gone." He turned over her hand and pulled the silver necklace from his pocket.

Gandrett's eyes drifted to her hand, surprise written clearly on her features, as she pulled back her hand to examine the small silver pendant set with splinters of emerald.

"Brax..." How different his name spoken from her lips sounded. Even when she was taunting him. She didn't know all the mistakes he'd made in the past, all the times he had drowned his moods in the burgundy wines of Ackwood in female company. Yes, she knew that everyone at court saw him as a spoiled brat, as an unworthy replacement for Josh... But he had opened up to her. Even when it had been just mere sentences of truth.

"Take it," he said and closed her hand around the necklace with his fingers, a smile that was about as confident as a little boy walking on thin ice on his lips. "Take it and think of me when you wear it, Child of Vala." *As I will think of you.*

Gandrett's hand hovered before her, Brax's gift weighing heavy in her palm as she watched him prowl toward the palace. Uncertainty wove its path down deep inside her chest and took root. *Brax.*

She was still staring after him when Nehelon's familiar voice—the emotionless one—tore her from her thoughts. "I chose Lim as your mount, as you are already acquainted."

Gandrett's head whipped around to face the Fae male, the black mare and bay gelding at either of his leather-armored shoulders. It was the same armor he'd worn the day she had found him climbing the walls of Everrun, only this time, there was no Brenheran coat of arms decorating his chest. He could have passed as a hired guard for any wealthy carriage-owner. So that was what she was supposed to perform as.

"You never told me his name," she said and reached her hand for the gelding's mane.

"He might be your only confidant once I leave you at Eedwood Forest." His face was tight as he glanced at her hand as if he knew what was hidden inside her fist, and she dropped it to her side, where it vanished between the folds of her skirt.

Nehelon blinked and reached for his mare's nose, caught looking.

"I am used to being on my own," was all she said and caught a flicker of emotion crossing his features even if he turned sideways to hide it, fingers petting the side of the mare's head under the plain leather bridle. "Does she have a name, too?" Gandrett eyed his horse, which seemed to stare her down with black eyes.

"Alvi." He didn't turn back to meet Gandrett's gaze as he offered Gandrett Lim's reins. "You can ride beside me or take the carriage. It is up to you."

Of course he wasn't going to delay their trip. Ever the soldier. That was how she saw him. Even if he was carrying the title of chancellor in this court. But to her, all she saw was someone born to fight, to kill. It was there in his muscled arms, in the powerful lines of his legs and torso as he pushed himself up onto his mount, Lim's reins still in hand. It had accompanied her every day since the moment she had fought him in the desert. Even if he had let her glimpse the man—the male—hidden beneath that warrior.

"I'll ride," she simply said and nodded at the carriage-driver who had jumped down from the seat do open the door for her. A hired carriage, not one of the ornately decorated Brenheran carriages she had spotted coming and going over the weeks.

Gandrett could swear a smile was tugging on Nehelon's lips as she reached for Lim's reins with her free hand, but the muscles in his jaw flicked, informing her he was biting back any emotion.

"We rest at noon and make camp at nightfall," he said and kicked Alvi's flank, setting the horse in motion.

The carriage followed suit, and Gandrett used the moment to slip Brax's gift in the pocket of her fine, cotton riding dress before she climbed up on the horse and caught up with Nehelon at the nearby gate.

As they rode out into the city, Gandrett's eyes saw it like a new world.

The half-timbered houses were still the same as was the calm water of the canal that wound along the road. But Gandrett suddenly noticed varieties of colors and fabrics that indicated the status some of the bearers had in the town. She noticed the smells of fried and baked fish and could distinguish them. She noticed how some of the people stopped to inspect the passing carriage emerging from the palace and how the eyes—especially the women's—lingered on Nehelon's powerfully built body. He inclined his head at some of them, and much to Gandrett's surprise, some giggled.

The music emerging from open windows and doors was a mixture of Sivesian folk songs and foreign tunes that could as well originate from the southern territories.

None of them reminded her of the prayer songs of Everrun, though. Those melodies were for the temples of Vala where the Vala-blessed priests and priestesses served, where one day, Surel may serve.

Automatically, her head turned south-east, and she rode in silence, wondering how her friend was faring while they slowly made their way to the draw bridge out of the city.

Nehelon quietly spoke to her of the details of the plan as the capital of the west disappeared behind them, sun kissing their faces from the east and fresh breeze speaking of the Northern Mountains. He spoke of how he was going to usher the wolf toward her with his magic once the Denderlain hunting party was within reach. In two days' time, if they kept a steady pace.

After a quick and quiet lunch, they switched to the carriage, giving their mounts some rest, and when night settled, the carriage driver helped Nehelon set up camp while Gandrett found a couple of bushes to see to her needs. When she returned, Nehelon was digging bread and cheese from a box and placing them on small, wooden plates he had perched on a tree trunk nearby where the carriage was parked at the edge of the forest, north of the Ackpenesor River.

"The carriage will take us to the outer edges of Eedwood Forest," he explained, glancing at her over the plate he was handing her. "Mckenzie packed fresh clothes for you to wear when you go *hunting*." The emphasis on the word reminded Gandrett what was expected of her. And her hair stood.

"Why bring a carriage at all?" She asked, ignoring the prospect of enamoring the enemy's son to be able to find her target. That's how she had started thinking about her task. A simple mission to retrieve a rich bastard's heir and use any means necessary in the process. She would go on many missions after this one. And she would do worse than deceive people. That much she knew from those few conversations she'd had with returning members of the Order of Vala. "We could just ride the whole distance."

Nehelon pulled more bread from the box, turning his back toward her. "Because if you are to arrive exhausted and dirty, no one will believe you are who you claim to be." He handed one plate to the driver, who nodded in acknowledgment. "Don't worry about Farlon," Nehelon added as he noticed Gandrett's unsure glance at the man. "He is one of my most trusted men."

Farlon inclined his head at Gandrett. "Pleasure, Miss Brayton."

Gandrett forced a smile. "And who exactly am I to claim to be?"

"Gandrett Starhaeven."

Gandrett felt a laugh build up in her throat. A real one. He couldn't have picked a more stupid name.

"Sounds like a fairy princess," she commented, a hint of a laugh escaping with her answer.

In response, Nehelon gave her a daunting look.

He didn't comment. A fairy princess. None of the fairies—the Fae—were alert since they had been sent into dormancy a long, long time ago. Thank the gods none of them were. And that it was him she was speaking to. Any other Fae might have decapitated her for merely joking about Fae royalty. He *should* scold her for even taking the word in her mouth. If anyone found out just how much he knew about Fae princesses, he would find himself chained up in ribbons of iron in no time. He should—

He watched her eat in silence, his own Fae temper recoiling somewhere to the back of his consciousness at the sight of her eyes in the light of the small fire they had risked. Two nights before he'd drop her off at Eedwood Forest, and with Farlon nearby, he wouldn't stand a chance to figure out if it was true, that she had magic running in her veins.

"Sleep," he finally ordered as she set her plate down. "Tomorrow will be a long day."

To his surprise, Gandrett didn't object but instead curled up on her bedroll and closed her eyes.

22

The first fingers of Eedwood Forest appeared at about the same place where Ackpenesor and Eedpenesor met, where Alencourt lay a day's ride north. Gandrett reached for the place where her mother's necklace was sitting together with Brax's thin silver chain, hidden under the collar of her dress, and leaned out the carriage window.

Alvi and Lim trotted at the back of the carriage like faithful dogs.

The grains had been sown and it wouldn't take long before the now dark brown soil would disappear under a blanket of pale green. Her family was probably out on the fields, overseeing the development of the seeds they'd planted like they did every year.

A tug on her heart let her sigh into the passing breeze.

"When you return with Joshua," Nehelon said behind her as if he had read her mind.

She settled back on the leather bench across from him and tried to focus on the task ahead. Tomorrow she would part ways with Nehelon, and she would be on her own.

"How long have you been in Lord Tyrem's service?" She asked it just so she wouldn't think of how close her family was right now if she chose to turn north at that moment—if Nehelon let her.

The latter played with the pommel of his sword. "A little over ten years." He didn't look up.

"Why him?"

"Because—" Nehelon stopped, nostrils flaring.

"What is it?" Gandrett wanted to know as he leaned forward and directed his eyes at the horizon ahead.

"We are in the borderlands between east and west where most incidents occur," he explained, eyes intent as he pulled his sword.

Gandrett leaned forward, trying to see what was inciting the sudden alarm in his eyes.

It took her a while to make out the tendrils of smoke against the light.

"Denderlain is giving his mercenaries free rein again," he said through clenched teeth. "We need to get into the forest as fast as possible."

The smoke became more visible as the wind changed direction. It couldn't be more than a couple of miles ahead.

"Every other month they roam this region and burn down the houses of people who remain loyal to Lord Tyrem."

Gandrett stared at him. The Meister had told all the details about the conflict. Nehelon had told her some. But seeing the devastating results was something different.

"We need to go help whoever lives in the houses they are destroying," she demanded, her own hand now clenching her sword.

But Nehelon shook his head. "Lord Tyrem's men are out there in the villages fighting as we speak. Besides, you have a date with the young Lord Denderlain." His eyes said something different. *It's too dangerous.*

"Farlon," he called out the window, "into the forest, now."

It took them an hour until they reached the denser part of Eedwood Forest where the carriage began to slow them down. Nehelon informed her he had planned to enter the forest as late as possible without risking visibility so they wouldn't lose time. All during that time, Gandrett sat, quietly fuming that the Fae male was preventing her from helping someone in need.

"Vala would have wanted me to go help," she murmured more to herself, but of course, Nehelon's Fae ears picked up her words.

"Unless you are Vala-blessed, Vala would want you to stay the hell away from fire," he retorted, blue-diamond eyes dangerously sparking. "The last time I checked, you weren't able to manipulate water."

"Were I Vala-blessed, I wouldn't be stuck with *you*." She gave him an icy look, and Nehelon lowered his gaze as if searching for words but didn't speak. Frustration furrowed his brows, making him look more human than she had ever seen. And as she stared and stared at him as though she could punish him with her mere gaze, his eyes snapped up, locking on hers.

He wasn't sure if he'd imagined it, but that spark in her eyes...

"Say that again," he dared her and leaned closer, staring her down.

"I wouldn't be stuck with you, Lonnie." Gandrett smirked, unyielding.

Nehelon couldn't tell if it was the sunlight or if the gold in her eyes grew more intense as she held his gaze, unfazed. "You know what? If it makes it easier for you, I'll walk the rest of the way. I'm sure if I *flirt*—" She dragged out the word. "—with the wolf, it'll come right after me. Or better," her fingers reached up to her chest, touching something hidden under the compact fabric of her dress, "he might even take me home and offer for me to stay so I can snoop around his cave."

Nehelon studied her, open-mouthed as her temper broke through the perfectly-crafted mask she had been wearing for the past month. So much anger. So much suppressed pain.

Gandrett's face was close enough for him to touch her, her scent, even if mixed with dirt and sweat of their journey, filled the narrow space between them. All he needed to do was lift his hand from his sword and—

"You know what, Lonnie?" she continued like a ram. "Why don't I mention to the next person I see what you truly are? Once your little secret is out there, I no longer need to fear you." Her eyes tightened. "Even if you'd kill me for revenge." She spat those last words at him, making his breath catch in his throat.

"Kill you?" He'd never do that. Never in his life could he fathom the thought of ending her.

"That's what you are thinking, isn't it?" Her voice hitched as her words rushed out. "That's what you'd do if I chose to run and go see my family instead of Eedwood Castle. That's what—" silver lined her eyes, drowning out that spark he thought he'd seen, and within a moment, that tear fell—

His hand was there before he could remind himself to be cautious, fingertips grazing the salty line down her cheek. Gandrett didn't cringe. She didn't fight, and all he could think of was that no one had the right to make her feel this way. No one.

A sob shook Gandrett, but she didn't turn away. Couldn't. Too hypnotizing were Nehelon's eyes as they bore into hers in swirling shades of blue. And his fingers on her cheek—

She almost didn't notice she was crying. Almost. Hadn't it been for the wetness that kept coming from her eyes. Ten years since she had last cried. And now, in front of *him*? The Fae male who had taunted her, brutally pinned her against the wall, mercilessly brought his sword down on her—

He sat spellbound by her tears, knees an inch from hers, and his hand lingering on her skin despite the rocky movements of the carriage through the forest. He had let her rage at him. If he'd noticed her call him Lonnie, he didn't show. But one thing was different about him.

The mask was gone. The stone-cold, emotionless warrior who had been her shadow in the palace of Ackwood was gone.

So was the furious Fae male who had bruised her wrists. What remained were eyes, deep like the sea of time, full of its sorrow, too. And a yearning that so far she only knew from the high priests and priestesses when they plead to Vala for forgiveness for the sword-fighters' missions.

It was enough to let her shut her eyes so she would not tumble into the hidden world behind the blue mystery. The gods knew she wanted it. Wanted to lean into his palm, let the burden on her shoulders ease, if only for a moment—

As if he'd read her mind, Nehelon adjusted his hand so he cupped her face, thumb brushing away the moisture under her lashes. "You will learn over time, Gandrett, that who you believe me to be and who I am are not exactly the same." He paused, now running his other hand over her forehead, down her temple on the other side of her face. She didn't open her eyes, not yet, the callouses of his broad hands caressing her skin triggering a sensation she had never experienced. "And I am not sure that's a good thing," he added.

For a long time, the warmth of her skin in his palms was all he knew, his words losing all meaning. Her tears had ebbed, leaving her lashes in the shape of half a star, but regardless, her eyes remained closed as if she was seeking sanctuary in his touch. He leaned closer until his face was mere inches from hers, and her features, now relaxed and calm between his hands, dissolved before his vision, leaving him with the sensation of her breath on his lips.

Something stirred inside of him. A long-forgotten emotion that had led only to loss and pain in the past. And before she could blink her eyes open, he drew back enough to escape the draw of her quiet beauty.

PART TWO

A COURT
OF DECEIT

Nehelon stood watch while Gandrett washed up in the nearby stream then dressed in the fresh, midnight-blue riding gown Mckenzie had packed for her. It was more revealing than the green one and definitely not meant for practicability as much as to impress Armand Denderlain.

She stepped into her boots, fastened the broad golden belt around her waist, and braided her hair back. Then she slipped both necklaces on, hiding the pendants between her breasts under the gold-woven fabric.

"Who rides in a dress like this?" she demanded as she emerged from the bushes that separated Nehelon and the carriage from the stream.

"You, apparently," Nehelon joked. He actually joked, lips relaxed despite the caution that had snuck back into his eyes.

She tried not to think about it. Tried not to think about the words he'd spoken in the carriage either. *You will learn over time, Gandrett, that who you believe me to be and who I am are not exactly the same.*

She shook her head and folded the dirty green gown on her way back to the carriage where Farlon was waiting with a pack and two bedrolls.

"I'm sorry I can't take you further." He looked sorry, too.

Nehelon patted the man's shoulder—a gesture that was as natural from a human as it was shocking from the contained male. "Thanks for bringing us this far," he actually thanked the man before he dove into the carriage to pull out a bundle of clanking metal. "We have all we need."

Farlon inclined his head and climbed back onto the carriage seats, picking up the reins from the leather bench. The horses stomped, eager to get out of the trees.

Gandrett waved as Farlon maneuvered the carriage to turn around in the narrow space and found the man smiling at her as he steered the horses back onto the path and away. "Good luck," he called over his shoulder. Gandrett couldn't tell if he had spoken to her or Nehelon.

As she placed her bedroll on the ground and slumped—as far as the tight bodice of her dress allowed it—Nehelon had laid out an assortment of weapons on his own bedroll and was kneeling before them on the mossy forest ground.

"For me?" she asked, assessing the variety of blades and the beautifully carved bow sitting in the dimming evening light filtered by the thickening crowns of trees above them.

Nehelon picked up a short dagger. "This should fit under your dress on your thigh," he explained, focusing on the shiny blade as he weighed it in his broad hands.

Gandrett glanced down at her skirts and wondered if—even if there was the dire need for a blade—she would ever manage her way through the fabric in time. It would be hard if she had to retrieve it herself, too.

"And this," Nehelon laid down the dagger and chose a small, curved knife instead, "Will fit into the bodice. He glanced at the spot between her breasts where the two pendants were already hidden and buried his lips.

Gandrett placed a hand on her chest as if she could deflect his gaze. "It might stab me while riding," she pointed out, focusing on the practical details as she ran her hand down to her navel.

"Not if you do it right." With unsettling force, Nehelon jumped up and was beside her with two strides of his long legs. He reached out a hand, evading her doubtful gaze—"Allow me."—and as she didn't object, he grabbed the seam of her neckline right above her breasts with two gentle fingers and pulled.

Gandrett didn't breathe.

Much to her surprise, his calloused knuckles didn't brush her skin as he slipped the blade into a hidden compartment that seemed to run from right under her nose down to where she had placed her hand on her stomach.

"Mckenzie had this installed for you so you can slit Denderlain's throat if he ever gets too close." He pulled back his hand but remained kneeling before her, eyes now lingering on her face.

The hard shape of the blade winding along her chest and stomach made her sit up straight, raising her face closer to his. "When you see her, tell her I said thanks."

Nehelon smiled a crooked smile that made Gandrett wonder if that blade was poking through her skin as he said, "The compartment was Mckenzie's idea, but the blade is mine." He turned to the side to pick up a pack and opened it while getting to his feet.

"Thank—" Gandrett halted. *Never thank a Fae or you'll be eternally in their debt. A debt they will make you pay over and over again.* Gandrett remembered the words from her childhood. The legends of the heartless creatures of Ulfray. "Thank the gods you brought weapons," she corrected, her heart not nearly back to normal speed.

And she was sure he could hear it.

Lim and Alvi were grazing, side by side, by the nearest tree where the sun had allowed a small patch of grass to grow, their chewing a slow beat to the fading bird voices and awakening forest nightlife.

"You should eat." Nehelon handed her a piece of fruit cake then scanned the trees around them. "Tomorrow morning, you're going hunting."

Gandrett shuddered as he rubbed his fingers, cake crumbs falling to the ground, then flexed his fingers and rotated his wrist in a slow circle.

She felt it before she saw it. Twigs and leaves were growing like a natural wall around them, enclosing them the way the earthen circle had in the desert.

"We don't want that wolf to find you early," he explained, but there was no smile on his lips now. Just the cautious expression that he had been wearing in the carriage before.

With those words, he rolled up the bundle of weapons and shoved it under his pillow then laid down, eyes on the patches of sky visible through the canopy of leaves.

His magic resonated in the air long after the wall had grown. Gandrett could almost taste it. She hadn't been able to in the desert. Perhaps because of the wind relentlessly carrying away any fragrance. But now, it was clearly there, the scent of his magic, a mysterious layer, hovering above her and enclosing her as she stretched out on her bedroll, too, the blade in her bodice a constant reminder of his fingers, of the gentle tug on her clothes as he'd sheathed it.

For a long while, she lay there listening to the sounds of the forest until the horses had fallen silent, until she could no longer remember the whistle of the biting winds of Calma.

It was only when her eyelids drooped that Nehelon murmured, "Promise me something, Gandrett." Her eyes flew open at the sound of his voice, but she didn't dare speak. "Promise me you'll return from Eedwood."

"I have a bargain with Lord Tyrem," she simply said. "It is in my best interest to return with Joshua Brenheran safe and sound."

"I know you do. But that's not what I mean." He sighed. A deep and heavy sound as if he was trying to escape centuries of memories. "Promise me you'll return to *me*."

*D*own, *down the slippery stairs, down, down into the dark,*
Addie Blackwood chanted in her mind as she followed
the rough steps that led to the hidden well. Her hands
weren't shaking with fear the way they had that first time.
After a year at lady Linniue's household, she had gotten used
to the darkness that veiled the woman. That veiled the whole
damn court.

Addie's steps echoed in the stone shaft leading under the
north tower of Eedwood castle. Eedwood fortress would be
more suitable. For that's what it was. A fortress, impenetrable
from the outside, inescapable from the inside.

She couldn't count the times she'd tried. Tried and failed.
Failed and been punished for her recklessness.

If she had a choice, she'd rather return to her prison in the north. Where the nights were frosty and dark and the days even colder.

Addie glanced at the wet stone beneath her boots, her hands clutching the bucket she was to fill for the lady. Every day a couple of times. That was the only thing she was allowed to leave Lady Linniue's wing of the castle for.

She couldn't remember when she had last set foot outside the castle. Cross the courtyard under the disdainful glances of the Denderlain guards, yes. But that was about it. The only time she saw the fields and forests was through the windows and glimpsed the sea in the east...

The East Sea sparked like molten gold in the morning sun whenever she made it to the highest windows of the north tower. There, she was alone—really alone. Not the way she was alone when she slept on a sack of straw by the fire in the servants' dormitory. Slaves' dormitory.

Today, she hadn't made it there in time to take a breath and clear her mind before she returned to the tedious chores she was expected to do—and did for Lady Linniue Denderlain.

The surface of the water rippled in circular lines as she dipped the bucket in to fill it up for the second time today. The first time, she had spied Lord Hamyn and his son as they were mounting their horses to go on the annual hunt in honor of Demea. How she hated the goddess of the hunt.

Armand, in his hunting jacket, his hounds barking and howling from excitement. He had raised his hand, and the party had set in motion. She didn't know why they still bothered to go on that specific hunt when they were hunting every day. Not wolves, like this tradition demanded, but people.

The innocent souls of Sives who didn't declare loyalty to House Denderlain as so many of the families in the heart of Sives never would.

Sometimes she watched the smoke rise behind the edges of the forests when she directed her eyes west, toward her home.

But today, Addie Blackwood did not dare look east, for she knew what would happen if Hamyn and Armand Denderlain brought back the wolf as planned—

There would be a feast. And a dance. And the highlight of the celebrations would be the heads of those noble men and women their mercenaries had collected over the winter, and who were now starving in the cells under the castle—fortress. No way in. No way out. Unless you wore the blue and yellow coat of armor of House Denderlain.

Addie shuddered, pulled out the heavy bucket, and made her ascent back to daylight.

Gandrett ran. She ran as she had never run before, the dress restricting her from gulping enough air down and the dagger strapped to the inside of her thigh making her grit her teeth when it hit her knee every time she made a turn. Behind her, paws dug into the moist forest ground, claws slithering over tree trunks as the wolf pushed her to her limits, herding her.

Vala help her, Nehelon was right when he said that there would be a moment she'd hate him. Last night, he said it when she had asked why he wanted her to promise.

Right now was that moment. Not that she hadn't hated him before. That's how it had started off in Everrun. That's how it had remained until that moment when he had let her glimpse that there was so much more than the emotionless bastard he let on. Then, her stomach had started doing weird things.

As for now—she hated him again. Why couldn't she just fight the wolf and bring him down? Why wait for Armand and his hunting party to come rescue her? What if they never came?

A growl, too close to let her think of anything but how to put one steady foot ahead of the other, shattered through the trees, and the beast was before her. Gandrett jammed her boots into the ground, almost losing balance, knees barking when she came to a sudden halt.

The wolf had cut her off, forcing her to either run back toward where she had left Lim in a clearing Nehelon said was safe. The hunting party would stop by there, he'd said, and find her abandoned horse as the first clue there was something wrong. She had made sure to leave footprints in the direction Nehelon had pointed, and it hadn't taken long for the gray-furred beast to show up. The Fae male had done a job better than promised. *It will look as if the wolf was really about to kill you.*

Gandrett frowned and reached for the bow he'd handed her this morning, pulled an arrow from the quiver and nocked it, eyes on the gaping maw of the beast.

Tried to.

The bow snapped in two halves where Nehelon had said it would.

Damn you, Fae bastard! Where was the Denderlain hunting party?

The wolf had been chasing her for too long to believe Denderlain would find her easily.

And it was coming closer, head lowered, eyes gleaming with bloodlust. Gandrett went through her training in her mind. She had never fought wild animals—other than the adolescent boys at the priory.

With the arrow in her hand and the few in her quiver, she would be able to wound the beast enough to enrage it, but not defeat it. Not without the bow Nehelon had manipulated to break.

I have confidence in your skills. He'd smiled at her, a ghost of that cocky grin from their first encounter making his eyes gleam.

Maybe *he* had confidence. As for Gandrett—her hands were shaking as she debated how much longer she could go without pulling that knife from her cleavage. It was a last resort. Weapons should remain hidden so Denderlain wouldn't get suspicious. That's why he hadn't given her the hunting knife she'd asked for to strap to her belt, so she appeared even more like she had no clue what she was doing. No threat. A harmless lady in need of Denderlain's aid.

Gandrett bared her teeth at the thought and grabbed a second arrow with her free hand, watching the wolf prowl toward her, claws sharp as needles piercing deep into the mossy ground with each step it took.

"You don't have anything better to do, do you?" she snarled, readying the arrows to ram them into the beast's chest or neck should it attack.

The wolf stared back at her, growling again as it studied its prey. Easy prey, too easy.

Then it leaped off the ground, a gray thunderstorm, coming at her. And Gandrett braced herself for the impact of claws and teeth.

That wasn't how he'd planned things. Not like that.

Nehelon leashed his rage and unleashed his magic as he heard the deadly growl through the forest. He didn't need the birds to tell him what was happening even though he had instructed a few to follow Gandrett through the woods, to alert him if things went wrong.

They had. He could feel it in his very core as the forest shuddered with her scream—

And Denderlain's horses and hounds were nowhere near her. If he didn't react, she might die.

How he wished he'd had time to pick a wolf and tame it so he could order it to protect Gandrett rather than let a random one eat her alive. But that took time. The wilder, the more predatory the animal, the more difficult.

Tendrils of power probed their path through the tree branches and roots until he found her, too far away to draw his sword and strike the wolf down, but he made the closest willow grow some branches that put a leash on the beast so he could at least pause it until his arrival.

The wolf struggled under his power. He didn't need to see it to feel the wild energy, the fury of the predator. It was a fully-grown male, ready to sink its teeth into the girl he needed to save his world.

So Nehelon ran. He ran like the wind, commanding the latter to carry her scent toward him, to tell him if she was alive. Until he could hear her heartbeat, slow and weak instead of thrumming of fear as he'd been expecting.

When he broke through the thicket, the wolf was growling in his prison of willow rods, some curling around its flanks and haunches, some around his neck and maw.

"I'm sorry, friend," he said to the wolf as he scanned the area for Gandrett, "but this woman is not meant to be your meal."

He spotted her near a tree trunk, chest moving with slow, labored breaths, her gold-flecked eyes hidden behind her lids.

"Gandrett." He was on his knees beside her, his own heart uncertain of whether to gallop at the pace of panic at her motionless form or the pace of quiet relief at her flat breath and remaining heartbeat. "Open your eyes."

She didn't respond. Neither did she open her eyes or twitch, nor did the rhythm of her heart change. *Unconscious*, he diagnosed and sniffed. The iron tang of blood filled the air, and when he scanned the scene, he found a spot of crimson blood at the bark of the tree behind her.

And a matching spot on the side of her head.

Nehelon cursed violently. What had he been thinking? He should have stayed closer.

His hand reached for hers, squeezing gently.

No response.

His free hand reached for her chest, checking if the knife was still there and careful that the knife was the only thing he touched. It was there—resting solid and lethal between her breasts. He swallowed at the thought and turned his attention to her thigh where, without lifting her skirts, he could tell that the dagger was still strapped and sheathed.

He should have listened to her, should have given her a hunting knife to protect herself from the wolf. His mind had been set on Denderlain and Denderlain only. That she'd need protection from him, but from the wolf—

"I'm so sorry," he breathed as he studied her shape, stroking over her forehead with one hand before he rested it there, ready to heal her. Just enough to be certain she'd survive the attack. It was a miracle the wolf hadn't shredded her apart with its claws. He scanned her body for more wounds, scratches he had missed, and when he found none—only a half-torn sleeve—he let his magic flow into her. In the background, the wolf continued his growls.

It tingled in his fingers when he touched her with his power. A sensation that slowly spread through his hands, his arms, and ventured into his chest where it lingered for a long moment until he let go as her scalp knitted itself together enough so he was convinced she would wake up again.

"I am so sorry, Gandrett," he repeated. And as he drank in her slender shape, her waist so small his hands might fit around it if he dared hold her, he sat back on his legs, knowing that this might be the last time he saw her. She had promised she'd return with Joshua so she could see her family again. Not for him. She hadn't promised that. And it had torn him apart, still was tearing him apart that she couldn't give him that little. He would never ask anything of her. Never demand. Not the way the men in this world did. For his world—the world of a different time, of a kingdom that was unscathed—no longer existed. Unless she made it back to him.

"If you can't promise me," he leaned down, bracing one hand beside her head, the other one brushing along her temple, "I promise I will make sure you make it back in one piece." He studied her face. The thick rim of lashes, which were two dark half-moons against her sun-kissed skin, her lips pale from fright and unconsciousness. "Back to *me*." And he closed that gap between them, brushing his lips against hers ever so slightly. Just to feel what it could be like if he had a choice—even if Vala would damn him for this.

He lingered. A moment. Two. Even the wolf had gone silent ensnared in the willow branches.

And it was one moment too long.

Her mouth opened, not for him but to suck in a breath as she opened her eyes and found him so close. Too close.

He pulled back enough to let her sit up, but she remained on the ground, eyes shuttering as if she wasn't certain she was dreaming, her expression dazed. But no word rose from her lips though the color returned to them with every breath she took anew.

He wanted to tell her, wanted her to know that she was the key. That he needed her. And that this had never been meant to happen.

But the whinny of horses and howling of hounds closing in stopped him dead before he could even find the words to say it.

They were coming. Denderlain and his hunting party. And it was time for Nehelon to leave.

So he squeezed her hand once before he got to his feet. "Don't forget I promised."

With those words, he freed the wolf and vanished into the thicket.

The trampling of hooves, too many of them, too close, and excited barks woke her. And there were voices—

Gandrett blinked her eyes open to find Lim's black eyes gazing down at her as if to inquire if she was all right.

In response, she groaned, alerting the riders of the other horses and their hounds alike.

"Are you hurt, Miss?" a middle-aged man asked as he slid down his horse. "Did it get you?"

Gandrett tried to shake her head but found the throbbing too painful. So she just blinked.

What happened? She remembered the cracking sound of a whip that had followed the wolf as it had launched itself toward her. She had tumbled back to escape the beast and positioned her arrows before her chest, bracing herself to pierce it in whatever way she could. But something had swirled the animal to the side, making its shoulder hit her rather than its claws and teeth. Instead, the impact had propelled her into the nearest tree trunk at which's roots she was now sprawled.

Then there were those memories of *him*. His calloused hands on her forehead, his breath on her face. And his lips—

As if in trance, she gingerly reached up and touched her fingers to her mouth. A kiss. Had he kissed her? She couldn't tell if it had been a dream, if she had seen him there or imagined him so close to her face, his mouth warm and gentle, kindling a sensation Vala would damn her for.

And his words—

Don't forget I promised.

Promised what?

"I don't understand, Miss," the man said with pity.

Gandrett realized she had spoken aloud.

"What happened?" This time, Gandrett moved. With all her strength, she braced one hand at her side and lifted her head.

Her mission. She had to make sure Armand Denderlain found her...

The man looked back over his shoulder and called, "I need help here." To whom, Gandrett couldn't tell.

If this was Armand, even if he wasn't pretty, at least he seemed to care that she could hardly move. Lim nudged her with his nose as if to make sure she was really awake this time.

She let her head drop back into the moss and groaned.

"We found your horse a couple of miles back in the clearing, and when no one showed up to claim it for a while, we started looking," the man explained, bushy eyebrows raising. "He belongs to you, doesn't he?"

Gandrett nodded carefully and looked past Lim's legs at the massive, gray shape that was perched on a tree trunk.

"You killed it," she breathed as her surroundings blurred in and out of focus. "You—"

A pair of polished, black boots stopped right before her and a voice, smooth like satin, said, "Did the beauty awake from her eternal sleep?" It wasn't really a question.

Gandrett's eyes followed the boots up to black leather pants and a hunting jacket in blue velvet—blue like her dress. And atop the midnight-blue, a pale and elegant face greeted her with a smile.

Gandrett blinked.

"You are safe, Miss," the owner of the face spoke, his lips curling at one side as he noticed she was staring at him. "The beast has met its deserved end."

Gandrett felt the urge to raise her eyebrows and ask if he was serious but remembered Mckenzie's final instruction: smile.

So she did. It was a joke of a smile compared to what she had mastered in the weeks at Ackwood, but a smile anyway. A smile with the same lips which might or might not have been kissed by a Fae. Gandrett swallowed, her mouth suddenly gone dry.

The young man returning her gaze seemed to wait for something. So she searched for words but found none.

In the meantime, the man kneeling beside her had placed his hands on her head, inspecting the source of the throbbing pain.

"She hit her head pretty hard," he reported to the man in polished boots. "Apart from that, she seems unharmed."

The one in midnight-blue nodded. "And have we learned her name yet?"

"No, my Lord."

While Gandrett shuttered her eyelids to clear her vision, the boots descended toward her shoulders, shoving aside the other man, and the young man crouched down beside her and cocked his head, exposing a ponytail of honey-blond. "So," he studied her with depthless, hazel eyes, "does the sleeping beauty have a name?"

Gandrett tried to speak, but as she opened her mouth, no sound emerged.

"Lord Armand," the middle-aged man with the concerned look spoke cautiously, "maybe we should get her some water."

So this was Armand Denderlain. Gandrett blinked at him, acknowledging that despite what had gone wrong, something had gone right. She had found Armand Denderlain.

"So get her some water," Armand hissed at the man, who stumbled to his feet and scurried away.

"You are lucky we found you," Armand said blithely, "The beast was coiling to spring when I sent my arrow right between its eyes."

Gandrett's stomach roiled.

Armand read her twisting face as fear and said, "Don't worry. I'll make sure you make it out of this forest in one piece."

Meanwhile, the other man returned with a waterskin, which he held out for Armand, who took it to offer it to Gandrett. "You should drink," he suggested as she didn't lift a hand to take it, and opened it for her before he led it to her mouth. "I'd truly like to know what birdlike voice goes with a face that Nyssa herself would envy."

Gandrett opened her mouth, intending to say she served the goddess of life, not the goddess of love, but remembered that she was not to give away who she was. Armand, however, took the opportunity to pour some water between her lips, and she sat upright, coughing the liquid that had been going down the wrong pipe back up in a spray.

Armand chuckled, his hazel eyes gleaming with amusement. "Is it really that bad?"

Great. She hadn't even spoken a word, and already she had embarrassed herself. That wasn't how she had envisioned facing the enemy—the startlingly handsome enemy—but with a strong voice to speak for herself, with legs to carry her. Instead, the young lord pulled a silken handkerchief from inside his jacket and handed it to her with a leather-gloved hand.

Gandrett gingerly took the fabric and wiped her face and the splatter of wet on her chest and stomach, fully aware Armand's gaze was following where her hands went.

"Thank you." She folded the silk and was about to hand it back to him.

"Keep it." He just smiled. "A token from the man who saved your life."

Gandrett was about to slap his smirking face with her fist for that statement—a token from the girl who kicked his ass.

"So you don't forget me when you return to—" He cocked his head. "Where did you come from exactly?"

Gandrett internally frowned and fashioned a painful smile. "From the south of Eedwood," she told the lie Nehelon had provided her with. "I rode up to hunt in Demea's honor, and when I was about to rest after the three-hour trip north—" She paused, pulling up her trained frightened face.

"The wolf attacked you," Armand finished her sentence, understanding in his eyes.

"It chased me all the way here..." Gandrett managed to authentically shake, voice raw. "Then..." Her eyes searched the forest ground for her broken bow. "Then, the bow snapped... I don't understand it. My father inspected it for me before I left. He is a merchant specializing in carved weapons and jeweled blades." She gave just enough context to hint toward

her alter ego's family's wealth. Armand's groomed eyebrows
rose. "If it hadn't been for you..." Her words tasted sour on
her tongue. Wrong. If it hadn't been for him, she would have
pulled her knife and dagger and slaughtered that damned
beast. But this way, she was bound to act like a helpless little
girl in need of saving.

She shoved aside the memory of Nehelon kneeling before
her on the mossy ground, his lips—

A dream. It couldn't have been anything else.

"I am most certainly pleased I chose to follow your footsteps into the thicket. Otherwise—" He gestured at her in general. "—I would have missed this."

Gandrett watched his hands, hidden under a thin layer of
black leather, as they elegantly waved along her form, waterskin still clasped between his fingers.

He held it out for her again with a smile. Less amused,
more genuine this time. "You should drink. Shock makes people do the weirdest things." A low chuckle followed his words.

Gandrett took it with her free hand and led it to her lips,
aware that most of the other men were now staring in their
direction, apparently bored having inspected the slain wolf for
several minutes.

"If I offered you a hand," he rose back to his feet, "would
you take it and let me help you up, milady—" He cocked his
head. "I still don't know your name."

"Gandrett," she said and looked at him from under her
lashes the way Mckenzie had shown her. The way that had
made Brax pause while he spoke. "Gandrett Starhaeven."

Armand held out a hand, face tense as he bit his lower lip
while he waited.

For a moment, Gandrett considered ignoring the gesture and simply staggering to her feet on her own. But this was not about what she felt like doing.

So she managed her temper and tucked Armand's handkerchief into her sleeve before she placed her calloused hand into his gloved one.

He responded with a gallant bow. "It's an honor to meet you, Lady Starhaeven." He pulled her up with a powerful tug on her hand, making her half-tumble into him.

"The pleasure is all mine." Gandrett stifled a groan as she balanced her weighed and failed, sagging into him, and his arms caught her around the waist before she could hit the ground again.

She fashioned an apologetic look, hoping to web some mystery into her gaze as she glanced up at him, his head towering above her as he stabilized her.

He just continued smiling. "I was going to ask you which direction to take you to the edges of the forest so you can make your way home, but—" He tried to set her back on her feet.

This time, Gandrett purposely let her knees buckle. No. He couldn't send her off. Then all would have been in vain.

"But it seems you need more than an escort back to the road." Something in his face informed her he was pleased about it.

"I think I need a healer," was what Gandrett said in response, attempting to sound ladylike and not like she wanted to hit him over the head with her spare arrows. For her family, she reminded herself. She was doing this for her family. A deep breath, as deep as was possible in the tight bodice, helped her stomach his answering smirk.

"We have the best healers in all of Sives at the castle."

There it was. Her ticket in. And she swayed again, trying to ignore the tightening of Armand's arm around her.

The gray crow perched on Nehelon's shoulder sang of Gandrett's success.

He had stayed behind, listening, hidden in the treetops, far away from where any of the hunting party could spot them. Far enough that not even his Fae sense could make out if Gandrett was all right.

So he had summoned the bird, asked it to bring him the news of the girl with the depthless eyes and the heart of iron. A heart that would destroy him eventually.

And when the bird whispered to him that Gandrett was riding with *him*, that they were on their way to Eedwood, he pictured Armand Denderlain's smirking face and how entertaining it would be to plant his flat hand on his fine-boned nose.

Nehelon's fists tightened at his sides. This was what he had wanted. What he had promised Lord Tyrem. That he would find a way to bring back Joshua. And Gandrett was that way.

And what a stupid fool he was. He couldn't have just made sure the wolf didn't kill her; he needed to let those strange sensations take over. Who was she but a mortal—?

He rested his head against the tree trunk, closed his eyes, and dismissed the bird with a wave of his hand.

26

When Addie made it to the top of the tower this time, the sun was painting the courtyard in fiery orange. She had taken the water to Lady Linniue and made sure the lady had all she needed before she left to her sanctuary high up in the quiet north tower. Just a couple of minutes of peace and quiet.

She blinked into the sunset from the highest window of the stairwell until the clattering of hooves disturbed her moment of silent rest.

The shouts of men carried up, bouncing off the rugged stone walls, words incomprehensible but urgency obvious. Addie shielded her eyes against the sun and leaned closer to the window, trying to spy what was going on.

Servants were emerging from the castle, running to meet the hunting party halfway into the yard.

"Careful," someone barked.

Not someone. He. The young lord on his chestnut horse, his voice like a thread of silver.

Addie spotted him at the center of the party, right next to Lord Hamyn, who cleared his path out of the group, and on the other side, a female shape on a bay horse, half-collapsing from the saddle as one of the servants helped her down.

"Bring her to the west tower," the young lord snarled at the man who gently lifted the woman. "And get a healer."

Addie watched the cluster of business disperse as he jumped off his horse, the image of spring, and handed the reins of his horse to one of the stable boys now buzzing between the riders.

The young lord was already following the injured woman inside when he called over his shoulder. "Make sure to get the pelt of that beast in one piece."

Addie's gaze followed the direction he was speaking and found, perched on a wagon at the back of the party that had hardly made it inside the gates, the lifeless shape of a massive gray wolf.

So they had been successful hunting.

Addie turned back to watch the young lord dash inside, the doors of the west tower bouncing closed behind him.

There was a lot of whispering when Gandrett regained consciousness. Several voices, some upset, some confused, some concerned judging by the sound of it.

"Ahh, there you are," a wheezy, female voice greeted before she could open her eyes.

The whispering went silent.

"She's awake," the voice spoke to whoever had been conversing beside her.

"She doesn't look awake." That voice, Gandrett knew. It was the same that had been speaking to her all the way back to Eedwood. And she could hardly remember a word other than the reassuring phrases he had thrown in between cocky comments. The voice of the man who had ridden beside her until she had blacked out.

Hands touched her head in professional assessment. "She is lucky to be alive," the wheezy voice stated and pushed something cold against the throbbing wound on the side of Gandrett's head.

Gandrett flinched, taking in her surroundings with adjusting eyes. Someone must have carried her to a bedchamber while she was unconscious she concluded from the deep blue curtains that folded around a four-poster bed at the other end of the room. Fading sunlight that filtered in through the narrow windows made the gold embroidery on the fabric lines of pale flame.

"See?" the woman said. "I told you she is awake."

Gandrett grimaced and opened her eyes. Heavy. Her eyelids were so heavy.

Perched atop the crimson armrest of a sofa at Gandrett's feet, Armand Denderlain was grinning in welcome. "I can't make up my mind whether I like you better asleep or awake," he said, grin broadening.

Gandrett frowned. It slipped onto her features before she could help it.

To her surprise, Armand leaned forward, one hand braced on the backrest of the sofa and said, "Awake." He nodded to himself. "I think I like you better awake."

Gandrett suppressed the urge to kick his face with her foot.

Behind him, a woman, maybe in her forties, rolled her eyes as if asking, Will he ever stop talking?

"I don't care if awake or asleep, as long as I get you out of here." The woman said grumpily and grabbed the young lord by the collar of his jacket. "My patient needs rest."

Gandrett coughed at the sight of no steel shooting up at the woman from Armand's side. Instead, he laughed. Actually, he authentically gave a heartfelt laugh that brightened his hazel eyes into an amber tint.

Behind her, someone cleared his throat. "He still acts like a four-year-old, doesn't he?"

Gandrett glanced up and found the middle-aged man from the forest behind her, lips pursed, not at Armand but at the woman who shook her head, eyes speaking that he didn't know the half of it.

"Ignore them." Armand shrugged off the woman's grasp and settled down on the edge of the sofa close to Gandrett's knees. The smile was still there.

A smile that reminded Gandrett of her little brother's carefree laugh.

Was this the man who Nehelon had called Hamyn Denderlain's right hand? A man who commanded an army? Who was involved in the abduction of Joshua Brenheran?

Could evil laugh like that? It was the only question she should be asking herself.

"How are you feeling, dear?" The woman gave up on Armand and stepped past him, sitting by Gandrett's hip, wiping her hands in her white apron in a subconscious motion before she reached for Gandrett's hand and searched her pulse.

Gandrett touched her head with her other hand and found dirt in her hair. At the priory, she had been used to it, hadn't cared. Here, it was vital that she impressed. Nehelon, Mckenzie, Brax, and of course Lord and Lady Brenheran had made that clear.

The woman crinkled her freckled nose as she spotted Gandrett combing it out with her fingers, her chocolate-brown curls dancing forward as she whispered, "The only thing that can help with this is a bath." She straightened again, her greenish eyes still twinkling. Then she glanced up at the man behind

Gandrett—"Go fill the tub."—who bustled away at her words, murmuring something, and after a door was opened, the sound of running water filled the air.

"Clean her up, Deelah," Armand said, not an order but a request. "I'd like to take her to the dance tonight."

Gandrett cringed and silently cursed for not yet having mastered her reactions. She knew that a dance would be coming. Lady Brenheran had told her. And suggested Gandrett hurt her ankle so she had an excuse when she was asked to dance.

Now she had a thorough headache to top the dull pain in her back and legs.

Armand read Gandrett for a moment. "That is, if you wish, milady." He raised one eyebrow in expectation of her response.

No, or, gods no, was what she wanted to say. What she said instead was, "It would be my honor, Lord Armand."

Armand stiffened on the armrest. "I didn't tell you my name." His eyes tightened the slightest bit.

"Your hunting companion called you that in the forest," Gandrett hastily explained. She didn't fail to notice the heat rising in her cheeks.

From embarrassment. What Armand made of it seemed to be something very different.

For he winked at her and got to his feet. "I'll have someone bring you a dress." With those words, he sauntered to the black, wooden door.

Deelah waited for the door to shut behind him before she sighed. "Let's get to work, then."

Gandrett swallowed the groan that threatened to escape her as she made it to her feet. A dance. That was good. Good. For some reason, she wasn't able to convince herself. Even if a dance would present her with the chance to get an overview of all the faces at court. Eventually, she'd need a plan to find Joshua.

So, first the trust and protection of Armand Denderlain. Everything else had to wait.

With Deelah's help, she got to her feet.

"You'll be fine in no time," Deelah reassured her as the man met them at the threshold of the bathroom before he hurried out the door with a nod at them.

Gandrett had no other choice but to believe the woman, so she let her guide her to the steaming tub and sit her down on a plain, wooden chair beside it.

"Are you a healer?" Gandrett asked as the woman reached into her apron to extract a small bottle. She poured the contents into a bowl of hot water that sat on the shelf behind her. Then, she dipped a piece of fresh cloth into it and cleaned the wound on Gandrett's head with professional lightness.

The woman shook her head. "Just so long in this court that Armand comes to me with anything." She smiled. "And he used to have injuries just like yours all the time—" She stopped as if she had said something she wasn't supposed to. "The young lord asked me to clean you up—so here I am."

The pain in Gandrett's head subsided as the woman worked away.

"Can I go in this dress?" Gandrett asked, more to make conversation. Anything to learn more about Armand.

"Silly girl," the woman pursed her lips. "We'll find you something worthy of being the young lord's escort for the night."

Something in the woman's eyes told her this wasn't the first time she'd done this—patch up a girl and dress her.

"Now, get out of that dress and into the tub." An order. "You don't only look like you slept on the forest ground; you also smell like it."

Gandrett felt her cheeks turn red again. She hadn't had a chance to really clean up since the quick wash up in the stream, and she had ridden and run and sweated in this dress.

She was about to reach to her waist to take off that wide band of gold then yielded, remembering that she was wearing blades in her bodice and beneath her skirts. Privacy. She needed privacy to hide the weapons now and put them under the new dress later.

"Before I bathe, I need to—" She glanced around, stopping at the small adjacent chamber that stood open. Perfect.

"Relieve yourself?" Deelah asked and dumped the cloth in the bowl. "By all means. Go ahead. I'll be waiting in your room. Call me when you're in the bathtub."

"My room?" Gandrett wondered if she had heard correctly, but Deelah just shrugged.

"Today, it's yours, tomorrow—who knows?" And with a thoughtful look on her face, she left the bathing chamber.

Addie Blackwood rubbed her fingers dry on a rag before she picked up Lady Linniue's satin robe. She should be wearing gloves when she touched it. The lady would not be pleased if she found stains or smudges of dirt on it. That's why Addie had scrubbed her hands with soap for minutes before she came anywhere near it.

"I hear my nephew has brought home another trophy," Lady Linniue conversed with a breezy voice. "Hamyn visited earlier, and I tell you he wasn't speaking about the wolf."

The other woman laughed. Addie had seen her in Lady Linniue's chambers before. Isylte Aphapia of Ilaton. A trusted friend of Lady Linniue's and almost as much of a gossip.

Addie kept her head down as she smoothed out the gown and prepared it for wearing, unlacing the sides so Lady Linniue could fit it over her head.

"They say he had to hit her over the head to get her here," Isylte murmured and laughed.

"A merchant's daughter from the south of Sives," Linniue wondered aloud. "Whatever made her go on that hunting trip, the gods were too busy to keep her out of Armand's path."

Addie held her breath at the mention of the young lord's name. She had seen him run after the unconscious girl. But...

"I don't know what has been going on with my nephew, but ever since Aphra's death—"

Addie remembered the months of darkness that had followed the unexpected passing of Lord Hamyn's wife—of Armand's mother. The weight of ruling had fallen on the young lord's shoulders even if his father was still called Lord of Eedwood. Hamyn wasn't a born Denderlain. Aphra had carried the bloodline, and now that she was dead, her only son had taken on her tasks.

A shadow crossed Lady Linniue's face as she stared out the window into the falling night outside. "My sister was the only thing that could have saved this court." Her words were flat—almost as if she wasn't noticing she spoke them.

She turned, teacup in hand, all of a sudden a smile back on her face. "The dress, Addie," she said across the room to where Addie was still, unnecessarily, smoothing out the skirts of the gown.

With an efficient movement, Addie was on her feet, picking up the folds of satin in the process, and rushed to the lady's side, who had set down her teacup and was now holding out her arms, allowing Addie to slip off her bathing robe.

Isylte Aphapia watched her with mild interest as she stripped the robe off the lady until she was only in her underthings, then flitted the Denderlain-blue satin over the lady's head, making sure it didn't catch on the pearl-decorated pins in the lady's hair.

"Gorgeous," Isylte complimented Lady Linniue. "Absolutely gorgeous."

Linniue turned on the spot, hardly giving Addie a moment to tie the laces along the sides of the waist, then clicked her tongue. "The shoes."

Addie knotted the last lace in a hurry then dove for the blue satin slippers that sat by the fireplace.

"I suppose we'll find out if this one lasts longer than the last one," Linniue dryly said and gave Isylte a knowing look.

"If he even brings her to the dance tonight," Isylte added.

Addie knew those talks. It seemed to be the young lord's hobby to collect pretty women somewhere in the streets of Eedwood—also in the forest, as she'd learned today—and bring them back to the castle for a while. His way of distracting himself from the darkness that she still sometimes spotted in the young lord's eyes on the rare occasions when he rushed by in the hallways. The rare moments her heart gave a short sting of despair.

"Let's hope this one doesn't talk as much," Isylte prompted.

Linniue just picked up a necklace of silver and pearl which she draped around her throat before she hooked her arm in her friend's—"Let's see."—leaving Addie behind to clean up and prepare the bedchamber for the early hours of the morning when Lady Linniue would return, drunk with the thrill of the night, and Addie would have to climb back into the hidden well to refill the bucket.

No matter where Gandrett looked, there wasn't a spot in the bodice of this gown where she could place that knife.

She had discretely stored the dagger at her thigh when Deelah had left her in her chambers after draping her into a low-cut, midnight-blue gown made of thin velvet for the bodice and chiffon for the skirts, which were a lighter shade of blue and glittered like stars with little crystals that had been sewn onto the delicate fabric.

The thought of laying the knife into the thin wrapping around her breasts without any protection from the sharp blade made her hair stand for more than one reason. It was his blade—Nehelon's. While the thought of carrying his weapon made her feel that she was not as alone as she truly was in this court, the idea of his blade on her naked skin came with the thought of his hand there as well. Gandrett eyed herself in the mirror and made a face.

So Gandrett gave up, discarding the blade in her pillow-case, shoved the string-like strap back up her shoulder, and paced the room, eyes scanning walls and windows for anything that may be useful should she need to flee.

She had glanced out the windows earlier, finding herself to be at least two floors up in the castle with the Eedpenesor flowing by the foot of the walls like a raging snake. There was no way out of here.

She went through the floorplans and maps in her mind, trying to remember every line on the scroll that had sat between her and Mckenzie, first, and then Nehelon. For some reason, the features of his face dug their way to her consciousness first.

Damn Fae male. Gandrett flung herself on the sofa and pouted at no one until a knock at the door had her shooting upright.

She didn't make it to the door before it sprang open, and Armand Denderlain's elegant shape sauntered in, nothing less graceful than a desert lion, his face bright with anticipation.

"I am at a loss for words." He placed his hand on his chest as if she'd just fired an arrow at him and blinked. Once. Twice.

Gandrett wanted to scream at him to get the hell out but smoothened the thought—as entertaining as it would be to kick his ass—and said, "Milord is too kind."

His smile widened.

Perfect. She thanked Mckenzie for telling her what to say, when to smile, how to act. Her natural instincts would have had her ripping open her skirts and challenging him to a duel to know if he was worthy of even one of her smiles.

Not if she believed the hints Deelah had thrown her in the bathing chamber.

He walked right up to her, close enough to touch her, then reached into his pocket and pulled out a necklace with a crystal the size of an eyeball.

The first thought that came to Gandrett's mind was that if she had this, she wouldn't need a knife at all. One strike in the face with a jewel that size would take out even Nehelon.

Argh. Nehelon. There again was the Fae male, prominent right where her focus should be on the enemy before her—the smiling enemy. With lovely, hazel eyes.

Gandrett sighed through her nose. The only relief she allowed herself.

"If you don't like it," Armand said with a raised eyebrow, "I can run back to the family trove and fetch you something different."

Gandrett surveilled him for a moment, trying to figure out if he was serious—she'd have loved to have sent him running just to get the chance to give him a vulgar gesture as he turned his back.

This was the man who fully supported his father in keeping Joshua Brenheran prisoner. The man who sent mercenaries to the villages at the center of Sives to force their allegiance.

And here he was, offering her a clunky jewel which's size reminded her of the bells the cows in the meadows around Alencourt wore.

He hesitated before measuring her with observant eyes. "You are not one for jewelry, are you?" He made up his mind. "And then I thought I needed to bring something big to impress you. You know," he dangled the necklace before her face. "With your father being a merchant for jeweled weapons... I thought you were used to rocks this size."

Yes, rocks. Indeed. But the dull, gray ones that cut your knees when you fell from exhaustion during training in the Calma Desert. Vala help her.

"It's..." She shuttered her eyelids, hoping he'd let it go. "It's just—" She searched for words—lies. "—it's just so beautiful, and I can't take any gifts from you." She had already taken Brax's necklace—which securely rested under her pillow with her mother's. And Nehelon's knife and dagger. If she took another gift, Vala might never forgive her.

"Not a gift." Armand grinned that full-hearted grin again. "I'll need that back after tonight."

Because that's how long she would stay here. One night. Like the others, if she believed Deelah.

"Then keep it." Gandrett's words were out before she could restrain herself.

She expected Armand to kick her out, to get upset, to show his evil nature, the one that the Brenherans had warned her about.

But nothing. He just dropped it on the sofa behind her and offered his arm. "Shall we?"

27

Armand led her down a torch-lit hallway followed by a twisting stairwell where the distant sound of music greeted them alongside the scent of spring herbs and blossoms. She marked every turn they took, every door, every painting. She'd need those for later when she went exploring on her own.

"It's older than the Battle of Ithrylan," Armand commented on her seemingly random glances. Just another girl impressed to death with the wealth and pompousness of the young lord's home.

"It's—" Suffocating. "—breathtaking."

He smiled and tucked his free hand behind his back as he led her down the next flight of stairs.

Gandrett followed along, one hand lifting the hem of her skirts just enough so she wouldn't fall over them, and quietly counted the stairs.

Music filled the air by the time Armand led her into a wider hallway, his eyes, Gandrett noticed, on her rather than the guards in black positioned in regular spacing along the walls. They must be close to the dance, for ahead of them, at the end of the hallway, lights greeted them with the warm shades of fire.

"Wait until you see the great hall," Armand chuckled from the side as he commented on her gawking.

Garlands of flowers were draped over the columns right where the light emerged together with a carpet of voices, all cheerily and happily chattering. She swallowed and let the Denderlain heir lead her forward and into the great hall.

She had no words. Not because the flowers from the columns spread all across the ceiling and walls of the great hall—she had seen arrangements like that in Everrun—but because of the sheer size of the space they filled, the people in finery floating through the open space, carrying glasses of sparkling wine and the music...

An orchestra played the songs she remembered from her childhood. More refined than the simple versions on a piano or a lute she knew, but they were the melodies that brought her back to the smells of grain in summer and fresh bread in her mother's oven.

Gandrett forced her heart to stop singing with it.

She needed a clear head—something that would not be easy considering the scent of flowers smashing her brain into a fuzzy substance. *Focus. Find the exits. Mark details.*

"After today's hunt and a party like this, Demea will surely make certain you'll never miss a shot in your life." Gandrett gave Armand an appreciative glance.

He just shrugged—"I never miss a shot anyway."—and stepped into the hall, pulling Gandrett with him.

She hid her grimace, faking interest in the wall behind them, and spotted a wide set of stairs at the far end of the corridor that led away from the festivities. The entrance. This led to the entrance. She knew from the maps there was only one stairwell in this castle that was wide enough for ten armed guards to walk beside each other, and it led to the main gate in the south-west.

As if to confirm her thought, a breeze of fresh air blew into her face, accompanying the guests in finery stepping past them from the direction of freedom.

"Wine?" In the meantime, Armand had taken the opportunity and waved over one of the servants carrying trays of delicate, crystal glasses, picking up one of them and holding it out for her with his free hand.

Never. Gandrett had sworn an oath to Vala. Her body, that of a fighter, needed to be pure at any time to keep at full strength and mental clarity. She was about to shake her head then reconsidered. No one could know what she was. If she even pretended to drink that wine, it wouldn't raise unnecessary questions.

She un-looped her arm from his and took the glass from his long, sure fingers, swirled it, raising it to her face, and took a whiff. "Beautiful," she remarked. "The color, the bouquet." She had picked up some phrases during her time in Ackwood. Nothing that would pass her as an expert but enough to keep her inconspicuous.

He smiled and took a glass for himself before he led her further into the hall, Gandrett dodging the poofy skirts of swirling dancers.

At the end of the hall, a dais hosted a wide table filled with foods on silver platters. On the throne beside it, Hamyn Denderlain sat and watched in boredom how his court was enjoying itself.

It took Gandrett a while before she noticed people staring at her, some whispering behind their lace fans as their eyes devoured her like a sensation.

"Ignore them." Armand took her hand, his calloused fingers firm around hers. "They stare at anyone I bring to our parties."

Gandrett wasn't certain she wanted to laugh or cry at his words. So she decided to put on a mask of polite smiles and keep it for the rest of the night.

"So you do this frequently, milord?" she shuttered her eyelids and pretended to nip at the wine.

"Do what?" He grinned.

"Rescue young women and bring them back to your castle to show them what life could be like?" She wanted to sound charming, tried, but the words came out a tad sharp.

Armand laughed. "Only when it serves my purpose."

"And what purpose may that be?" She withdrew her hand from his and took a step closer to the dance floor, leaving Armand with the view of the cascade of curls Deelah had created, and smiled at the young man on the other side of the dancing crowd.

"That, milady, is my concern," he stepped on the dance floor, blocking the young man on the other end from view, and held out his hand, "not yours."

Gandrett eyed him, breathing through the annoyance the young lord induced despite his pretty face, and said, "I'm afraid this room is spinning without me even having to dance." She gestured at the spot on her head that had been bloody when she woke up in the forest.

Armand's hand remained extended in front of her, his eyes insisting she take it.

So she took it. She could always fake a sprained ankle later as Lady Crystal Brenheran had suggested.

The young lord's eyes flared with excitement as she set down her glass on a nearby table, placed her hand in his, and let him pull her to his chest.

Vala help her. This was real. She had envisioned how she would have to lie, pretend, snake her way into Armand's interest, and here she was, already in his arms. One of those locking around her waist as he pulled her into a spin and into the moving row of dancers.

Gandrett stumbled along, praying to the goddess that she wouldn't stomp on Armand's feet, and let him pull her further, further around the dance floor.

Until they passed by the young man who had smiled back a minute earlier. His eyes—

"For someone who lay splattered on the forest ground couple of hours ago, you dance exceptionally well," Armand commented on her uncoordinated movements as he steered her away from the man.

Gandrett cocked her head, trying to see past Armand's broad shoulders, but he kept adjusting his position so all she saw was the silver embroidery on his black jacket.

For someone who dances with a different woman every night, you're an exceptionally bad liar.

Gandrett sucked in a breath as Armand stopped in the center of the dance floor, staring down at her with narrowed eyes.

By Vala, had she spoken aloud? Judging by the tight look on his face, she had. What had she done? She couldn't jeopardize this mission by her thoughtlessness. She should apologize then and there—

Armand burst into laughter, his hazel eyes sparkling with delight. "I don't think anyone has ever spoken to me like that," he gasped between his rolling laughter.

Around them, people were staring as Gandrett took a step back, measuring the young lord's fit of amusement.

"I didn't mean to—" Gandrett stopped, no longer sure if an apology would make it better or worse.

But Armand waved off her words and grabbed her hand instead. "Come," he said, still chuckling as she let him lead her off the dance floor with curious gazes following them and whispers growing louder behind them. "Let's get something to eat."

Gandrett was only half-there as Armand guided her along the rows of tables and waved at a servant, whom he murmured something to before he guided her to the dais at the end of the room.

As she climbed up the stairs beside him, Lord Hamyn lifted his head and swept a gaze of distaste over Gandrett, then turned to his son. "You didn't have anything better to do than to bring her to the dance?"

Armand fashioned a smile that would have made Brax's pale. But his eyes were cold. Solid amber rather than golden honey.

"I was thinking you were going to keep that sort of entertainment to your own chambers," Hamyn continued, his eyes still on Gandrett as if he was trying to solve a riddle made of poison and thorns.

Gandrett thought of Everrun. Of the citadel and its thundering waterfall. Of the Meister and his lectures about obedience and discipline. About the unforgiving wind in the desert and the countless nights she had stayed up despite exhaustion, just to go over certain moves in her mind. To become the best. Vala's blade—that's what they called her at the priory.

And Vala's blade didn't waver with the words of a tyrant—a sexist tyrant, it seemed.

A gust of air escaped her nose as she dialed down her temper, little by little, her hands remaining relaxed at her sides, right where she would keep them to pull a sword the next moment.

No. She wouldn't let his words get to her.

Across the dais, by the edge of the fish-laden table, a movement caught her eye. Someone was staring at her—not the way the whispering crowd by the dance floor had, but a different type of movement. Fast and elegant like a cat on the hunt.

Gandrett tuned out Armand and Hamyn Denderlain, eyes tracking the shadow that was now hurrying for the alcoves of darkness in the wall behind the dais, until Armand's hand grabbed hers and pulled her around to the buffet of fish delicacies she could hardly keep down.

"Don't worry, Father," Armand said over his shoulder with a cool lightness that might have even made Nehelon gape in awe, "my chambers won't stay un-entertained either."

Furious. It didn't even closely describe how she felt as her steps, surprisingly light, breath unexpectedly calm, carried her back up the stairs.

Beside her, Armand was quiet. Eyes on the polished stone beneath their feet, hand clasping hers with too much force.

But she didn't complain.

His chambers. That's where he was going to lead her.

And she had a mission to accomplish. Gain his trust and protection so she would last long enough in Eedwood castle to have a chance of finding Joshua.

She didn't ask questions as he led her past her own chambers and further down the hall to black double doors, a silver star engraved on each of the wings. She didn't fight as he opened them and motioned for her to enter, nodding at the guards positioned on each side of the entrance with a smirk.

She didn't gawk at the midnight-blue tapestry, golden threads woven into it in intricate patterns, or the scent of the sea that carried from the miles-away shore through the widespread balcony doors on a chilly breeze. Only when she spotted the bed—wider than the four-poster bed in her own chambers and glazed in gold and midnight-blue—did she yield and swallow the lump in her throat.

Armand, no longer bothering to smile, sauntered to the other end of the room where he dropped into a wide, blue, velvet chair and eyed her like the hunter who had brought down the wolf.

Gandrett fought her fury with the soothing sensation of Nehelon's dagger strapped along her thigh. She would reach for it if needed, Joshua or no. Vala's child. Even if she hadn't chosen it. She wouldn't let an arrogant, royal brat take her oath away.

Her fingers curled at her sides as she stared him down. A polite smile still sat on her lips, but she was ready to destroy him if he as much as lifted a finger against her.

"You're different from the others," he said, face not warming toward her. "I think I'd like you to stay."

Gandrett tilted her head, unsure if anything she could say would make the situation better. The small portion of fish she had managed to force down her throat with a smile earlier didn't help the nausea creeping up on her.

"My father acts like that with all of them," he shrugged, "but you..." He got to his feet, eyeing her with cool interest. "You're different. He outright hated you."

Delight crept across his features, and Gandrett didn't dare inquire what exactly it was about it that made him so happy. But his face turned serious again as his gaze grazed over her body, lingering on her arms. "You have many scars, Gandrett Starhaeven," he noted, brows knitting into a frown.

She cringed. Her scars. As thin as they were, as many were they. She hadn't thought about them when she had slipped into a gown with nothing but midnight-blue cords to hold up the bodice, slinging over her shoulders. She hadn't given it a thought. But now—

Armand's attention was on them and them only. He sauntered closer, surveilling every inch of bare skin with an eagle-like glare. Her arms, her shoulders, whatever of her back wasn't covered by her curls. The unscathed skin on her chest where the dress exposed the beginning roundness of her breasts. They lingered there until the sound of a loosed breath filled the air. Not hers.

"You bare a lot of scars for a wealthy merchant's daughter," Armand noted, gaze still on that spot where no scars lay.

She felt it, the cognitive dissonance that arose inside the young lord like tendrils of water rising when Surel lifted her hand over a pool to summon it. Fast. She needed an explanation. And fast.

"Money doesn't make men any less cruel," she said coldly, her heart raging in her chest from true, authentic fear. "It only buys the silence of those who witness it."

At her words, Armand recoiled as if she had struck him in the face. He ambled back to the chair and slumped there, face not showing a hint of the laughing, taunting boy she'd thought him to be. "There's a door behind that tapestry," he waved a hand at the part of the wall with the strongest accumulation of gold threads. "It will take you to your chambers."

The corridor didn't take her to her chambers. She had no idea where else it could lead for it hadn't been on any of Nehelon's maps.

Gandrett followed the narrow passage to the first door she could find, hidden under layers of dust and spider webs so heavily that she had almost missed it, then had cracked it open and checked whether the air was clear.

It was. But instead of taking her to her own chambers, she found herself in a side corridor that bore little to no light. She followed it long enough to know she couldn't be anywhere near her chambers. Too long had she been groping along the rough stone walls not to know she must have long passed it.

Lucky. She had been so lucky that Armand hadn't pushed for more information. That he hadn't insisted on that entertainment.

She could only imagine what his situation with his father was if he found such delight in upsetting him.

And she... Gandrett found absolutely no delight in being a tool in someone's games. For that, she figured, was the only thing she was.

The tunnel turned right and descended in shallow stairs, into the gloom of complete darkness.

Turn around. That's what she should be doing. But she was already in motion, away from Armand, no sound other than her footsteps accompanying her into the blackness. She wanted to know where the tunnel ended. Armand had already told her one end went to her chambers, so she must have chosen the wrong door. And this one arm of the tunnel might be her ticket to snooping around the castle. And one day, maybe also her escape route.

So she continued into the darkness while Armand was convinced she was tucked under the blankets. The dance would probably continue into the morning hours, and no one would come looking for her. Still, if they did, they wouldn't find it suspicious if she wasn't in her own chambers, for Armand had made it so very clear what he intended for their night together.

It was only when a soft whisper disturbed the echo of her slow footsteps that she halted, one hand braced on the wall, the other lifting her skirts to reach for her dagger.

The whispering stopped.

Gandrett held her breath. She could hardly see her hand before her face, but far ahead, there was a spot of light.

"Who's there?" Gandrett asked in a low but steady voice. She had spent enough days in the dark tunnels of the citadel to keep her calm.

No answer.

Something moved near the light, as if she had disturbed it, and skittered away too fast for her to make out anything.

With cautious steps, she followed the light, pulling her dagger as she moved along the doorless wall. The temperature had dropped, making her shiver in her sleeveless gown, and the stone under her fingers became slippery.

Cold. So cold. She was sure her breath had turned into puffs of haze before her face could she see it.

She could bear it no longer. What was this place?

The light she had seen didn't seem to come any closer even when she continued walking for a minute until her breath hurt in her lungs.

She had to turn around—get out before she would freeze alive down here.

With heavy legs, she made the turn, hilt of her dagger threatening to stick to her hand from the glacial cold. Her steps were slow. Slower even now that her path was uphill. And no matter how much she pushed herself, her legs were growing heavier with each step. As if they were made of lead.

Her breathing was shallow when the temperature rose slightly as she made it to a sharp left turn she couldn't remember taking before. But she didn't stop. Anything but going back into the freezing cold.

One step after the other. Up and up. Until her knees buckled and it was all she could do to creep forward, away from the ice behind her.

She made a mental note to tell Nehelon what a bastard he was to send her into this hell. If she ever got out of there. Vala help her, she was on her hands and knees, dragging her skirts through the dust as she forced herself to keep going.

And then, the darkness lifted like a veil, and a breeze of warmth touched her shoulders and back. Her eyes adjusted, and she noticed footsteps nearby. Right behind the wall beside her. The door beside her.

She lifted one weak hand to the rusty knob above her head and turned.

Addie Blackwood's heart almost stopped when the wall beside her opened and a dirty, female shape slumped into the corridor, right where she had been about to set her next steps, with a groan.

She wasn't one to be startled easily. Vala knew, she was used to surprises—bad ones mostly. Her time in the mountain prison in the north had most certainly taught her that no matter how bad things got, it could always get worse.

"Are you all right, Miss?" She set down her bucket and knelt by the young woman whose eyes were blinking as if she was struggling to keep her focus. In her hand, she was clutching a dagger.

Addie tried not to shy away from the blade and touched a hand to the woman's forehead. Cold. That woman needed help.

And her lips were an unhealthy shade of blue, as if someone had pushed her out into the snow the way the guards had done to her in the north. The most northern point of Neredyn, even beyond Lands End, where a solid blanket of ice and snow-covered the mountain ranges.

The woman didn't speak but instead rolled to the side and braced herself on her hands and knees, crawling forward until her feet had made it out of the doorway.

Addie peeked through the door, catching a glimpse of dim light and gray rock.

"Don't," the girl said through gritted teeth and kicked—with what seemed like her last strength—the door shut.

Addie watched it melt into the polished stone wall of the corridor she had been following, leaving nothing but smooth surface and no hint of the door the girl had just crept through.

She was tempted to run her hand over the stone to ascertain herself she hadn't dreamt, but the girl had cowered over her knees beside her and was shivering uncontrollably, her shoulders and arms left bare by the elegant gown she was wearing.

"Come," Addie took the girl by the arm and pulled her up with a force that made her muscles scream and picked up her bucket. "We need to get you somewhere warm." The girl let Addie tug her along, stumbling beside her as she led her toward the servants' kitchen where a flame was always kept alive in the oven in case any of the courtiers fancied a late meal. "How ever did you get there?" She asked as she dragged the quiet girl down the stairs and into the familiar space that smelled of herbs and bread and stale bothenia ale.

While the nobles had been dancing, every servant who could spare a minute had cheered to Demea's blessing that the young lord had ensured by killing the wolf. Her heart picked up pace at the thought of him. Even if he had never noticed her in the shadows of Lady Linniue's chambers, she had been there when he visited. It happened rarely but often enough for Addie to notice how handsome his face was from up close, how his hair looked like molten honey when it trickled out of his ponytail.

"We're almost there," she reassured the girl and wrapped one arm around her cold, shaking shoulders.

The heat hit Gandrett like a blow in the face.

"You'll be fine, Miss," the servant girl kept repeating as she led her into the empty kitchen, her light-blue eyes spilling worry as she spoke. "You'll be fine."

She sat Gandrett down on a three-legged chair, which she had pulled up to the stove where a pot of something hearty was steaming along.

Gandrett tucked her dagger between the folds of her skirt, wrapped her arms around her torso, and watched the fog rise. "Thank you."

The girl started but smoothed over her expression fast. She hadn't commented on the weapon nor attempted to take it away. "Maybe you should eat something," she suggested, eyes still a little nervous.

Gandrett scanned her head to toe. She wasn't wearing anything better than rags sewn together into a dress. She hadn't spotted a servant in the Brenheran household or here who was dressed like that. "You're probably right," she said to the girl, waiting for her reaction, which was similar to when she had thanked her.

Shaking her surprise, the girl hurried to a cupboard and pulled out a bowl then picked a spoon from a drawer.

"Here," she handed her the bowl after filling it up just enough that it didn't spill in Gandrett's shaking hands. "This will help."

Something in the girl's eyes told Gandrett she knew exactly what she was talking about.

She eyed the girl over her bowl as the hot scent of Sivesian spices and bothenia stew filled her nose, easing some of the shudders.

"It's not the fish they serve upstairs."

For a fraction of a second, Gandrett was tempted to tell the stranger that she had no interest in the fish they served upstairs. That it still sat in her stomach like a salty lump that had frozen in the tunnels.

"What was that?" she asked eventually, deciding she'd let the girl reveal what she knew first.

The girl shifted her weight, exposing poorly made boots under the hem of her skirts. "I have never noticed a door there." She looked to the ground as if following Gandrett's gaze. "It disappeared right after you closed it. As if it was never there."

They both kept silent for a while, Gandrett stirring her stew and sipping from the spoon in regular intervals as the girl stood, pretending she wasn't there at all.

"I've never seen anything like it," Gandrett mused.

The girl remained silent.

"What's your name?"

"Addie." Her voice was low as if she didn't want to speak.

Gandrett asked anyway, her limbs slowly warming by the stove, "Who else knows about those corridors?"

"If anyone knew, they would surely not tell me." Addie averted her gaze, scanning the polished surfaces of the kitchen with weary eyes instead.

Something in her demeanor told Gandrett that Addie had little to gain in this court and little to lose in her life. A kindred spirit.

"My name is Gandrett," she offered and found Addie blinking at her in surprise.

"The trophy," she whispered, then clasped her hand over her mouth, eyes turning wide.

Gandrett didn't know if she even wanted to understand what had been done to the kind girl that she was so afraid of speaking wrong.

"Armand's trophy?" Gandrett asked, more to clarify the meaning of Addie's words than because it was outrageous to call her that.

"Well... the lady he brought home from the hunt, I mean."

Gandrett smiled at Addie, imagining how Armand must have spread the news in the castle about the lady in need to whose rescue he'd so bravely come. No need to add that it wasn't Armand who had saved her. It had been the annoying, brooding Fae male who might or might not have kissed her while she'd recovered from a blow to the head.

"I didn't mean to upset you," Addie added, fear now plain in her eyes. "Please don't tell the young lord I said anything."

Her reaction made Gandrett wonder yet again if she had misread Armand. If he was indeed the evil the Brenherans thought him to be and not the hurt boy seeking his father's attention.

"I won't tell if you don't," Gandrett whispered, glancing at the kitchen door. "No one can know I wandered through hidden corridors in the wall."

Addie nodded in silent agreement. And who would believe a servant girl in rags if she told that the young lord's trophy had stumbled into the hallway through a door in the wall that was no longer visible? Sad as it was that Addie's word wouldn't hold against that of a lady was to Gandrett's advantage.

However, she herself knew exactly how not having a voice felt. At the priory, she hadn't had one until she'd become Vala's blade. And before, as a daughter of farmers, a child...

She finished her stew in silence. All the time Addie waited, standing on the side as if taking leave was even scarier than staying.

And all that time, an unspoken question hung in the air between them: how could Gandrett have been half-frozen on a mild spring night in a castle with hearth fires in every chamber?

Gandrett didn't let herself think about it too much. She had no idea how long she had been down there. Only that Armand had sent her in.

Had he known he was sending her to her potential death? Was that why he brought home another girl every second day—if she trusted what she'd pieced together? Was Armand even more dangerous than she could have imagined?

"I have no clue where we are in the castle, Addie," Gandrett said with a smile, forcing any thought about the icy cold and the whispering in the tunnels from her mind, "Would you mind showing me how to get back to my rooms?" She went through the maps in her mind. The servants' kitchen wasn't anything that had been displayed in the plans Nehelon had laid out. Just a general servants' area on the ground floor between the north and the east tower. She must have been several levels underground in those tunnels. A shiver crossed her shoulders, and she shook her hair over them, hoping to hide the goosebumps that rose on her back and neck. "My rooms are in the west tower, I think, somewhere near Lord Armand's chambers," she added, attempting to look lost but wasn't sure Addie bought it.

The girl took her empty bowl but didn't give a sign of whether she would help.

"I would go on my own and ask the next guard I can find to escort me back, but somehow I think that would raise more questions than it would be helpful." She glanced at the dagger in her lap, and Addie's gaze followed her.

"Were you running from someone?" she asked lowly but not weakly. "The young lord? Is that why you are carrying that?" She gestured at the blade.

Gandrett shook her head. "I thought I saw something behind that door," she explained as truthfully as she could without giving away any bit about her mission or what had happened with Armand or in the tunnels.

The girl pursed her lips, eyes still on the blade.

Gandrett picked it up, pulled up her skirt on one side to sheath the dagger, then smiled. "I won't need it when I'm with you."

Addie's face relaxed, and she nodded. "Come," she picked up her bucket and gestured for Gandrett to follow her. "I'll show you the way."

andrett marked every turn, every door, every narrow
window on the way back to her chambers. The path
Addie was leading her wasn't the route the members
of this court were taking, but a narrow corridor that seemed
to be exclusive to servants, some of which glanced at Gandrett,
her dirty clothes and probably face, too, as they bustled along
to take care of their chores during this cheery night of Demea's
celebrations. She marked those faces, too, and was relieved
neither Deelah nor the middle-aged man who seemed to be
reporting directly to Armand were among them.

After a couple of minutes of ascent through narrow
stairwells, Addie pointed left where the corridor split.

"This leads to the west tower," she said, face unreadable. "Follow the main corridor, and you'll end up right by the young lord's door." Something bitter entered her tone, but Gandrett didn't dare inquire.

"Thank you, Addie," she gave the girl a half-smile. "If there is anything I can ever help you with, let me know."

Addie's eyes widened, but she said nothing as she smiled and disappeared back the way they'd come.

Gandrett didn't waste any time looking after her, but instead took the left path and followed it with a tight chest until it opened into the wide hallway Armand had led her down earlier that night. She loosed a breath. She was safe—or as safe as anyone could be in this castle.

She made her way, sneaking from doorway to doorway until she got to familiar black doors engraved with silver stars. The guards were gone, and Gandrett didn't stop to marvel at the carving before she ran to her own chambers, the rustling of her skirts the only sound filling the air.

She had never been more relieved to see a door close behind her. As it clicked shut, she closed her eyes and leaned against it, resting her head against the wood behind, and she took deep breaths, trying to calm her beating heart. She was lucky those guards were no longer at Armand's doors or they might have—

"How nice of you to return," Armand's voice greeted her from the other end of the room, making her heart stop and her eyes snap open. "I was beginning to wonder if I am really that terrible of a host."

To Gandrett's relief, there was no anger on his features as he rose from the crimson sofa where she had woken up only hours ago.

"I was coming here to—" He stopped mid-sentence, eyes going distant, and he shook his head. "I don't really know why I came here." He rubbed the bridge between his eyes with two fingers as if he was thinking hard. "Anyway, I found your chambers empty."

Gandrett was still recovering from the shock. She knew what her dirty clothes and face must look like—like she had tried to run. She braced herself and decided to take the same approach she took during a sword fight. Assess her opponent, find his weaknesses, bring him down.

The dagger on her thigh weighed heavily as she took a step toward the young lord.

"Didn't you know it's impolite to intrude into the chambers of a lady uninvited?" Mckenzie's words. "I could have been... indisposed," she chose her wording carefully, watching his face change to confused. He was in a strange mood. She could tell from the look on his face, his eyes still looking her over.

"You don't look *indisposed* to me at all, Lady Starhaeven." He pulled his lips upward at the edges, the resulting smile not in the slightest resembling anything she had seen on those features before. "Dirty, but not indisposed. Have you been out on a night stroll?" he offered, smile tightening. "You could have asked me to join."

"You sent me away," she poked, and by the flare in his eyes, she knew she had found it. His pride was what weakened him.

And that was probably why he had come to her chambers—to make sure the impression she had of him wasn't weak. "You'll probably kick me out in the morning anyway... as I was useless for your *entertainment.*"

There it was. No restraint lingered in her words, no leash keeping her thoughts to herself as she hit him with words she knew would trigger him in his pride.

She needed to keep a clear head even if she was drained. She had almost frozen down there in those tunnels. Did he know? Had he sent her there and was only checking in to see if she had survived.

Armand's smile had vanished, leaving his features blank.

"Where were you?" he asked flatly.

Gandrett took another step closer. If she made it past him to her bed, she could grab Nehelon's knife from her pillowcase. Then there was still the dagger on her thigh even if she had no intention of revealing her legs before him. How she yearned for her plain acolyte uniform so she'd be able to fell him with a few jumps and kicks.

"I won't ask again," Armand eyed her with a gaze that didn't allow for defiance.

So Gandrett took another step and changed her tactics, giving him an icy look. "I slipped in your secret, little passageway so I went to find someone to bring me clean clothes to wear." She took another step, getting close enough to her bed to dart for it if he attacked.

But his eyes shuttered. "What?" He stared at her as if she didn't make sense.

Oh, this was already so off-track. Where had the illusion of Lady Starhaeven gone?

Gandrett sighed through her nose. "I slipped." She couldn't bring herself to tell him about the icy caverns under the castle, the whispering shape in the dark, the minutes she'd thought she'd freeze down there. "And now let me go take a bath so I can get an hour of sleep before you kick me out." She stepped even further toward her bed, making it look like a subconscious gesture.

He didn't seem to notice.

"Why didn't you come to *me*?" His voice was raw, eyes two hazel disks that let Gandrett glimpse a different Armand than the one she'd met.

The words were on her tongue—ready to be released. *Because I don't believe you would have helped me.*

He read them in her eyes anyway. "I saved you in the forest, Gandrett. I brought you back to Eedwood castle to have my healers look after you." His throat bobbed. "Do you think I wouldn't help you with something as easy as fresh clothes?"

His answer left her empty.

Armand sat back down on the sofa and crossed an ankle over his knee. His hands dug into his hair as if he was trying to make sense of something, pulling strands out of his ponytail.

Gandrett watched him, taking the moment of silence to breathe and remind herself that she wasn't there for Joshua Brenheran, no matter how much any captive deserved to be freed, but for her family—to see them again.

"You're right, milord." She sought his gaze and sat on the edge of the bed, hands in her lap. "I should have come to you instead."

He gave her a nod as a sign of appreciation. "What makes you think I'll kick you out in the morning?" His features were open, not the cocky, cheery, young man or the evil lord she had expected, but someone with an honest interest in her thoughts. She swallowed.

"Word spreads within the castle," she said with a shrug. The conversation had taken a turn from which there was no going back anyway.

His lips curled. "Gossip spreads fast in this castle," he agreed, "but only the gossip I *want* to be spread." He winked, some delight returning to his face.

"So it's not true?" she asked unsure how to actually phrase the question.

"That I bring home a different girl every other night?" He leaned back and crossed his hands behind his head. "Absolutely." He gave her a wicked grin, and she wanted to stick out her tongue at him. But before she could embarrass herself, he added. "But not for my entertainment the way my father thinks—the way I let the entire castle believe."

Gandrett braced herself for the revelation while he measured her from across the room, probably weighing whether he could trust her enough to share his secret.

Apparently, he did, for he said, "My sole entertainment is to torment my father with the embarrassment of bringing home one floozy after the other." He chuckled to himself.

Gandrett's jaw dropped.

"He hates you. I could tell from the look on his face." He seemed to be enjoying the memory. "I'm not going to let you go that easily."

Gandrett exhaled a breath of relief and worry. She had achieved a milestone for her mission—not being kicked out, earning Armand's trust. But the fact that he had decided to keep her at the palace only put her from one sort of prison into the next. Yet, that was what her entire life was going to be like—wasn't it?

"Who says I'd like to stay?" she asked, keeping all emotion from her voice.

In response, Armand's gaze fell on her bare arms, on the thin scars she never wasted a thought on. "My father might be a different type of cruel, but your scars tell me you could do with some time away from that."

He didn't need to point his finger for her to know what he was referring to. So she played along. Not really played, considering the Meister was the only father figure she'd had in the past ten years.

"We can send word to your family if you'd like," he offered, "tell them that you were injured during your hunt and we are keeping you here until the wounds heal."

He didn't need to say that he wasn't referring to the blow to the head in the forest.

Intimate. This conversation had turned so intimate so fast, touching layers of herself Gandrett had never dared question.

She laced her fingers together the way they did at the priory for meditation hours, just to have something familiar to hold on to. "I don't think anyone will miss me." She made it sound like a sad truth. And it wasn't as far from the truth as she wanted to make herself believe.

Armand just smiled. A warm and open gesture. As if he had shed his masks and only now she was seeing him. "All the better. Then I won't have a guilty conscience keeping you to myself."

As she returned his smile, he laughed the way he had with Deelah.

Addie's footsteps echoed off the rough stone as she carried the filled bucket up for the third time that day. Even though it was late at night—more early morning—Lady Linniue had demanded another one. So she had made the arduous way down to the well once more, her mind still on Gandrett. How she had practically fallen into the corridor through the stone wall. How the door had sealed behind her. The icy cold of her skin...

She was the young lord's guest, and yet she seemed to have been on the run from something. From him? That would surprise her. For even when he pulled off that heartless, cocky, womanizer noble to perfection, she could see right beyond that facade where the pain over the loss of his mother still stung deeply.

With a gaze out the window, she could tell that dawn would be breaking soon. The music in the castle had ebbed away, and the last guests were leaving in their carriages, singing and swaying, probably drunk with sparkling wine and the music.

When Addie knocked on Lady Linniue's door, a young man opened it, a dismissive look in his emerald eyes as from the room, the lady's voice demanded, "Leave the bucket, and make yourself scarce."

So Addie did.

Lim greeted Gandrett with a whinny as she entered the stables the next day, his head bobbing up and down in something that could be interpreted as enthusiasm.

Her head hurt again, whatever potion Deelah had rubbed onto her wound obviously having worn off. Gandrett didn't spend a moment thinking what that liquid might have been, for there were other, more pressing things keeping her mind busy.

"Are they feeding you well?" she asked, half-expecting the horse to answer. Nehelon's horse.

She wondered what he would make of the news she bore. That Armand Denderlain wasn't half the villain the Brenherans imagined. At least, not when it came to how he treated the women he brought home.

She and Armand had talked until the sun had risen, and she couldn't tell if it was the wine he had retrieved from his room once they had gotten into a flow, but he had poured out his heart about his mother's death and that he thought his father was responsible for it. Responsible in what way exactly, he still intended to find out.

Whether or not he knew about the icy tunnels under the castle, Gandrett couldn't tell. With no word he'd spoken had he given away even the hint of it. Still, Gandrett knew better than to trust a noble who had a moment of trust. His trust had been part of her mission. And now, it was time to get to the core of it.

Lim nudged his nose to her arm and nibbled at the loose gray sleeve of the dress Deelah had brought for her this morning. She patted his nose, thinking about whether or not it was a good idea to ask Armand to go on a ride with her. Just to see how well guarded the castle was, to get a better impression of the immediate terrain around the massive stone fortress. She hadn't had a chance on her way in, given she'd fallen victim to the aftermath of her encounter with the tree trunk.

But Armand was probably still between his sheets, sleeping off the excitement of the night.

That left her with some spare time to explore the inconspicuous parts of the castle. The main corridors on her level and the level below. The hallway leading to the great hall where the remainders of last night's event had been scrubbed away by busy hands and the courtyard that had led her to the stables.

"Feel free to look around," Armand had invited her before he'd tumbled through the hidden door behind the painting of the castle, "but by all means, let me sleep in."

She had done exactly that and taken off by herself, smiling at every guard, pretending not to notice the whispers behind her back, curtseying at a yawning Lord Hamyn Denderlain whose eyes were shadowed with dark bruises as if he hadn't slept at all, and not cringed at the bark he'd given her as he'd noticed her by the stairwell.

Much to her satisfaction, the dress she wore today accommodated both weapons Nehelon had given her. It was also warmer than last night's gown. A blessing Deelah thought practical rather than pretty even if Armand might have probably preferred the latter.

Lim whinnied again as Gandrett remained in her thoughts for a while.

"What's wrong, buddy?" She ran her hand over the soft fur on his neck and was about to take a step back from the wood that separated her from the horse's stomping hooves when she noticed a crow on the windowsill to the courtyard.

At her glare, it cocked its head, reminding her surprisingly of the fat bird that had followed her around at the priory.

"Shoo." She waved her hand more to reassure herself she wasn't going crazy but that those murky eyes were really focused on her.

The bird didn't move. Instead, it hopped closer, settling right between Lim's ears. The horse stomped again but kept its neck still.

It was only when the crow clicked its beak that Gandrett noticed the small item tied to its leg. It cocked its head again, waiting.

Gandrett glanced down the long clean-swept corridors to both sides, finding no soul besides the hay-chewing horses in their stalls.

With quick fingers, she reached for the crow, Lim lowering his head to help, and carefully extracted a small scroll from the cord around its leg. The crow clicked its beak at her, still waiting, so Gandrett unfurled the parchment and read.

If you read this, it means Riho found you alive and on your own. If you want to deliver a message, talk to him. He'll find me.

Gandrett attempted to control the pace of her heart as her eyes flew over the scripted lines. A message from Nehelon. And a channel to the outside world.

"So you are Riho," she said to the bird which, again, clicked its beak, expectation brightening its eyes. "I have a message for Nehelon."

Addie watched Gandrett across the yard from the windows in the stairwell. She looked better than last night. Not as cold, not as bothered, scared even. Her chestnut hair was flowing behind her in soft waves rather than the thick curls from the night before, and her stride, even if she concealed it well, her movements reminded Addie more of that of a warrior than of a lady.

Maybe it was the angle or that she had seen Gandrett sheath that blade in such efficient, professional movements that she couldn't forget the sight of it.

More—definitely more than she let on.

Addie didn't linger, her bucket weighing heavier than normal in her hands.

She couldn't wipe the sight of the young man from her mind; how he had studied her while she'd set down the bucket before the door. How his hand had darted for it that moment she had let go and taken a step back. Eyes like gems. Emerald and glowing even in the dim light of the night.

Addie shuddered and continued walking.

She made it to the lady's floor and was about to cross over to the east tower when footsteps carried through the usually empty corridor.

Addie stopped in an alcove where a set of steel armor was propped on a low dais. A relic of wars long gone past. Not the type of war that was now plaguing Sives. Addie saw the soldiers leave under Lord Hamyn's command and small groups riding out under Armand's command. Whenever they returned, there was blood on their hands and ash staining their uniforms.

She didn't want to think about what they were up to while they were gone. Who they killed and who they spared. As long as a good portion of them returned safely—including the young lord.

The footsteps stopped, and Addie's heart picked up pace instead. Invisible. That's what she was in this court, and it was better than being at the focus of Lord Hamyn's temper or Lady Linniue's gossiping. Only the young lord was someone she would like to be noticed by—just once. Even if he wouldn't see anything more than a dirty slave clothed in rags.

"Who's there?" a cautious male voice asked.

Addie held her breath, her bucket cutting into the inside of her fingers as she pulled it closer.

"I know you are there." The voice trembled.

Addie didn't speak. Didn't dare as much as think.

The footsteps continued, coming closer until Addie could see a pair of brown boots. The rest was covered by the suit of armor.

But the man wasn't the only one who had been spotted.

So fast Addie couldn't brace herself, the man was upon her, hard grasp restraining her, forcing her forward out of her hiding place.

She didn't struggle. She had learned in the prison in the north what defiance brought with it.

So she held still, letting him drag her forward, water spilling from her bucket as she stumbled along.

"You." The man blinked at her with emerald eyes.

Addie blinked in response. It was the young man from Lady Linniue's room.

As he eyed her with what appeared to be relief, Addie dared to take a better look at the sharp angles and broad planes of his face now that daylight brightened his features.

"I thought you were—" He loosed his grasp on her upper arms, probably leaving bruises where his fingers had been placed. Addie didn't flinch. And the young man didn't finish his sentence.

There was fear written on his features, distorting them slightly but doing nothing to hide how handsome he was.

His eyes darted in both directions as if making sure they were alone. Then his hand shot out, clutching hers, and he fell to his knees. "Help me."

His eyes kept staring at her, regardless of her inability to react, his grasp tightening on her hand. But despite the memories of violence the force of his hand induced, he didn't seem to intend to hurt her.

"Get me out of here before it happens again," he pleaded, face ashen.

Addie searched for the shreds of courage the prison in the north had left her with and knelt as well, bringing her head to the same level.

She hadn't given it a thought, but before last night, she had never seen the young man.

"Who are you?" she asked, setting down her bucket and grabbing his hand in an attempt to peel his fingers off hers.

"Later," he urged and held her gaze. "You're Lady Linniue's servant. You know your way around the palace. Get me out of here." The young man seemed to be about to vomit his guts up.

Addie considered offering him the bucket but then shied away, considering the consequences that would surely follow once the lady found out what she had let this young man do to the water inside.

It wasn't as if anyone had ever told her what exactly that water was. Why it was so crucial for Lady Linniue to have it available in her chambers at all times, why Addie was woken in the cold dead of night just to make the cumbersome path down under the north tower and back up again. Addie never asked. She knew from the prison in the north what could happen to people who asked too many questions.

That was probably why Lady Linniue had brought her in from there. And she would be eternally grateful to the gods for that small mercy. At least she wasn't pushed out in the snow at any sign of disobedience.

"Even if I wanted to—" Addie considered. Her chest tightened at the despair in his eyes.

She couldn't betray the lady. The price she'd pay would be...

What if the lady never found out? What if...

"Tell me your name," she demanded. "And I might think about it."

Memories of days that she'd hoped to escape the prison in the north flashed in her mind. She would have given anything for the opportunity to flee. Would have paid any price. Even if no one would ever believe that prison existed. She'd tried in the first weeks at Eedwood castle to find an open ear, find someone who helped her get back home.

But when she had mentioned Lands End, they had only laughed at her. So she stopped. She kept to herself. She no longer looked for a way out. For even if the castle looked like an average one, she knew how well guarded the walls were, how no one entered without permission.

Even the Brenheran brutes who had intruded this past winter only to be fought off by those relentless guards—guards under the young lord's command, she reminded herself—had failed to achieve whatever they had come for. So she had heard the other servants talk.

"Joshua," the young man said quietly, his gaze never yielding, begging her to hear him.

Addie's heart stopped as she looked him over, their hands locked between them in a pull-and-grasp struggle. His hair was a golden brown that reminded her of the fine horses in the stables, and his clothes were the same finery he had worn the night before.

"Why are you running, Joshua?" The question was as simple as it was damning.

Joshua's chin sank to his chest. "I have been trying to escape since the day I got here. I can't even tell how long I've been their prisoner."

She had heard the servants whisper about a prisoner. A noble one. From the Brenheran household. That was who the Brenheran brutes had come for that night—

"Joshua Brenheran." The pieces fell into place as Addie's hands went taut in the Brenheran heir's grasp.

He glanced at her, broken. "Help me. Please."

Nehelon picked up the hunting knife Gandrett had wanted to bring on her mission, the one he had denied her, and ran it over the log of wood for the millionth time. He hadn't counted the number of carvings he had made nor had he assessed their quality. The only thing he knew was that whatever he intended to carve, he ended up with a miniature-Gandrett in his hands.

A miniature-Gandrett he pulverized with his magic so no one would ever learn how much her allure sang to him. And it wasn't her face—he remembered every freckle on her cheeks, every fleck of gold in her eyes, every imperfection that made her so much more perfect—but it was her fierce heart that drew him in. Unyielding. Determined. Vala's Blade. They didn't call her that without a reason. Strong in so many more ways than just her fighting.

Nehelon sighed at the figurine between his fingers and snapped the fingers of his other hand, making it disappear into a cloud of dust. He watched the cloud carry into the skies from his position in the crown of a tree where he had made his temporary residence in the forest of Eedwood.

An upset caw disturbed his musing as Riho hopped onto his shoulder.

"Hello, friend," Nehelon flipped the knife in his hand and stuck it into the branch beside his knee the moment he spotted that the note was gone from the bird's leg.

Riho clicked his beak with impatience.

"Is she all right?" he asked unnecessarily. The absence of the small scroll of parchment was indicator enough that Gandrett had gotten his message.

Riho stalked up on Nehelon's shoulder until his beak was close to his ear and started whispering.

He loosed a breath. "Are you certain that's what she said?" he asked the bird. "Beneath the castle?"

Riho cawed as if offended Nehelon would even consider he could have misheard.

If what the bird said was right, that there were frozen caverns under the castle, then there was more to worry about than simply getting Joshua back. He cursed violently and creatively then pulled a piece of parchment from his pack and a pen from his breast pocket and started writing.

Don't go investigating in those tunnels again. Find Joshua and escape.

He didn't add the words pressing on his heart, that he would rather she stayed away from Armand, too. With the practice and control of centuries, it was easy to dismiss them. Almost like the dormancy the rest of his kind had fallen into.

He tied the message to Riho's leg and watched the bird take off, head resting against the tree trunk behind him.

It had been a long time since he had last heard of caverns like that—icy cold despite spring weather. The last time had been when the dragons of Lands End had befallen Neredyn. He shuddered. Those days lay in the past—centuries in the past. And what he remembered of the attacks wasn't pretty. Sacked cities, fields of dead soldiers who never even got a chance to lift their sword before the Dreads of the Skies rained flames upon them. It was still a miracle that they had been defeated.

Lands End was nothing more than a myth by now. A small settlement by the Northern Mountains that hadn't been re-populated after the dragons had died out. If Gandrett had encountered frozen tunnels, it could mean only one thing: someone was worshipping the god of dragons, attempting to summon the Dreads of the Skies

ddie sat in the servants' dormitory, knees pulled to her chin, and prayed that Vala would forgive her. Joshua Brenheran had sought her help—even if their encounter had been mere coincidence—and she had left him there in the hallway with little more than a pointer toward the gates. What had she done?

He had pleaded with her, had been on his knees. And she had chosen her own skin over his escape. Her own peasant skin.

Now, two days later, she hadn't seen any sign of him—neither in the hallways nor in Lady Linniue's chambers.

She had prayed to Vala in the prison in the north, and the goddess hadn't given a hint she cared—until that day Lady Linniue had marched into her cell, by the icy plains of the Northern Mountains, and brought her to Eedwood castle. And not one minute late. She might have frozen to death up there.

So now she had chosen the lady over Joshua Brenheran. No matter his pretty face. She had heard the rumors that Tyrem Brenheran was seeking to reign over all of Sives, that Ackwood wasn't enough any longer. And that his reign may be one of terror. At least that was what Isylte Aphapia of Ilaton said whenever she brought news from Ackwood. The lady seemed to travel a lot, given that her homeland was south of the mysterious and sleeping forests of Ulfray.

It didn't make her feel less guilty. She hadn't asked what it was he was scared would *happen again*. All she had done was calculate what Lady Linniue would do to her if she helped a Denderlain prisoner escape. But her conscience had kept her from informing the lady that her late-night visitor had tried to make a run for it.

Maybe he had even made it... But in that case, she would have probably heard about it by now.

With a grunt, Addie curled up on her side and blocked out her thoughts as best she could—the way she had learned to do during the freezing nights at the prison by Lands End.

Armand had made himself scarce over the past couple of days, and Gandrett had taken that as a sign that she could take the liberty to explore more than the obvious areas where her snooping didn't seem suspicious. There was nothing worth looking for in those parts of the castle anyway.

So Gandrett had decided to take a different approach and head down the corridor where Addie had brought her and see what the servants knew.

The guards at Armand's door smiled widely as she strolled past, playing with a lock of her hair and fluttering her eyelids at them. She had perfected that move over time, and it seemed it secured their lack of questions about where she was going or where she was coming from.

Oddly much freedom for a stranger in Denderlain court, but then, here she was nothing more than a merchant's daughter who liked to be called *milady*. Here she wasn't Vala's Blade. No one feared her for her fighting skills or her cunning. She had done her best to keep her head down except for those few times when she had run into Lord Hamyn, who always snarled at her, asking her if she didn't have some bedchamber she needed to attend to.

And she kept nodding every time he asked, making his eyes gleam with fury. She never failed to curtsey, to use the politest version of her fake smile—anything to help in the endeavor to keep Armand entertained. Even if it was in a very different way from what the rest of the court thought.

Gandrett went over the maps in her mind before she turned into the servants' corridor. She checked back over her shoulder three times, making sure she had taken the right path even though her training wouldn't betray her like that.

It was Nehelon's last message that had cautioned her to double-check every single door she stepped through, just to make sure it wouldn't disappear the second it closed behind her.

Through Riho, she had been able to inform Nehelon about the frozen tunnels beneath the castle, the whispering shadow, and that she was almost certain Armand wasn't going to kick her out after all—not after that first night. Secretly, she wondered if Nehelon would spend even half a thought on what may or may not have happened during that night. She also found herself contemplating that kiss that may or may not have happened in the forest and kept shoving the thought aside when her lips started tingling.

Busy chattering greeted her as she approached the kitchen. Servants in different uniforms darted in and out, carrying foods and ingredients in one or the other direction. No one heeded her a look until she passed by the storage room which led her even further than where Addie had led her.

"Need anything, Lady?" A short man with a heavy southern accent stopped on his path to the kitchen, a basket of eggs in his hands.

Gandrett seized the opportunity. With the same, polite smile she wore on all of her strolls through the castle, she laid one hand on her stomach and said, "What do I need to do to get some of that fresh bread I smelled on my way down here?"

The man chuckled. "That would be Poul's bothenia crust." He leaned a bit closer, apparently entirely at ease with the friendly guest strolling through the servant area. "He makes that for us only." His free hand waved at the buzz of people that were filing in and out of the kitchen.

Bothenia bread. Gandrett's stomach grumbled for real. She hadn't eaten bothenia bread since her childhood.

"It smells lovely," she grinned. A real grin. "Do you think Poul would make an exception for me?"

The man beckoned her to follow him, so she did, returning to the kitchen where she'd been warmed by its stove after the intermezzo in the frozen tunnels. She fashioned an impressed look at the sight. Everyone was going about their business, cutting vegetables, washing and slicing fruit, and in the corner by the stove, a man with little gray hair and a bemused smile was talking to the dough he was kneading on a wooden board. Steam rose from the pots on the stove beside him, spreading the smell of something sweet and spicy.

The man beside her called, "Hey, Poul."

Poul looked up, his hands remaining invested in the dough.

"I have someone who wants to try your secret bread."

Poul laughed at the sight of Gandrett's fine dress, the golden belt around her waist. "You can try, milady, but you might need to ditch that if the taste is to your liking."

Such bold words. Poul must feel at ease in this castle or he wouldn't speak to a stranger like that. Especially when her clothes clearly identified her as one of the inhabitants of the fine rooms in the higher floors.

Gandrett didn't mind. Only wondered.

Addie hadn't seemed that content. She'd even had a hard time looking Gandrett in the eye. Also, those servants were dressed way better than Addie's rags. Instinctively, she scanned the room, hoping to spot the girl and be able to ask some indiscrete questions. They already shared one secret, so maybe the servant girl was the only person she could truly trust in this court. Even if Armand had opened up to her about his frustration with his father, his suspicions. That didn't make him an ally. He was still top on the suspect list of keeping the Brenheran heir in the dungeons of Eedwood castle—

"I warn you," the man with the basket of eggs said as Poul abandoned his kneading, strolled over, and picked up something small and round which's crusty surface showed every imaginable shade of light brown. Gandrett's mouth watered. "It's addictive."

Gandrett didn't hesitate as she took the bothenia crust from Poul's floury hand. She only took the time to murmur a quick thank you, hypnotized by the smell of a happier childhood.

Poul chuckled as she groaned at the taste. "Don't get anything this tasty at your fancy dining table, do you?"

Gandrett wanted to strongly agree but held back when her gaze fell on the embroidered hems of her sleeves. No, she wasn't one of them even if she sure felt like it. At the priory, she was nothing more than a servant of Vala. Standing in this kitchen reminded her painfully of how much she missed Nahir's helpful advice. What would she say if she knew Gandrett was flirting and batting her eyelids at nobles to win them over?

"What are you doing down here?" It was Deelah's voice that brought her back to the present. The middle-aged woman cocked her head, brown curls sliding over her shoulders in disarray. "Does he know you're down here?"

Poul grinned at Deelah's frown. "Don't worry. She is in good hands."

"That's not what I'm worried about," Deelah growled and headed over to grab one of Poul's bothenia crusts. "It's what the young lord will think when his *guest*," she dragged the word out, giving it more meaning than Gandrett would like to hear, "prefers the company of some kitchen brutes rather than his refined company."

Poul roared with laughter as he returned to his dough. "Says the brute who used to be his babysitter."

They all laughed, and Gandrett ached to join in. Only, there was more in Deelah's words than she had spoken. She wanted Gandrett out of that kitchen.

So Gandrett thanked Poul for the bothenia crust, which she nibbled on her way out the door, closely followed by

Deelah, who showed more sign of relief on her lined features than Gandrett had felt when Armand had informed her he was going to keep her at the castle for a while.

"What's wrong, Deelah?"

The woman wiped her hand in her apron then grasped Gandrett's forearm with a firm grip. "Don't you dare go wandering down there alone ever again." The woman's green eyes gleamed with fear as she spoke.

"Why?" Gandrett simply asked, trying to not let show that she had registered the emotion.

Deelah pulled Gandrett to a halt at the corner where Addie had sent her off to her chambers. "Armand is a good boy—man," she corrected. "I've known him his whole life, and sometimes I was more of a mother to him than Lady Aphra, the gods cradle her soul." Her fingers dug harder into Gandrett's skin. "But there are others here at court who don't like seeing him settle for someone."

She started walking again, glancing back and forth along the corridor as if anxious they might be overheard, and didn't stop until they, passing Armand's door—the guards positioned there inclining their heads—made it to Gandrett's chambers. There, Deelah pulled Gandrett on the couch beside her and stared her down with a look that reminded Gandrett intensely of Nahir. "Armand hasn't been the same since Lady Aphra's death," she said in a hushed voice.

Gandrett didn't interrupt. Any information was better than having to search the entire castle for a captive whose face she'd only know from the similarities to the Brenherans with whom she had spent a month.

"Lord Hamyn..." Gandrett couldn't suppress the mention of that thought.

"Not only him," Deelah whispered.

Gandrett raised an eyebrow. This was a conversation she hadn't expected. Deelah was actually worried about her.

"I haven't kept my position in this castle for over twenty years because of Lord Hamyn's kindness but because of Lady Aphra, the gods cradle her soul. And after her death, it is by Armand's will only that I am still here." The woman held Gandrett's questioning gaze. "Armand doesn't deserve to carry out his father's bloody orders. Especially not when the only reason he is still Lord of Eedwood is because Lady Linniue declined the offer to rule long ago, giving her sister the throne instead."

Those were secrets, weren't they? How could she spill them in front of a near-stranger?

Gandrett studied the woman's eyes, the sparkle as she spoke of Armand with the affection of a mother rather than a servant.

"Why are you telling me this?" Gandrett asked truthfully.

Her lips curled in response. "Because in all these months, you are the first and only one worth talking to." She pursed her lips, hesitating before she continued, measuring Gandrett's face.

Gandrett willed polite emptiness onto her features.

"If Armand is to choose a bride to continue the Denderlain line, I want her to know exactly what she is getting herself into."

Gandrett's heart pounded. "Bride?" She panted, for once unable to keep her calm.

Deelah knitted her forehead into horizontal lines. "Lord Hamyn is not a Denderlain by birth but by courtesy of Armand, who is the true heir to his mother's title and throne." She studied Gandrett with a careful, yet warm smile. "He could have taken it right after Lady Aphra's death, but he chose to drift into a life of too many girls and few true friends, isolating himself even more than his position demands."

Gandrett swallowed. She had heard it before from Mckenzie's and Brax's lips why they didn't envy Joshua for being the one to inherit the West of Sives. But with Armand—

"If you are to be his bride one day, you will learn that Hamyn Denderlain doesn't exactly look forward to being replaced on the throne."

The throne. The way she said it reminded Gandrett why she was here. Why it was crucial she found Joshua and brought him back to Ackwood. Hamyn Denderlain was putting pressure on Lord Tyrem and Lady Crystal by holding their son hostage. That might clear the way for him to extend his reach even further west, once all those central-Sivesian villages had changed allegiance and hung blue-and-yellow banners from their windows instead of burgundy-and-gold.

So Gandrett let the woman believe what she wanted to believe and reached for her neck where the necklace Brax had given her hung alongside her mother's, pendants hidden beneath her dress.

"I haven't seen Armand this cheerful in a long time," Deelah said with a knowing look, folding her hands on her apron. "So whatever you are doing to him, keep it up." She winked, but her lips were tight. "And watch out who you trust in those halls. The kitchens have ears of all kinds, and you never know where a servant's loyalties lie."

"How do I know with you?" It was the first and only answer Gandrett could think of.

Deelah nodded in approval. "I want what's best for Armand. He's like a son to me, and if he has set his eyes on you, I want to protect you from harm so he can be happy."

Gandrett huffed, taken aback by the simple truth of the words Deelah had spoken.

And the implications for Gandrett.

If Armand really was looking for a bride—

"Thank you for the warning." Gandrett weighed the risk of asking, deliberating for a long moment before she spoke, "What kind of ruler would Armand be? Would he want east and west to unite?"

Deelah's face filled with pride. "After decades of bloodshed, Armand would want peace." It was a simple answer so full of hope that Gandrett didn't dare ask any further.

So she made a mental note to give Armand more credit the next time she saw him.

Even if the memory of the frozen tunnels still leaked into her bones.

Nehelon be damned. She needed to figure out what was going on under this castle. Gandrett waited until Deelah had closed the door behind her before she jumped to her feet and wheeled around, darting for her pillow to get the Fae male's knife.

With quick fingers, she checked Nehelon's dagger, which was strapped to her thigh, then changed into the emerald gown Deelah had put in her room last night. The one that had enough space to accommodate the extra knife in her sleeve where she wrapped a piece of cloth around her forearm and bound the blade to it before she pulled the sleeve over it.

Not one minute late, for the door bounced open, and in came Armand Denderlain, face frosty as the mountain ranges in the west and north, no hint of the *good boy* Deelah had just talked about. He didn't bother to give her a look before he flung himself on the crimson couch. "Will there be a day when being a Denderlain will get any easier?" he said by way of greeting, smoothing out his bloodied tunic. A sword hung by his side, the tang of iron still fresh from whatever battle he'd fought.

Gandrett, petrified by the fact that he had almost walked in on her hiding a smuggled-in blade, eyed him with what she hoped was more surprise than fear as beads of moisture were forming under the mass of hair that covered her neck.

Armand waved a lazy hand at her. "You, I suppose, dear Gandrett Starhaeven, are one lucky girl that your father doesn't care what happens with you."

With all the force of will she had, Gandrett sat on the edge of the bed and folded her hands in her lap. "And why would that be so, milord?"

He looked her over with the lackluster eyes of a desert mole and raised a hand as if saying, *Isn't that obvious?*

It wasn't.

"You know what my father expects of me?" He didn't wait for her to think up an answer before he continued. "Slay the enemy."

Gandrett hid the thrill his words induced. The enemy. House Brenheran. She didn't speak for fear her words might stop whatever rush of words may come from his lips.

"Over and over again. And I, being a good soldier—" He swallowed.

Gandrett knew that look. Armand Denderlain was deeply unhappy. It wasn't just that he made his father responsible for his mother's death, but that he despised anything and everything the man asked of him. She knew because that was how she felt about the Meister.

Gandrett saw two paths before her: one shining bright. The path of pretending to be something less than she actually was. To hide her strength, her skill, her mind. The path Mckenzie had taught her, the path Nehelon and Lord Tyrem would push her to take. The other—

Gandrett sighed through her nose, besieging Vala for her guidance before she got to her feet and crossed the room to sit on the sofa beside the frustrated Denderlain heir. "Why are you telling me this, Armand?"

His eyes found hers when she addressed him by his name rather than his title, warmth returning to his face, his lips twitching ever so slightly. "Because you're the only one in this court who couldn't care less who or what you are." He laid his fingers on her hand, which was resting on her knees. "That kind of freedom—" He stopped himself, scanning her face for emotions that weren't there. "The freedom to choose who you want to be."

Gandrett's face almost twisted at his words. Freedom. That was the reason she was there. Not because she had it, but—

"You are a lord's son..." She considered Deelah's words. "A lord, actually. Can't you make your own rules?"

He weighed her words, his eyes on her face, searching.

"No matter what rules I make, it won't stop the hatred, the loss of innocent lives." He brushed his fingers across hers once before he pulled back his hand and leaned back, resting his head against the sofa. "That war has been going on for too long."

"So make your soldiers stop threatening the people of Sives in order to ensure their loyalty."

"My father does that." He rubbed the bridge between his eyes with a blood-crusted hand.

Gandrett shuddered at the thought that he hadn't even taken the time to wash off the blood of whoever he had fought— or worse, killed—before storming into her room. "And you gladly follow his commands," she pushed. She wanted to know if it was true. If he *was* part of the groups who burned down houses and villages who defied Denderlain.

Armand stopped rubbing and turned his head, eyes wide. "I should lock you up in the dungeons for the way you speak to me," he said with a solid gaze. Then a smile cracked over his face. "I should have after the dance."

The memory was still fresh in Gandrett's mind. The music, the horrible fish... The young man who had smiled back at her from across the dance floor, his eyes so familiar—

Gandrett launched to her feet as it struck her. Familiar. Green. Emerald. Brenheran eyes.

She hadn't been close enough to be able to say for certain, but... She rubbed her fingertips against her temples, pacing the space before the sofa.

Armand pulled his feet closer so she wouldn't stumble over them.

Forgotten were Armand's words. His confessions of the person he wanted to be. The person he probably already was.

"You don't really think I would lock you in the dungeons," he remarked from the sofa as her pacing didn't stop.

But Gandrett was already trying to figure out if it could be true. "Why not?" she griped at him, letting more sharpness into her voice than any of her tutors in Ackwood would appreciate. "You already have a history of locking up nobles."

She held her breath, feet still restless as she waited, waited, waited for him to reply.

He didn't.

So Gandrett brought her legs to slow, her mind to stop racing, and eventually, her feet halted right before the young lord. "Is it not true, what the birds whisper?" She couldn't help but think of Nehelon and the crow he had sent. She would go on a trip with him all over again if that would relieve her from her duty to the House Brenheran, if it paid off what they had offered the Meister for her service.

Armand eyed her cautiously, and Gandrett quietly cursed. Damned be Demea and her hunt if she couldn't control herself enough to get Armand to speak.

"What do they whisper, exactly?" Armand had gotten to his feet, scanning her with lazy eyes. He stepped closer. And another step. Then leaned in until his lips were at her ear, hot breath tickling as he whispered. "You should know better than to think I'd ever lock you up, Gandrett. There are better things I could do with you."

Gandrett shuddered. It was a sensation like nothing she had ever felt before. Her blood started pounding in her veins. If she played his game, maybe she could coax something of value from his lips.

But, Vala help her—

What if this led down a path she wasn't ready for? A path she could never be ready for. Consecrated in Vala's name.

And she thought of something to say. Something that would draw a line so she wouldn't get tempted to inhale his scent...

She did.

And as she inhaled, her senses returned. Blood and sweat and dirt.

"You should take a bath." There was the line.

And Armand started laughing. Roaring with laughter as he pulled back. Then he turned on his heels and sauntered to the secret door, lifting one hand to wave as he pulled it open.

"Where are you going?" Gandrett demanded, fallen out of role completely, and Armand chuckled again.

"To take a bath."

He was half out the door when Gandrett remembered she even had a mission to accomplish.

"Can I have a tour of the castle tomorrow?" she asked, forcing enthusiasm into her voice.

Armand glanced over his shoulder, still smiling. "I will make myself available to entertain you, Gandrett." He sketched a bow then hurried out before she could respond.

Gandrett waited a solid minute before she soundlessly cracked open the secret door, straining her ears for suspicious sounds from the other end of the corridor as she gazed into the half-light.

There was nothing suspicious about it. At least no drop in temperature. So Gandrett set one foot after the other, the hem of her dress lifted an inch so she wouldn't make noise on the loose stones on the floor.

It took her about ten steps before she got to a turn, then she could already see the door she remembered led to Armand's chambers. No other door within sight, and no other turns where she might find the old, spider-webbed door that had led her into her-freezing.

The walls, all rough stone, were flat without any dents that would indicate there had ever been a door as she ran her fingers over the spot where she had entered the tunnels the other night. No door. Not even a hint of torn spider webs.

So Gandrett turned on her heels and snuck back into her chambers, closing the door behind her, settling for a hot bath instead.

A corridor, dark and cold. Her heart slowed so much that she was hardly capable of a clear thought. Her limbs felt so heavy. Gandrett made her way further and further, beckoned by the whisper that was waiting for her near the light.

It spoke in a language Neredyn had long forgotten.

Symbols, sharp as ice, drifted through Gandrett's mind, leaving her gasping for breath. They had no meaning to her other than pain.

The whisper got louder, and Gandrett's feet slipped as she groped her path through the darkness.

A heartbeat of silence. Then a scream—

Gandrett sat up in her bed, one hand on the knife under her pillow, the other one on the pendants around her neck. The scream still echoed in her mind.

Not her scream. A dream.

Bright sunlight greeted her from the windows, and the smell of bothenia crust filled the room.

"You look oddly awake for someone who was deep asleep two minutes ago," Armand, perched at the foot end of her bed, said by way of greeting.

With all her force of will, Gandrett managed to tune out the noise in her head and focus on the young lord in front of her. She left her hand under the pillow until he lowered his gaze to the tray sitting on his knees. Then she grabbed the blanket instead and pulled it up to her chin.

"Should I call the guards?" she wondered aloud only to get his boyish laugh in return.

"You would only summon *my* guards, which wouldn't be very helpful if you wanted someone to defend you from *me*." He smirked.

Gandrett didn't mention there were about twelve different ways to bring him down right now if she wanted, the cleaner ones involving a knife to his throat, the not so clean ones involving the steaming pot of tea and the red sash that had been wrapped around a small vase holding a yellow flower. She cocked her head, letting go of the pendants.

"Deelah mentioned you liked these." He picked up a bothenia crust and flipped it in the air, catching it with one hand before he took a ravaging bite.

"Why are you here?" Gandrett was still pushing back the nightmare as Armand set down the tray on the covers and slid an inch closer.

"You asked me for a tour of the castle. Here I am." He inclined his head. "At your service, milady."

Gandrett loosed a breath and extracted one hand from under the covers to pick up a bothenia crust, her smile half-real.

She couldn't help it. Despite the unsolved mysteries around Armand's person, there was something comforting about his presence.

"Breakfast first," she said and blinked at him, reminding herself that despite the growing familiarity with Armand, she should at least try to remain in character. Especially with the information Deelah had entrusted to her. "Then I want to see every last corner of this fortress."

Armand grinned, the sorrow of their last conversation forgotten. "I'll send Deelah to help you get dressed," he said, his glance wandering down to where Gandrett had failed to keep the blanket at her chin as she bit into the bothenia crust. "As much as *I* enjoy the view, the rest of the court shouldn't be so lucky." With those words, he got up and strode to the door—the one to the hallway.

Gandrett glimpsed down, finding the strap of her nightgown had slid down her shoulder. She cursed and leaned forward, pouring herself a cup of tea, and waited.

This way of living—people who brought breakfast to her bed, a hot bath at any time of the day, bothenia crust—it was more than Gandrett could have ever hoped for after all the hardship of her childhood, the years of fighting and honing her skills, the pain of the Meister's wrath...

And yet, even as she was a slave to the House of Brenheran, with a Fae male ready to snap her neck with a gust of air if she defied the orders of Lord Tyrem, she got a glimpse of what real freedom could be like. The freedom from the oath to Vala, freedom to think of a future for herself, maybe even with some nice man in her company...

Her mind drifted back to the powerful Fae who may or may not have kissed her, his eyes like blue diamonds, his silky, dark hair covering those pointed ears even when his glamour slipped. She didn't even let herself think of the force of nature he was when they sparred, how his muscles played under his shirt when he wielded his sword in his hands. No.

The door clicked and Deelah walked in, a conspiring grin on her lined features and a flowing chiffon gown slung over her arm. "You'll be spending all day in Armand's company," she said by way of greeting. Then, as she spotted the tray on the bed, she continued, "So he listened to my advice, for a change."

It was hard, so hard, to see how Armand and Deelah acted as if Gandrett had always been in their lives. It made her task even more difficult—because eventually, she would betray them.

33

Armand helped her down the stairs—she let him. After half a day of meandering through the hallways, most of which she had already seen, her stomach growled more from boredom than real hunger. She had devoured at least four bothenia crusts and ignored Deelah's comments about how she wouldn't fit in the delicate, dusty-blue gown now flowing freely like the ocean in the east they had been watching from the battlements on the north tower.

"I wish I could go there one day," she said, half a thought still on the glistening waters beyond the land that lay cleaved between two courts.

Armand grinned sheepishly and tugged lightly on her arm—a motion which would have a less trained girl sent stumbling into his arms. "I can take you—one day." He watched her descend step after step in graceful balance.

The balance of a fighter, not a lady, but she didn't let his thoughts wander there and said, "One day," and batted her lashes the way Mckenzie had shown her. The way that had made Brax stare. A smile stole itself onto her lips. "But first, I'd love to see the more secret places of the castle..." She felt her own heart pounding as she spoke. "The ones where no one will disturb us."

His answering grin was imperial, and Gandrett wondered if she was playing with a sort of fire that Vala wouldn't be able to quench with her water.

But she still had her dagger strapped to her thigh. If Vala wouldn't help, she would.

So he led her down. Down, down, down. Until they reached the empty hallways of the north tower, accelerating Gandrett's pulse with every step they descended. The light grew fainter as they entered the lower floors, and what chambers they passed were empty, not even a piece of furniture left.

"What happened here?" Gandrett's tension originated from something more than Armand's hand, now clasped tightly around hers.

As they moved past empty room after empty room, the castle felt less and less like the inhabitable space her chambers provided but like a tomb.

"What you see is the tower of the last Dragon King." Armand spoke as if that was something to be proud of. "What's left of it," he added with a grin.

Gandrett stopped dead. She had heard it in the countless lessons from the Meister that the dragons of the north had played a part in why the Calma Desert existed. Why the lands, once lush and fertile, now lay barren, hostile to any sort of life.

But there was more. She remembered bedtime stories about the Dragon King. How he had ridden on his snow-white beast. How he had bent the territories of Neredyn to his terror. And even Nahir had spoken of the legends. The Dreads of the Skies.

"He resided here for a short while during his reign," Armand continued, gently tugging on Gandrett's hand in encouragement to keep walking.

"That was a thousand years ago," she said flatly.

"It was." He laughed at the concern in her eyes. "There is nothing left of the Dragon King. My ancestors made certain of it."

Had Gandrett thought the tour *boring* before? She could now feel her muscles tighten as if they were readying for battle.

"How long did he..." She searched for the right word. "How long did he stay in Eedwood?"

"Just a few months," he responded, his voice melodious as he studied her from the side. "As we know from history, he had bigger plans than Eedwood. Than Sives."

It sounded so simple. And yet, the meaning of it was tremendous.

"No one ever comes here." He gave her a meaningful look. "We don't even need to shut off the corridors that lead to this tower."

As if to mock Armand, footsteps filled the hallway.

Armand stopped, pulling Gandrett to a halt with him. His free hand was at his sword before she could think about digging up her dagger. No. Not yet. She would see first if there was danger before she exposed her disguise.

The footsteps came to a sudden stop. As if they had followed the sound of their own, and whoever it was, was now trying to localize them again.

Gandrett saw him first. Like a beam of light, he was staring down through the partially-lit corridor. His clothes a shade of golden brown as was his hair. She didn't need to see his eyes to know it was him.

Then, Armand spotted him and drew his blade. "What are you doing here?"

Joshua Brenheran. She knew it was him not from his eyes alone but from the way he walked—like Brax. Thank Vala, he didn't seem hurt. On the contrary, he appeared well—too well.

Also, he didn't run from Armand even if the latter approached him with a blade in hand.

"Stay here," Armand hissed at Gandrett, who had little time to even consider what was going on.

But she remained where she was, her eyes absorbing every detail, every last one of Joshua Brenheran's graceful steps, as he walked up to Armand as if they were companions rather than enemies.

"Lord Hamyn asked me to deliver a message, Lord Armand."

Gandrett's blood froze, and Armand stopped a couple of steps away from Joshua Brenheran, his sword at the ready. "Speak," he ordered, voice all commander and nothing like the Armand she had gotten to know, the one who grinned and smiled and joked, who disdained his own father for what he did to their homeland.

"He is waiting for you in his study," Joshua said flatly. "He says it's urgent."

Armand nodded and dismissed the man, waiting for him to disappear behind the corner before he sheathed his sword and returned to Gandrett's side. "I am sorry for the interruption, but it seems this cannot wait."

The look on his face told her that he wasn't at all in the mood to respond to his father's call, but some part of him still had to be loyal despite how differently he saw things from his father.

"Who was that?" Gandrett asked, not ready to let the opportunity pass. Yes, she had stayed behind, observing only and trying to make sense of what she had witnessed, but couldn't find one logical reason why Joshua Brenheran would be here willingly.

"Just a messenger." Armand's eyes, as flat as his voice, stared ahead rather than at her.

"He didn't seem like *just a messenger*." No. He seemed like the man she had come here to retrieve.

She laid a hand on Armand's arm, bringing herself to smile at him with what she hoped was understanding. "Don't worry about me," she hoped she cooed. "Go. We can continue our tour tomorrow." He turned to look at her, some light returning to his eyes. "I'll find my way back on my own. Just back there, right?" She pointed in the opposite direction of the one where Joshua Brenheran had left. "Your father is waiting."

He bought it even if his gaze remained an enigma in hazel.

Gandrett waited until his footsteps disappeared then wheeled around, gathered her skirts, and ghosted toward the corner Joshua Brenheran had turned, hoping to find a trace of where he might have gone.

She found herself in an empty corridor similar to the one she came from, but there were more doors and some alcoves hosting suits of armor probably as old as the castle itself. Yet, no sign of her target.

Her training set in as she screened the doors, the slits underneath, for signs of movement. Nothing.

She inched forward along the hallway, glancing out the window to check whether someone might see her from the yard, then moved closer to the side with the alcoves between the doors, making sure she didn't get caught.

Then she heard footsteps again, not too far ahead. So she sped up, her own silk slippers almost soundless on the polished stone, and found Joshua's outline descending a staircase.

She followed, leaving enough space so she wouldn't give herself away but stayed close enough so she wouldn't lose him. Down, down. They had to be on the ground floor by now, still descending. Then, the footsteps stopped.

Gandrett halted, holding her breath as she listened intently. Nothing.

As she turned the next corner, he wasn't in the dim, windowless corridor, which didn't seem to lead to any kind of rooms.

She turned, checking behind her. Had she missed an exit?

Her breath slammed from her lungs as a rough hand wound around her throat, pulling her backward into the stone wall behind her.

"Why are you following me?" His voice was like ice as he leaned over her, his breath like a cloud of frost.

Gandrett's hands shot up to fight off his iron grasp, but he was strong—

"Again. Why are you following me?"

She fought for air, gasped for it, but his fingers were too tight. The dagger. She had to get to that dagger before he—

"I should just snap your neck," he mused, not reminding her even a fraction of what she had heard of him. "You're lucky the lord's son takes interest in you, or I actually would."

Now. She had to do it now. With all of her concentration, she let go of his wrist, for pulling on it wouldn't free her, and plunged her elbow into where she estimated his stomach to be.

His hand dropped, and he cursed—long strings of violent curses, including the mention of Shaelak.

"The god of darkness is not interested in me," she snarled at him as she wheeled around, finding him doubled over. She had been lucky and hit the spot right between his ribs that made one want to hurl.

With fast fingers, Gandrett pulled up her skirt and drew the dagger.

It weighed comfortingly in her hand, the twirled hilt providing solid grip as she grabbed Joshua's shoulder with her free hand, one foot hoisting him against the wall with a quick push. No time for artful combat. This wasn't training. This was life and death.

Joshua cursed again as he noticed the blade at his throat.

"It would be easier to free you if you worked with me," she said as she studied his surprise face.

Surprised and furious. No, he wasn't the least bit concerned about the blade. Just... annoyed, it seemed.

"Joshua Brenheran." Gandrett set her foot back on the ground, her eyes scanning the young man towering over her for weapons. He bore none. "That's your name, isn't it?"

He cocked his head, strain replacing his annoyance for a fraction of a second, but didn't answer.

"Tell me if I'm wrong, and I'll walk away," Gandrett offered. But she knew by the sneer that graced his lips—Brax's lips, Mckenzie's lips—that she was right.

"Tell me," his grin widened into a violent baring of his teeth. "How is my father doing? The old fool," he hissed, hands balling into fists at his sides as he cursed yet again. This time there were syllables woven into the fluent string that she had never heard before—at least not when she'd been awake.

"Joshua?" As the first thrill of having found her target wore off, concern set in.

And fear.

Fear that finding Joshua Brenheran had been the easy part of her mission.

His hand knocked against the wall behind him. Knocked at first. Then, he slammed his knuckles into it until he was bleeding.

Gandrett leaped aside, her blade not moving an inch from his throat. What was he—?

She didn't see it coming. With all her training, all her experience in bringing down warriors twice her size, she didn't see it coming when his bloodied hand slammed into her nose, setting her face screaming with pain.

She heard herself gasp before the world went black.

Three days. He hadn't heard from her in three days. Nehelon couldn't even begin to describe the growing sense of unease that formed in his stomach.

Riho had checked in, reporting what he saw of Gandrett on his patrol-flights over the castle grounds every day. But it wasn't nearly enough to allow Nehelon to sleep at night. Not *nearly*. Especially when the last time the crow had spotted her was two days ago.

He flicked a leaf from his arm and leaped off the tree, landing with nothing more than a soft thud. Beside him, Alvi threw back her head.

"I know." He patted her neck, losing his hands under her thick black mane. "It's been too long. We have been stagnant."

The horse stomped one hoof and huffed at him, eyes inquiring.

"I don't know when she's coming back." He forced himself to believe that it was a given that she would.

But deep in his chest, he felt that it might not be more than wishful thinking. That something was wrong.

Gandrett's head throbbed as she woke. She couldn't remember the last time someone had knocked her out that easily... Yes, the wolf. But this?

The image of emerald-eyed Joshua Brenheran didn't leave her mind. He was there with every throb, his smirk, his flashing teeth. His broken knuckles—

It was the smell that hit her first. The sharp odor of grime mixed with the iron tang of blood.

She rolled over on the ground, which seemed to be solid rock covered with gravel, cold and wet.

Wet, right where she had laid flat on her stomach. She must have relieved herself while she had been out. She shuddered. That hadn't happened since the Meister had let one of the older boys fight her till she was bloodied and broken and went out cold, and he had locked her in one of the underground chambers of the citadel in Everrun so she would learn what it was like to wake up disoriented and in pain. To learn the humiliation of no longer being in control of your own bodily functions. She had been barely thirteen then.

How she had hated him. How she had spent day and night after that to become the best. Just so she would never have to experience that again.

Yet, here she was, face caked in dried blood, gravel sticking to her cheek, and shivering from the cold that was seeping through the thin layers of chiffon.

She managed to crack her eyes open and found a narrow beam of light where she expected to be a door. No movements outside. No sounds.

A push of her hands against the ground sent a gasp of pain from her lips, but she didn't stop. Up... she needed to get to her feet... knees at least, so she would heave her body off the cold ground. And so she could assess her surroundings. Regroup.

It took a couple of attempts until she knelt, cowering over her knees, her back protesting as she tried to sit up. What had he done to her?

Judging by the soreness in her limbs and spine, he must have just dumped her into whatever dark room this was.

Gandrett clicked her tongue and listened to the sound as it bounced off the walls. Close walls. A small space. Stone walls, probably, just as the rest of the castle.

For a long time—Gandrett lost track of time as she sucked in sharp breaths between her teeth, fighting the cold and pain— she just knelt there, arms wrapped around her chest, hands tucked under her arms, and waited for her strength to return. Then, slowly, she straightened, and with time, her eyes adjusted to the dark enough to see the outline of the narrow door under which flickering light danced. Firelight, no daylight.

Her stomach churned, knees wobbling as she pushed herself upright, hands searching the dark for the closest wall to lean on.

She found it just a step forward. Rough stone, moist and covered in something soft and spongy. Some type of moss perhaps?

The touch of the cool, water-binding layer on the wall had her noticing her mouth was dry as sandpaper. She swallowed once. Twice. Until the movement of her lips let her taste blood.

She had to get water and, quickly, clean her wounds before they got infected, drink something so she would have the

strength to fight her way out the next time the door opened—
if it ever opened again.

Gandrett's shivering got worse at the thought Joshua Brenheran might have put her here, not to keep her prisoner but
to let her rot.

A surge of panic ran through her, causing her to stumble
toward the door. Her shoulder stung with pain at the impact,
and her shaky hands groped their way along the sides, looking
for a doorknob, a keyhole, anything that would help her deter-
mine what kind of cell this was.

Calm down—that was what she needed to do. Breathe. She
had trained for situations like this. And even if deep down she
had always known someone would come for her if she didn't
manage on her own, she had never let herself grow lazy. She
had always managed. Always found a way out. She would find
a way out of this, too.

Facts. She needed to collect facts. Anything that gave information about where in the castle she may be.

She slid her hands further along the walls, marking the
size of the cell—not dramatically small but just big enough
that she could lay sprawled on the floor. Her assessment had
given no indication of windows. She had to be underground.
And they had been in the north tower when Joshua had surprised her and probably broken her nose—she reached up and
gingerly lay her fingers on its bridge. A firework of white-hot
stars erupted before her eyes at the painful contact. But it
cleared her senses, her mind.

With two strides, now knowing the dimensions of the
cell, she crossed the room back to the door and pushed. It
didn't move.

She searched the edges for hinges and almost yelped in relief as her fingers bumped into metal cylinders on which's top she could feel the circular head of a bolt. It wasn't fortified. Even if the door was locked and showed no sign of door handles on the inside, it might be possible to unhinge it.

Even if it was probably solid steel, the weight of a small horse.

All she needed was something to shove under it and—

She darted to the ground, testing the width of the door by shoving her fingers into the opening beneath it. Just big enough to get half her palm in. But she loosed a sigh of relief as her fingers curled around the bottom. Two inches of solid steel separated her from the drafty, cool air on the other side. A weight she could never lift on her own, but with the right tools—

Gandrett was on her hands and knees, gritting her teeth as the gravel dug into her kneecaps through the thin fabric. If she had her dagger—Nehelon's dagger—she could use it to try to pry the door open somehow. Force the blade into the groove at the side where the lock had to be.

Her mind kept swapping options for alternatives as she ran her palms over the ground and found some bigger stones, a small log of wood, and collected them in her lap, wrapping part of her skirts around them so she wouldn't lose them again.

Scanning the ground took her a solid minute even with aching limbs. But at least the activity kept the shivering at bay despite her dry throat paying the price for it.

She was panting by the time she had made her way to the second wall. Nothing. There was nothing of use in the small space.

No. It wasn't time to give up just yet. She had two more walls to go.

Frantically, her fingers searched. There had to be something. Anything.

But there wasn't. So she unwrapped the stones and wood and placed them by the door.

There was one final option. This room consisted of more than walls and a floor.

Holding her breath, Gandrett lifted her arms above her head and braced herself for the disappointment.

It didn't come.

The ceiling was low enough for her to feel spider webs in the corner where she started. So she gritted her teeth and jumped, every fiber in her body aching as she coiled, then pushed. But with her hands, she hit solid rock.

Solid rock and metal. Something clinked as she landed on the floor.

She jumped again. This time a little bit further ahead. The chain clinked again. It had to be a chain.

The next time Gandrett jumped, she hooked herself into the metal and prayed to Vala this was her way out.

The chain came crashing down with an earsplitting bang with Gandrett rolling to the side just in time to dodge the avalanche of debris it brought raining down.

She kept her hands over her head, cowering in the corner by the door until the gravel stopped falling. Then, when silence fell once more, she leaned against the mossy wall and reached for her skirt where she ripped off a piece of fabric to shield her mouth and nose from the dust.

But she couldn't sit still for even one moment. There was a chain somewhere in the darkness before her. The fact that solid iron had ripped out of its anchor in the ceiling told tales of how old this cell had to be. How weak the chain might even be.

Not only the chain, if she was lucky.

So she bound the piece of chiffon at the back of her head to keep it from slipping then ripped off more strips, which she wrapped around her hands so her palms wouldn't slice open on the rocks before her.

She had just started to crawl forward when she noticed that the beam of light had disappeared in the settling dust. Not the dust. It was blocked by the gravel that she had put in motion.

So she started digging, slowly shoving rocks aside until she noticed rays of light in the haze, and it was pulling out into the draft.

Good. This way she would still get enough fresh air.

But her body already protested with every scraping of gravel, every lifting of her arms as she reached into the dirt again. Until—

There, under her fingers, the cold, rough surface of rusty iron.

Gandrett closed her fingers around it and pulled. Pulled even if her muscles were screaming.

The chain moved an inch then another. And slowly, so slowly, Gandrett gathered the entire length of it before her knees. What she would have given to be able to see. But this way, she had to measure the chain by the number of arm lengths she had hauled toward her.

Still, Gandrett didn't allow herself a moment of rest. There were only two outcomes to this. In the better case, she would use the chain to throttle Joshua if he ever came back for her, and in the other, the iron between her fingers had to pull that door out. Either way, there was a chance it wouldn't work and she would end up in Vala's eternal gardens. But she had to try.

Even if the man she was supposed to rescue was the one who had put her in here. She had to try, for her own promise, for her family.

With shaky hands—no longer from cold but from exhaustion—Gandrett braced herself on the wall beside her, one end of the chain in her hands, and pushed herself up.

If the anchor of the chain had broken, there was a good chance the iron door wasn't the most stable either. But she would go for something smaller, more delicate first.

She fingered the chain links, measuring their diameter with her index finger before she ran her hand over the hinges of the door.

Vala be thanked, they were close enough in size that it was worth a try. So Gandrett looped the chain, one chain link over the top hinge, a second one over the bottom hinge, flexed the chain and shouldered it before she leaned against the wall, bracing herself, and grasped the chain tightly. She bit back a scream as she pulled sideways with all the force she could muster.

The screech of metal on metal told her that the links were grinding against the hinges, straining under the pressure as much as she did.

But they held firm.

And her strength was coming to an end.

In the soft afternoon light, Hamyn Denderlain, lounging in his throne, looked almost like the father Armand remembered from the years of his childhood. Almost. Hadn't it been for the sour face.

"Father." It was all he needed to announce his presence. The guards inclined their heads as he walked up to the dais, his father's milky eyes shifting toward him.

"Ride out immediately," his father commanded. "There are more villages revolting against our methods."

Armand kept his face blank except for that smile he had perfected. Not the smile he used to give his mother. The smile he gave Deelah. The smile he even sometimes found himself giving Gandrett Starhaeven.

This was the second time his father summoned him in two days. The first time, the Brenheran heir had played the messenger. Strange—so strange to have him sneaking around the castle. But there was really nothing anyone could do about it. Not as long as both his father and aunt Linniue agreed he was to stay.

"Now," Hamyn Denderlain tore him from his thoughts.

Armand nodded at his father and turned on his heels, some of his guards falling in step behind him.

As their commander, he wasn't concerned about his tail, but he would rather have some moments to himself to check in on Gandrett. She hadn't been in her chambers when he'd returned from the last turmoil his father had asked him to smother. Not that he had truly smothered it. Not the way his father would have wanted it, with heads rolling and limbs missing. He had long outgrown his father's view of things. Armand wanted peace. And peace was not gained by bullying your people into submission with a sword and a torch.

He rushed down the main stairwell then took a sharp turn into the courtyard where his eyes scanned every corner for Gandrett.

It was only hours later, and he hadn't seen a trace of her. Neither had he had a chance to inquire with Deelah how his guest was doing.

Something tightened in his stomach. The bile-raising sensation of missing some detail. Of failing to ensure her safety.

He had brought Gandrett here. It was his responsibility to keep her safe. Even if his father would probably not mind one bit if she disappeared into thin air.

And then there was the questionable presence of Joshua Brenheran.

And the way he had eyed her at the dance... The way he had gazed at her through the corridor when he had delivered the message the day before...

Armand balled his hands into fists as he strode right for the stables, guards at his heels.

"Do you need us to ride out with you, Lord Armand?" one of them asked.

But he shook his head at them, reaching for the reins of his already saddled horse before he hoisted himself into the saddle, eyes already at the opening gate. "I'll do this on my own."

And with a nudge at the horse's flanks, he was riding out to right what his father had done wrong. Even if it took him farther from the first spark of hope he'd felt in twelve months.

"I'll be back for breakfast," he whispered as he gazed over his shoulder at the west tower.

She had tried. Not only once but several times until warm liquid dribbled down her hands and the blood started spilling anew from her nose. Every time, the hinges had groaned, but they had not moved even remotely enough to break them apart as she'd hoped they would.

Gandrett was leaning against the door, calming her breathing, her legs unstable as she heard the noises outside. Footsteps. *Light* footsteps. Too light for Joshua Brenheran's tall frame or for the heavily-muscled guards she had spotted all over the castle.

She balled her hands into fists, sucking back the hiss as they closed around the blisters and scratches, and turned around.

Her fists landed on the heavy iron with a thud.

Outside, the footsteps yielded.

"Who's there?" Her voice almost brought tears to Gandrett's eyes.

Not Deelah's voice but the only other female voice she had listened to long enough to mark its accent—the accent of central Sives—and its cautious melody.

Gandrett heaved a breath. "Addie."

Addie Blackwood took the shortcut down to the well since Lady Linniue wanted the water without delay. It wasn't one of her planned walks down the spiral staircase, but she had been woken in the dead of night by Linniue's chambermaid, whose eyes had been red from either lack of sleep or tears, Addie didn't dare be the judge of it.

So she had gotten to her feet, sleep beckoning her to do the opposite, and had taken the shortest route to the north tower. She had made it halfway down the corridor that led to the entry to the well when a noise stopped her dead.

No one ever came here. Sometimes she even found herself talking to herself in these hallways just to fill the air with sound. To make the descent into the darkness less sinister.

"Who's there?" She held her breath, heart in her throat as she waited for a response. Anything was better than the looming threat in the silence that followed. The type of silence she had lived through too many times at Lands End.

"Addie." The voice was muffled, barely audible, yet it had clearly spoken her name.

Addie gasped. It was a female voice, so it wasn't Joshua Brenheran. She had been spending the past days glancing over her shoulder at every turn, dreading to find the young man spying her in the hallways.

Shame. Deep, heavily-weighing shame tightened her chest. And even if she was a coward for hoping she could avoid him, she had no words to say to him that could justify that she had denied him assistance. Even if she had only hidden him, bought him time...

Another thud. "Addie, I'm here," the voice repeated. "Help me."

The corridor was lit by torches stuck in metal hoops on the walls in irregular intervals, but there was no sign of whoever had called her.

"It's me," the voice said, "Gandrett."

Gandrett. What was she doing down here?

"I am locked in a cell."

Addie swallowed. There were several doors down here, each of them so ancient they could hardly be functional. "Keep talking so I can find you," was all Addie said and started walking again.

Gandrett spoke something about bothenia crust and tea and about Armand, but Addie could hardly understand a word as she continued down the hall until the voice was so close it could be only one of the two doors she had halted before.

Addie looked them over. Both solid iron, rusty on the outside and handle missing. But gravel was leaking from one of them through the slit above the threshold.

"I'm here," Addie informed Gandrett and set her bucket down. Linniue would have to wait another minute.

It took a short moment until Gandrett's fingers appeared under the door, pushing the gravel forward. "Get me out of here." Her voice, clearer from up close, sounded tired, strained. "Please."

Addie ran her gaze over the rusty iron. No doorknob. Just one dark keyhole and no key within sight.

"I can't," Addie noted outside the door. "We'll need a key."

Gandrett's head pounded as she rested her cheek on the ground. The bottom of Addie's worn, leather boots was the only thing she could make out through the slit. But at least there was air, and she sucked it in between gritted teeth. "You need to hurry, Addie," she urged.

"Move away from the door," Addie warned and left Gandrett with barely enough time to roll to the side.

There was a brief silence followed by the thud of Addie's shoulder slamming into the door.

But the door didn't move.

"I tried this already," Gandrett chuckled darkly, strength leaving her.

Addie cursed lowly outside the door.

"What?" Gandrett prompted. "What is it?" How she wished she could peek outside to see what Addie saw, to hear what Addie heard.

Addie let her wait another moment before her voice appeared in a whisper near the slit under the door. "Someone is coming."

The gods have mercy. If Joshua was coming back for her...

There was only one person in this castle who might be able to help her. So Gandrett damned the consequences of asking for him because the alternative was so much worse.

"You must get Armand, Addie," Gandrett whispered, crawling back to the door. "Do you hear me?"

Addie murmured her affirmation.

"Find Armand, and bring him here." Gandrett swallowed the curses that brewed on her dry tongue and, instead of releasing them, added, "Go, before it's too late."

Addie's footsteps were bustling away just in time as the clicking of polished boots approached from a distance.

Up. She needed to get up so she could meet whoever would open the door head-on.

Mobilizing whatever was left of her strength, Gandrett grabbed for the chain again and lifted it with her as she stumbled to her feet.

Closer and closer, the footsteps came, and Gandrett's heart was beating too fast. She needed to calm and gather her strength.

One deep breath. Two. Three. The fourth time she inhaled deeply, the boots halted before her cell. Gandrett took a step to the side so whoever would open it couldn't see her right away but would find a heap of debris in the center of the cell instead.

The metallic sound of a key scratched against the door, then the click as it turned in the lock.

Gandrett exhaled, air blowing from her lips in a slow, steady flow. She had stopped shaking.

Chains in hands, she squinted her eyes, readying for the light the opening of the door would allow inside and the handsome face of Joshua Brenheran, which she was going to strike with the rusty metal between her hands.

The door slammed open with a bang and bounced back from the stone behind it, rattling in the damaged hinges until one of them gave way, and the door tilted back and came to a halt, leaning against the wall.

Armand returned with blood on his hands. As happened so many times.

And as with so many times, he despised himself for having to do what he had to do. *For a peaceful Sives.* He kept thinking it, kept saying it to himself. It was the last thing his mother had asked of him. *Peace for Sives.*

And then his father had let her die like an animal. His father who had sworn an oath to her, to protect her, to love her, to...

His father, who he allowed to keep the title of Lord of Eedwood so he could pave the way for something greater than his own lordship. That's why he had helped his mother to retrieve Joshua Brenheran from Ackwood. Because she had wished for a better future for Sives where neither House Brenheran ruled nor House Denderlain, but both. That's why he had agreed.

Lord Hamyn Denderlain held no love of a Sives that was ruled by any other than the house he had married into. And for a little while longer, he could let his father believe he was in control, that he ruled, that his son made his people bow at his feet. Armand shook his head to himself. If his father knew what he was doing whenever he was sent on a mission out there, he would hang. That's why he rode alone or took only his most trusted soldiers—the soldiers who had already been trusted by his mother.

He climbed off his horse and handed the reins to the stable girl who was on duty in these ungodly hours of the morning. She swished back her braid and gave him a smile then led the horse back into the stables where she took off saddle and bridle and rubbed it down.

Armand watched as she worked, her young hands barely reaching the neck of the horse.

"That one has been restless, Lord Armand," the girl said as she noticed him leaning at a pillar in the shadows.

Armand followed her gaze to the stall which contained Gandrett's gelding. The horse stomped his hooves as if noticing the attention.

"Is he sick?" Armand asked, sauntering to the stall, and laid his hand on the beast's neck. It cringed.

"I cannot tell, Sir, but the stable master says he has been like this for the past two days." The girl didn't stop working on Armand's horse as she spoke but grabbed a fresh piece of cloth and cleaned the horse's face. The worn, gray fabric turned red as it touched its forehead.

"Not his blood," Armand commented as her eyes widened with concern. "Not mine either."

The girl didn't say a word after that, and Armand made to leave. However, a movement in the stall's corner caught his eye. A fat crow was hopping along the edge of the wooden feeding trough.

He reached to the side where they kept dried corn for the horses and extracted a fistful.

"Here." He tossed it past the gelding right into the feeding trough. "Make sure you get some before he," Armand jerked his chin at Gandrett's horse, "eats it." And with those words, he took his leave, giving a short nod at the stable girl.

The guards at Armand's chambers barked at her when she claimed she needed to speak to the young lord. But Addie Blackwood didn't let them turn her away that easily. Not once she had made up her mind.

"He'll want to know about this. Trust me." She squared her shoulders, ignoring their disdainful looks at her rag-dress.

"Lord Armand had a long night," one of the guards—the kinder one—said, and it wasn't amusement on his face but some apologetic frown.

Addie didn't let her mind wander to what might have kept the young lord up all night—most certainly not Gandrett. She clasped the handle of her bucket more tightly.

If nothing else, their words reassured her that he was indeed behind those black double doors.

She considered her options against the two heavily-armed men and decided words had to do. She wouldn't stand a chance if she tried to fight her way past them.

"Please, let him know I am here." Pleading was as much against her nature as it was to pick up a sword and fight, but Gandrett needed help, and her best shot at being able to speak to the young lord was if she convinced the guards this was about life and death—because it was. "Someone who he seems to be quite attached to is in danger."

The kinder guard, the one with the heavy eyebrows, raised one of the latter. A question and a sign of understanding.

"What does a servant know about the young lord's... *attachments*?" the other one asked with a sneer.

Addie considered screaming, but that would only make her less credible. She needed to keep her calm the way she had in the prison in the north when they came to mock her. The more she fought, the worse it would go. Only when she outsmarted them with words did they stop. That might have been the reason why they had handed her over to Lady Linniue eventually. Because she was *no fun*, as they had called it.

"Tell him his guest is in need of his aid and I know where to find her." It was all she really had to say.

"You are not the first of our servant girls to try and make their way into our lord's chambers," the sneering guard countered, making Addie's head pound with anger.

"Never," she said lowly but not weakly. "Never." And with a motion so quick she was surprised neither of the guards saw it coming, she yanked her bucket back and propelled it between the two gaping men, the iron hitting right between the silver stars on the doors as if she had aimed there.

It clattered to the floor, filling the hallway with the thunder of iron on stone before it rolled to a halt in front of the kinder guard's feet. His other eyebrow rose while the second guard had already darted for her, one arm restraining her around shoulder and throat.

To all of their surprise, the door sprang open, and a sleepy young lord stood barefoot on the threshold in silken pajamas, face half-hidden by his tousled honey-gold hair. Addie suppressed the urge to stare but focused on the guard behind her who was now pulling her forward and pushing her to her knees before the young lord.

Her kneecaps protested as they hit black stone.

"What's going on here?" Lord Armand asked, his gaze inquiring with the guards before it fell on the bucket and then on her.

Addie internally cringed. This was not how she had imagined it would go when the young lord noticed her for the first time. Not at his knees, in dusty rags, forced to bow by a guard who tugged her head down by her black braid. Not like this.

"This creature wouldn't give up," the guard said to the young lord. Then to Addie, he said, "Here he is. Now take a good look at him while he tells you that he has no interest in scum." He chuckled by her ear. "It will be the last look you get."

Addie didn't dare glimpse the young lord, but she had to. There was no other alternative. Not if she wanted to buy Gandrett a chance of getting out of that cell.

"What do you have to say for yourself?" Addie's heart all but stopped as the young lord spoke to her, voice not harsh as she'd expected, as she had heard him speak to his guards; or arrogant as he spoke to his aunt, Lady Linniue; but a tired, troubled voice that made her cringe all over again. Not from fear but from worry over why the young lord might feel that way.

"Gandrett," was all she could muster with the breath left in her lungs as he crouched before her, measuring her face.

"What is wrong with Gandrett?" Alarm now rang in every word, and Addie gathered all her courage and looked him in the eye.

His eyes, hazel and gold, a mirror of the emotion in his voice, stared back at her.

"She is in trouble," the words fell out of Addie's mouth. "She asked me to come get you before it is too late—"

Armand studied her as if making up his mind whether to believe her or laugh out loud. Then he shot back to his feet and turned on his heels. "Release her," he said to the guard as he walked back inside his chambers, voice the calm before a storm.

And they did.

All three of them eyed each other—Addie looking at the two guards, and the two guards considering each other and Addie, neither of them having the answer to what was going to happen.

Then the young lord returned, wearing boots this time, carrying a bloody sword in his hand.

"Lead the way," he said, and Addie started running.

Gandrett's mouth fell open in a silent scream. Had she remained where she had been standing a few moments ago, she might now be dead—either from the impact of the door on her skull or from breaking her neck being pushed back into the debris in the cell.

A long shadow flickered in the now fire-lit space, and Joshua Brenheran's voice carried inside like a promise of pain, "I hope you're not under that heap of gravel. It would be a shame if I didn't get to kill you."

Gandrett tightened her grip on the chain and dared a glance around the room, just to know her surroundings, to know of the traps, the potential additional weapons. The walls were black stone covered with some purplish moss that didn't seem to depend on daylight, and where the chain had been lodged in the ceiling, a crater remained, big enough to fit her head in. But there was nothing but the rocks on the ground and the chain in her hand that would help her overpower Joshua Brenheran.

The shadow started moving, a counterpart to the escaping haze. Gandrett didn't move. Not yet. The element of surprise worked only once. And she had to make it count.

He neared another step. And another. Then the tip of his sword was visible from the side. Gandrett rallied her strength and let him take another step before she hurled the chain like a whip, watching it wrap around his blade, and tugged it free from his grasp.

His responding growl was nothing less than lethal. The sword clattered to the ground between them and Joshua Brenheran had already drawn a dagger—Nehelon's dagger—by the time she bent, trying to pick it up. Gandrett hurled back the chain, leaving the sword where it was before Joshua could launch at her with the new blade gleaming in his grasp.

"You should not fight me," he warned her, teeth bared, emerald eyes piercing through the dim light. "It will only make your suffering longer."

He took one feral step toward her, dagger ready to slice into her.

She needed to find his weakness. She had caught him off guard before in the hallway. All she needed to do was—

"I am here to help you, Joshua," Gandrett tried. If there was any truth to what the Brenheran family said about their heir, then she had to find a way to get him to stall rather than to fight. To listen. "Your father sent me to get you out of this castle."

Joshua didn't seem human as he waved her off and took another step. "My family is *glad* I am gone." He laughed darkly. "The black sheep of the Brenherans. A stain to my family's honor." He spoke, it seemed, more to himself.

Gandrett didn't stop him. As long as he had something to say, he wouldn't kill her. So she didn't stop him.

"It's a surprise my *father*"—he laughed as if that word was a joke—"even let me live. A Brenheran by name and blood, but—" His eyes grew distant as if he were listening to something.

Gandrett strained her ears, trying to make out any sound but the slow shifting of Joshua's feet on the gravel-covered ground.

Now. It had to be now.

With another—last—surge of strength, she let the chain lash against Joshua's neck, and as it wrapped around his throat, she pulled hard enough to fell a tree, but Joshua didn't even tumble. And he didn't yield.

"You vicious creature." His face distorted, all handsomeness relinquished by the grimace, and his free hand grabbed the chain, now pulling Gandrett closer as if he were hauling in a boat.

Gandrett, no matter how hard she dug her heels in the dirt, couldn't hold her ground. Not as Joshua released his full strength and tugged, sending her stumbling forward until she came to a stop an inch from his dagger—Nehelon's dagger.

A surge of fury filled Gandrett's chest, strong enough to burn the fear for her life and dulling the pain in her face, in her limbs, in her torn palms. Nehelon's dagger. His diamond-blue eyes flashed before her, centering her, and felling her rage.

"Give me that dagger," was all she said.

Joshua cocked his head in response, seeming confused by her demand.

"The dagger, Joshua Brenheran. Give it to me."

He did no such thing, but his confusion grew, spreading wide on his features. His grasp on the chain, however, held fast.

"A friend gave it to me, and I would not want to return to him without it. So give me the dagger. I won't say it again."

As Joshua's lips curled into a cruel smile, the leash on Gandrett's temper snapped, and she tugged on the chain with all her force, grabbing the blade of the dagger before her with one already injured hand.

It cut into her palm, sending searing pain up her arm, but she didn't let go. The blade shook between her grasp and Joshua's, but she didn't yield. Even when the blade turned hot like a branding iron between her fingers, she didn't loosen her grasp. She held Joshua's gaze, staring him down until he flinched, sucking in a breath of surprise.

"Magic—"

Armand's breathing was ragged by the time they made it down the stairs. He never took this corridor—even though he knew of its existence, knew where it led, he never took it.

"How much further?" The servant girl kept running ahead, her legs fast as a doe's as she leaped around corners, braid bouncing on her slender back.

He could still feel the looks on his guards' incredulous faces as he'd taken off with her. But he'd care about that later. Right now, his ray of hope needed his help, and he would run until his lungs bled if he had to.

"I don't know how long she's been in there," the girl panted as they flew down the next flight of stairs. Never in his life had the castle felt that unnecessarily large to him. "But if we don't make it soon..."

Do you have any idea how she got there? Wherever that *is.* He wanted to ask. But he saved his breath for running.

"She didn't sound good when I left and"—Addie flung out her hand, holding on to the wall at the corner she was turning—"and someone was coming." She didn't pause for a second to see if he was catching up. "She was scared, Sir."

It was when they made it to the bottom level of the north tower that Armand's chest tightened. The north tower was the last place he'd seen her. What if she had never left?

They made it past another turn and then down into the underground levels where the ancient dungeons of a time long before the Dragon King were located.

The humid smell of mold climbed into his nostrils as they entered a long, torch-lit corridor.

"Almost there," the girl panted and pointed ahead, this time glancing back over her shoulder, her face panic-stricken.

He heard it then, Gandrett's scream. A sound shaking him to the core of his bone marrow.

His legs automatically pushed harder, as if in answer to the horrifying sound of pain, and he darted past the girl, sweat sheathing his neck.

It couldn't be far. Just—

In the corridor, coming into view as he made it past the next corner, a shape was cowering on the floor, hands raised before her face and shaking uncontrollably.

Gandrett.

She was wearing the same elegant, dusty-blue dress as the last time he'd seen her. Only now it was hardly recognizable, covered in dust and something darker he hoped wasn't her blood.

Armand skidded to a halt in front of her and dropped to his knees, his sword hand still firm on the hilt of his sword while his free hand hesitated midair as he noticed the deep gash on her hand.

His strength almost left him as she lifted her head, exposing her face. Blood. There was so much blood on her lovely features. Her nose was swollen, dribbling fresh blood on top of the crusted one covering her lips and chin. Dirt glazed her cheeks and every inch of skin that wasn't covered by her gown.

"What happened?"

He was still waiting for an answer when the servant girl joined him on the ground. To her credit, she didn't hesitate one second as she noticed Gandrett's injuries, but reached into the pocket of her dress and extracted a handkerchief. "It's clean," she commented as Armand gave her a doubtful look and grabbed Gandrett's sliced-open hand to bind it with the cloth. Then she took Gandrett's other hand, which, to Armand's horror, was covered in countless little cuts and scratches, and she made Gandrett apply pressure on the bound wound.

"I think I killed him," Gandrett whispered and glanced over her shoulder into the open cell behind her.

Armand froze. There were boots visible from his angle. Familiar boots.

He jumped up, leaving the girl to tend to Gandrett's wounds—"Wait here."—and made his way to the cell, a looming dark hole behind her, to find out who she had been speaking about.

Joshua's motionless body lay sprawled over a heap of gravel, his dark tunic and pants covered with dust. But what held Armand's attention wasn't the fact that Joshua didn't move but the burn marks encircling his throat. The stench of singed flesh filling the small cell made Armand cover his mouth and nose with his free hand.

Beside Joshua, a long chain sat on the ground, part of it incinerated.

What had happened?

He darted to the Brenheran heir's side and gently nudged his shoulder. It couldn't be. If he was dead, all his efforts, all the efforts of his mother would have been in vain. All those years—

If Joshua was dead, there would not be a true king of Sives.

To Armand's relief, Joshua's chest was slowly rising and falling, but his injuries looked bad. He needed a healer before the wounds could get infected. As did Gandrett.

"Can you hear me, cousin?"

Gandrett held her breath as Joshua's groan drifted from the cell. Alive. He was alive. And she wasn't a killer.

Her heart beat a bit more lightly but remained the same darkened lump it had turned into the moment the dagger had started to glow.

Magic. She couldn't even begin to comprehend how it was possible that magic had erupted from her hands. Never in her ten years at the priory had she ever had a spark of magic—a sword-wielder, yes, the best one, but magic? Vala had not bestowed that gift upon her.

So how could it be possible that the blade had heated in her hand, that it had burned Joshua, that the chain around his neck had seared into his flesh?

She was remotely aware that Addie had returned with Armand. A welcome rescue under different conditions... But not with magic involved. The magic that had run through her hadn't been the calm stream of the Vala-blessed water mages but something different. Hot and angry magic. Some rogue energy that had saved her from Joshua Brenheran. And yet, it had damned her. If anyone found out, her fate would be to be exiled to the dormant forests of Ulfray to live her life in the wilderness of the Fae lands... if she was lucky. If she wasn't that fortunate, she would meet her end through magic-haters before she ever made it to the borders of the Fae territories.

She knew that when Armand returned from that cell, there would be questions, and she wasn't certain if she could find plausible answers to any of them. He would know something was wrong.

And once Joshua woke up to tell the tale...

Her face stung as Addie dabbed the fresh blood off her lips, but Gandrett didn't complain. She was still trying to make sense of what had happened in that cell, the slightest of hope remaining that she might have hallucinated.

"We must get Joshua somewhere safe." Armand appeared at her side, face weary. "And you need a healer."

Addie had stopped torturing her face with the cloth and folded her hands in her lap, bloody cloth and all. "We can hide them somewhere in the higher levels of the north tower," she suggested quietly as if embarrassed to speak at all.

When Gandrett looked up, she found a silent understanding between Armand and Addie as if they both knew exactly there was something more than just their recovery at stake. For Gandrett knew, the wounds on her would heal once she could clean up, get some water to drink, and then rest for a day or two. Joshua would most likely survive if a healer tended to his burns, or so she hoped. But her hopes of ever dragging him back to Ackwood had been incinerated when she realized just how strong he was.

He wouldn't go willingly. And she wouldn't have the strength to make him.

"People will start looking for him," Addie noted. "We need to hide him." Some ghost of guilt crossed her features that Gandrett didn't understand.

Armand touched Gandrett's shoulder with a light hand. "Can you get up and walk?"

Gandrett studied him for a short moment. He was wearing night-blue silken pajamas and boots. Under different circumstances, she would have made a joke about it, but now, she just nodded. It didn't matter if she could stand and walk. She had to in order to get out of here.

So she pushed herself up and set one wobbly leg in front of the other until she swayed. Addie caught her around the waist, not commenting on the wet stains at the back of her dress. Gandrett hid her embarrassment and made a silent promise to reward Addie for her aid later.

Beside them, Armand appeared, Joshua Brenheran's limp body draped over his shoulders.

"Not in the north tower," Armand said to Addie. "Gandrett goes back to her room, and Joshua we'll hide in plain sight." Gandrett felt his gaze on her as she stumbled along, mouth too dry to say a word, head spinning. "I'll keep him at my own chambers for now."

Riho didn't bring news when he returned at first light, instead, dropping a corn-seed in his hand, he cawed by way of greeting. It was the third day without news from Gandrett. If it took another night, Nehelon swore, he would go to Eedwood himself and turn the castle upside down until he found her.

He had even prepared a message for her, saying exactly that. Riho cocked his head as Nehelon tied the tiny scroll of parchment to his leg. He was just finishing up as it hit him like a surge of wind running through his blood. Magic.

Clear and bright like a bolt of lightning. He hadn't felt something this strong since—

He didn't allow himself to go there. It had been over a century...

"Did you feel that, my friend?"

Riho cocked his head to the other side in a silent question.

"Magic, Riho." Nehelon leaned back against the tree, probing through his system for a trace of the sensation he had just experienced.

But it had already subsided. A bright light in a dark world that had flickered for but a moment and had left the darkness that came after even more blinding.

With a sigh, Nehelon sent Riho in the skies. "Find her," he told the bird even if he knew it was out of his hands.

A ddie refused to leave Gandrett's side as she dismissed the girl with heartfelt words of thanks. As did Armand.

He had taken Joshua to his chambers and sent one of his loyal guards, both of which had not asked any questions despite the horrified looks on their faces when they had assessed the condition Joshua and Gandrett were in, to get reinforcements—only from his inner circle, he had demanded, and Deelah.

While Gandrett had washed and changed into her sleeping gown and wrapped a robe around her shivering body, Armand had overseen Joshua's treatment. Only now that Joshua was asleep, he had come through the secret passageway together with Deelah, and the woman was now cleaning the wounds on Gandrett's hands. No burn marks there, Gandrett had noticed. Just the deep cut from Nehelon's dagger.

Deelah didn't ask questions either but patiently worked on Gandrett's hands while Armand paced the room in an elliptic path.

"I can do this myself," Gandrett commented between two sips of water she drank from a glass Addie was holding to her lips.

"It seems you can do more than that," Armand noted from his position by the wall.

Gandrett knew by the look on his face that he knew. She could tell by the deep furrow between his brows that he was debating what to do with her—or Joshua. But he didn't speak until Deelah was done with her hands and left with a bucket full of bloodied water.

"Use this for your face." She placed a small bottle on the table before she headed out the door, a weary smile on her lips.

"She's not going to say a word to anyone," Armand claimed as soon as the door closed behind Deelah.

Gandrett loosed a breath, as did Addie and Armand. The three of them stared at each other for a long moment, Gandrett close to the point of falling asleep sitting up. If it weren't for the fear that she would be kicked into the forests of Ulfray before she ever had a chance of finishing her mission and seeing her parents again. Then, if she *did* have magic, wouldn't it be better to stay as far away from them as she could.

Eventually, Armand stopped looking at her as if she was a hybrid between a branding iron and a porcelain doll and sauntered over to sit next to her on the crimson sofa. All the while Addie still stood, shifting as if she was about to make an excuse to leave.

"You are staying here," he said with a voice that was more commander than a young lord.

Addie, to her credit, didn't shy away from his tone but simply said, "Lady Linniue will be wondering where I am."

The light of recognition flashed in Armand's eyes. "So that's where I have seen you before."

Addie cringed. "The Lady doesn't like to be kept waiting," she murmured, her electric blue eyes wandering to the secret passage between Armand's and Gandrett's chambers.

Armand gave her a tentative smile. "When you get there, you can tell my aunt that it is my fault you're late."

Gandrett tried to piece together the information while Armand leaped to his feet once more to pick up the bottle Deelah had left. With quick strides, he vanished into the bathing chamber, from where he emerged a few moments—and the sound of running water—later.

"I can do this," Addie offered as Armand returned to Gandrett's side where he set down the metal bowl he'd filled with water and dipped a fresh piece of cloth into it.

Armand waved her off. "You've done enough already," he said, glancing at her as she was still fidgeting. "Why don't you sit down and rest?" he suggested. "You must be exhausted."

Addie felt her jaw drop and had no control over it. Never once had anyone in Eedwood castle offered her to take a seat and rest. Especially not Lady Linniue. But the young lord's stare was so compelling that she set foot after foot without even realizing it. Only when she reached the table and sat down did he release her from his surveillance.

"Good," he said and turned back to Gandrett.

It was hard to watch the way he looked at her, his measuring gaze, the unspoken words on his lips. There was an undeniable bond between them. A sort of closeness that made her heart ache for someone she could confide in.

"I want the whole story, Gandrett," he demanded, words gentle despite the urging tone in them.

He pulled the cloth from the water, wrung the excess fluid from it, then touched it to the side of Gandrett's nose where, after she had washed all blood away, a gruesome, swelling bruise was distorting her beautiful face.

She flinched but didn't complain. "He came out of nowhere," she said, sounding not even half-convincing. "And then he locked me in that cell and left me to rot... I think."

Armand's lips pulled up at one side as if he found her lie adorable. "You need to lie better if you want to lie to me, Gandrett."

He looked so different from the way Addie remembered him, now in black pants and a blue tunic instead of the silk pajamas, but hair still disheveled as if he'd just climbed out of bed. There was something heartbreakingly beautiful about this amused, caring side of him—despite the fact that he was caring for someone else, and the sorrow in his face had vanished only for a brief moment.

"Maybe you want to enlighten us—" he turned to look at Addie, those eyes inquisitive, "I never asked for your name."

Addie shifted in her chair, suddenly very much aware of the rags she was wearing. But she squared her shoulders and cleared her throat. "It's Addie." She considered bowing her head but decided that for this one moment, while she was sitting at his grace, she would not be the servant girl but the one who had rescued Gandrett from the man whom she had denied help once.

The guilt rumbled in her chest as she held the young lord's gaze.

So she told the story of how she had been on her way to get something for Lady Linniue—she left out the details of her routine to go to the hidden well—when she had heard Gandrett's call for help. Of how they'd heard footsteps, of how Gandrett had asked her to get him.

But Armand wasn't satisfied. "That's all?"

Addie nodded, so he turned back to Gandrett and dipped the cloth in the bowl again and dabbed it along the bridge of her nose, seeming absorbed.

"Addie, why don't you go take a look at how Joshua is doing?" he said without taking his eyes off Gandrett's face.

Addie got to her feet but hesitated. "He's deep asleep, isn't he?" After seeing in what shape he had left Gandrett, she had no desire to be next on his list. And after having denied him help once—

"Deelah gave him something, so he'll be asleep for a while. Plus there are guards right by the door. And the passageway is open. So if you call, someone will come, whether it's me or my men at the door." It was clear by the way he said it that she was dismissed.

So Addie pulled up every ounce of courage she could muster and headed for the young lord's chambers.

His gaze was a weight on her heart. Not because there was pity in it or concern but because of the infinite tenderness as he touched the moist cloth to her cheek, then to the corner of her mouth, and along her lower lip, which she must have split when she had hit the ground face-forward.

"What's really going on, Gandrett?" he asked, his voice a low melody, almost singing to her to trust him. "What did you do to my cousin to end up in our ancient dungeons?"

Gandrett froze. "What did you just say?" She didn't care for whatever appearance she was supposed to keep up. He had seen her in a dress that she had soiled herself in. He had seen her bloody and distraught. And now he was tending to her wounds—almost like a friend.

Armand pulled back his hand and rested it on his thigh, eyes alert. "What did you do to end up in the dungeons?" he repeated.

"Not that," she gestured with her good hand. "The other thing."

He squinted his eyes, trying to read her, but Gandrett didn't have much strength left before she'd black out from exhaustion, and she wasn't going to waste it on trying to feign patience. "The other thing about Joshua being your cousin."

Armand didn't respond, face hardening as if he were damning himself for having said too much.

"You are aware what Joshua's last name is?" She couldn't stop herself. It was almost the same way it had overcome her when she was provoking Nehelon. The image of the Fae male's incinerated blade flashed through her mind. Magic. She had done that.

Armand probed her gaze as if trying to read whether it was worth lying to her.

"Brenheran," she answered for him. "His name is Joshua Brenheran."

Armand didn't look the slightest bit shocked.

He knew.

Of course he knew. He had been behind it from the start. He had hidden Joshua when the Brenheran mercenaries had tried to free him under Nehelon's command. He—

"You're shaking, Gandrett," Armand noted, voice calm, controlled.

He dropped the cloth in the bowl, laced his fingers together, then took a deep breath as if he needed to build up courage before he closed his eyes and said, "What if I tell you I am not who you think I am?"

Gandrett had expected many reactions, but not this one. "Then, who are you, Armand Denderlain?" Her face exploded with pain as she grimaced at him, but she didn't yield. "Is that even your real name?"

His eyes shot open, all the worry gone, the hazel-gold that was left so vulnerable it smothered Gandrett's rising anger.

"Yes, it is my real name," he said, his lips curling at the sides for a moment, "and yes, I am the rightful Lord of Eedwood and regent over the east of Sives—in theory." He sighed through his nose, probing Gandrett's gaze as if expecting her to slap it. "But I am not the man the world thinks I am. I don't ride out there to strike down those villagers who defy my father's rule, I don't kill for pleasure. All I want is peace for Sives."

His words filtered through the haze in Gandrett's head, but they didn't make sense. Not yet.

Yet, he didn't halt to give her time but poured out his heart, "By bringing my cousin home, I am fulfilling my mother's wishes for a peacefully united Sives."

"How can he be your cousin if..."

"Aunt Linniue and Lord Tyrem Brenheran," he simply said. "She gave up her throne when she was pregnant with Joshua and left it to my mother with the promise to, one day when Joshua was old enough, allow him to rule in Eedwood as king of Sives."

His words hung heavy in the air. So heavy that Gandrett didn't dare speak.

"My aunt took ill when Joshua was a baby, and she gave him to his father to look after. Of course, a marriage between the two houses was something unthinkable. It has been a thousand years since Sives has last seen a king, and with his Denderlain and Brenheran blood—Joshua is the rightful heir to both thrones and could be king of Sives. A true king."

It took Gandrett a while to process. If this was true, she had been sent on a fool's errand. If Joshua Brenheran—Joshua Denderlain—*was* the rightful heir to both reigning houses of Sives, this could be the end of war.

Then she remembered how Joshua had threatened to kill her—for what? What had she done, except for calling him by his name, that he had locked her up and threatened to kill her? Would someone like that be a good ruler? Either as lord over the west of Sives or as its king.

"But he is dangerous." Gandrett knew from the way Armand looked at her that after what he saw in the cell, he wasn't convinced Joshua was the dangerous one.

"You tell me, Gandrett," he said with some heaviness. "Who attacked who down there?"

"He locked me up in a cell and left me to rot," she bit at him.

"Why?" Armand demanded. A simple question, one that she had asked herself a moment ago.

"I don't know." She folded her arms across her chest.

"Joshua doesn't just attack people," Armand claimed, "I have spent enough time around him to know he isn't a bad man."

"A good man wouldn't want to kill me," she countered.

"What did you *do* to earn his disfavor?" Armand asked, all gentleness gone from his voice.

Gandrett swallowed. Could it be that there was more at stake than even Nehelon knew? That maybe Joshua didn't *want* to return?

The room was like the young lord himself. Elegant threaded with amusement and a heaviness that pushed down on Addie's shoulders like a boulder of granite. Vases with small, colorful flowers sat on every surface like little suns to contrast the dark tapestries. The four-poster bed was beautiful, carved, and covered in Denderlain-blue silk sheets. She didn't dare look there for longer than a second, for on the couch by the window, Joshua Brenheran started twitching.

She inched closer, uncertain if it was wise to be within the man's reach.

His eyes were closed, features relaxed. Only his fingers and toes moved every now and then as if he were having a nightmare.

So she decided to be brave and pulled up a chair to sit beside him.

He appeared younger than that time she had refused him help. Shame crept up on her together with the painful realization that if she had aided him back then, Gandrett might have been spared.

His tunic had been unbuttoned halfway down his chest, exposing bandages covering the heavy burn marks she had spotted on their way up here. What was visible of his chest was smooth skin stretched over hard muscle. The body of a trained fighter covered in the elegant clothes of a noble.

Addie averted her gaze and rolled her feet back and forth to pass the time.

The young lord had undoubtedly kicked her out because he had things he wanted to discuss with Gandrett in private. They would make a beautiful pair, the two of them. She could almost see them strolling through the castle together, the young lord with his elegant, cunning stride and Gandrett with her graceful, feline movement. And the thought of it hit her right in the heart.

Don't be silly, Addie. She folded her hands in her lap and looked out the window where the clouds were slowly turning pink and orange in the morning light. Beneath, the Eedpenesor snaked through the landscape in curves of sparkling gold. She absorbed the images, archiving them for the dark hours of her life that were sure to come once she returned to Lady Linniue empty-handed.

A groan breaking from Joshua's lips made Addie tear away from the beauty of the lands that she was never to walk again.

When she found Joshua's face, he was blinking his eyes open. Two glazed, emerald disks that searched the room as if unseeing.

"What..." He coughed and grimaced, the peaceful rest gone from his features. "Where...?"

He tried to prop himself up on his elbows and failed, ungracefully plunging back into the silver-threaded pillows.

Eyes slowly focusing, he glanced to where Addie had shrunk back into her chair, praying to Vala he wouldn't attack her.

"You..." He lifted a hand and reached for her, making Addie almost topple over with the chair. But the look in his eyes changed to that haunted gaze he'd given her when he had pleaded for her help.

"There are guards outside," she said, a promise that if he as much as lifted a finger against her, she'd scream for them.

He rolled to the side, groaning through gritted teeth until he was half sitting up. "Help me," he whispered and grabbed her hand with what seemed to be agonizing effort.

There was no aggression in his eyes, nothing of the man Gandrett had been so afraid of but fear. Authentic, deep-rooted fear.

Addie's heart pounded in her chest, threatening to break her ribs. The words were there on her tongue. I can't. But she had spoken them before, and she could not face herself another minute if she repeated that mistake.

"What are you so afraid of?" The words came out in a mutter, hardly seeing the light of day, but it was enough to let Joshua Brenheran rest his back against the sofa and exhale a stuck breath.

"Where are we?" He searched the room for details, and when his eyes fell on a portrait of the young lord with his mother hung near the secret door, he found his answer. "Armand Denderlain's rooms?" His face was incredulous. "What am I doing in Armand Denderlain's rooms?"

Addie heaved a breath, finding that if she wanted to do it right this time, she had to get answers. And in order to get answers, sometimes you had to offer some truth yourself.

"We found you in the dungeons," she said and smoothed out her rags over her thigh. She couldn't remember the last time she had worn real clothes. "I am not certain what happened exactly, but you were injured." It was the truth. Other than that Gandrett had been locked in that cell earlier and both of them had been in really bad shape when she and Armand had gotten to them, there was hardly a detail she knew, other than, "Is it true you locked Gandrett in the dungeons?"

Joshua's eyes tightened with realization. A realization he seemed to not particularly enjoy. "So that's her name?" He reached to his side, to the now-empty spot at his sword belt, and Addie glanced to the secret passageway, debating whether to call Armand now or wait until she had gotten something of worth from Joshua.

"Who else knows I'm here?" he asked, gaze suddenly full of fear again.

Addie leaned forward a tad, trying to read the depths of his eyes. What was going on in his mind? Why beg for help then lock up a defenseless lady?

"Just the young lord, Gandrett, and I."

The expression on his face didn't relax. "He's not going to tell her, is he?"

"Who?"

"Armand," he clarified. "Tell my mother."

Addie scratched her temple as she tried to understand how the young lord would be able to inform Lady Crystal Brenheran of anything.

"You're aware I am a servant in this house and I don't have communication privileges with the outside world," she merely said.

Joshua's eyes did that thing with the realization again. "Not Lady Brenheran," he whispered. "My mother—Linniue Denderlain."

Addie's heart stuttered to a sudden halt.

"It's a secret," he said through gritted teeth as he pushed himself forward and rested his elbows on his knees, face oddly close to Addie's. "No one knows but Linniue and Armand. Even Lord Hamyn is oblivious of my Denderlain blood." He spat the words as if it was a stain on his soul.

The fear in his eyes was still there, so Addie repeated, "What are you so afraid of?"

He reached for her hand and clutched it as if she was a lifeline. Addie didn't dare pull it back as she studied the scabbed knuckles. It wasn't a fresh injury. "It's happening over and over again. I lose control over my mind, my body. Almost as if someone else were commanding my actions."

Addie saw the conflict flash across his features, his eyes turning a shade darker with the pain of his story.

"When that girl—Gandrett—" He coughed again from the strain of sitting up. "When she followed me into the depths of the north tower, I was compelled to get rid of her." Shame filled his features, and he slowly shook his head then cursed at the pain it caused him. "As I am compelled to get rid of anyone who finds out about me."

Addie realized it might be time to call for aid, for everything he was telling her now meant he'd need to rid himself of her later.

His hand tightened around hers as he read the fear in her eyes. "No, please," he murmured. "Please, don't run from me." His voice was soft, soothing. "Who else can I trust in this castle but someone who has nothing to gain from my presence?"

His words stung and comforted her at the same time.

"When I asked you for help last time, I had one of those rare moments of clarity when I am in charge of my own mind and thoughts. Why do you think I did anything to avoid crossing your path afterward?"

Addie didn't have an answer. All she could do was stare at those emerald eyes as they helplessly searched hers for answers.

"I wanted to spare you so if I ever got a moment like that again, you would still be around, so I could convince you to help me." He loosened his grasp on her hand as if intending to let go but lingered. "I didn't let myself think about our encounter. I convinced myself you didn't exist, that it had been a dream. All of it so once I was back under that spell—whatever it is—I wouldn't sell you out to myself." He searched for words. "That I wouldn't sell you out to that version of myself that seems compelled to stay at this castle and keep my identity hidden, no matter the cost."

Addie slowly withdrew her hand and sorted her thoughts. "And now, you are having one of those rare moments?" she simply asked.

There was nothing between them but the raw words spoken. He didn't look at her as the servant she was, and she didn't see a noble but a man in need of help. A man who was about to break apart from the fear of losing control over his own self.

"Now is one of those rare moments." His eyes shone with gratitude for merely hearing him out, for not trying to run, for not calling for guards.

"And in the cells?" Addie's voice shook with tension.

"Compelled to kill her. I didn't kill her the first time I had the chance." He glanced at the scabbed knuckles of the hand that had released hers. "It was all I could do to keep in control, rather hurt myself than kill her. And I managed to convince my compelled self that locking her up to kill her later was acceptable."

Horror filled his features as he looked into the past. Addie didn't dare interrupt.

"If she hadn't stopped me..." His voice trailed away.

Addie felt her heart ache for the young man before her. So strong, and yet that strength meant nothing if he wasn't in control of it.

"Do you know what it's like watching yourself harm someone? Not being able to stop?" The haunted look returned to his features.

This time, it was Addie who reached out for his hand, gently brushing her dirty fingers over his wrist. "I am sorry."

He looked at her. Really looked at her. And his emerald eyes tightened ever so slightly. "Who would have thought that my mother's servant would become my trusted ally?"

Addie knew he wasn't asking for an answer, and she didn't have one except for that one truth she had no one in this castle. That she, as much as he, was a prisoner here.

"How badly is she hurt?" he asked, shame yet again on his features. Addie could read him so easily. Every emotion plain on his face as if his features were the clouds in the skies, telling by their color and shape whether they would begin to storm and rain or pass and leave sunshine.

"Her face looks pretty bad." Addie didn't go into the brutal details of the swelling or the black and blue bruise that was developing along her nose and lips. "As for the rest of it, she needs food and rest." Addie watched Joshua's eyes darken at her words, and she could almost feel how sorry he was. How little he had wanted for this to happen. Instinctively, she rubbed her thumb over his hand in small circles. "You saved her by hurting her like that," she reminded him. "It was a better option than killing her."

"It should have been I who was locked up in that cell." Joshua turned his head in disgust at himself then cursed as he moved the burnt areas around his neck too much. "I deserved every little inch of what she did to me." He waved his bandaged hand at his neck and flinched.

"What exactly is it that she did to you?"

39

"You didn't abduct him," Gandrett thought aloud. "You brought him home."

Armand eyed her with calculating cool. "What would a merchant's daughter know of the politics in my court?"

Gandrett blinked at the question, realizing she had said too much. Heat flooded her as he stared her down. "Isn't it common knowledge that—"

"Not common knowledge. No," was all he said. "And no one but the inner circle of his court even knows Joshua Brenheran is here." He was on his feet, pacing again, the bowl swaying in the wake of his rushed movement. "Probably no one outside Ackwood castle knows he's been gone for years. It would make the west look weak."

Wasn't there an easy way out? A solution she could fight out with her sword, for that was what she was good at. That was why the Lord of Ackwood had bought her from the Order of Vala to retrieve his lost son.

Vala help her, there were no words she could say to make Armand any less suspicious. Nothing. She couldn't even run, her body too weak after the strain of the day—or more than one. She hadn't had a chance to ask.

And she, sure as Shaelak reigned over darkness, couldn't return to Lord Tyrem Brenheran empty-handed.

"Who are you, Gandrett Starhaeven?" Armand had stopped before her, his expression as if someone had dragged him through the mud. And as she didn't respond, "We both know you used magic down there." Gandrett's stomach knotted as adrenaline rushed through her system, wiping all exhaustion away as her instinct for survival set in once more. His gaze lowered to her bandaged hands. "The question remains: did you use it to defend yourself or to attack?"

Gandrett couldn't help registering some sort of fascination flickering in his eyes as he ran his hands through his hair like sorting that honey-gold mess would straighten out his problems, too.

"I don't know what happened down there," Gandrett said truthfully. "The only thing I know is that I *was* defending myself and that Joshua locked me in that cell right after you left to speak to your father."

He froze, all agitation vanished, his lips paling as he took her in as if he was seeing her for the first time. "Gods above, Gandrett, that was three days ago."

Three days? That explained why she had been near exhaustion even before Joshua had attacked her in the cell.

"How can you be even standing?" He still bore that same look, but his voice had turned devastated.

Gandrett attempted to smile but gave up as her injury stung at the strain. "I'm not standing, Lord Armand," she said and gestured at the sofa. She had endured worse, had spent longer without food, without knowing when she'd see the desert sun again. Yet, here he was, giving her that look that could have meant she was Vala made flesh.

Armand didn't laugh. His lips didn't as much as twitch. "Aren't we past you calling me *Lord* Armand?" His face was unreadable as he measured her, gaze slowly swiping over her as if he was looking for something, some hint to give her away.

"What am I supposed to call you, milord?" She thought of the days she'd spent preparing with Mckenzie exactly for this, for deceiving Armand Denderlain, for making him believe she was something she was not.

But he didn't fall for it. He didn't seem pleased at her words, the way he had in the beginning when every not so deliberate statement had sent him laughing. No. Armand Denderlain had finally caught on to it that something was wrong with her, and he had done so at the worst possible moment. When her target was finally just one room away.

"Call me Armand."

Now it was Gandrett who stared as Armand returned to her side and picked up that bowl, placing it in his lap. He reached into the water, wrung out the cloth, and continued where he had left off earlier.

"After what happened, I think we are beyond titles"—his eyes narrowed as he leaned closer, cloth brushing over her cheek—"and beyond lies, I hope."

It was an honest offer, she could tell by the look in his eyes—so open, so vulnerable.

So what if she told him the truth? That she had come here working for his enemy? That she had befriended him only to betray him? That she was neither a lady nor a merchant's daughter, but a Child of Vala, that she would not marry any man and what Deelah had hoped for would never happen?

Neither of them felt like the right thing to say—not yet. So she said, "Thank you, Armand, for coming to my rescue." She gave him a long look—not the flirtatious type that Mckenzie had taught her and that she had perfected during her hours spent with Brax, but a deep look that let him, she hoped, glimpse into her soul. "I didn't deserve it." *That* was the truth.

Truth. He had told her the truth about Joshua. All those years since he had found out he even had a cousin. Then, the day his father had ordered him to bring Joshua to Eedwood under the impression he was abducting his enemy's son to have a tool to pressure him.

That's what his father had been doing all those years—using Joshua against the Brenheran family. To keep at bay their efforts to win over central-Sives and slowly push back the Denderlain troops that were scattered over the territory in strategic positions, ready to strike the moment Brenheran made a move.

The month he and his mother had spent convincing his father to let Joshua live in normal chambers—even if they were guarded like a prison, but with humane conditions—rather than the dungeons. All that time, keeping the truth hidden from his father. For if Lord Hamyn Denderlain knew that Joshua was not only Tyrem Brenheran's son but also Linniue's, he would have executed him on the spot.

So Armand had played by his father's rules, kept his head down, little by little, bought Joshua more freedom so he could spend time with his mother, so that he could see for himself that the House of Denderlain wasn't the snake-pit everyone in Ackwood believed it to be. So Joshua would one day proudly carry both names and step on that throne and rule, not as lord of Ackwood or Lord of Eedwood but as king of Sives.

Now that vision—everything he had fought for by keeping Joshua a secret, by putting up with his father's moods, his hunger for power—that vision his mother and he had fought for, what he had promised to her, didn't matter. If Joshua was the type of man who locked Gandrett in a cell for three days, only to go down and finish her off himself... Raw emotion threatened to burst from him. Devastation.

Joshua had been so peaceful, so noble all those times they had talked. All those afternoons spent together when Armand had snuck away to meet with his cousin. The picture of a united Sives, the Sives his mother had dreamed about, they had painted together, building for the day that they were ready to set the crown upon his head. For Sives to be ready.

"I didn't deserve it." Her words were like a blow to the head, and he studied her for a long moment, feeling less the lord everyone expected him to be and more the man he wanted to be.

"If you asked me again, I'd help you," he murmured as he watched the swelling on her nose reduce under the touch of

Dragon Water. Probably the only gift the last Dragon King had left behind in Eedwood. Deelah had left a flacon of it for him so he could get her back in shape. So no one noticed just how badly she had been treated in this palace. His chest hurt as he took in her face. Her beautiful face, brutalized by the Hope of Sives. "I don't care if you have magic, Gandrett." He glanced at the bowl. "Magic is all around us. Even if we can't see it."

He felt her breath against the inside of his wrist as he reached to clean the other side of her nose.

"You're not going to report me?" Her eyes were wide like those of a chased animal, but her voice was steady.

Never. "What would I do if they tossed you over the Ulfrayian border? Who would make me laugh? Who would entertain me?"

For some reason, his response didn't put her at ease the way he'd hoped. So he took a steadying breath—the sort he never usually took with women, and said, "You may have your secrets, Gandrett, and I have mine." He allowed his free hand to brush a strand of hair from her forehead. "But before you, I never met a woman I even wanted to share them with."

He listened to his own words as he spoke them. Pathetic. Desperate. And yet—the truth.

Gandrett pulled out of his touch. Answer enough that what resonated in his words wasn't an option for her. At least, not now that she had just escaped death. He bit back the bitter aftertaste of rejection and dipped the cloth back into the water to dab the magic liquid on her lips for one last time.

"Deelah will be back with food soon," he changed the subject, hoping to give her the feeling of not being pressured.

Gandrett remained silent. Deep in thought, it seemed a struggle that he couldn't even begin to understand unfolding on her features.

The bruises were already a light shade of purple when she finally spoke again, "If Joshua becomes king of Sives—" Horror won the upper hand.

"The last time I saw him fight anyone was when they brought him to Eedwood," Armand admitted with shame. The memory of his cousin in chains. That first time he had spoken to him, explained to him why he was there, that there was Denderlain blood running through his veins. And then the curiosity. That first meeting with aunt Linniue—

"I don't know what got into him."

"He was about to kill me, Armand." Gandrett held his gaze as she spoke, her moss-green eyes weary. "He said it. He was unstoppable. So strong—too strong. I have never fought anyone that strong—" She bit her lip and flinched as she realized there should have been a bruise where her teeth dug into her lower lip. "What did you do to me?"

She touched her face with cautious fingers, probing along the parts that had been injured an hour ago, and surprise spread under her hands.

"As I said," he found himself capable of a smile, "you have your secrets. I have mine."

But she was smarter than that, her eyes darting to the bowl in his lap. "The water," she said and realized that she wasn't the only one using magic here—even if his type of magic came from a hidden well at the bottom of the north tower that only a few people knew about, including him, his late mother, and aunt Linniue. He knew that Addie, the servant girl was the one to fetch it from the well every day, and Linniue had been using it since the day she had fallen ill.

"It has healing properties." That was all he was going to tell her about it, he promised himself. He had already told her too much. But for all that was worth, she *was* different from everyone else he had met. There was a quiet form of beauty in her that he had never seen before, someone whose heart and soul was blessed by the gods and untouched by the corruption of the Sivesian courts.

For a moment, she looked like she was going to ask questions, but then she yawned as if the relief of pain had paved the way for sleep, and when he murmured that it was okay if she rested, that he would be right here when she woke up, exhaustion had already taken over her body, and he set aside the bowl and slid his arms around her shoulders and knees. He lifted her with ease and carried her over to her bed where he tucked her in. It was when he pulled the covers over her that the front of her robe slid aside and revealed two pendants resting on her chest: a small silver one showing the grains of Sives, and one that held shards of emerald. The twin to the necklace Joshua Brenheran was wearing around his neck.

40

Magic. Addie was still trying to wrap her head around it. Gandrett had used magic on Joshua.

The last mages had disappeared when the Fae had gone dormant in the forests of Ulfray, and whatever mages were left were either the Vala-blessed, who all of Neredyn adored like the goddess herself, or those unlucky few who were born with it and who were exiled into Fae territory. A meal for the wicked.

Joshua had told her word for word how Gandrett had followed him almost three days ago, how he had punched the wall to prevent himself from snapping her neck. How he had fought the urge to kill her until he no longer had been capable of lying to his compelled self. Looking at him was like looking at a man with two souls in his chest.

And Gandrett—

Addie had known something was off with Gandrett after the girl had fallen through the wall. Had she used magic back then?

"Fire," Joshua continued, "is a type of magic that is most definitely not the magic of a Vala-blessed, so we can rule that out."

She had spent the past minutes trying to figure out how it was even possible. "You have been compelled to remain in the castle for years, and you are wondering how it's possible someone has magic?" Addie's words came easily as she spoke to the Brenheran heir, for who she saw wasn't nobility but a prisoner with a soul broken as much as her own. And equal. "How do you think it works?"

She thought about the last time she had seen him when he had been in control of his senses and actions. "What is different now—" She held his inquisitive emerald gaze. "What's different from an hour ago when you wanted to kill Gandrett?"

"I don't know." He glanced at his bandaged hand, slowly flexing it as if to test if it still worked. It did. "I was on my way to see my mother for tea when I—when my compelled ego— decided to go and finish off the girl."

His mother—Lady Linniue. A shudder ran through Addie as she imagined the lady as a loving mother. The only thing she could manage was to conjure that image of the lady the day she had brought her to Eedwood castle with the words, "Be grateful it is I who came to get you. At least with me, you'll be serving a greater cause." She hardly had dared to wonder what that greater cause might be, the prison in the north still too fresh in her mind. The freezing cold, the screams. And the ceremonies that she had listened to from afar—prayers to the god of dragons, the offering of sacrifices. What if it was all connected? The magic, the freezing cold as she had found Gandrett in the corridor that first time, the spell that someone had put on Joshua. All the while she was spinning her theories, Addie didn't interrupt but gave him an encouraging nod.

"It's only recently that she calls me to her chambers for tea—she used to come to my rooms." His eyebrows knitted together. "Sometimes at the weirdest hours of the day," he noted. "She says I'm ready."

"Ready for what?" Addie wanted to know and had the intuition it would be bad—if it was connected to Linniue, it had to be bad.

But Joshua shook his head. "I don't know." He gave her a look that didn't let her wish for anything good. "But I know that sometimes I black out after my visits with her."

"Do you think it has something to do with her?" Addie almost didn't speak the words even if the thought was nearly tangible in the air. Accusing someone's mother—especially if that mother was the one holding her fate in her hands.

Joshua didn't seem upset as he considered her words, his good hand extracting a necklace from in-between the fabric of his half-open tunic. "My mother ordered my kidnapping," he said, face hardening. "If she is capable of that, I think her capable of worse." He didn't seem like the lost son who had been reunited with his mother but haunted by his forced presence at her side. "Whatever that spell is that she put on me—if it was her—it must have worn off last night and also that day I ran into you in the north tower."

Addie hid her shame as he brought up that day she had denied him help.

"What did you do differently then?" she asked quietly. She could almost smell the answer to the riddle Joshua Brenheran presented.

And there was something in his emerald eyes. A horrible realization that made Addie dread the words he was about to speak.

"I missed my visit with my mother," he said with an ashen face. "Both times."

His words triggered something in her. Something that she might have been pushing away for too long. It *was* all connected. Even the task she had been brought here to do. "Do you think it has something to do with what your mother is sending me to procure for her every day?" she proposed cautiously.

He eyed her as if she were speaking in mysteries. "I don't know what errands you run for her," he said, his good hand sliding up to his neck to probe the bandages, "just that whenever I see you, you are carrying a bucket with you."

"The water from the well in the north tower," Addie explained, knowing that if he ever fell back under the spell that compelled him to do such horrible things, her life would end.

The air between them went taut.

"You know that I remember everything but those blackouts I had," he whispered. "Everything."

Addie shook her head, indicating she didn't understand what he was trying to say, but he no longer looked at her. He had gone into his own mind where he seemed to be piecing things together.

"Linniue told me the story about whose tower the north tower used to be a long time ago." He eyed her briefly as if checking whether or not she could follow before he was back in his thoughts. "The last Dragon King. It was the last Dragon King's tower. His home, from where he flew out to slaughter and conquer." There was revulsion in Joshua's voice. "And his dragon slept under the castle in caves it dug with its claws, its magic seeping into the very soil under this Fortress."

Addie's breath caught at the thought of the Dreads of the Skies—the last one of them—having left their magic under the foundations of the castle. Maybe not just there, but also—

"The water." Her hand darted to her side for the bucket that wasn't there.

Now it was Joshua who couldn't follow her.

"The water Lady Linniue keeps requesting. It's from the hidden well under the north tower. It's," she hardly whispered, "Dragon Water." It had to be.

"Dragon Water?" Joshua raised an eyebrow as if he didn't know what to make of her conclusion.

But Addie didn't care. She didn't give him a moment to ask questions but offered something no one else had yet believed in this castle. "Before your mother brought me to Eedwood castle, I was a prisoner in Lands End."

He stared. It was all he did.

"Everyone knows that Lands End is where the dragons used to reside." She took a steadying breath. "But what nobody knows is that of the prisoners who go to Lands End for whatever crimes they committed, none return. Not alive." Addie saw them before her, the cells in the dark caves, the cold—cold that went not only under your skin but right into your heart. "There was something more there than human evil, and the nights they worshipped Shygon," her voice shook at the mention of the god's name, "the cold and the darkness seemed to grow worse than on others. They sacrifice them." She had pushed it so far from her mind, the destiny that had awaited her in Lands End. "To Shygon."

Joshua looked positively dead, his skin a shade of chalk-white that any corpse would be jealous of, his eyes a stark contrast to his pale-pink lips. "They pray to the god of dragons?" he asked in a whisper.

Addie nodded, unable to repeat the words. It was forbidden. The last one to have done it had been the last Dragon King. And he had brought destruction over Neredyn.

"If what you procure for my mother is Dragon Water—" He rested both hands on his thighs and his eyes widened. "Do you think my mother worships the god of dragons?"

Addie almost burst from gratitude that he had said it first. The god of dragons—or the god of forbidden magic—that's what all of Neredyn called him *if* anyone dared speak his name.

"One thing I can tell for sure," she replied, voice anything but steady, "there is magic involved, or your mother wouldn't be able to control you."

"We don't know that for a fact," he said too quickly, but she could tell by the look in his eyes that he had come to the same conclusion.

"So, if she does—" Addie glanced at Joshua's bandaged neck, his hands, and then back to his face where emerald eyes looked at her in wonder. "The question remains: why?"

He didn't cringe at her words but glanced past Addie to where Armand had appeared in the secret door. Addie jumped to her feet, habit taking over.

"I should kill you," the young lord said through gritted teeth. "I should lock you in a cell like the animal you are." He had drawn his sword and held the tip of it high enough that it came to rest on Joshua's collarbone as he walked up in a few quick strides and planted himself before his cousin. "I should impale you for what you did to her. You had no right—"

Joshua, to his credit, didn't move. "It might be a mercy, cousin." His eyes were bleak as they held Armand's furious gaze.

His words made the young lord yield, though. "We had an agreement." He lowered the tip of his sword to the height of Joshua's chest, not seeming to notice as Addie inched forward.

Armand's fury was intimidating. A facet of the young lord she had never before appreciated. But she rallied her courage anyway, searching deep in the well of her heart for the words that might spare Joshua Brenheran—and save the young lord from the biggest mistake of his life.

"How many times did I want to hit your face on the delicate tea table in my chambers," Joshua said with a dark kind of humor.

He stopped as Armand's hand twitched, bringing the blade dangerously close to his skin. He gave Joshua a feral grin. "I'd like to see you try now."

Addie didn't think as she stepped in front of Joshua, pushing the flat of the young lord's blade aside with her bare forearm. "You'd make a mistake killing him."

Armand's eyes wandered to her, incredulous and wide, but there was a warning there.

"Why did you lock her up in that cell?" he asked, not moving his sword. "What did she ever do to you?"

Joshua was quiet for a long moment before he said, "She offered to help me get back to Ackwood."

Armand's blood turned cold. "She offered *what*?"

Joshua, half-hidden behind Addie's slender shape, was about to repeat what he had said, but Armand was already wheeling around, pacing rather than spearing his cousin like he wanted to.

He had seen the necklace on Gandrett. The same necklace that Joshua was wearing. A Brenheran heirloom.

There were three of them—one for each of Lord Tyrem's children. And one of them had to be running around without it right now. It wasn't Joshua for sure since his necklace was visible beneath his unbuttoned tunic.

"Tell me who she is," Armand demanded. "Tell me now." He could hear the urgency in his own voice, the shaking, the loss of control.

Years. He had spent years with Joshua, getting to know him, plotting how they would eventually put him on the throne. How the future king of Sives would bestow peace on both halves of the territory. And all this time...

"I don't know who she is," Joshua said calmly. "At the dance in honor of Demea was the first time I ever saw her."

At least it sounded like he was telling the truth, but... "How can I know you're not lying now?" Armand hissed.

To his surprise, it was the servant girl who responded, "Because he wasn't himself when he locked her up."

It took Armand a moment to understand the words she had spoken.

"Someone put a spell on him," Addie explained before he could ask specifics. "We suspect his mother."

To his surprise, Joshua nodded.

"He has been under a spell since the very first day he came here," Addie added.

From the very first day? Armand stopped and watched the clouds pass by his windows, his mind racing. If what they claimed was true and Joshua hadn't been himself—

And as Addie and Joshua told him everything they had figured out—the Dragon Water, about which he added he knew had healing properties, that the last Dragon King's dragon had resided under the castle, the suspicion of aunt Linniue worshipping Shygon, the god of dragons—it all made sense. Painfully perfect sense. That Joshua had stopped fighting from one day to the other. That he had roamed the castle freely, never as much as asking to send a message to his family. That he had been perfect. Perfect and invisible, his identity a secret to all but a few. Armand broke for his cousin's fate of a mother who had given him away just to bring him back as a prisoner—even if his prison had been in his mind.

"Was any of it real, cousin?" The question was as simple as it was scary, the answer of it defining whether what he'd been working toward—what his mother and he had been trying to achieve—had all been a lie. He turned around to face his cousin, who looked even paler than usual.

Joshua's face was unreadable as he said, "I told you I would have given anything to smash your pretty Denderlain face into the coffee table so many times." He exhaled a long breath and gazed at the ceiling as if calling for Vala's aid. "The goddess knows, I have been occupied with two minds in my head—the one that grew to agree with your plan, and the one wanting me to get you to spill every detail of the plan to have something to hold against you one day."

"So that's what she wants?" Armand prompted, betrayal thick in his voice. "She wants to rid herself of me?"

Joshua shook his head. "I have not the slightest idea what her ulterior motive is."

"Not her love for her son, for sure," Addie added darkly, and both of them gave her a look that could only be described as pained agreement.

"But she has been encouraging me to make my plans with you." Joshua glanced at him with those green eyes that seemed haunted. There was truth in them. Even if there were so many open questions. Why would Linniue spend years deceiving this court if she wanted her own son on the throne? "I don't know what she is waiting for... What her plans are." Joshua sighed through his nose, frustration and pain plain on his face.

Armand's own mind was trying to grab a hold of what was going on—what had been going on all this time, unnoticed. That all he had been working toward might have been a lie. And Linniue? Could she truly be behind this? He'd known his aunt to be eccentric, difficult even, but this? Deceive her entire family about the father of her child, only to one day use her son against all of them? Was it truly Linniue alone, or was Joshua deceiving him as well? Was there even a spell?

"And where is that spell now?" Armand returned to the sofa where he planted himself in front of Joshua, sword still in his hand. "How do I know you're not lying right now?"

"Because if I were, I would not be sitting here telling you this but would rip your sword from your hands to ram it into your stomach."

Joshua's words were as harsh as they were convincing. His cousin had never raised a finger against him. Never... And it had taken long for him to trust Joshua. With his Brenheran heritage and his claim to what should have been Armand's... If his mother hadn't paved the way for trust, he might have been convinced this was purely Joshua's craving for power. But with all they had been working toward, with what he had promised his mother, with the proof of Joshua locking up Gandrett in the dungeons and attempting to kill her—

It couldn't be him.

It had to be Linniue. If they were right. Even so, betrayal by the aunt he had known his entire life was hardly any easier than by the cousin he had been seeing as the future of Sives.

"Our plan is still intact, Armand," Joshua said to him, his green eyes like clear waters. "That is—" He rested his back against the sofa, exhaustion creasing his forehead. "If we can make one adjustment."

Armand raised one eyebrow as he waited, still uncertain what or who to trust.

"Get me out of Eedwood. Return me to my father's side. Take over your own lordship of Eedwood and end your father's reign of terror so together we can build up the future."

Armand listened, his heart quickening as he heard the words he had hoped would one day be spoken. And yet he couldn't enjoy them, the bitter taste of betrayal weighing heavy on his heart.

"You as the Lord of the East while my father remains Lord of the West until the day he dies. And *then*, I will take my throne and rule over all of Sives with you as my chancellor."

Armand didn't respond. Not to this. But his gaze fell on Joshua's necklace once more.

41

When Gandrett awoke, she was tangled in blankets, and where her stomach was supposed to be, a gaping pit of hunger demanded bothenia crust. By the candlelight, she could tell that it was past sunset even if the lack of daylight triggered alarm in her system. The last time she had woken, she had found herself in a pitch-black cell somewhere under the last Dragon King's residence in the north tower by the future king of Sives. She was still trying to wrap her head around it—that her mission, the big mission she had been sent on had been only half a mission because the truth was Joshua belonged to Ackwood as much as he belonged to Eedwood. And if he was the cruel type of person she had gotten to know him as, then either there was something very wrong with him now, or his family had a very mistaken image of him.

Gandrett rolled over to glance at the secret door and found it open, but there were no sounds other than the rumbling of her stomach and the crackle of the hearth fire. She would have remained in bed just to enjoy that she hadn't been cleaved apart by Joshua's sword, hadn't it been for the pressure in her bladder that couldn't wait. She padded across the room and hurried to the bathing chamber,

When she returned, a clicking sound from the window made her hand twitch to where her sword normally hung on her belt. Another click. Gandrett couldn't spot anything from her position by the door, so she inched forward until outside the window she made out the fat, feathery shape of Riho, the crow.

She loosed a breath and stumbled toward the window, catching herself on the windowsill.

Riho clicked his beak at the glass once more, impatience in the gesture as far as that was something one could see in a bird's behavior.

So Gandrett unhooked the window and opened it just enough for the crow to hop inside.

"What are you doing here?" she asked him, and as he held out his leg for her to retrieve the small scroll of parchment, Gandrett dove for it and untied it with surprisingly healed hands.

She remembered the Dragon Water, and a shudder ran down her back. What else was going on in this castle that no one had warned her about?

Riho cawed lowly and waited for her to read Nehelon's message.

She stared at its contents, hoping she had misread, but when she read it for the third time, it still said, *If I don't hear from you by tomorrow, I'll turn the castle upside down until I find you.*

Somehow, it sounded like a threat.

So Gandrett lowered her head to Riho's and whispered. "Tell Nehelon I found Joshua and that I am no longer sure Joshua wants to return. Tell him I will try to get out as soon as I've eaten."

She kept everything else to herself. The magic she potentially had performed, the days she had been locked in a dungeon under the last Dragon King's tower. It was nothing to put into a brief message delivered by a bird. Especially if she was still trying to make herself believe the magic hadn't happened.

Riho took off with another caw and what Gandrett could swear was relief in his circular, black eyes, leaving Gandrett to deal with her hunger for answers as much as the hole in her stomach.

She hadn't lied when she had told Riho she'd get out of there soon. But first, she had to find Armand and Addie to figure out what had happened to Joshua.

With quiet footsteps, she made it back to the bed where she picked up her water glass and drained it before she pulled Nehelon's knife from under the pillow. Then she got her old dress—the one with the secret compartment in the bodice—from the wardrobe where Deelah had hung it after she'd fixed it, and quickly changed.

As she sheathed the knife in her bodice, the memory of Nehelon's tug on the fabric shook her for a moment, closely followed by the memory of his lips on hers. A memory, or a hallucination?

So she made her way to the secret door and slipped into the passageway.

Armand had slept better. He would have preferred not to sleep at all, but the fact that he had ridden out for one of his many fake-missions the evening before rescuing Gandrett caught up with him. Fake-missions where he didn't silence anyone who spoke against Denderlain but spent his time promising the people of central-Sives a better future, a peaceful future, if they endured just a little longer, and returned with the blood of one of his father's loyal men on his hands instead. One of those men who were willing to torture to get people to turn on Brenheran.

The conundrum of Gandrett's magic and her necklace might have something to do with it too, or the fact that he was sleeping on the rug before his bed, where he had fallen asleep after a long discussion with Addie and Joshua.

They had decided that until they were absolutely certain where the spell that had bound Joshua originated from, the latter should remain hidden in Armand's chambers.

Addie, however, had taken off in the early afternoon to return to Linniue so his aunt wouldn't suspect anything. His guards had retrieved her bucket and he had filled it with regular water before she'd left, to prevent anything from happening in case their suspicion about her was true—that it was Linniue who controlled Joshua and it had something to do with the magic in the Dragon Water.

On the sofa, Joshua's regular breathing was a comforting layer of sound. At least his cousin was sleeping well, unplagued by a second mind overpowering his. Hours and hours they had spent trying to understand the limits of the spell's power. And Joshua had patiently explained in detail whatever Armand had asked—and Addie, who seemed to put a lot of effort into helping Joshua, given she had denied him help once. Armand's mind was still spinning at the thought of having a second presence locked in his head with his own mind that sometimes was already too much to bear.

How did Joshua stand it, having his own wishes, his own opinions smothered for years and not break?

Joshua had laid out how the second presence in his head prevented him from ever bringing up that he wished to return to Ackwood or that he was even exposed to that constant internal struggle of not being able to speak his own mind. What a relief it must be for his cousin to finally say the words—that someone had been guiding him through Eedwood and potentially even picking through his brain to gather information.

He had spoken about the nights and days he had spent wishing for them; those moments when the spell got weaker—over time, it seemed—and how he still always ended up back in those shackles of his mind. Linniue's men must have been keeping their eyes open for his movements through the castle, or he would have managed to escape that one time he had broken the spell—or that it hadn't been renewed.

Armand's head threatened to burst from trying to understand how it worked. And from the horror his cousin had endured for such a long time without as much as a word of understanding.

"What got me through those years," Joshua had said, and it warmed Armand's heart, "were those hours spent planning with you." That though he had been under a spell that had prevented him from even attempting to leave, there had been someone—who hoped for a better future for Sives. And that Linniue had been wanting him on the throne as well, only there seemed to be something more she desired. Something bigger she had been working toward.

It was impressive how Joshua had been keeping track, all those years, of all those thoughts that had been his own, and how he had managed to stay sane. The only thing that still wasn't clear was how much time he had truly missed during those blackouts and what had happened during those hours or days or weeks.

So they all were convinced there had been someone controlling Joshua's mind. The only question left was if it was truly Linniue who did that to her son.

Armand turned to the side, trying to shut out his thoughts, when the sound of Gandrett's voice disturbed him from the open door to the secret passageway.

"Armand, come quick," she called, "it's back."

He was on his feet, sword in hand, and rushing to the secret door before he could even give a thought to what she might have meant was back. Too urgent was her tone, too terrifying the thought of her getting into trouble again.

A brief look at Joshua informed him the future king of Sives was fast asleep. The guards at the doors were not going to let anyone in or out.

When he made it to the corridor, Gandrett was standing halfway in, hand on the wall and a mixture of fear and excitement on her now completely healed features. Gods, had he ever acknowledged how beautiful she was?

"Do you see it?" She whispered, now that her eyes had spotted him in the doorway.

Armand closed the gap with a couple of quick strides, sword at the ready, his eyes on her, alive and healthy—and possibly the biggest liar of all times. For some reason, he didn't care about the latter as much as he should have as long as the former applied.

"What is it?" As he asked, he saw it.

There was a door etched in the thick, stone wall. In a small alcove that he had passed countless times, there was a door.

He blinked, clearing his vision and hoping he had not seen right.

"Good," Gandrett commented, "You see it too." There was relief in her voice as if she had been doubting the existence of the entrance they both were staring at.

Armand reached out his hand and examined the door, the spider webs that had been torn in front of it. He could have sworn the door's temperature was a tad cooler than the stone surrounding it.

"Where did it come from?" he mused aloud, fascination and alarm mingling in his stomach.

But Gandrett didn't give him time to think. She grabbed him by the forearm, hand firm and unyielding as he attempted to pull it open.

"Listen to me," she whispered, her eyes sparkling in the torchlight. "I came across this door the first night you sent me back to my chambers. I've been in there."

What? "Why didn't you tell me?" He remembered very well that night she had returned to her chambers, looking like someone had dragged her through the dirt. He had felt guilty for using her to provoke his father, had felt, with her history, she might understand him, better than anyone, his difficult relationship with his tyrant father. How she had deceived him—

"There was no indication I could trust you," she plainly said, all ladylike words, all smiles, all pretenses gone, replaced by a fierceness that was illuminating the dim air around them.

He wanted to ask if she trusted him now, if that was why this time she had called for him. But he couldn't bring himself to. Too much did he dread the answer she had in store.

"There are tunnels behind this door," Gandrett continued, "and I don't know where they lead, but we had better get a warm coat, or we won't make it out of there again."

He stared. At her bravery, at her practicality, at her not being any of the things every other girl he had met was. "You are intending to go in there?" he asked.

"Preferably just you and I," she nodded. "I wouldn't want to risk anyone else seeing what's in there."

Armand tried not to sound like a frightened boy as he asked, "What's in there?"

The flesh on Addie's back was raw from the beatings with the rod. She had endured it before at Lands End, and here in Eedwood, when Linniue's guards caught her at her attempts to escape. So she bit down on her tongue and swallowed the pain.

"So..." Linniue strolled around her with a smile, making a small circle around the bucket beside her. "Can I expect you to do a simple task such as delivering a bucket of water properly next time—and not a day after the order?" Her voice was so sweet, almost as if she were talking to her friend Lady Isylte Aphapia of Ilaton—only, her fingers were still gripping the rod that had gotten acquainted with Addie's blood instead of the teacup that she usually carried around the chambers.

Addie nodded. Not because she agreed she would do better, but to herself that she could do this—endure this and not break. Only until the lady let her out of her chambers again, and then, back to the young lord and the future king of Sives. A shudder ran through her at the thought of the events of last night. Could it be that there was hope? Hope in the shape of Armand Denderlain and an emerald-eyed prince—for that was who Joshua was. A prince of Sives. Probably the last if they didn't manage to put him on the throne.

She shifted her feet, eyes glancing for the door. So close, she might be able to run... only to be dragged back by Linniue's guards. Who knew how many other people in this castle were under her spell—

"Don't even think about it," Linniue answered Addie's silent pondering and lifted her rod.

Addie cringed where she stood.

"I have different plans for you tonight." She opened the door and called for one of the men guarding it, who saluted and on Linniue's beckoning, grabbed Addie by her arm and dragged her to her knees. "I made a mistake assuming you would understand the importance of your task—your only task," Linniue hissed as she bent down enough to look into Addie's eyes. Linniue's gaze beamed in a darker shade of the young lord's hazel, and there was no warmth there. "As you have been trained in Lands End."

"Trained," Addie repeated, trying to make sense of the lady's choice of words.

The response was a lash on her back.

Addie gritted her teeth as she panted through the pain. She should have known better than to provoke the lady, and any sign of being a coherent being with thoughts and opinions seemed to fall into the category of provoking.

Linniue giggled at Addie as she grabbed her hair out of nowhere and pulled her head back.

Addie tried to free herself, but the guard didn't loosen his iron grip on her arm. Instead, his second hand grasped her by the chin and forced her mouth open while Linniue exacted a flask from the pocket of her dress, wheeled the lid open with one hand, and lowered it into the bucket before she brought it to Addie's spitting lips.

"Drink up, Addie," Linniue cooed, her eyes sparkling with insanity. "It will soon be over."

Addie coughed up the water Linniue forced into her mouth, no longer a single doubt in her mind that it was Linniue who had spelled Joshua Brenheran. It was the water that she used for it—

Only, the water in Addie's bucket was from Armand's bathing chamber. A different sort of excitement rose in her as she remembered the scent in his chambers—wildflowers and something that she couldn't identify that was very masculine. She thought of that scent, the people she was doing this for, as she fell into her role and finally gulped down the water and stopped fighting.

Let Lady Linniue think whatever she was doing had succeeded. All she needed was to get out of here alive to let the young lord and the future king know that it was Linniue who was doing this.

"Your commitment to your task will have much improved after I am finished with you." Linniue giggled again and let go of Addie's hair in favor of a knife she picked up from the sideboard where a silver tray was waiting with a variety of utensils, none of them promising an easy death.

Addie held her breath as the guard tore open her dress on her shoulder and Linniue let the blade hover over the bare skin, murmuring in a language she hadn't heard since Lands End.

The language of the dragon lords.

She was doing it—Linniue was doing it, praying to the god of dragons. Addie recognized the songlike murmur, even some of the syllables she had heard in Lands End so many times. And she knew what it meant—

A scream escaped her as Linniue brought down the blade on her shoulder and didn't stab, but carved something on the part where skin stretched thinner over the bones. She screamed and screamed until she tasted the salt of sweat and bitterness of dirt on the hand the guard shoved over her mouth.

"Hold your breath for later when the real fun begins," said Linniue as she was done, leaving Addie's shoulder dribbling with blood. Then, she stepped back and gave Addie a smile. "From now on, you will not only obey me to a full extent. You will have the honor of being part of my inner circle."

Addie silently sobbed through the lady's words. *For Joshua and the young lord. For a better future.*

"Lead her into the caverns." At her command, the guard dragged Addie back to her feet and forced her forward to the wall that looked the way it always did—except that there was a door.

Addie didn't fight. All she needed to do was to get through this and get out alive to tell Armand and Joshua. She had to.

If Linniue had been performing the spell on her, Addie didn't notice any sign of it. Maybe it would come later, and she would be forced to betray the only allies she seemed to have in this castle, no matter how unlikely it was at all a servant girl had allies. Or maybe the spell hadn't worked because of the fake Dragon Water.

Either way, she wordlessly walked into the corridor that the guard exposed as he pushed open the door and shoved her into the chilly air.

Gandrett. Addie thought of Gandrett and the first time she had met the girl, half-frozen, as she'd fallen through a door in the wall that had sealed itself back in place, leaving no trace it had ever existed.

A magic door.

As was this one.

Addie braced herself for the cold, the shiver that ran across her bruised and bloody back as painful as her carved-up shoulder, and stepped toward her fate.

42

Of course, Armand had wanted to go first. Gandrett wouldn't have expected otherwise.

Now that they had made it halfway down to the colder areas of the tunnel, she was already wondering if she should have left Armand behind, if it would have been smarter not to involve him at all and just get it over with. She pulled the coat he had lent her more tightly around her and followed him down that path that had almost destroyed her last time.

She could have simply ignored the door and grabbed Joshua and run instead.

But, it seemed, the castle had a message for her, showing her the door—or it had something to do with her sudden magical abilities, which were as unproven as Nehelon's kiss. It could have been Joshua incinerating the chain and the blade—only, what incentive would he have had to destroy the advantage he'd had over her?

Gandrett felt Armand's eyes on her as she pushed past him to examine the frost that was collecting on the stone walls. It melted as she brought her torch closer and trickled down the stone until it froze back to it out of reach of the fire's heat.

"This must be the dragon lair that Joshua talked about," Armand said out of the blue.

Gandrett was still chewing on what Armand had told her about Joshua's split mind and how they suspected his aunt for putting a spell on him to prevent him from running.

To a certain degree, it made sense. At least, it explained how the Brenherans could have described him as such a saint when he had attacked her here and tried to kill her.

After giving her a summary of the discussion he'd had with Joshua and Addie, Armand had been awfully silent on their way down here even though she could almost feel that he carried words on his tongue that if he didn't speak them now might never be spoken. For before the first light of day, Gandrett would be gone. And if they were right about Joshua and the spell, this time, he would come gladly.

"Did Joshua say anything about when he's returning to Ackwood?" she asked just to make conversation.

But Armand's sigh was answer enough that this was a story that might take longer than the endless stretching darkness before them.

However, he grabbed her hand and pulled her over so she faced him. There was no sound other than the crackling of the torch, and the air smelled of ice and fire.

His gaze wandered down to her chest and back to her eyes, face unreadable. His fingers pulled her hand up toward him, and he examined her calloused palm with a brush of his thumb. "These are not from sorting jeweled weapons," he noted, looking at her as if he was seeing her for the first time.

Gandrett swallowed. So it was time. Time for the truth, or as much of it as she thought Armand could handle.

"I came here with a mission, Armand." It hurt more than she had thought to admit that she had been lying to the young lord, the man whom she had been told was the enemy when in reality, he was the one trying to save Sives. Her heart ached for him as his eyes turned shadowed. "To bring Joshua Brenheran home."

He let go of her hand and reached for her neck, almost making her let her training set in and bring him down before his fingers brushed against her throat. But he wasn't attempting to harm her. His fingers picked the thin, silver necklace from her skin and weighed the pendant in his palm.

"Joshua has the same necklace," he said with a voice that sounded like defeat rather than anger. Gandrett would have never believed that she would wish for anger instead. "It's a Brenheran heirloom, he once told me. There are only three of them in all of Neredyn, and the one you are wearing is not his." It was there, the silent question whether she was one of them—a Brenheran. Or just some stranger, unlucky enough to be bestowed with the task.

Gandrett's pulse quickened to a speed at which she was sure, if Nehelon had been there, he'd have forced her to sit and calm down before she said anything, did anything. An heirloom for the Brenheran siblings. And Brax had given her his. The younger Brenheran's emerald gaze and his outrageous smile flashed before her eyes—*Think of me when you wear it, Child of Vala*—and all of a sudden, she felt dizzy. Brax hadn't gifted her just any necklace. The pendant, threaded with emeralds, was a token of the Brenheran bloodline, something more personal than any other thing he could have possibly given her.

And now, it had given away her ties to Ackwood.

Armand's hazel gaze was patiently measuring her as she made up her mind whether or not the truth was something she should give—could bear giving.

But Armand didn't pressure her.

"I came running when you called for help once. And I told you already that if you asked me again, I'd help." He let go of the necklace and took her hand again, a gentle touch this time, full of curiosity and expectation rather than the resignation from before. "You can trust me, Gandrett." It was there in his eyes that he didn't want to think about the consequences of helping her, of what it would do to him, that it was a decision made by heart rather than the logic he, as a lord of Eedwood should be following.

It cost her all of her force of will to bring herself to speak the words, "Lord Tyrem Brenheran hired me to bring back his son," and they sounded bleak in the frosty air. The unpretty truth that she had been lying to him from the second she had laid eyes on him—even before, when she had let that wolf attack instead of slaying it with one swift move of Nehelon's—now incinerated—dagger.

But Armand just nodded as if he wasn't surprised. After all the other revelations of the night, it did indeed seem like her little secret was the least of his problems. For once, it made them allies—true allies. For if he cared about his cousin enough to lay down his own right to rule just to see Joshua on the throne of Sives, it would be the smallest of favors he could do him to get him out of Eedwood and far away from the people who had been controlling his mind. "You have always been too wicked-mouthed for a lady," Armand said with a grin, all those thoughts on his face.

His acceptance hurt more than a slap in the face. It let her writhe in the guilt of lies. Hadn't Armand been anything but kind to her? Hadn't he shared his own thoughts, his emotions with her, regardless of who she was? And she had not once found it in herself to trust him enough to tell him who she was. A liar, unworthy of Vala's love. "Don't you care that I am a fraud?" It was as much a question to her goddess as it was a question to the man before her.

But Armand shook his head. "I am a fraud myself." He shrugged. "A lord pretending not to be one. A secret rebel fighting my father's terror-rule instead of the people he sends me out to kill when they don't swear fealty. A leaf in the wind, belittled, laughed upon by his own father, putting up a show so no one sees who I truly am—" He smiled an apologetic smile. The smile of a man who had nothing to lose.

Gandrett took a deep breath, bracing herself for what she was about to say, then found she was able to return his smile. "It doesn't matter what any of them think," she said and meant it. "The only thing that truly matters is what you think of yourself."

She ran her fingers over the back of his hand, and the smile vanished as his gaze fell on her mouth as their breaths became puffs of fog between them. Something tightened in Gandrett's stomach—

The faint sound of approaching footsteps made both of them jump.

Gandrett's hand flashed into her coat where it withdrew Nehelon's knife from the bodice of her dress. She sent silent words of thanks to him, hoping that she wouldn't be in his debt if he didn't hear them, and shrugged at Armand, who was eyeing her as if now he was wondering if he had been right to say he didn't care.

But he didn't speak. Neither of them did. Because far ahead, in the distance where the chilly draft was coming from, a light appeared.

Armand's hand froze to his sword, almost literally, as he drew it back and placed it on its hilt, the warmth of Gandrett's hand immediately a phantom touch contrasting the icy steel.

There, at the end of the tunnel, outlines appeared, dark spots before a soft light.

So quick he couldn't protest, Gandrett grabbed the torch from him and suffocated its flame on the ground. Instincts. She was acting on instincts like some of the best fighters in his army. An army he hoped would one day protect the borders of Sives rather than fight a war on Sivesian soil, where the lush green of meadows and the light gold of ripe grains should reflect the color of the lands and not the crimson of its own men and women's blood.

He blinked into the darkness, letting his eyes adjust, Gandrett beside him still like a statue.

The dragon lairs of Eedwood. Not a legend. He still wondered why that door had never shown for him, never revealed itself to the true Lord of Eedwood. Perhaps it was Gandrett's magic that had triggered it. Even if, when he had spoken about the conundrum of Joshua's compelled actions and how lucky she had been to have been able to stop him, she had denied she had ever used magic before, that she had even known she was carrying it within her, maybe the door had known. Maybe the dragon magic buried deep under the castle had known.

He glanced at her outline, loose strands of hair floating behind her in the draft.

Had she told him what her mission was, had he known sooner, he might have turned the castle upside down in order to help her. Even if eventually Joshua would have never agreed to leave—but, by the gods, Armand would have tried. It didn't matter who she truly was. A mercenary or even a random girl pushed into the wrong path. He had never seen an image of Mckenzie Brenheran, but the similarities with Joshua were nonexistent, so he excluded that option. Even if the pendant on her chest suggested otherwise. One thing was certain. She wasn't the Lady Starhaeven she had been letting him believe, but something much, much more. And may it be reckless, but the thought of her having so much more depth to offer was exciting, thrilling. A kindred spirit in this godsforsaken world.

He inched closer, feeling the energy brewing in her.

"Last time I was down here, I saw someone," she whispered, leaning toward him without compromising her center of gravitation. "They fled when I called out to them. I don't want to spook them this time."

Without waiting for his assessment of the situation, she started moving, slowly and noiselessly like a ghost. Armand followed, fascination and concern fighting to gain the upper hand as they slowly descended into the darkness of the tunnel and toward the figures that had stopped far away enough that it was impossible to tell who they were.

Addie tumbled into the darkness, Linniue and her guard behind her, the former wrapped in a Denderlain-blue coat lined with white fur, the latter grunting with every step, as if he knew exactly what was about to come and was only half-excited about it as he pushed her further and further into the cold.

With half a thought, Addie wondered if he was like Joshua, if he served Linniue without consent. Or if he truly believed that what he did was right.

As for herself, she couldn't find any indication that her mind had been clawed into by the lady behind her. No traces of compulsion besides the hands that were roughly shoving her on and on.

She didn't fight the guidance, no matter how much her back hurt, no matter how the cold air made her shudder as it kissed the open wound on her shoulder. Appearance was all she thought about for now. She had to appear as if she was already under that spell Joshua and probably half the castle-guards had fallen victim to. And she needed to be convincing enough to get the lady to speak freely so she could collect whatever scraps of information to carry to the young lord and the future king. And to Gandrett, whose life she had saved and who had a secret of her own she carried with her.

Magic didn't scare Addie as it did most people in Sives. Even if she had grown up on a farm, she had been exposed to all sorts of people over the years. People who had crossed through the north-east of Sives and passed by her parents' house, seeking shelter for a night or two. And her parents, may the gods cradle their souls, had helped whoever they could. Until that night their farm had been set on fire. "Brenheran sympathizers," the cruel people who had done it had hissed as she had escaped the flames. And instead of killing her—an orphan by then—they had taken her to the prison in the north. A girl no one would miss to rot in the ice and snow of the mountains.

But now she knew better. Shygon worshipers. That's what they were at the prison in Lands End. And the inmates were vessels to be sacrificed eventually. To the god of dragons. For what reason, she could only suspect. But there was a reason Neredyn was grateful that the dragons had been eradicated. The Dreads of the Skies had plagued the lands too long, and what few had bonded with humans had caused destruction and terror wherever they had gone.

So Addie steeled herself for the cold that she was used to and kept putting one foot before the other, head high, and in her mind, she chanted a prayer to Vala, hoping the goddess of life would remain with her.

As the tunnels grew darker, Linniue stepped past her, the bucket in her hand, the fine lady actually taking the chore Addie normally did. It was clear that to her it wasn't ordinary water, that it was something so vital she didn't entrust anyone else with it. At least not now that she had retrieved the bucket from Addie.

"Where are we going?" Addie kept her voice steady, interested, without letting show the desperate need to figure out if she was going to get out of there alive.

Whatever Armand had planned to get Joshua out of Eedwood, Addie hoped he was going to do it soon. That if she didn't return, he wouldn't wait to save the future of Sives.

"You'll see, my faithful servant," Linniue said with a smile. "We are almost there."

Addie watched her step as the path wound into the depths under Eedwood castle, trying to keep track of where she was, to mark the turns in case she needed to run... Not that she was in any shape to run. It was an endless walk through the darkness, each new breath filling her lungs with more icy air than the one before. But at least the faint, blue light grew brighter as they finally slowed.

Linniue's skirts fanned out to the side as they stepped into a circular open space where in a gigantic stone bowl, a slow, flickering, faint-blue flame was burning.

"Dragon fire," Linniue whispered, her eyes lighting up like a child's as she admired the deadly flame.

Addie knew dragon fire from legends, from the balls of flame that the Dreads of the Skies had spat upon their enemies. But this—

She stepped forward on her own accord, joining Linniue in her marveling. "It's—"

"Beautiful," Linniue finished for Addie.

Horrifying had been the word Addie would have chosen, but she nodded anyway, hair shifting over her carved shoulder, and she sucked in a breath through her teeth. "What does it do?" she asked instead.

Linniue eyed her with a smile of anticipation. "It is our bridge to the one god of dragons. Shygon, the Bestower of Power."

Addie shuddered at the mention of the name. She knew that it was said that Shygon gifted strength and power—but for a price. The price of blood and life.

"You are so lucky, Addie," Linniue set the bucket down near the altar in front of the flame and reached for Addie's hands as if she were reaching for a friend. "Your sacrifice will gift my son eternal greatness."

Addie's heart raced. So that was the plan. One life—*her* life—sacrificed for the power of another.

Suddenly the pain in her back no longer mattered. She needed to get out of there, or she'd end up on that altar. Was that blood on there?

Dark stains and streaks decorated the rough stone, making her guess she wasn't the first one to be brought down here.

Time. She needed time.

"How does it work?" Her voice was a meek sound in the dome-like chamber that rose around the flame, light spreading into the two other corridors that led away from it.

Linniue's smile spread wider. "Since this is the last time you'll be asking questions, I'll be generous and grant you your answers." She squeezed Addie's hands, eyes shining with something that Addie could only name madness. Linniue was mad. "Even if I let you live, the spell I put on you will make sure you won't speak a word about it, ever."

Addie nodded, in her mind clinging to the assumption that the spell couldn't be complete without Dragon Water. She had drunk normal water as Linniue had chanted the words. Not Dragon Water.

"My son is almost ready for his big day. The future king of Sives." Pride filled her eyes as she tugged Addie forward. "While your life slowly fades, he will gain strength, power, bestowed by the god of dragons. Your blood will be the medium to bring his power to life."

Words. They didn't make sense.

"Why me? Why now?"

Linniue pulled her closer to the altar, swaying backward as if she was inviting Addie to dance. "You have fulfilled your task, bringing the water that bound my son to my will for the past year. The girl doing it before you met her fate the day before you arrived."

Addie suppressed a gasp. So that had been it from the beginning? She had been brought here to serve and then die?

"What an honor, Lady Linniue," Addie said, every inch of her body screaming at the flat-out lie.

But that was what she was supposed to act like, wasn't it? Like a smitten slave. "It's an honor to die for him."

Addie's eyes darted to the corridors behind Linniue, both of them dark holes that no one could tell where they led. But did it matter? Anywhere that was away from *her* was good.

With a quick glance over her injured shoulder, she measured the distance to the guard behind her. Three long strides. If she was quick, she'd make it to the other side of the altar before he'd be able to react. But then, one well-thrown blade could easily bring her down. Even the touch of a hand on her back probably would. Too raw the tissue, too fresh the wounds.

So Addie played for the only factor she could influence—time. Even if time would be her certain death if she stayed in the freezing cold with her rag-dress much longer.

But even that would not be granted to her. For Linniue nodded at the guard, who approached them and shoved Addie forward to the broad side of the altar while Linniue led her by one hand as if in a procession.

With horrified eyes, Addie noted that there were shackles hooked into both ends of the stone. Two that would fit around her wrists and two that would fit around her ankles. She twitched, aching to do anything but stand and watch as her own life was being offered to a god of destruction and terror. A god of creatures that had no regard for human life. Shygon, the god that should have been forgotten.

Armand's arm and sword were a reassuring presence at Gandrett's side as she groped her way along the wall, Nehelon's knife in one hand. There were three figures by the light down at what seemed to be the end of the tunnel, and this time, she would approach slowly enough to make sure she saw their faces.

The cold grew with every step, making it harder to remain so still. But she was so close to finishing her mission, so close to figuring out those last details, that she couldn't stop now.

So she took one icy breath after the other and moved forward until voices made her yield.

Not voices. But one particular voice she had heard before in a dream. A whisper, speaking in the language Neredyn had forgotten. Or should have forgotten. For some odd reason, the words the icy air carried toward her made sense. A summoning of the god of dragons, the offer of a vessel in Shygon's name.

Armand tensed beside her as they witnessed what they had been suspecting: someone was praying to the god of dragons, and as far as Gandrett knew, that included blood sacrifice.

They had made it halfway down the corridor when the bluish light revealed its shape as a flame. High and wide, set in a bowl of stone, and seemed to flicker tall into the chamber that the tunnel opened into. The three shapes paid them no heed. Too dark was the tunnel that was swallowing their movements.

Another few steps, and Armand froze beside her. "Addie." It was less than a whisper but enough to make Gandrett stop and grab his forearm.

She took in the slender shape that stood between a woman in a big dress and a tall man, and her breath caught in her throat. Armand was right. That was Addie down there. And the chanting whisper was—

"Linniue." It was Gandrett who spoke this time, and Armand's infinitesimal nod was enough to confirm she had guessed right. "She's going to kill her."

Gandrett couldn't tell if it was her or Armand who charged first as they rushed down the corridor, blades at the ready, and stormed into a dome-like chamber where Linniue and a man in the armor of the Denderlain guards blocked Addie's path, forcing her toward the stone altar behind her.

Addie saw them first, eyes horror-stricken and skin as pale as the frost covering every inch of the room. Even the flame seemed to be made of ice rather than heat.

While Linniue seemed to have fallen into a trance, chanting in the ancient language of the times of dragons, the guard beside her very well noticed the intruders and pushed Addie against the stone before he drew a second blade and planted himself between Linniue, and Gandrett and Armand.

As he approached with slow, solid steps, Nehelon's knife suddenly felt like a toothpick in her hand. But she had defeated men with less than that. And Armand was right next to her, his longsword ready to strike.

Before the first blow fell, Gandrett noticed Addie sliding to the ground, face down, and exposing a back covered in lines of blood. What had they done to her?

Then the guard's sword hit Armand's blade with a powerful strike, and Armand engaged the man in combat, buying Gandrett time to take care of Addie and Linniue.

The latter hadn't so much as realized that someone else had joined their little ritual but continued her chants, arms spread wide and eyes closed. Gandrett snuck up from the side, half a thought on Armand's aunt as she crouched down beside Addie, checking if the girl was still alive or if they had come too late.

Addie groaned at Gandrett's touch, the bare skin of her shoulder like ice, and there was a symbol carved into her—a symbol Gandrett had seen before in her dreams. Only this one was crimson with Addie's blood, while the ones in her dreams had been a turquoise-blue like the flame above the altar.

"She's alive," Gandrett said to Armand and tried pulling the girl up by her arm, but Armand's shout of warning reached her just in time to turn and parry the guard's blow, which would have surely hit its target in her back, with a twist of Nehelon's knife, the curved blade somewhat helping to direct the force of the guard's sword away from her. Caught off guard, the man landed on the altar, cursing as he pushed himself off the edge and attacked again.

Armand had already joined her, tugging on Addie's arm as if he wasn't certain Gandrett had assessed the girl's condition right.

"We need to get her out of here," Gandrett said to him over her shoulder, this time, boots ready to kick the guard's blade out of their trajectory. "If she doesn't die of her injuries, she'll surely freeze to death." She spun, letting the guard stumble into the empty space between Linniue and where Armand was crouching on the ground beside Addie, eyes wide as he watched her keep the heavily armed and armored man engaged in a battle he couldn't win—even with little more than a toothpick in her hands.

The guard attacked again. This time, Armand took the blow with the flat of his blade before sending the man tumbling away with a push of his foot.

Not bad. Armand was fighting well—given that they had one injured and one religiously frantic to consider.

"What do we do with your aunt?" she asked, eyes on the guard who was restlessly coming for them again and again as if someone had erased all common sense. But his blades were still sharp, his blows still deadly. And it took Gandrett all her attention to not simply throw Nehelon's blade to silence him forever. That wasn't how she had been trained at the Order of Vala. Killing an opponent was the last resort—always. So she kept at it, taking turns with Armand, their strength slowly fading, and hoping that it wouldn't be too late for Addie, while Linniue's chanting turned from a whisper to a song, and eventually faded.

The silence that fell was sudden and dreadful, and when Gandrett looked up, Linniue was smiling at her from beside an array of blue-glowing symbols which was the altar in front of the fire.

44

Nehelon cursed creatively at the first rays of sun peeking through the canopy of leaves. How long had he slept? An hour was what he had allowed himself. That had been after Riho had circled toward him from the night-sky, cawing urgently the news that he had found Gandrett. Also, the message that she would be on her way the second she'd eaten. No indication of what had happened to her, his mind was already flipping back and forth between anger and worry for her life. No clear statement about whether or not she was bringing back Joshua. What did it mean, *She wasn't sure he wanted to return?* And most certainly no specifics about where and how she would exit the castle. Almost as if she wanted him to lose his mind.

He leaped off the ground, grabbing his sword in the process, and whistled for Alvi who came trotting from the nearby stream.

"It's time," was all he said to her, and the mare understood, black eyes blinking as she nudged his bicep with her nose, eager to see Lim again. "I hope she brings him," he added. "If not, we'll have to go in later and do that for her."

Alvi nodded and stomped her hooves as Nehelon reached for the saddle and bridle and readied his horse for the most significant ride in a century.

"My nephew's new toy," Linniue cooed as Gandrett's eyes met hers. The guard stopped his attacks as if halted by Linniue's words. "And Armand." She glanced at the ground where Armand was crouching beside motionless Addie. "What ever are you two doing down here?" She didn't give them a chance to respond as she said with a wicked smile, "Nevermind. I had planned to take down the *Lord* of Eedwood much later, once Joshua is on the throne, but this way I am getting an early reward."

Her gaze wandered to the altar lit up with the light of the symbols carved into stone. Armand straightened, planting himself between his aunt and Addie.

"Why her?" he asked, voice husky.

Gandrett noticed from the side that Armand's free hand was signaling something with tiny gestures.

"Why?" Linniue shook her head, annoyance slipping through her mask. "Always those same questions. Why? How does it work?" She glanced down at Addie, that annoyance turning more pronounced. "I have been waiting for almost a year to get her ready, you know?"

"Ready for what?" Gandrett's voice was carried by the freezing haze that escaped her mouth.

The symbols started pulsing beside her as Linniue took a step closer.

"What is this place?" Armand demanded.

Linniue's lips twitched. "Welcome to the temple of Shygon."

Gandrett's breath caught. "The god of—"

"Of dragons, my dear. That's the one." Linniue took another step closer and rested her palm on the ignited stone, face ecstatic. The guard stepped to her side, marveling at the altar. "I wanted my son to be here to do the honors," she spoke as if only half-aware they were there.

Armand started gesturing again, pointing down at Addie, opening and closing his hand, and then swishing it aside.

It took Gandrett a moment or two to figure out what he wanted to tell her.

But she couldn't just leave him there with the crazy one. She shook her head.

"Grab her," Linniue ordered with a nod at Addie's lifeless form.

Gandrett stepped to Armand's side, blocking the path, Nehelon's knife ready to take out an eye.

"Allow me, milady. I am not certain she is even breathing." The guard's statement was punished with a slap of Linniue's slender hand in his face. He winced and engaged Armand in battle with one well-placed strike of his sword while he seemed to ignore Gandrett.

"Why are you doing this?" Gandrett tried the one thing that had always helped her. A moment to figure out the opponent's weakness before the attack. Linniue didn't let go of the altar but raised one hand toward Gandrett with a smile. "You're sure asking many questions for one of Armand's numerous conquests."

For some reason, her words hurt more than a blow of a sword. She was just about to tell her how wrong she was about her nephew, how he was the true hero of Sives, the true unifier of a land plagued by war and terror, and that she'd better show him some respect—the true Lord of Eedwood—when Linniue's eyes turned milky, and she opened her free hand toward Gandrett.

A streak of blue flame surged from Linniue's palm, sending Gandrett stumbling to the side, and she landed next to where Addie was slowly turning blue on the frozen ground. Somewhere behind her, metal was battering down on metal.

Before she could spend a thought on what was happening, flames licked in their direction once more, and she threw herself over Addie. Flames hit Gandrett's back in full force, their touch like little blades made of ice rather than the hot, singeing fire in the hearth she had left behind in her chambers. A groan of pain beneath her filled her chest with relief. Addie was still alive.

The pain in Gandrett's back was nothing compared to what she had endured less than a day ago. She just needed to get to her feet, and she'd pin Linniue's other hand to the altar, too.

"Dragon fire," Linniue giggled, ecstatic, marveling at her hand. "I wish Joshua could see this."

"I am most certain he'd love to see it," Armand's hands circled Gandrett's arm, lifting her from Addie. "Before he hands you over to my father so justice can be executed."

Gandrett scanned the room for the guard, half-expecting him to appear out of nowhere and stab Armand in the back, and spied him on the ground, throat slit and eyes rolled back in their sockets.

Her stomach lurched.

Linniue's hysterical laughter filled the dome. "Lord Hamyn doesn't get a say in this," she said and let blue flames dance at her fingertips.

Gandrett needed to put an end to this before she hurt Armand.

"He only hears what *I* want him to hear; he only sees what *I* want him to see." Linniue let her fingers slide over the blue lines in the stone as if she were tracing the symbols.

"He's under your spell, too?" Armand spat the words, little shock in them but laced with true disgust. "Who else?" he asked, voice harsh like thorns as he inched toward his aunt, sword at the ready. "Is it only Joshua and my father who you enslaved through your spells? Or am I also your victim, just oblivious?"

Linniue jerked her chin at the dead guard. "All my guards are under my spell. Not *my* spell. Shygon's spell. It's the god of dragons who gives power. My power comes from him. So will Joshua's. As for you," she pointed her finger at Armand as if it were a dagger to pierce through his heart. "If it hadn't been for your mother and that nurse-maid she hired for you, you would have been long gone."

Armand had turned paler than he already was in the frosty air at the mention of his mother.

"Your mother knew everything about this place. Every dirty little secret. Every passage, every tunnel." She stopped, her milky eyes faking pity as Armand wordlessly listened. "What? She only told you about the Dragon Water? How well it heals injuries? She wanted a good son. A proper son. And an impeccable successor. Someone who would lead Sives back to peace."

Gandrett had heard about Armand's mother's wish to finish what she had started. A better Sives. A peaceful Sives. With the true heir to both lordships as king.

"If your mother hadn't hired a Vala-blessed to protect you, you would bow to me the way they all are or will be very soon."

Gandrett's heart stopped. "Vala-blessed," she repeated in a whisper. "Deelah is a Vala-blessed."

How could she not have noticed? The kind, humorous woman who had tended to her from her first day at Eedwood was a Child of Vala. A Vala-blessed, with the mission to watch over the heir of Eedwood. To protect him from evil with her prayers to the goddess.

Armand blinked, wordless.

"So how did you find out about these caves, Armand? Did Deelah finally tell you?" Linniue ignored Gandrett's realization.

Armand broke free from his momentary petrification. "How dare you manipulate *my* court? Your own son?" His voice was deadly. Icy, making the frost on the walls and ground appear like a spring breeze. "He would have taken the throne without your interference, aunt. And he would have been a good king of Sives."

"King of Sives," Linniue laughed, flames flickering between her fingers. "Who is speaking about a king of Sives? Joshua will be Emperor of Neredyn. Sives is just the beginning."

Mad. She was mad.

"All I need is for you to hand me the girl"—She pointed at Addie—"so I can finish what I've started—before I finish the two of you."

Armand hesitated a moment too long as another surge of blue flame erupted from Linniue's hands. It hit him in the chest, throwing him back like a ram.

Gandrett darted to his side, her own spine protesting as she bent down to assess his state.

His eyelids fluttered a couple of times as he blinked away the force of the impact, features twisting as he cursed away the pain.

"We need to get her out of here," Armand hissed, eyes on Addie, "before it's too late."

Gandrett followed his gaze to where Addie was slowly freezing on the ground. There were only two ways this could end: either they got her out before Linniue could get her hands on Addie to sacrifice her to the god of dragons, or they'd have to stop Linniue.

Just as if Linniue had heard her thoughts, she sent a wave of flames toward Gandrett, making her stumble back a step. But no matter the pain, she remained on her feet. She couldn't—wouldn't give up until Linniue was defeated, or the third outcome would have to happen, and that was something Gandrett didn't even want to think—she would have to end Addie herself so whatever horrible sacrifice to Shygon would be prevented and even worse consequences be stopped.

"Take her," she urged in a whisper. "She won't be able to walk, and I can't carry her."

He didn't give any indication he was going to lift Addie from the ground. Instead, with a whirl so fast it surprised even

Gandrett, he darted for Linniue, sword lifted over his head in preparation to strike. He attacked like the wolf he'd slain to protect her, fast and deadly. And he'd come so close. So close—

Blue flames surged toward him, hitting him in the chest once more and causing him to drop mid-leap like a sack of flour. He hit the ground with an echoing thud where he remained as lifeless as Addie.

"Nooo!" Armand had given enough, sacrificed more than any of his people knew. He didn't deserve to die here, underground where no one would ever know—let alone believe—how he'd met his end. He was the future of this court.

Gandrett braced herself for the all-consuming fury in her and let her instincts take over.

Linniue was still smirking at Armand's sagged shape as Gandrett flicked her arm, releasing Nehelon's knife, sending it right toward Linniue's heart.

The woman screamed in fury as the blade got stuck in her shoulder.

Only her shoulder. Where Gandrett never missed a target, anger and real emotion had made her sloppy. She loosed a string of curses.

But Linniue had already regained control over her body, now sending lances of fire toward Gandrett, keeping her busy dancing and whirling between them, left with nothing to defend herself from such an attack.

At a glance, she saw that Armand was still down.

Linniue dragged Nehelon's knife from her shoulder with a smile, stopping the attack for a moment, giving Gandrett time to catch her breath.

Behind her, Addie's breathing had turned shallow enough to tell that she was fading.

"If she is dead, I can always use your lover," Linniue said, nothing human in her voice. Her hand never let go of the altar almost as if she was drawing her power from there.

No. Not Addie. Not Armand. No one would be sacrificed to an outdated deity of terror and blood.

Gandrett's hands trembled.

No one would harm her friends. *No one.*

Heat washed through her. Energy. She couldn't tell where it originated from, only that it was there and that it was strong. Way stronger than when she had incinerated Nehelon's dagger and the chain around Joshua's neck.

And the ground began shaking where her feet stood on the frost. Linniue halted, the smile that hadn't left her face despite the stab-wound on her shoulder now fading, Nehelon's knife clutched in her hand.

"What is this?" Linniue asked, eyes on the dragon fire illuminating the room. "Is it you, my Lord?"

Was she speaking to Shygon? By now, nothing would surprise Gandrett.

But the tremor in the ground didn't come from the god of dragons. It came from within her, and as Linniue realized that the ground was cracking open between them, she stumbled one more step backward.

What was happening? Last time her magic—if it truly had been hers—had manifested as fire. As burning heat, able to melt steel. What was unfolding before her now wasn't even remotely comparable. If she didn't find a way to stop, the canyon that was spreading would swallow them all.

Gandrett didn't dare move for fear the crack would move with her and swallow Armand, who was so close to the ground rift that part of his arm hung into it.

"Armand," she called, voice raw with strain.

To her relief, he lifted his head with a groan, and as he noticed the gap clearing his shoulder, he gave a solid curse.

"Get up," she cried, hoping he would understand without explanation that this wasn't the time for heroism but to save his own ass. "Now!"

He crawled to all fours then inched away from the canyon.

Stones were beginning to crumble from the ceiling.

But Gandrett didn't dare move as much as an inch, anxious she would make it worse.

"Stop it." Armand had realized what was going on, eyes wide with something more than fear. "Stop it or you'll bring down the castle."

"There *must* be a sacrifice," Linniue screamed from the other side of the canyon, voice half-mad.

Gandrett didn't know what would be worse—if she managed to stop and Linniue got to sacrifice Addie or if they all died in an attempt to halt her from beseeching the god of dragons for power.

Before she could make up her mind, an avalanche of stone fell from the ceiling, cutting Linniue off from them. Gandrett threw herself back over Addie, protecting the girl from the rain of gravel while Linniue's shriek tore through her mind like a bolt of lightning.

The trembling stopped, and the rift yielded as the energy in Gandrett came to a halt. She panted, sweat beading her forehead and neck, making her shiver in the stirred cold.

"Get Addie out of here," Armand said. An order this time. "I'll take care of my aunt." His tone promised violence.

So Gandrett obeyed. With her last strength, she pushed herself up enough to slide off Addie, who no longer groaned, and tried to heave her off the ground.

"Watch out!" Armand's warning came too late as Linniue sent another line of flames after Gandrett. They brought her flat to her stomach where she landed with a rib-shattering crash, and the moment she was down, Linniue aimed for Armand, attempting to do the same.

Gandrett's anger flared again. Linniue couldn't win. Not like this. So she summoned that heat that had incinerated the dagger. That heat that had saved her from Joshua. And released it on Linniue.

The sound of more gravel falling and the hissing of fire on ice filled the air.

Then a scream followed by a whimper. Gandrett couldn't prop herself up enough to tell what had happened, but Linniue's voice returned to that whispering chant from her nightmare, speaking those prayers to the god of dragons until they ended in a gurgle.

Armand felt the tidal wave of heat flooding through the chamber, leaping over the canyon too wide for even him to jump across. He ducked away, shielding his face, and with gritted teeth, waited for it to fade. So strong. Her magic was like a force of nature. If she truly hadn't known until recently, it had surely occurred at the perfect moment to save their asses.

The air tore from a scream. His aunt's scream. A sound that pierced him to the marrow of his bones. Then the muttering in that strange tongue began, making his hair stand on his neck.

But only so long—

For it soon got weaker and weaker until it faded into a whisper and ended.

The heat—probably deadly in any other environment but the frosty caves of the last Dragon King's dragon—subsided, and Armand dared to lift his head and peek over the rocks.

On her island of stone, enclosed by half-incinerated boulders and canyons, on the glowing altar, lay Linniue Denderlain, Gandrett's dagger sticking from her blood-drenched chest, one hand still clutching it tightly where she had pushed it into her own heart, and lines of crimson were starting to drown the symbols in the stone.

45

Armand's voice was the first thing she heard as he muttered her name, close enough to her ear to tell her he had made it through Linniue's attack, that he had been able to at least crawl over to where she must have collapsed.

"Can you hear me?" His voice was raw like the void in Gandrett's chest where her magic must have been a moment ago—or a lifetime.

A warm hand touched the back of her head, stroking over it so gently she wondered if it could be him. Sobs were breaking the silence otherwise filling the chamber.

With a swimming head, she tried to piece together what had happened—what she had done. The canyon. The collapsing ceiling.

Out. They needed to get out.

Dust and stone pushed into her cheek, cutting into it as she shifted her head to glance up at Armand. She sucked in a breath through gritted teeth.

"Thank Vala." Armand's face was above her in an instant, one hand gliding under her neck and shoulders as she rolled to the side in a slow and rocky movement. "I've got you." With some effort, he pulled her up into his arms, cradling her against his chest, shaken by more sobs.

"It's over," he whispered in between, arms closing around Gandrett more tightly.

Gandrett just rested there for a moment, letting his rocking movements take her away from the horror of what she had done.

"Linniue?" She shot out of his embrace, nearly hitting her head on his chin, and blinked at the thin lines the tears had cleared along his blood and dirt-smeared cheek.

He shook his head, and Gandrett knew who those tears were for.

"She betrayed my mother. She betrayed me. She betrayed all of us." His voice hitched.

Gandrett couldn't tell if she had ever seen someone so broken. Even the children they brought into the priory every year cried from fear, from being homesick—not from the deep-rooted sense of betrayal that shone from the hazel depths of Armand's eyes.

There were no words that may soothe him, not when the pain was that of a fresh wound to the heart, so Gandrett sat up and wrapped her arms around him, pulling him tightly to her like she used to do with her brother when he was little, like she had done with the new arrivals every spring at the priory. Like she hadn't been held since the day she'd stopped crying.

Over his shoulder, she could see Linniue's body draped over the altar, blood streaming from her pierced chest. It hadn't been Gandrett who had killed her, but Linniue herself who had plunged the dagger into her own heart. What had been her last words? *There* must *be a sacrifice.*

Gandrett didn't dare consider the meaning of Linniue's words or the consequences of her actions. For now, all she could think of was the broken man in her arms and the sensation of relief as the glowing of the symbols faded and the flickering of the flame of dragon fire above Linniue's body dimmed.

"We need to get out of here," Armand reminded her. "And Addie, too."

Gandrett pulled away, releasing him from her arms to turn and check on Addie.

The girl still lay face down on the ground, but the blue tint on her skin had vanished—as had the frost on the ground.

To Gandrett's surprise, the icy air had turned warmer, letting her breath leave her mouth and nose unnoticed, no clouds of haze hovering before her face as she exhaled. She glanced over her shoulder and noticed that dragon fire had almost gone out, making it nearly impossible to see.

"Help me." She grabbed Addie's legs from the side, waiting for Armand to lift her torso. "Carefully," she cautioned as the blood on the unconscious girl's back started to spread on her clothes. "We need to get her out *now.*"

They didn't look back as they groped their way along the now lightless tunnel that led back to Armand's chambers, nor did they wonder about the sudden warm breeze that seemed to wash through the air. All Gandrett could do was put one step after the other, and again and again, until the dim, flickering light of a torch beckoned them from afar.

Her legs almost gave out under Addie's weight as they stumbled toward the light where a worried Joshua greeted them, rushing to aid them with Addie. Gandrett's heart started racing in alert anew, and it cost her all her willpower to remind herself that the Joshua who had locked her up and tried to kill her wasn't this Joshua before her. The man whose emerald eyes were so much like Brax's and whose hands were reaching out to help rather than hurt. "Take this." He pushed the torch into Gandrett's hand at the same moment he reached under Addie's legs with the other, relieving her of the weight. Gandrett took the torch, and together they headed back toward the hidden passageway that connected Armand's and Gandrett's chambers.

"What happened?" Joshua wanted to know, his eyes on Addie's bloodied dress as he and Armand gently laid her down on the couch. His emerald eyes glanced up at Gandrett, who wasn't certain if she should be afraid of him or thankful for his help.

As Armand recapped how Gandrett had found the invisible door, how Linniue had brought Addie down into the dragon lair as a vessel for Shygon—a blood sacrifice to buy Joshua power—Joshua listened in silence, his hands busy with the vigilant movements of cutting open Addie's dress from the shoulder down. He lifted the fabric inch by inch, so slowly that no additional tissue would tear from her wounds, and folded the dress to the sides, leaving her hips and legs covered.

Only when Armand mentioned that Linniue was dead— how she had died—did Joshua pause and look up, deep sorrow shadowing his features. "I wish I had been there to stop her," was all he said, and there was silent mourning in his movements as he walked to Armand's bathing chamber.

Armand stepped to her side as she bent over Addie's back, examining the wounds—bruises with bits and parts of split skin. The horrible evidence of being beaten with a rod.

She swallowed as phantom pain spread on her own back and arms. No more. After she got out of there, after she delivered Joshua to Ackwood and stayed with her family for a year, she would no longer live at the priory. She would be sent on missions all over Neredyn, far away from the place that had scarred her so deeply.

"She is barely breathing," Armand noted with a huff of exhaustion.

"Don't you have any of that Dragon Water left?" Gandrett didn't look up from the array of blooded streaks as if her gaze itself could soothe them.

Without another word, Armand darted from her side and followed Joshua into the bathing chamber from where they emerged together, carrying a bowl and one of Deelah's flasks, along with a fistful of towels.

Gandrett took a towel from Joshua's fingers and reached into the bowl before she gingerly dabbed at the wounds, careful not to hurt Addie more than necessary. The girl had suffered enough.

A groan escaped Addie's lips, flooding Gandrett with relief. She was coming around.

"You're safe, Addie," Gandrett told her and placed one hand on the girl's forearm. "You'll be fine."

Armand added a few drops from the flask into the warm water in the bowl, took a piece of cloth himself, and joined

Gandrett in her efforts from the other side of the sofa, his eyes cautiously on Addie's raw back. "She's lucky to be alive," he murmured as he got to work, watching as skin slowly knitted itself back together where he touched it with Dragon Water.

When Gandrett studied him as he dabbed along one long slash, she noticed that his hands and face were clean, all traces of those tears gone, but the endless sorrow in his eyes remained.

"Maybe I should clean up, too," Gandrett realized, a welcome excuse to buy some time to sort her thoughts now that she knew Addie would be all right.

When she laid down her towel, Joshua was there to take over, his face serious and full of gratitude despite the loss he'd suffered.

She nodded at him, unable to speak, and trudged back to her chambers, the open door that led to the temple of the god of dragons which had become Linniue's tomb costing her a glance as she passed by. There was no icy draft kissing her skin, no blue light, no sinister whispers—only darkness.

Her legs sagged the moment her bed was within reach, and she let herself sink onto the soft covers. Just one short moment of rest. It was all she asked.

Gandrett woke what had to be hours later, stirred by the sensation of another presence in the room. She bolted upright, hand reaching for her side in reflex to where her sword should have been. Where it would be again as soon as she made it out of this castle.

"Why didn't you send word you needed help?" a familiar voice asked from the side, and Gandrett spun on the spot, her already-strained heart threatening to burst.

She found him perched on the windowsill, dark hair illuminated by the rising sun, making him look as if he was wearing a crown of light.

"Don't tell me you can fly," she asked, her voice hardly a breath, but she knew he would hear it. Nehelon's Fae ears didn't miss anything.

Slowly, as if not wanting to make a sound, he climbed down from the windowsill, setting one foot then the other, onto the wooden floor. As he walked toward her, tense as a desert lion on the hunt, she could make out his features against the light. Her stomach tightened—

He looked paler than she remembered, face calm, professional as he assessed her head to toe, his gaze lingering on her torn and dirty dress, the stains of blood—her blood, Addie's, Armand's, she couldn't tell. When his eyes reached her face full of conflict, his glamour slipped ever so slightly, and those exquisite, diamond-blue eyes turned rich with expression. And she beheld his mouth—that mouth that may or may not have touched hers. A tingling sensation ran through her lips like the echo of a dream.

"No," he whispered as he stopped at arm's length, "But you wouldn't believe how fast you can climb if you have the wind at your disposal."

For a long moment, Gandrett just stared at the impossibility of his presence. A beautiful illusion who had tossed her into this mess and had now come to retrieve her. She couldn't tell if he was upset, if he would yell at her, if he would stand like a handsome statue for the rest of eternity.

And she didn't care.

He was here.

"Must have been quite a meal," he said, lips twitching at one side. And as she didn't respond, "Riho delivered your message." He took another step. And another. Hesitant in a way she had never seen him, eyes probing hers like a million facets of light boring into her soul.

And before Gandrett could gather a clear thought, his arms were around her, careful at first as if he was anxious not to break her apart, then crushing her tightly to his chest.

His scent was as she remembered it—no scent in the human world compared to it. No flower, no type of wood.

She took a deep breath, letting it wash over her, a cleansing breeze that soothed her mind, her aching chest where her magic had poured out and left a gaping hole.

*A*live, his eyes seemed to say as he let go of her after what seemed a moment or eternity, Gandrett couldn't tell. Too lost had she gotten in the depths of his arms, cheek resting against the leathers on his chest, listening to the steady beat of his heart. A heart that had been beating for a long, long time before she had even been born. Probably before her parents and grandparents and their grandparents had been born. A creature as eternal as the snowy mountains and the flowing waters of Neredyn. Something ached deep within her chest as she studied him, his face so much higher up than hers.

As if he had read her thoughts, his gaze wandered down to her mouth, to where dirt and blood were still covering her face. He brought a broad hand to her cheek and let it rest there, her skin heating under his palm. His thumb strayed down to the corner of her mouth, a stroke so light she couldn't tell if it was really there, and her pulse picked up speed. His thumb slid further, crossing the curve of her lower lip, lingering.

Vala help her, the sensation brought her far from anything her life as a Child of Vala should have in store. She sucked in a breath, her lips falling open as if she could inhale his touch.

And his gaze wandered back to meet hers, different. Deep. Full of wonder and mystery, and a lifetime of memories that she had never noticed once. She stood on her toes to bring herself an inch closer to the enigma of blue diamond, and as if her movement reminded him who he was, who she was, his eyes iced over just as she noticed a hint of that softness that she had glimpsed in her dream—in reality—in the forest.

Gandrett stepped away, feeling the calluses on his hand scraping over her cheek as she slid her face out of his touch.

"Joshua," she remembered.

Nehelon crossed his arms as she took another step away from him. His face was unreadable.

"I am glad you are not forgetting about your mission," he commented without sounding at all glad.

She hadn't. She had fallen asleep, leaving Armand and Joshua alone tending to Addie. She had promised to be back immediately. And now it had to be hours later, and she was wasting her time indulging in an emotion that had no room in the life of a Child of Vala.

She left Nehelon without an explanation as she ambled into the bathing chamber where she washed her face and hands and, without bothering to look at the mirror, darted back across the room right to the hidden passageway that led to Armand's chambers. "Stay where you are," she ordered in a whisper. "Better—hide."

Nehelon only raised his eyebrows, for once, it seemed, at a loss for words.

"Don't believe for a moment that I will let you go on your own." His words came from right behind her where he had snuck up on her on silent Fae feet.

With a leap that almost brought her face-first into the open door to Shygon's temple, she avoided his breath on her neck and turned. "It's not just Joshua over there." She pointed with her thumb over her shoulder. "The *enemy* is in the same room." She mocked Nehelon, herself, anyone who had ever called Armand an enemy by the way she emphasized the word.

Nehelon just stared, unfazed by her explanation, and it occurred to her that he hadn't asked her what had happened since she had awoken to an image of the gods on her windowsill.

"How long have you been here?" she asked in a whisper.

Nehelon shrugged at her question. "Long enough to know that you succeeded to a full extent in coaxing the *enemy* around your little finger."

Gandrett stared at him with incredulous eyes.

"He checked in about a hundred times while you were asleep," he explained, a sour expression gracing his sensual lips. Gandrett feared the worst. If Nehelon still thought of Armand as the enemy...

"No, I didn't kill him." He lifted his hands in defense. "When after the ninety-eighth time, he still didn't do anything but stare at you from the doorway and sigh, I decided it was time to introduce myself."

Gandrett's heart almost stopped.

"Don't worry," he said between clenched teeth. "I didn't harm a hair on his head." He paused, a flash of mischief brightening his features. "Not after I put a sword to his throat and let him tell me the whole story. I can't wait to hear your side of the tale." As fast as the flash had appeared, it was gone, leaving Nehelon's gaze pensive. "Why didn't you send word you needed help?" he asked, voice raw.

"I had help," she retorted. What had he done to Armand? To Joshua and Addie?

Gandrett's heart ached from the way his eyes bore into hers as if he could see right into her mind. Right into her soul. Whatever he found there, he stepped closer once more, one hand on his heart. "Why didn't you send word you needed *my* help?"

His words were a dagger to her heart. What could she tell him? That she had spent hours pondering if that kiss had been real. That she had been too proud to ask for his help after everything that had happened? That she knew that it was impossible to get into the castle with all the guards watching... "Linniue's guards, Lord Hamyn's guards," she mused aloud and turned on the spot. She needed to get to Armand and Joshua. Maybe they had answers.

As she stormed into Armand's room, he and Joshua both looked up from the table where they were taking a meal. Addie's slender shape was wrapped up in sheets on Armand's bed, thick pillows tucked under her head and shoulders.

"Deelah brought this earlier when she checked on Addie," Armand gestured at the plates in front of him. "There is some for you, too." His eyes wandered over to his bed. "Addie will sleep at least a day, Deelah predicted, but she'll be fine."

He didn't seem surprised at the tall, intimidating male who was following Gandrett into the room. Neither did Joshua.

"And for you, too, Nehelon." Joshua beckoned for the Fae male to join them at the table. Of course, what they would see when Nehelon came closer was a human man; a terribly strong and handsome soldier. A warrior with the looks of the gods and the fierceness of entire armies. What Gandrett saw, however, was that image from the forest. A different Nehelon, a Fae Nehelon, who was trapped in his glamour, forced to hide from the world in plain sight for Vala knew how many centuries.

To his credit, Nehelon didn't hesitate as he joined the others at the table and picked up a round little something.

Bothenia crust. Her stomach growled a greedy melody.

Gandrett took a steadying breath. She had survived the priory. She had gotten into Eedwood. She had found Joshua, defeated Linniue. And she would not fail so close to the end. She would get out of this castle and bring Joshua back to his father.

But first, she would eat. As she had told Riho to tell Nehelon—she'd leave as soon as she'd eaten.

So she prowled toward them with all the grace of a starved goat and sat in the chair that Armand had pulled out beside him.

"Why didn't you tell me you were working for Lord Tyrem's chancellor?" Armand asked, his gaze weighing heavy on Gandrett. So heavy she didn't dare look up from the bothenia crust she'd picked up. She bit into it, taking her time to find an answer to his question while her mind was going elsewhere. How would they get out of the castle? How had Nehelon gotten in unnoticed? He had failed before—even if then he had been with humans and had to take a human approach when this time, he'd simply used his Fae senses and Fae abilities to climb up the tower. Riho had to have told him where to find her.

Her gaze met Nehelon's as he shook his head almost unnoticeably.

"I must say, I was surprised to find him in your chambers when I checked in on you." Armand's words were a mixture of worry and accusation, but mainly there was a male coldness in his tone that wasn't directed at Gandrett at all.

Nehelon's gaze was still on her as he responded for her. "It might have something to do with your guards fainting on the battlements," he suggested with raised eyebrows.

Joshua shot Nehelon a dark look, and Nehelon lowered his gaze.

"We're all on the same side now," he said with the tone of a diplomat and the wisdom of someone who knew what it meant to have two minds battling in his own head. "Let's act accordingly."

Armand nodded, gnashing his teeth.

"While you were sleeping, my cousin, Nehelon, and I had a chat," Joshua opened. "Armand will help us get out of this castle unnoticed."

Nehelon didn't flinch at the mention of the blood relation between Joshua and Armand, which meant, either they had talked about that, too, or he had known all along and hadn't found it worth his time to tell her. She put it on the list of things she'd probably never have the courage to confront him about and met Joshua's gaze.

"So, you're coming with us?" He had locked her up the first time she had told him she intended to bring him home, and it had been Linniue's spell making him do it. But now that he was free, his mind seemed set, for he nodded and glanced at his cousin.

"I am going home," he said, the sorrow a ghost damping his smile and preventing those emerald eyes from shining brightly. "And when the time comes, I'll take up my crown."

Nehelon nodded at his words, eyes flickering to the chamber doors every now and then.

"We'll need to leave soon," he said with a calm voice, his role as Tyrem Brenheran's chancellor in perfection, "if we want to use the momentum of confusion."

When Gandrett asked Nehelon for an explanation with a gaze, Armand leaned closer and said, "While you slept, I did a control round in the castle." His hazel eyes were dark with shadows of exhaustion. "It seems most of the guards on duty on the battlements were under her command... Her spell," he corrected.

"Did they really pass out as Nehelon said?" Gandrett asked.

Nehelon bit his bothenia crust and chewed, his gaze going back and forth between Gandrett and Armand.

"They did," Armand confirmed. "Now, the best men from my own, personal guard are in command of making sure each and every one of the spelled ones gets rest, and then we'll need to sort through them and see who remembers what happened or who is still loyal to Linniue's cause even with the spell lifted."

"When you say we—" Gandrett wondered if maybe it was wrong to leave him with this mess. Maybe she should stay and help. At least here she wouldn't be alone. With a Vala-blessed watching over Armand, she'd have someone to confide in.

But Armand finished her thought. "I will ask Addie to stay and help. I don't know if she has family to return to, and I won't stand in her way if she does want to leave—but if she is willing to help, I'll set her up in your chambers, Gandrett, so she can learn that Eedwood castle is more than the terror of aunt Linniue she got to know."

"May the gods cradle her soul." Gandrett lifted her gaze to the ceiling and sent a silent prayer to Vala for letting them escape from Linniue's madness in one piece.

"May the gods cradle her soul," the others repeated, Armand and Joshua's eyes filled with sorrow.

After a moment of silence, Armand said, "I asked Deelah to bring a pack of supplies to the stables. Your horse, Gandrett, and a horse for Joshua will be saddled and ready when we get down there." He glanced at Nehelon, not seeming completely certain if he could trust Nehelon. "Will you require a horse, chancellor?"

Nehelon shook his head. "I will ride with Gandrett until we make it to the forest where I left my horse."

Armand raised an eyebrow but said nothing.

"Well, then." He pushed away from the table and stood, wineglass in one hand and eyes on Joshua. "To a brighter future for Sives," he toasted.

"To a brighter future," Joshua replied and raised his own glass—filled with water—before he stood.

"Let's get out of here."

47

Lim whinnied as Nehelon entered the stables, the cheerful sound of an old friend's greeting. Beside him, Gandrett was quiet. Too quiet for all the horrors she'd endured over the past days. Had he known... Had he even had an idea of what had been going on, he would have come earlier. He would have broken down doors and walls just to make sure Gandrett made it out alive.

Now pensive, as a shadow at his side, the Child of Vala was like a ghost of who he'd met in Everrun. Something had changed. And he wasn't only thinking about her magic. For of that, he was certain, after Joshua's and Armand's detailed depictions of what she had done.

The lump of stone in Nehelon's chest felt like a beating heart once more—beating and throbbing with every thump.

He rubbed Lim's nose and promised him that they were going to see Alvi.

In the stall next to Lim, a second horse was saddled in the colors of the Denderlain guard, and by the doors lay two packs and waterskins.

Joshua led the horse out of the stall and to the back door as Armand had asked while Gandrett hesitated, waiting for Nehelon to make a move. Her shoulders had been hunched since she had hugged Armand goodbye before they had exited into the yard.

Too long had their arms remained around each other. Armand's hands too tight on her waist, his words too close by her ear. Nehelon had heard them as he had heard hers. A promise that she'd come back for him.

He suppressed the urge to rip out the door to Lim's stall with his bare hands, and opened it like a civilized human instead. Lim trotted to the door behind him, Gandrett following suit.

Outside, the west side of the building lay in shadows as Armand had promised, and while Joshua was already on his horse, Nehelon let Gandrett get onto Lim first. Then, with a murmured apology to the horse for having to carry both their weights, he grabbed Gandrett by her hips and shifted her behind the saddle, ignoring the sensation that allowing himself to grip her flesh like that instilled in him, before he climbed into the saddle in front of her, swinging his leg over Lim's neck.

Gandrett grabbed his Denderlain-blue cloak Armand had given each of them by the shoulders as Nehelon nudged Lim's flanks, and the horse set in motion. He was grateful she didn't wrap her arms around his torso, for he wasn't sure he could trust himself not to fall apart at her touch. He needed to remain focused on getting her out first. On getting all three of them out so Joshua could return to Ackwood palace and Gandrett's mission would be fulfilled.

When they arrived at the side gate in the north, Armand was waiting as he'd promised. Unlike before, there were no guards by that entry, nor on the battlements above them.

"They'll be back soon," Armand answered Nehelon's unspoken question. "You should hurry."

Joshua inclined his head as he rode past his cousin in front of them. The future king of Sives nodding his farewell to the Lord of Eedwood, the hood of his Denderlain-blue cloak hiding his features.

"I'll send word about developments," Joshua promised.

"As will I." Armand bowed, his elegance worthy of a prince itself.

Joshua hesitated before he led his horse out the gate. "Make sure Addie is all right," he said, worry lacing his voice. "And tell her she won't be forgotten."

When it was Nehelon's turn to ride through the gate, he stopped Lim and inclined his head at the young lord he had underestimated so dearly. His nobility, his bravery, his good heart. "Thank you, Lord Armand, for keeping Gandrett safe during her mission," he said and was about to nudge Lim forward when Armand looked up, but not at Nehelon.

"Tell Addie I said thank you," Gandrett said behind Nehelon's shoulder.

"I will." Armand smiled. "Thank you for keeping *me* safe, Gandrett whatever your last name is."

Behind him, Gandrett's heart quickened and he could have sworn he heard a chuckle.

Before she could respond, Nehelon kicked his heels into Lim's side, and the horse bolted out the gate, trailing Joshua along the path that followed a line of bushes and led into the forest in the distance—ten, fifteen minutes maximum if they kept up that speed.

She hadn't thought it was possible, but she would miss Armand. For the first time in years, someone had opened up to her because he had chosen to, not because he was stuck with her in isolation in the desert. And he reminded her of her brother, the way he'd smiled when he was little. With half a thought, Gandrett wondered what Andrew would look like today. A young man of fifteen years, almost sixteen. If his blond hair was still curly, if his dimples were still there.

But not yet. They needed to make it to the forest first and back to Ackwood.

"Alvi is waiting a little bit south from where we enter the forest," Nehelon said over his shoulder, his voice familiar and yet strange. "We're going to go off the path the moment we're in the shelter of the trees."

Joshua was riding in front of them, glancing back only once or twice all the way to the forest, probably reassuring himself that they were still there, and the terrain was becoming more uneven, Lim's steps less steady.

As the welcome shade of the first trees swallowed the view of the castle, Gandrett glanced back one last time. No one was following them. They had made it.

She didn't dare hold on to Nehelon more tightly than clutching his cloak until they stopped in a hidden clearing where Alvi was grazing lazily in the morning sun. As Lim spotted her, he made a joyous leap to the side, forcing Gandrett to grab Nehelon's biceps in order to keep herself from falling.

He didn't comment but swung his leg over Lim's neck again. The horse stopped as if he knew what Nehelon wanted to do, and he slid off the horse's side, out of Gandrett's grasp.

She didn't dare frown at him with Joshua watching them from where he was waiting a bit further into the clearing. But when Nehelon offered his hand to help her down, Gandrett swallowed her pride and placed her fingers in his, allowing him to catch her as she followed his lead and flipped her leg over the saddle, sliding down Lim's flank.

Nehelon's free hand caught her by the waist and lingered for a long moment as he let her glide to her feet, his eyes deep and open. "I wouldn't mind sharing a horse with you all the way to Ackwood, Gandrett," he said with a hint of a smile, "but I am almost certain Lim wouldn't mind sharing his burden with Alvi."

Lim threw back his head as if demonstrating his agreement.

So Gandrett took Lim to the black mare who was fidgeting with anticipation.

Nehelon followed his steps, almost soundless on the forest ground. In the shade by the trees, Joshua had sat down on a fallen tree trunk and was sipping from his waterskin while Nehelon greeted his horse and rearranged one of the packs to her saddle. Gandrett joined Joshua, silent beside the future king of Sives.

"You know that without your help, I wouldn't be here today," he said, voice solemn, emerald eyes clear and serious.

Gandrett shook her head. "If it wasn't for me, you wouldn't have ended up with those scars. She hardly dared look at his neck and hands, which all, despite the healing properties of the Dragon Water, held scars—nothing as bad as what a natural healing process would have left him with but still scars to tell a tale of Gandrett's magic.

Joshua pulled his collar up, covering the evidence.

"If it weren't for you and your magic, my mother would have killed another innocent." He lifted his gaze to the canopy above them. The greens were a darker shade than the first springy sprouts she had observed on her ride from Everrun back to Sives with Nehelon a month and a half ago. How much had changed since then, her magic being only one of the many things within her that had recently scared her. She stole a glance at Nehelon, who was absently massaging Alvi's ears, his own, pointed ones probably intently listening to their conversation.

"I am sorry about your mother." Gandrett placed one hand on his arm in comfort. "I wish there had been a way to stop her without—"

"You didn't kill her, Gandrett," Joshua interrupted, face stern as he relieved her of her guilt. "She made a choice to drive that knife into her own heart. It was *her* choice." His fingers curled around the air in his palms. "She made her choice long ago when she decided to put a spell on me so she could manipulate me into becoming something I never wanted to be. My own mother—" He shook his head.

"And it still hurts," she said, fingers squeezing his arm.

He nodded, that sorrow filling his eyes again. "It still hurts," he agreed.

That night after miles and miles of riding, Gandrett couldn't find sleep, even when Joshua was already deep in dreams.

"I wonder if he has nightmares," she whispered to Nehelon, who had been sitting like a statue on his bedroll, eyes on the small fire they had risked. "After years of sharing his mind with another presence—" Gandrett could only imagine the horrors he had endured and to what degree it might have scarred the young prince. A prince. That was what Joshua Brenheran was.

Nehelon got up from his bedroll and noiselessly prowled to hers, where he sat down beside her.

Gandrett curled herself into a sitting position, resting her chin on her knees.

"Will *you* have nightmares?" he asked, sincere concern in his words. He picked up a piece of wood from the ground between his feet and played with it. "After what you've seen down there," he didn't need to say *in the temple of Shygon* for Gandrett to know what he was talking about, "it wouldn't surprise me."

As Gandrett tilted her head, shoving her forearm under her cheek so her knee wouldn't dig into it, Nehelon's eyes studied her with caution as if he didn't fully believe she was truly there.

Gandrett herself couldn't fully believe she was truly there. Too much had happened in Eedwood—

"Does it scare you?" he asked. Words she would have never expected of him. Words that didn't come with any mockery or pitfalls. "Your magic, I mean."

Gandrett searched her chest for the hollow space that had throbbed this morning but couldn't find it. She didn't know what kind of magic it was that she had, only that she had almost killed Joshua with it, and hadn't it been for the icy cold in the caverns, she probably would have killed Linniue and Armand.

"A little." It was an understatement, but admitting to fear wasn't something she was used to.

As if Nehelon understood anyway, he nodded and held up the piece of wood before her.

It burst into flame at the top of his hand, dissolving into ash before her eyes.

Something in Gandrett's chest stirred.

"I felt it," Nehelon whispered. Gandrett blinked—a silent request for what he was talking about. "I felt your magic awaken, Gandrett."

His eyes sparkled in the firelight while pieces of ash still floated before him.

Gandrett didn't speak for lack of a response, just locking her gaze on his.

"You will need training, or you will expose yourself." His eyes were full of wisdom, of history, and it occurred to her again that he wasn't human, that he had roamed the realms of Neredyn for centuries and longer, and that he would when she was little more than the ashes floating between them.

She knew he was right. She could feel it even now as he spoke, that space in her chest that had replenished over the past hours, that would soon be brimming with power.

"I don't want to hurt anyone," she admitted, offering the truth about how she felt for once.

Nehelon turned to the side, propped up on one arm, and brushed his fingers across her cheek in response. "You won't," he promised. "I won't let you."

Gandrett held very still, anxious he would continue and anxious he would stop.

"I will be there to guide you," he breathed as he leaned in, the thrilling, nameless scent that promised his presence filling the space between them. "You won't be alone."

She took a deep breath, indulging in the thought of speaking those words which had been following her around since that moment in the forest, but Nehelon was faster.

He dragged his thumb across her lips, straightening up as he cupped her face in both hands, bringing his own to level with hers. His breath was a rush of heat on her skin, and his glamour was slipping, exposing the full beauty of his features and letting Gandrett's pulse thump in her throat. It had to be so loud it might wake Joshua.

But Nehelon smiled. A sweet smile that didn't match the torment in his eyes. "One day, Gandrett Brayton, I will kiss you..." His finger traced her lips in a slow curve that made her breath catch. "One day, when I'm a better man."

The next morning, they were back in the saddle before the sun rose, taking the most direct route to Ackwood, stopping only to water their horses and to rest and eat when necessary.

By the time the monumental drawbridge and the statue at the main gate over the water became visible two nights later, both Gandrett and Joshua had told Nehelon the full story of what had happened at Eedwood castle. Nehelon didn't interrupt often. Only when he learned both his dagger and his knife hadn't made it back out of Eedwood did he voice his complaint. But Gandrett noticed a smile as he fretted. And whenever his gaze met hers, his eyes seemed to be saying, *Alive. You are alive.*

Mckenzie's squeal of delight set the entire courtyard on red alert as Joshua climbed off his horse, his hair shimmering in the afternoon sun like molten gold.

They had stowed their Denderlain-cloaks away into their packs the moment they had made it out of Denderlain territory, and they'd arrived in Ackwood with their dirty riding clothes telling tales of their journey.

Gandrett observed from her spot between Lim and Alvi how Mckenzie wrapped her arms around her brother, both laughing and crying at the reunion. Nehelon had left the two horses in her care as he had prowled off to inform Lord Tyrem and Lady Crystal their lost son had returned. Which gave Gandrett a moment to breathe. After almost four days of riding side by side with Nehelon, she still hadn't had a chance to bring up the one topic that wouldn't let her sleep at night. She had caught herself studying him from the side countless times, never able to figure out if those curves of his lips had touched hers. And if it had been so, if Vala would forsake her.

She handed the reins of both horses to the stable boy who had come to retrieve them and headed for the closest guard, who drew his sword as he saw her approaching. There was something she needed to do.

"Unarmed," she said by way of greeting, cocking her head and lifting her hands, palms outward.

The guard didn't seem convinced. Gandrett recognized him to be the mountain of a man she had put on his back that first day in Ackwood. A grin broke onto her features. "Sorry for last time."

He gave her a sour smile in response.

"Where can I find Brax?" she asked, one hand absently wandering to the silver and emerald pendant on her chest.

"In the gardens, Miss Brayton," he said, not seeming certain he was doing the right thing giving her the information, and knowing that if he didn't, she could easily make him.

His uncertainty seemed to grow as she thanked him and curtseyed before she strode through the gate that led to the gardens under the palace windows.

She found Brax sitting under a tree, back resting against the trunk, a book open on his knees. His black hair was moving in the warm breeze, the sun painting patterns on his pale skin through the branches above his head, and his black jacket was open, exposing the collar of a casual, white tunic. Gandrett stopped at the corner before stepping out of the shadow of the wall.

She didn't think she had ever seen him in a different color than black. And his face... He looked so peaceful. A slight smile on his lips, one hand flipping the page every now and then while the other played with the grass beside his hip.

Her hand tightened around the necklace he had given her, and she pulled it over her head then weighed it in her palm.

Think of me when you wear it. She had thought of him many times during those days in Eedwood.

And now that she knew what his gift truly was, what it meant to him, it was time to give it back.

He looked up at the same moment she stepped out of the shadows, making herself walk as ladylike as she had learned with Mckenzie. And even though her clothes were dirty and sweaty and smelled like the miles they'd covered over the past days, she held her head high as he closed the book and jumped to his feet, a hand smoothing over his hair.

"What are you reading?" she called at him, and he tucked the book under his arm with a grin.

"You came back," he said, not answering her question, already sauntering toward her, the slight arrogance he usually wore returning as if he was falling into a pattern.

Gandrett nodded, her own strides slowing as he approached her with sleek grace.

"Is he—" He stopped himself as if he was anxious to ask and even more afraid of the possible response.

"Joshua is back." Gandrett nodded, and before she could brace herself, Brax's arms were around her in a bone-crushing hug.

"You really did it," he said into her hair. "You brought him back."

Gandrett nodded again, unsure if Brax would even notice she was moving, so tightly was he holding her against his chest.

"Vala knows why she sent you here," he murmured before he let go. "Thank you."

His eyes were on the gate she had come from, probably searching for a sign of his brother—his half-brother as he would soon learn if he didn't already know. But that wasn't Gandrett's story to tell.

"He's with Mckenzie in the yard," she said, expecting Brax to bolt that direction the moment she finished speaking.

But he remained where he was, his gaze returning to her face, eyes full of a different emotion. "*You* came back," he repeated in awe as if that had been something impossible to consider. A miracle.

"I thought you believed I could do it," she teased just to ease the tension.

Brax nodded. "I believed you could do it," he said, his voice turning deliberate. "I just never thought you'd come back—long enough to say hello."

Gandrett played with the silver chain in her palm, pondering whether it was the right thing to do, return it to him. She held his emerald gaze, new depth to his humorous eyes making her pause a moment longer than she cared to admit.

But as she lifted her hand between them, exposing what she had been clutching between her fingers, his shoulders slumped an inch.

"Had I known what this is, I would have never accepted it." It had to be explanation enough.

But Brax shrugged and took her hand in his, tilting it from side to side, the sunlight igniting specks of emerald reflections on her fingers. Gandrett marveled, wordless, not just at the dancing green light but at the warmth of Brax's palm under hers.

"It is mine to give to whoever I choose," he said, no arrogance in his words but a tenderness that didn't match the teasing young man she had gotten to know during her time in Ackwood. There was no trace of the shameless flirt who had made her cheeks flush or the chivalrous noble son who had escorted her through the halls of the palace day after day. It was Brax as she had spotted him reading, imperfect and vulnerable, and at peace.

His hand closed hers around the necklace and lingered until Gandrett tore her gaze away from his long, pale fingers, how they contrasted with her sun-kissed skin.

"Keep it." His lips parted into a smile that was like the sun itself.

And he stepped past her, falling into a jog as he headed for the yard.

48

G andrett's old rooms looked exactly like they did when she had left them—including the bathing chamber, which was already prepared with steaming water as she made it there, her muscles exhausted from the days on horseback and the nights on the ground.

She closed the door behind her, slid out of her dirty, sweaty dress, and dropped the fabric where she stood, leaving a collapsing heap of midnight-blue streaked with dirt and half-washed-out stains of blood. Who knew when the next time would be that she would get hold of a tub like that? Most certainly not in her parents' house, and even less than that at the priory in Everrun.

The water hugged her sore body like the touch of the goddess of water herself. A groan escaped Gandrett's mouth as she dipped her hair in the water and started scrubbing at her head, watching the dirt float and slowly dissolve in the heat.

When she was done, she wrapped herself in a thick towel and studied the plain, functional dress that had been laid out for her on the bed next to her clean acolyte uniform.

"Take the dress. It suits you better," Mckenzie said from the door, an apologetic look on her face. "They told me to come get you—and that you're up here."

Gandrett fixed the towel with her hands just in time as Mckenzie ran toward her, arms wide and face beaming. Words of gratitude rained down on Gandrett's shoulder as Mckenzie squeezed her tightly. Gandrett waited in silence, so many thoughts filling her own mind that she didn't have one single word to say in response.

But she mustered a smile.

Mckenzie waited in the hallway while Gandrett got dressed, and as they walked back to the great hall, Gandrett thought back on those first steps she had set into Ackwood Palace. The uncertainty, the fear of Nehelon, the hope of freedom, the pressure to prove herself.

Now she could walk up to the table where Lord Tyrem was lounging in the same chair as he had been in that first day, Lady Crystal to his right, and Joshua to his left, next to Brax, already deep in conversation with his parents. As she approached, they looked up, Lord Tyrem's eyes rimmed with the red of recently-fallen tears, his features appearing younger as he glowed with joy.

"Nehelon didn't lie when he told me you could do it," he said by way of greeting, "And what a rescue—Nehelon and my son here have told me all about it." One of his hands rested on Joshua's forearm, the other one clutching Lady Crystal's, who eyed her son who wasn't her son with what appeared to be mixed feelings. Gandrett wondered how hard it must have been for her to bring up someone else's child. The lovechild, potentially, of her husband and her enemy.

From the shadows by the columns, Nehelon's diamond-blue gaze was resting on her, thoughtful.

Gandrett didn't let her own look hover but took another step closer to the reunited family where Mckenzie had taken up the spot beside her mother and was beaming at Joshua with the same admiration her brother Andrew had beamed at Gandrett.

Brax pulled out a chair for her, beckoning her to sit.

But Gandrett didn't take the offer. She had completed her mission, had retrieved Joshua from a situation even worse than what any of them could have imagined, and brought him home.

"You have held up your end of the bargain," Lord Tyrem said and got to his feet, walking up to her with the steps of a proud lord, a warrior, a father who had gotten back his son. All those facets of him were there in his straight posture, his gleeful expression, the jeweled sword and knife at his belt. "So I will hold up mine."

Gandrett's heart beat like a prayer drum. Home. She would go home. See her mother, her father, and Andrew.

Lord Tyrem reached into his jacket and extracted a small leather pouch, which he unceremoniously held out for her.

Gandrett waited, unsure of whether it was right to take it.

As Lord Tyrem shook it, metal clanked inside. "You don't want to go to your family empty-handed," he said and let it hover between them until Gandrett reached for it with hesitant fingers.

Not a payment. Not a gift for her but for her family. Vala couldn't begrudge her if she took it. "I don't know what to say, my Lord." The pouch weighed heavily enough to tell her the contents could feed half of Alencourt for a winter.

"Take it as the gratitude of an old man who got back his son." He smiled more widely, reaching out with one arm toward Joshua. "Now, I don't want to keep you," he said and dismissed her with a gracious gesture of his hand.

Gandrett inclined her head at Lord Tyrem as she thanked him, and when Joshua joined his father, the latter wrapping an arm around his shoulders, she dipped her chin again. "Goodbye, Future of Sives," she said and returned Joshua's grin.

"There will always be a place for you here at Ackwood," he said and inclined his head in return, "after everything you've done for this family."

Gandrett took his words and tucked them away in her heart right next to the knowledge that eventually she would return to Everrun where her journey had begun. With a curtsey for the Brenheran family, she took her leave, a weight lifting from her shoulders.

The stained glass windows of Ackwood Palace tinted the hallway in familiar patterns of crimson and gold as Gandrett walked down the stairs, away from Lord Tyrem's great hall.

Handing over Joshua had been quick and, thank Vala, Nehelon and Joshua had already told the tale of Joshua's rescue. They graciously had left out details about how exactly Gandrett had defeated Linniue as they'd promised on their journey back from Eedwood. Her magic, Nehelon and Joshua had agreed, was something to be kept a secret—for now.

She knew Nehelon wouldn't tell a soul, for she had knowledge of his little Fae-secret. As for Joshua, Gandrett could only rely on all the stories of his pristine heart she had heard of from his family—the Brenheran part of his family.

Now that Lord Tyrem had dismissed her with a verbal pat on the shoulder and a small bag of gold for her family, there was nothing holding her back. She was going home.

Had someone told her a year ago that she was going to see her family again, she would not have believed them. And now, she had bargained for a whole year and would not return empty-handed.

"Lim and Alvi are eager for a ride." Nehelon appeared beside her, a pack slung over his shoulder and a smirk on his face.

"I thought I was free to go." Gandrett didn't stop. Too close were the gates, too close was her temporary freedom.

Nehelon fell into step beside her. "You didn't think I'd let you go alone." He watched her with raised eyebrows. "Not after what happened last time."

Gandrett suppressed a whimper when, as if in response to his words, her magic stirred.

They walked in silence, passing by the guards who saluted Nehelon and eyed Gandrett with cautious glances. The girl who had rescued Joshua Brenheran.

Gandrett gave them a smug grin before she stepped out into the yard.

The gold in her pocket clinked as she patted her skirt. Her sword yet again was a comforting weight at her hip, her dress fresh and hair clean. Gandrett Brayton was going home.

49

U nder a blanket of ferns, in the shadow of trees so ancient they could tell the history of the world, something stirred. An old and dangerous magic that had been sleeping for centuries, dreaming of the day that the forests of Ulfray would awaken. It had felt a surge of power in the north where an echo of the past lingered like a memory. It growled and flexed and opened an eye, winding and writhing from its sleep.

The north had awoken, and it was ready to answer its call.

ABOUT THE AUTHOR

"Chocolate fanatic, milk-foam enthusiast and huge friend of the southern sting-ray. Writing is an unexpected career-path for me."

Angelina J. Steffort is an Austrian novelist, best known for The Wings Trilogy, a young adult paranormal romance series about the impossible love between a girl and an angel. The bestselling Wings Trilogy has been ranked among calibers such as the Twilight Saga by Stephenie Meyer, The Mortal Instruments by Cassandra Clare, and Lauren Kate's Fallen, and has been top listed among angel books for teens by bloggers and readers. Angelina has multiple educational backgrounds including engineering, business, music, and acting. Currently, Angelina lives in Vienna, Austria, with her husband and her son.

Made in the USA
Columbia, SC
30 June 2022

62551771R10281